Advance Praise

"There are multiple ways to tell the story of Black Liberation. But the novel by new author Wendy Shaia, *The Black Cell*, provides a roadmap of possibility, telling the story with passion, purpose, and people; characters that you will feel you know from the first page to the last."

— A. Adar Ayira
Anti-Racism/Anti-Oppression Educator
Baltimore, MD

"In *The Black Cell*, author Wendy Shaia draws on America's recent history to paint a provocative portrait of its near future. What will it take for true Black liberation? How far will white people go to enforce white supremacy? No form of resistance is off the table as *Black Cell*'s riveting and complex Black characters take dramatic personal journeys in a time of tribulation. *Black Cell* illuminates the many facets of Blackness and the destructive power of whiteness. Shaia's ruthless perceptiveness in depicting the mechanisms of a racist society is equaled by the finesse of her draftsmanship in crafting the inner lives of characters shaped by— and resolved to dismantle by any means necessary—those mechanisms. This provocative page-turner imagines a 2024 reprise of our Trump-inspired white nationalist nightmare.

Bursting with suspense, it will shake readers as it ponders what might go down when Americans feel forced to pick a side."

— Lawrence Lanahan, author, *The Lines Between Us: Two Families and a Quest to Cross Baltimore's Racial Divide*

"A compelling first novel written by Dr. Wendy Shaia is reminiscent of a contemporary version of the television series, *The Wire*. Set in Baltimore, Shaia's detailed account of the individual and community effects of systemic racism is poignant and raw. The novel, through its characters' experiences, exposes the painful truth of how white supremacy intentionally oppresses Black people, whether through legal, political, social, and economic structures. The grave consequences of this injustice, and what can happen when Black people aim to dismantle the power regime, are gut-wrenchingly exposed. *The Black Cell* is a good choice for those who are interested in expanding their anti-racist readings to include fiction, and those who strive to understand the Black experience in the United States."

— Jennifer Swanberg, Ph.D., Professor of Health Sciences

"Wendy Shaia has increased the volume on voices that are often not heard by magnifying the existences of Baltimoreans that are often not seen. Through her intense and real storytelling, Wendy introduced us to the Black people of Baltimore, that they are alive and living through the traumatic effects of racism. She captured the struggles and complexities of inferiority of Black people which is the constant effort to be heard, seen and to feel normal. She shared the multiculturalism of Black people, the Black Diaspora on a smaller scale; the city of Baltimore is truly alive with a purpose to survive. Wendy powerfully demonstrated that freedom is the ongoing existence between humanity or violence, rage or calm, and me or you."

— Barbie Johnson-Lewis, LCSW-C
President, Board of Directors, National Association of Social Workers MD Chapter
Founder, Lotus Healing Services

The Black Cell is an engaging and powerful read. I could not put it down, I was so enthralled. Wendy Shaia does a beautiful job of weaving more distant history with current history into a dystopian (though, not too distant) future which both feels omniscient and hopeful. Omniscient because it isn't hard to see this coming to pass given our recent history as a nation and the full history of anti-Blackness in this country. Hopeful because what Wendy has done is provide us a way to activate our own radical imaginations about community building around mutual aid, resistance, and self-defense.

She shows us that as Black people, we have power when we can unite against white supremacy and she lays out the complexities within and outside of the Black community around organizing. Further, she very deftly teases out the various ecosystems in which Black people live and by which our senses may become dulled to the realities of white supremacist culture and systemic racism in ways that humanize the characters and the struggles they have as they learn a more complete history of the United States, the Black freedom struggles, and the realities of the present moment. While weaving history throughout, she never loses sight of the present struggle for full liberation and charts a multi-pronged path forward in the tradition of Marcus Garvey, Angela Davis, Malcom X, and others.

This book is a must read for all Black people and non-Black people alike because she takes on education, politics, criminal justice, and media and illustrates there is much for each of these institutions and those within them to learn about the ways Black children and adults are viewed and treated as well as the myths that uphold white supremacy and anti-Blackness.

I am looking forward to utilizing this book in my professional development sessions, can see this book being used in literature and critical studies courses from education to communication studies, and think it will make an excellent book club pick. Few books leaving me wanting more like this one has; I cannot wait for the sequel."

—Xyanthe Neider, Ph.D.; Anti-racism educator & professional development facilitator

Honoring My Community

I would like to thank my incredible family: Clinton Devereaux, Domino Devereaux, John Thomas Shaia, Mikko Shaia, Timothy Shaia, and Tyler Shaia. I am grateful for the time and space you gave me to work, all the meals you brought me as I sat hunched over my computer, and your never-ending belief in me. Clinton, you are my greatest champion, and I will never be able to thank you enough.

Thank you, also, to my amazing sister-friends: Gayle Carney, A. Adar Ayira, and Mishka Migacz, who patiently listened to me fuss and worry, read my drafts, and encouraged me to continue. Gayle, I am so grateful for all the free work and consulting you provided for my website. Thank you, Renee McSwain, for pushing me to "walk through that door." So much #blackwomanmagic.

I would like to acknowledge my editors: developmental editor Kimberley Lim; copy editor Rebecca Spencer; writing coach Mark Spencer, and Caleb Mason of Publerati. Your gentle guidance has significantly shaped this novel.

Finally, I would like to recognize the elders and ancestors who walked before me and in whose footsteps I dare to tread. Thank you for reminding me that I have a voice, and that you have already paid the price for my success. I hope you find these words worthy.

THE BLACK CELL

A Novel

by Wendy Shaia

PUBLERATI

THE BLACK CELL

"History is the landmark by which we are directed into the course of life. The history of a movement, the history of a nation, the history of a race, are the guideposts of that movement's destiny."

— Marcus Mosiah Garvey

"If you are silent about your pain, they will kill you and say you enjoyed it."

— Zora Neale Hurston

This book is dedicated to all those working towards Black liberation. We see you. We thank you.

And for Corey, this is your revised life story.

Chapter One

Corey knew it was his fault his mother went to prison. He thought about it every time he looked at her, and the way his heart quickened, and his breath caught in his throat when the thought rose up in him, made him want to stay away. Even now, seven years later, as he slowly made his way towards her one-room studio apartment, the thought crept up around him like a cloud of smoke from a cigarette that refuses to extinguish, no matter how many times you step on it. He ground his heel firmly into the thought, and yet it wafted up from the pit of his stomach, up his spine, around his waist, across his chest and wrapped itself around his neck, squeezing. He rubbed his hand slowly across the back of his neck and over his jaw as he walked, suddenly hot from the weak winter sun. He lifted his baseball cap and wiped his forehead.

Old Bubba, who sat every day on an old folding chair in front of an abandoned building drinking from a bottle in a brown paper bag, nodded at Corey as he passed.

"'Sup?" Old Bubba mumbled, peering at Corey through half-closed eyes.

Corey paused and offered his fist for Old Bubba to bump. He shrugged. "You know."

Old Bubba nodded again, smacked his lips in preparation, and took a long sip from his bottle as Corey moved on. The neighborhood hadn't changed much since Corey's childhood. Every third building was still vacant and boarded up, except where the boards had been pried from the windows and doors by squatters or had rotted and fallen off over time. Those buildings resembled grotesque faces with gaping black eyes and mouths. Sometimes errant trees sprang up inside the buildings and grew out of the windows or holes where the bricks were missing. When Corey was young, he sometimes had nightmares that he was walking down the street and the houses with big black eyes bent towards him, the trees reaching with long, thin arms. He would wake up terrified and panting, and the next time he had to go to school, he walked in the middle of the street, just in case.

His mother lived on the same block on which he had grown up, but in a different building. He walked up the crumbling concrete steps and let himself into the building with his key. He stopped to open her mailbox, one of eight lined up in the lobby. Nothing. The only mail she ever got was the occasional statement from Social Security. Her utility bills went to Corey because he paid them. She got nothing else. Not even junk mail. It was as if she no longer existed, which was true in more ways than one.

He let himself into his mother's small, dark apartment. "Hi, Momma!" He forced a brightness into his voice he did not feel. "How're you doing?" He put his backpack on the floor by the door and walked over to her.

She glanced up at him as she sat slumped against the back of the couch staring at the television holding a cigarette with a long ash threatening to fall. "Doing okay," she said, her voice so low he strained to hear her. She slowly turned her attention back to the television. Everything she did these days was slow.

He perched on one end of the couch and pretended to be interested in the television while he watched her from the corner of his eye. She didn't look anything like the woman she used to be. This woman was thin and scrawny, with sharp cheeks and hips that looked like they might cut you if you rubbed up too close against them. Her eyes stared straight ahead like dull black coat buttons—old, tired, worn.

Seven years ago, his mother had been anything but tired and worn. Instead, she was full of life with a loud laugh everyone recognized the moment they heard it, and eyes that grew wide when she was excited, which seemed to be all the time. Folks couldn't get enough of her. The apartment was always full of neighbors and friends stopping by to chat, hanging around to see what she was cooking, asking for advice. Corey and his younger brother, Calvin, rolled their eyes when folks came around, as if they didn't want to share her. But really, they were proud their house was the center of the block. Corey and Calvin belonged to all the folks who came by, and the neighbors belonged to them. If they ever got locked out of the house there were ten doors they could knock on for help. By the time their mother came home, they would be sitting up in Miss So and So's house, eating chips and drinking juice or playing video games with her kids. Their mother knew, if they weren't at home, they were close by and well taken care of, unlike when they were in school, where the white teachers and staff acted as if someone forced them to come to work every day, as if they hated the Black children.

On the day his life changed forever, Corey went to school like a 16-year-old, tightly-wound spring just waiting to release. He should never have gone that morning, and Aunt Doreen told Momma not to make him go, but she wouldn't listen. Momma shook her long, curly black wig (chosen from her substantial wig collection) at him and pointed a perfectly manicured nail in the direction of the school.

"Go on ahead to school and get out of this house and take Calvin with you. Ain't no use sittin' around lookin' at me. I gotta call the liquor store, tell them I ain't coming to work today, and I'ma go on up to the funeral home."

Momma and Aunt Doreen left and headed towards the funeral home to see about Uncle Tony's body. Momma tall, wide-hipped, buxom and sure, with a stride that made men stand up straight and pay attention, and Aunt Doreen, petite and shapely walking next to her. They made a striking pair.

Corey and Calvin, headed toward the school, skirting around Old Bubba, who was nodding off in the middle of the sidewalk, one arm stretched out as if he had just stood up from his chair to reach toward the table for a pack of cigarettes. This time Calvin didn't ask if Old Bubba was going to fall or how long he could stand like that. Instead, the two of them just hurried along the sidewalk, trying to avoid the broken bottles and heaving pavement, huddled together, almost holding hands—but not quite, because that would make them punks. Uncle Tony was gone, and no one explained who had shot him or why. They just knew that two white cops had come to their door the day before, and Momma and Aunt Doreen had spent the day crying and the night drinking while a bunch of people came by to join them.

Of all the people in their lives, Uncle Tony was one of the best. Corey thought about Uncle Tony, and the five-dollar bills he used to give to his nephews whenever he came around. How he used to slap Corey on the back kind of hard, but not in a mean way. How they used to talk about girls, and how he had promised to teach Corey to drive. Uncle Tony was just cool. He was Momma and Aunt Doreen's youngest brother, and whenever they talked about him, they would suck their teeth and roll their eyes in a big-sister kind of way. But Corey knew they loved the way he messed with them and called Momma "Big-Boned Girl" and Aunt Doreen "Red-Boned Girl." When they scolded him for being involved with too many women, he called them old and told them not to worry, that he would take care of them in their old age. They would giggle and slap at him, then go into the kitchen and make him a big plate of whatever they were cooking. He would look at

5

Corey and Calvin and wink, as if to say, "That's the way you two need to handle them."

The thought that Corey would never laugh and joke with Uncle Tony again made his throat dry and his head hurt. But folks being shot in their neighborhood was not unusual. Practically every day someone in the neighborhood was shot, and no one ever seemed to care, besides the people who loved them. The cops would come around, pick up the body, ask a few questions, and go on about their business. There was never an investigation or a trial. It was as if their lives didn't matter. Sometimes Corey wondered if the same thing would happen to him some day.

And so, this was the only thing on Corey's mind when he got to his first-period class. He threw himself into his chair and put his head on his desk. He was so deep in his thoughts about Uncle Tony that he didn't hear the teacher talking to him. He had his face buried in the neck of his sweatshirt, and his hood up over his head, with his forehead resting on his forearms on the desk. The softness of the fleece inside his hoodie and the warm smells of fabric softener and deodorant made him want to close his eyes and drift away. How could Uncle Tony be gone?

Mrs. Minkus' voice broke into his thoughts like a shot through his head. He started and looked up. She was standing over his desk, very close, looking down at him. He sat up and bowed his head toward the desk, his chin on his chest, trying to block her out.

Her voice was sharp, "Corey, I'm talking to you. Take that hood off."

He tried to push her thin, beakish, pale face and stringy brown hair from his mind. Corey sat up straighter in his chair and pulled the hoodie up so it covered his nose and mouth, leaving his eyes exposed. *Why won't she shut the fuck up and go away?* He shoved his hands into the sleeves of the hoodie and closed his eyes. He was sitting up now. *What else did she want?* He wanted to go back to his thoughts.

Her voice broke through again, sharp and high-pitched, "Corey, I'm talking to you. I will not be disrespected in my classroom."

Corey felt her take a step closer to him, so close now that he could hear her breathing. He squeezed his eyes tighter. *Back the fuck off.* He wanted to tell her. *Back the fuck off. Leave me the fuck alone.* He wished he could say it, wished he could just lift his head and scream at her. He felt his skin begin to crawl, slowly at first. His heart pounded in his chest and the neck of his hoodie, which at first felt like a place to hide, now threatened to suffocate him. He felt sweat creep down his sides under his T-shirt. He kept his eyes closed.

Her voice was raised now, and there was silence in the rest of the class. Mostly. He didn't have to open his eyes to know the scene playing out between him and Mrs. Minkus was center stage in the classroom. He heard Talib snicker all the way across

7

the other side of the room. He knew it was Talib, could almost see him put his hand up to cover his mouth. Asshole.

Corey's skin felt as if it was on fire now, with a thousand tiny pinpricks of heat. They were crawling all over him at a rapid pace, on his body, his scalp. He wanted to jump up and run, but Minkus was standing between him and the door.

She kept going. "Why do you even come to school, huh? Why do you even drag your sorry butt to school if you're just coming here to sleep?"

He could feel the heat of her breath push past the hoodie and fan his nose. He willed himself to keep his eyes closed. He held his breath, feeling he would explode. He didn't want to smell her. His head pounded with a low rumble, like distant thunder coming closer.

"In fact, why do you waste taxpayers' money and my time trying to teach your sorry ass? They don't pay me enough for this. Get out of my classroom!" With that, she stood up straight, grabbed the back of Corey's hoodie by the neck and tried to yank him to his feet.

A burst of energy exploded from within him. He jumped to his feet, almost turning his desk over and knocking Minkus on her butt as she jumped back. The room disappeared for a moment as everything around him went dark. When the light came back on in his head he blinked rapidly.

"Don't touch me!" he yelled. "Don't you fucking touch me! I will *fuck you up!*'"

Minkus stepped back in surprise, looking as if she didn't recognize him. Corey was vaguely aware of a distant rumble, like thunder. He was at the door before he realized the entire class was in an uproar. Out of the corner of his eye, he saw Talib on his feet, his arms in the air, his long, thin body shaking in delight and amusement. Other kids were open-mouthed, laughing, gawking, pointing at Minkus as she stood beside Corey's empty chair. He stopped for a moment, confused that she held a hoodie in her hand, until he realized the darkness a moment ago had been her pulling his jacket right over his head. He didn't stop for long. The roar in his head was deafening as he ran into the hallway. It continued out into the street. Only when he burst into the empty apartment and threw himself onto his bed did the sound disappear. He pulled the covers over his head and slept.

Corey felt the rising smoke, just as real today as it had been seven years ago at school. He shifted on the couch and rubbed the back of his neck.

"Momma, you want some more soda?" he asked, still grinding his heel into the memory. The cloud of smoke kept coming. He grimaced. It had gotten so much worse. His mother's eyes swung slowly from the television to his face. They stayed on him for a moment, as though she wasn't quite sure who he was, before she answered.

"No, thanks, Baby," she whispered. She stared at him for a moment as she slowly raised her cigarette to her lips for a long

9

drag, before returning her gaze to the television. The cigarette ash landed on her lap and he reached over to brush it off.

"Thanks, Baby." He got the sense she might have been talking to anyone.

He watched her as she stared at the television. Something about her was absent. It was almost as if she had had the life sucked out of her.

Momma and Aunt Doreen came home from Watson's funeral parlor just after noon that day to find Corey asleep in bed with the covers pulled over his head and without the expensive Nike hoodie Momma bought him for Christmas, which she knew he left for school wearing. He woke up to find the roaring tiger at the foot of his bed, demanding to know why he was there and not in school. So, he told the story. When he got to the part about Mrs. Minkus grabbing him by the hoodie, Momma was out the front door and headed to the school before he finished talking. Aunt Doreen followed her as far as the corner yelling, "Now, Danasia, don't you go down to that school with no foolishness. You know how those white people get."

"I'm sick and tired of these folks. They did that shit to me. Now they want to come do it to my kids. They don't have no right to put their hands on him. No right! Tired of it!" Momma flung over her shoulder back at Aunt Doreen as she strode toward the school.

Corey stood at the door of the apartment building and watched her storm down the street. Even from this far away, he could see Old Bubba straighten up from his perch against a boarded-up building with two other men, drinking from a bottle in a brown paper bag. They were passing the bottle between them and exchanging toothless grins. Normally, Old Bubba would try to flirt with Momma, calling her Beautiful Queen, or asking her when she was going to come marry him. But not today. As Momma swung past Old Bubba, he stood up. There was something in the set of a woman's jaw or in her stride that lets a man know when it was best to leave her alone.

Corey knew, when he heard sirens and saw red and blue lights heading toward the school, that it was bad, and when it came to bad things between Black people and white people, the Black people usually lost. Calvin came home fighting back tears. He wouldn't say what he saw, just that they took Momma away in handcuffs and the principal told him to go home before school ended.

Momma didn't go to Uncle Tony's funeral the following week. In fact, Momma didn't come home for the next five years. For the first two years, Aunt Doreen took Corey and Calvin to visit her in prison, until Calvin refused to go anymore, and Corey and Aunt Doreen went together. Then Aunt Doreen got too sick with cancer to go, and Corey would go alone, every week on the bus.

At first, Momma was still fired up. She was going to fight to get out. Show them how the system abused Black children. Show them how the teacher put her hands on Corey first, and that she was just protecting her son, and that it was her right as his mother. She said she was going to tell them the teachers had treated her just as badly in that very same school, along with her sister and brother. But then the attorneys told her if she didn't plead guilty and stay quiet, she was looking at fifteen to thirty years for assaulting the teacher, even though she had only jabbed her finger at the teacher's chest. She needed to decide if she really wanted to fight because they were offering her seven years, and her pro bono lawyer suggested she shut up and take it. The lawyer even suggested he wouldn't fight as hard for her if she didn't take the deal, and that she didn't really have much of a chance of winning anyway. He hinted she come up with some ridiculous amount of money, ten thousand dollars or something crazy, to hire a lawyer who might be willing to work harder on her case. He knew Momma didn't have any money. She took the deal and got seven years. She did five years altogether.

About a year before Momma came home, Aunt Doreen died from that cancer, and they wouldn't let Momma come to the funeral. So, she didn't get to go to the funeral for either her brother or her sister. She was the last one living of her parent's children, if anyone could say she was even alive.

Momma was just forty-three when she got out of prison, but looked like she was sixty. That smooth, shiny brown skin was sagged and wrinkled, her hair was thin and short, she walked slowly with a slight stoop, and she looked older than her mother had looked when she died at sixty-five.

No one even suggested Momma look for a job when she got out, two years ago. Everyone knew that wasn't going to happen. She sat on the couch in her studio apartment and chain-smoked, Corey thought, waiting to die. He was thankful the disability checks paid her rent. At first people came to visit her, but she barely looked up at them, so they stopped coming and she sat there alone. Calvin rarely came around, because he was too busy smoking dope and getting himself arrested. The last time Calvin came by, a bunch of Momma's jewelry went missing, and when Corey confronted him, Calvin collapsed in tears and apologized. Corey threatened him with his life if he ever stole from Momma again, so Calvin just stopped coming. Maybe he didn't trust himself not to steal. Whatever the reason, Corey—glad that was one less thing for him to worry about—visited Momma every week and forced himself to sit with her and make conversation.

Sometimes, looking at her, he felt the pinpricks of heat on his skin and heard the roar of thunder in his ears like he had that day at school. Whenever this happened, he would fight it back. The right time would come, and he would get his chance to exact revenge. He didn't know how or when, but someone would pay for what happened to Momma.

For now, Corey came and went and made sure she had

13

everything she needed to the best of his ability. And he ground his heel into the smoking butt of his anger and guilt, never quite extinguishing it, but never allowing it to erupt into a full flame either. There would be time for that.

Tasia sat looking at four Pull-Ups on the dresser. By her calculation, they would last until morning. She tried hard to avoid using them by putting Sharonda on the toilet every hour that day. But Sharonda had no intention of using the toilet. She giggled and sang the alphabet while Tasia stood waiting for her to pee. Eventually Tasia would take her off the toilet and pull up the dry training pants. Sharonda would promptly pee in them and then have the nerve to pull at her butt and fuss about being wet. Tasia wanted to scream.

Now there were only four left, and Tasia didn't have any money to buy more. If she went to the corner store, the Korean shop owner would sell them to her individually for two dollars each, which was a rip-off because the ones they sold were some no-name brand and probably cost fifteen dollars for a case of one hundred. And, unlike the name-brand pants, they leaked through after a few drops of pee soaked in.

Tasia sat on the bed and reached for her wallet. She had five dollars, and hadn't been able to give Nana any money for food and rent this week. She sighed and buried her face in one hand while she ran the other over her twists. At least she was working at 7-Eleven tonight. If they would just give her some more shifts things would get better. Not for the first time, she thought about the packets of training pants on the shelf at the store. She was there alone most of the night. It would be so easy to slip one of the smaller packs into her purse. No one would miss it if she did it in the corner of the store where the video cameras don't reach. Sharonda walked over, garbling something unintelligible. She seemed to be asking Tasia a question. She reached up and pulled Tasia's hand away from her face. Holding onto her mother's hand she garbled some more. Her large, dark eyes searched Tasia's face as she tilted her braided head from side to side questioningly. Tasia's heart melted. Her daughter was asking if she was okay. She reached down and scooped the eighteen-month-old up into her lap.

"Mommy's okay," she said pulling the toddler close to her chest. "I'm okay," she whispered to herself.

A lump rose in her throat and she buried her face in Sharonda's soft, sweet-smelling hair so her tears didn't show. "I'm gonna be alright," she repeated. Her chest felt tight, like it did when she was about to have an asthma attack. But she wasn't. She just needed to calm herself down.

She heard the front door open and Nana called out. Sharonda sat up straight and looked at Tasia. Her eyes widened and she smiled brightly, showing two even rows of perfectly white teeth in the front only.

"Who's that?" Tasia asked. "Is that Nana?" Sharonda was already struggling to get out of her mother's grasp. As soon

15

as her feet hit the floor, she took off running.

"Nana!" Sharonda called out. Tasia heard her grandmother drop her bag on the table and knew she had picked Sharonda up by the squeal of delight Sharonda let out. Well into her sixties, Nana needed to stop lifting Sharonda like that.

Tasia walked the four steps from the bedroom to the front door. It took her only ten steps to walk through the entire apartment.

Nana was putting Sharonda into a chair at the kitchen table. Sharonda's chin barely cleared the table. Tasia saw the bag of Chinese food that Nana had brought in.

"Hey, Dimples," Nana greeted her. Nana was the only one allowed to call Tasia that, and had for as long as she could remember. Probably as long as Tasia had dimples, which was from her very start.

"You working tonight?" Nana washed her hands and began removing Styrofoam containers of food from the plastic bag. "I stayed to do some overtime, but I knew you had to work so I didn't want to come home too late." Nana scooped some fried rice and steamed broccoli onto a paper plate for Sharonda and handed her a plastic spoon. Sharonda put the spoon down, picked up a piece of broccoli and put it in her mouth. She gave Tasia a broccoli-filled, wide-mouth grin. She chattered words Tasia couldn't understand between mouthfuls.

"Keep your mouth closed when you're eating, Pookie," Tasia said. Everyone in their family seemed to have a nickname that had nothing to do with their real names. Some kids never knew their real names until they got to school. That wouldn't happen to her Pookie. "Yeah, I'm doing overnight—eight to six."

Nana unbuttoned and peeled off her big shirt that covered her gray and white striped housekeeping shirt. She always covered the uniform up on her way home because she didn't want Sharonda to come into contact with "that nasty-ass uniform." She laid the shirt over the back of a chair and began fixing herself a plate. She shoved a paper plate and plastic fork towards Tasia.

"I just don't like you being in that store at night," Nana muttered.

"I know, but I really need the shifts, and they've been cutting me back ever since Ahmed's cousin came from Pakistan. He gets all the daytime shifts and his greedy ass even wants to work at night sometimes."

Tasia spooned some food onto a plate. It was their second time eating Chinese food this week. If it wasn't Chinese, it was a chicken box. There were few other food options in the neighborhood. The next time she got paid, she would take the bus over to Howard Street to the Stop, Shop and Save. It was hard to carry groceries on the bus, but she didn't have much money, so she wouldn't be able to buy more than she could carry anyway. The lady at the Food Stamp office acted like it was her own money she was giving out so Tasia could buy food for Sharonda. She sighed and gave Tasia nasty looks during their meeting, finally turning her away because she didn't have all the necessary papers.

Tasia didn't know if she would go back. She needed the hundred dollars a month to buy food even though it didn't go very far, and she wasn't sure she was ready to deal with those people with their nasty attitudes and dirty looks. It was like they all came to work pissed off every day.

She worried whether Sharonda was getting the right foods to eat. The books she read when she was pregnant said both mother and baby should eat a lot of fresh fruits and vegetables and lean meats. Yeah, right. Where could you find that in West Baltimore? Chicken boxes and second-rate Chinese food was all there was. Not even Chinese people would eat that shit. All you could taste was salt. But she was starving, so she sat down at the table.

Tasia shoveled the food into her mouth and looked at her grandmother. Nana looked tired. Her face showed no lines, but Tasia could tell that her body was aching by the way she held her shoulders so stiff. At sixty-five it looked like she would clean classrooms and bathrooms at the university for the next ten years or more. She put her retirement on hold because her barely nineteen-year-old granddaughter went and "knocked herself up," and now Nana had to support all three of them. She sighed as she thought about it for the millionth time. How did this happen? What happened to "The Dream"?

It was a beautiful dream, too. Kenny was Tasia's first and only. He talked to her every day when she walked past him on the way to school, but she didn't pay him any mind. She was determined not to be one of them baby mamas pushing a stroller down the street. She was going to finish high school and go to college. She got good grades from elementary school—even when she had to get herself up and find her own way to school because Mamma was too strung out or hung over or hadn't come home from partying the night before. Tasia remembered getting herself to school in second grade and always being on time. But hunger was a constant companion, and she sat in class forcing herself to pay attention when all she really wanted to do was put her head down on the desk and sleep. Since Mamma didn't fill out the lunch form, she didn't get free lunch either, even though they were certainly poor enough. Many times, she didn't eat all day, and she was lucky if she could find something to eat when she got home. Sometimes Mamma would give her money to go get a chicken box. She didn't know where Mamma got money, but it was most likely from her current man. Mamma never seemed to eat—she just smoked cigarettes and sipped from a huge bottle of sweet wine.

No one at school knew how hungry Tasia was, and no one ever asked. Even when she sat alone in the cafeteria with her book while the other kids ate, no one asked. Even when her clothes were dirty because she didn't know how to take them to the laundromat, no one asked. Even when her clothes were clearly too small and her hair uncombed, no one asked. The teachers just wrinkled their noses up at her when they walked past and stayed more than an arms-length away. They focused their attention on the kids who talked back, fought the teachers, and ran out of class. Tasia didn't do any of those things. She got good grades and stayed to herself, hoping no one would hear her stomach rumbling. She was invisible.

"Nana," Tasia began. She hated asking her grandmother for money, but she didn't have a choice. She picked at her food, her appetite suddenly gone. "Sharonda is almost out of Pull-Ups." She glanced over at her grandmother. She was supposed to be taking care of Nana. What was she doing? "Do you—?"

"I got a twenty in my purse," Nana stopped her. "Take it and buy this child what she needs. Can't have you walking around with a wet backside, right, Pookie?" Nana reached across the table and touched the tip of Sharonda's nose. Sharonda squealed and tried to catch Nana's hand.

"Thanks, Nana. I'll pay you back," Tasia muttered. Nana smiled knowingly. They both knew it would be a very long time before Tasia could pay Nana anything.

Chapter Two

The shots rang out as soon as Corey turned onto Schroeder Street. Instinctively, he dove into the stairwell of a row house. Momma used to say that bullets don't have names on them, and there were many nights when his whole family lay flat on the floor, without a word, when they heard gunshots. It got so he could roll out of bed onto the floor during the night without waking. In the morning, he would find himself on the floor and, after he got up, he would look for news from the neighborhood grapevine about who got shot during the night.

It sounded as if the shots were coming from right behind him. He tried to bury his face in the space where the steps met with the brick front of the house. Out of the corner of his eye, he saw children running, their backpacks bouncing behind them. They disappeared around the corner, headed towards the school.

Damn! This was some shit for kids to have to see. He peeked out from around the steps. The street was empty. He looked up to see people gazing out their windows wide-eyed, but no one came outside. He looked at his watch. Several minutes had passed. He needed to get moving if he was going to get to class on time. His marketing professor was known to lock the door five minutes after class began, and Corey was on track to graduate in

21

ten months with a degree in marketing. He couldn't afford to miss class.

Corey emerged from his hiding place. His black jeans were dusty where his knees had hit the ground. He had scratched his arm on the house's brick front. It was a long, deep, bleeding scratch, from elbow to wrist. He wiped the blood on his jeans and cursed, noticing some of it on his light-blue graphic T-shirt.

Corey continued walking down Schroeder and heard sirens in the distance. "I hope they catch the motherfucker," he muttered as he walked. As he neared Martin Luther King, Jr. Boulevard, he saw a police car coming towards him, blue lights flashing. His heart sank as the officer in the passenger seat pointed at him. The patrol car pulled up with a screech and two white officers jumped out, guns already drawn. His hands instinctively went up in the air. He knew the drill.

Corey stood silently, hands in the air, avoiding eye contact with the officers. He knew better than to speak. They would just tell him to shut up, anyway. They stopped several feet away from him, still close to their patrol car.

"Turn around!"

Corey turned his back to them, his hands still in the air. *Don't make any sudden movements; stay smooth and predictable. Don't give them any reason to claim you were aggressive. Don't let them shoot you.* Perspiration slid down his sides under his shirt. His heart beat so violently it seemed to shake his entire ribcage with a bizarre drumbeat. He felt light-headed, as if he might pass

22

out, and his breath came in uneven bursts. He struggled to control the panic rising within.

"Walk backwards to me!"

Corey heard the sirens and screeching brakes of other police cars as they pulled up around him. *How many cars were there?* He struggled to walk backwards, finding it difficult to do with his hands in the air. His backpack felt as if it weighed one hundred pounds, and it threatened to pull him to the ground with every step.

A hand grabbed Corey by the neck and spun him around. The cop slammed Corey's head onto the hood of the car, face first. Pain shot through his head and down his neck. He cried out without meaning to. Tears flooded his eyes. His nose pressed against the car, and he struggled to breathe. A heavy hand stayed on his neck, pushing his facer harder against the patrol car. Someone was pulling his backpack and jacket off and cuffing his hands behind his back, but the hands on his neck never moved. He felt his legs kicked apart, nearly buckling beneath him. He forced himself to stay on his feet.

His first instinct was to struggle. The urge for self-preservation rose urgently in him. He wanted to lift his head, so he could breathe. He wanted to fight back against the hand holding him down. Instead, he opened his mouth and took deep breaths. *They want you to fight so they can shoot you. Just chill. Just chill.* He breathed deeply.

He was pulled upright into a standing position and was

23

surprised to see a large pool of blood on the white hood, running down to the bumper. It took a moment to register that it was his blood, and that it was still pouring from his nose. Blood also trickled from his forehead into his right eye. He was surrounded, two pointed guns at him, others poised and ready to fire.

There was a cop on each side of him holding a handcuffed arm. Someone else was behind him, going through his pockets and feeling up and down his shirt. He saw his phone and wallet tossed to someone out of his sight. When his pockets were empty, the cop behind him walked around and unbuckled his belt. *What the fuck was he doing?* He tried to look at the face of the Black cop undressing him on the street, but he could only see out of his left eye.

Someone lifted his feet one at a time, taking off his shoes. Hands moved from his ankles up his legs. At the same time, the Black cop in front of him was pulling down Corey's pants, exposing his boxer briefs. They pulled his pants down to his ankles.

"Yo, Man!" he protested. The Black cop didn't even look at him. He was having a casual conversation with the other cops, something about overtime. These motherfuckers were undressing him on the street and chatting as if they were sitting in the break room with coffee.

Corey felt hands in the waistband of his briefs. He looked down to see the cop's blue-gloved hands feeling around inside his underwear, which were partially pulled down, exposing his pubic

24

hair. He felt cold air on his backside. *What the fuck?* The cop's hands were between his legs, feeling and squeezing.

"Yeah, man. I told them that this denying overtime was gonna be a problem. Seems like Wilson and Jacobs were the only ones on the crew that got overtime this week," the white cop to his right said. The cop feeling him up finally seemed satisfied that Corey wasn't hiding anything under his balls and stepped back. He pulled Corey's pants up but didn't zip or button them.

The cop behind Corey pushed him towards the patrol car. The cops on either side of him held him up as his legs buckled. He willed his feet to move. Someone put a hand on his head and pushed him roughly into the back of the car. He pulled his legs in just before the door slammed. He was laying sideways, unable to sit up with his hands clasped behind him. His pants had fallen to his hips. He dug his feet into the floor of the car and pushed himself into a sitting position. As he did so, his pants slid to his thighs and the rough leather of the seat dug into his skin through his briefs. The cops stood around gabbing and laughing as if he wasn't there—as if they hadn't just undressed him in front of the whole damn neighborhood. As if they hadn't violated him.

Corey bowed his head. He could feel his nose swelling, his face covered with blood. His head throbbed and he could feel blood rushing around his temples. The cloud of smoke that usually drifted around him hovered overhead. He was aware of it, but he was in too much pain to feel angry. He just wanted to go home.

*****

25

By eight-thirty in the morning, Lisa knew it would be a difficult day. Her fifth-grade class was in an uproar. Even her normally calm kids were agitated and out of control. There was a fight between DeAndre and Justin in the hall outside her classroom before the first bell rang. As she stepped in to break the boys up, she wondered, yet again, what could possibly have happened between them so early in the morning. Neither boy would tell her what the problem was, as they stood on either side of her, with red, sweaty faces, their chests heaving, as they glared at each other.

"Well, if you can't sit in my class properly, you're both gonna have to leave," she pronounced. She eyed the long welt on Justin's cheek. The skin might be broken.

"Justin, go to the nurse's office and let her look at your face. Then go to the principal's office." She wrote out a referral for each boy. "DeAndre, you go straight to the office. I won't tolerate this type of behavior in my class." She held the slips out to the boys. They took them from her reluctantly, giving each other the side-eye. She held DeAndre back for a few seconds and sent Justin on ahead so they wouldn't resume their fight in the stairwell.

Walking back into her classroom, she noted that only half her class was present, and *that* half was already out of control, running around the room, laughing raucously, and throwing paper. Lisa was in no mood for this.

"Sit down!" she yelled. "Sit down right now or go to the

office." Only two students turned to look at her. None of them obeyed. Takara was running from one side of the classroom to the other, touching the window and then running back and touching the wall on the opposite side. Melanie started chasing her, both girls giggling. Some of the boys slumped in their seats with their heads on their desks. The few girls in their seats leaned across the aisles, talking and laughing.

Lisa shrugged. "It's your education." She turned to the board and started her lesson. She forced herself not to turn around to look at the class as she wrote out the math problems on the board. She kept her back turned as she talked through how to solve the problems. The noise level in the classroom seemed to escalate as she talked. When she was tired of Takara and Melanie, she sent them both to the office. *They could spend the entire day down there if they wanted. They didn't care about learning, so why should she? These kids were like little wild animals and their parents were, too.* Not for the first time, she thought about taking the pay cut and teaching in a different county. Maybe in upper-income Howard County, where she lived and the children would want to learn. It would be just fine with her if she never had to come to Baltimore again.

Her mother had warned her, when she took this job, that the people in Baltimore were "not like" her. At the time, she thought her corporate lawyer mother was being elitist. After all, her mother had grown up in a wealthy family in Black Connecticut Society, and tended to be overly dramatic about "the other half."

27

But over the past four years, Lisa had begrudgingly come to acknowledge that her mother was right. She had nothing in common with the students in this school, aside from the fact they were also Black. Some days she didn't even want to go to work to hear their broken English and deal with their bad behavior. None of them seemed to want to be there. If her own two daughters acted like that, she would have dealt with them harshly, but these parents were too preoccupied with their own troubles to care. She paused writing on the board for a moment and sighed.

Danielle, the other fifth-grade teacher, poked her head into the classroom. Her eyes took in the scene quickly. She walked over to Lisa. "Wild in the jungle today, huh?" Her smooth blonde bob bounced, her blue eyes twinkled. She turned to gaze around at the kids.

Lisa had another of those moments where she felt Danielle might have crossed a racial line. But she wasn't sure, and Lisa herself had just called the kids animals in her own mind, as she had many times before. But Lisa always felt guilty after her conversations with Danielle. It was one thing to talk about Black kids with other Black people—it was a different thing to entertain white people calling Black kids animals. But Danielle was a good friend, and their own children went to the same highly-ranked public school in the upper-class suburb of Columbia. Lisa didn't want to alienate her by being the "angry Black woman," so she smiled and nodded.

"I don't know what's wrong with them," she replied.

"Whoever knows?" Danielle shrugged and eyed the class. They were all seated now and zoned out, picking at fingernails and doodling on their notebooks. The room was quiet. "My class was the same, but I put on a movie and they've gone into full zombie mode. Forget testing prep. It won't make a difference to them, anyway. The movie keeps them quiet."

Again, Lisa felt uncomfortable, but it would be hypocritical for her to act as if she didn't think the same thing. In a good year, only thirty percent of students in her West Baltimore School scored proficient on Maryland standardized testing in reading, and only twenty percent in math. The rest scored basic or below standards. This year would be no different. *Why bother? These kids were being prepared to work the corner. Pimps, prostitutes, and pushers. Why should she work so hard?*

"Did you hear about the shooting over on Schroeder? Some type of drive-by gang thing," Danielle shook her head. "I just don't know what's wrong with these people."

"No, I didn't hear. When was it?" Lisa shifted uncomfortably. Some of the kids had perked up and were listening to the conversation, even though she and Danielle were whispering. Had the kids also heard how she and Danielle were talking about them? She hoped not.

"This morning before school. Some of the kids saw it," Danielle shook her head again and headed for the door. "I'd better get back before . . . " she nodded towards her room. "See you in the cafeteria!" she called over her shoulder.

Lisa sat at her desk, suddenly aware that many of the kids were looking at her. Nikya raised her hand.

"Y'all talking about that shooting this morning, Mrs. Wilson?" Nikya asked.

"Yes. I think so," Lisa replied. "Did you hear about it, too?" She was regretting the conversation with Danielle. The kids should not have heard that.

"I saw it. I was walking to school when they shot up that man in the car," Nikya said, almost in a whisper. "I think he dead."

Lisa leaned forward. "You did? You saw it?" Her eyes were wide. She watched Nikya nod and realized that several other kids were nodding as well. She sat silently for a moment as the sadness of the situation seeped in.

"How many of you actually saw the shooting?" she asked. Five hands went up in the class. She took a deep breath. "How many of you heard the shooting?" Every hand but two went up. The kids sat silently, looking at her. Even the boys who had been sprawled across the desk were sitting upright, their hands in the air.

Lisa felt her breath catch. "How many of you have seen people get shot before?" Every hand went up. Lisa's palms began to sweat, and she absently wiped them on her pants. She had been teaching fifth grade in this school for four years, and had no idea what her students' lives were like. In fact, she didn't know anything about the community in which she worked. She knew how to get from the highway to the school and back to the highway and was always grateful to watch the city disappear in her rearview mirror as she headed for her own neighborhood with its huge houses and rolling lawns. She spoke to parents only when students were in trouble. Now, she didn't feel like teaching and they didn't feel like learning. The air was too heavy, thick, and sad.

"Want to watch a movie?" she suggested.

Chapter Three

The bright sun hurt Corey's eyes, and he hesitated on the steps for a moment to get his bearings. His head hurt like a motherfuck. His face was tight and swollen and he wondered if his nose was broken. The cops refused to let him see a doctor during the four days he sat in that cell, and would not give him anything for the pain in his head. He could barely breathe through his nose.

He tried washing the blood off of his face when they let him go to the bathroom, but he was only given five minutes each time, and without a mirror, washcloth, or warm water, he had been unsuccessful. The dried, caked blood stretched his skin every time his face moved.

He stood in his socks on the steps, shivering. The cops had left his shoes and jacket on the street when they threw him in the police car. They returned his backpack, phone, and wallet to him, but somebody got a real nice pair of Chuck Taylors.

Devonte stood beside him. Corey could tell from his roommate's face he was pissed, but Devonte was a man of few words, and wouldn't say anything about this for a long while.

"Yo, Man. I'mma grab a hack. You don't need to be takin' no bus lookin' like this." Devonte stepped out into the street and stood for a moment waiting for a cab to pass by. Cabs knew folks were always getting released from the police station, so one would come along pretty soon.

At home, Corey stripped off his clothes and turned the shower up as hot as he could handle. He had sat on a metal bench, handcuffed to the wall for four days and now he could smell himself. Four days for nothing. No charge. Not even an apology. The cops treated him like shit. He would have lain down on the bench if they had let him. But they handcuffed him to the metal ring at the very end of the bench instead of one of the rings in the middle—he could only perch on the edge of the bench. So, he just sat there. For four days and four nights. He nodded off a little and thought a lot, and he fought to tamp down the curling tendrils of smoke that threatened to engulf him. He knew if he gave in to what he wanted to do, he would lash out at the next cop who came into the cell, and that would only make things worse. He needed to stay cool. He wasn't going to play into their hands. Finally, he was taken out to the front of the police station and uncuffed. They stuffed his wallet and backpack through the bullet-proof glass window and slid it shut. Just like that.

Apparently, when Corey didn't come home the first night, Devonte called every hospital in Baltimore looking for him. Then Devonte went to every police station in western and central Baltimore, and no one would acknowledge that Corey had been arrested. Finally, Devonte kept coming back to the Poppleton Heights police station, because something in the officer's face

33

when he asked about Corey didn't seem right. On the last visit, the cop behind the glass got up without a word and walked away from the window. Devonte just stood there until the cop came back and released Corey out the door to the holding area.

This was Corey's first arrest, and he had prided himself on making it to twenty-three without going to jail, unlike Calvin who, although he was two years younger, had been arrested several times. Corey had been stopped, stripped, harassed, and put in the back of police cars, but never arrested. Still, he knew what happened to him was a common experience for young Black men in Baltimore, and he was lucky he hadn't been held for months or even years without a charge, like some of the other guys in the neighborhood. They probably had only let him out because Devonte was so persistent, and they didn't feel like being bothered.

Devonte was all right. He was a good brother, someone Corey could count on since his scrawny ass first showed up in second grade. If he'd had a different roommate, Corey might still be sitting chained to that metal bench. Calvin certainly wouldn't have come looking for him. The only time Corey saw Calvin was when he was looking for money to buy drugs. Corey promised himself he would never forget how Devonte always had his back.

Corey let the water run over him for at least thirty minutes. He was alive. Charlie Davis hadn't been so lucky. Corey shivered as he thought of the white cop choking Charlie to death on Pennsylvania Avenue last year, simply because he panicked and struggled when the cops stopped him and threw him on the ground. Charlie's killing had been recorded by multiple cell phones. The videos went viral, leading to three days of unrest in the city. The killer cop was never disciplined and still had his job. There were promises of police reform, but nothing changed. The protests, the newspaper articles, even the new police chief, all led to zero change. The police still continued killing Black people on the streets of Baltimore without any repercussion.

"Fuckin' endangered species," he muttered, remembering the words of a rap song Devonte played for him once. *Another day in the jungle, they say we're the animals. But when they hunt us and kill us, just who are the cannibals?*

Devonte had been asking Corey for the past year to come talk to some folks he knew who were working to stop police brutality. Corey told Devonte he would go with him, but then was always too busy when the time came. He didn't tell Devonte that he didn't really believe there was anything Black people could do to stop police brutality—they were just wasting their time. This was the way it had always been, and nothing would change. Despite his recent experience, Corey wasn't sure his thoughts had changed, but maybe he would go the next time Devonte asked, just to hear what they had to say.

His reflection grew cloudy and faint as the smoke flowed around him with a fury he hadn't felt since the day he left his hoodie in Mrs. Minkus' hand. The force of the smoke threatened to knock him off his feet, and he gripped the edge of the sink to steady himself. He breathed deeply, willing himself to calm down. Blood pounded in his head, his chest ached, and he felt like there was a big ball lodged in his throat, like the penny he swallowed when he was six years old.

"Fuck y'all, too." He lotioned himself, threw on some clean sweats and tossed the black jeans, blue graphic T-shirt, belt, boxer shorts, and socks into the large kitchen trash can. He wanted nothing the police had touched. It was just as well they left his shoes and jacket on the street because he would have thrown them away, too.

Devonte was in the living room watching television when Corey came back from the bathroom. He glanced up with a look that said, "Aight?"

Corey nodded and headed into his bedroom and closed the door. He pulled the covers back. He was hungry. He had refused to eat the nasty food the cops brought him; he only drank the water and coffee because it warmed him in the cold cell. But he was far more tired than hungry. He crept under the covers and sank into his pillow. The smell of clean sheets, the weight of his comforter, the softness under his head pushed the smoke away. He sighed and soaked it all in. Sleep would come tonight. Tomorrow, there would be fury.

The small waiting room in the unemployment office was hot and stuffy. One of the fluorescent lights was flickering wildly, and it made Tasia's head hurt. Sharonda had been fussy all day, and she whined as Tasia bounced her on her knee. She tried offering Sharonda a small, fluffy elephant from her bag, but the toddler turned her head away and whined even louder.

"Noooo!" Sharonda cried. "Down!" She pointed at the floor and tried to slide off Tasia's knee. The lady behind the desk at the front of the room looked over and frowned. Tasia sighed and stood up. Balancing Sharonda on her hip, she walked around the room, skirting the rows of dark gray plastic chairs. Most of the chairs held people waiting for their numbers to be called.

Tasia looked up at the electric sign where the large red numbers changed each time one of the four workers was available. Just ten more to go and it would be her turn. Sharonda struggled to get down, squealing angrily. Tasia eyed the dirty gray tiles warily, not wanting Sharonda to put her hands and knees down on that floor. She placed Sharonda on her feet carefully. "Okay, but you gotta stay standing up. This floor is dirty."

Sharonda laughed with delight and waddled towards the front of the room, causing Tasia to hurry after her, trying to stay close in case she fell. As Sharonda ran, she stepped on the foot of a man sitting with his leg stretched out. She almost fell but kept herself upright and continued on.

The man hissed his teeth and looked sideways at Tasia. She mumbled an apology and ran to catch up with Sharonda, grabbing the toddler right before she ran around a desk. The woman sitting behind desk number four paused in mid-sentence as she talked to the man sitting across from her, peering over her glasses at Sharonda and then up at Tasia.

"You know she shouldn't be here."

"I know. I'm sorry. I didn't have nobody to watch her," Tasia mumbled. She felt like she was always apologizing to somebody. She picked Sharonda up and walked away, keeping a firm grasp on her, even though Sharonda fought to be put down. Tasia bounced as she walked, making Sharonda's butt rise from her hip for a second and then bounce back down again. Sharonda giggled and reached for Tasia's earring. Tasia grabbed her hand and kissed it.

"You like that?" She blew on Sharonda's hand and pretended to bite her fingers. Sharonda giggled more.

Tasia looked up at the numbers just as hers came up. She walked over to the woman at desk number four and sat in the empty chair. The woman did not look at her but kept her eyes on her computer monitor.

"Name?" Her fingers moved over the keyboard.

"Tasia Williams. T-a-s-i-a."

"Date of birth?"

"February 4, 2003."

"Okay. Age 21. How many kids?" The woman looked over her glasses at Sharonda. Sharonda dimpled at her and tried to reach across the desk. She loved to grab people's glasses.

"Just one."

"Age?"

"Eighteen months."

"And the father?" The woman looked over her glasses again, this time at Tasia.

Tasia hesitated. *What was the question?* "Yeah, she got a father." She replied.

The woman sighed. "Where is he? Does he support her?"

"No. I mean, I don't know." Tasia hated talking about Kenny.

"You don't know where he is, or you don't know if he supports her?" The woman leaned back in her chair, her fingers hovering over the keys. She sighed again while she waited for Tasia to respond. Tasia noted that the woman's smooth brown skin was perfect, but suspected she was about Mamma's age. What a difference between forty-five on heroin and forty-five on just plain old mean. Maybe mean was good for something after all.

"I don't know where he is. He doesn't support her," Tasia replied. She hated saying those words even more than she hated talking about Kenny. Maybe Nana was right and Black men were cursed.

"Humph!" The woman typed away at the computer. "Have you been to child support yet?" She raised her chin to look through her glasses at the monitor as she typed.

"No." Tasia whispered this time. She sat up straight, moving Sharonda to the other knee, and spoke louder, "I mean I went, but I have to go back with her birth certificate."

The woman paused and regarded Tasia for a moment over her glasses. She searched Tasia's face as if searching for something. Finally, she pursed her lips, shook her head and went back to typing.

Tasia walked out of the office with Sharonda on her hip and a stack of papers saying she wasn't eligible for unemployment benefits, even though her employer had reduced her hours. Her skin pricked, her eyes burned. Her throat felt dry and coarse and she wanted to scream. But she didn't scream. She didn't cry. She walked to the bus stop and sat in the shelter, buttoning Sharonda's coat. She relived the moments in the unemployment office, and the way the woman had looked at her—as if Tasia was trying to get over or something. As if 7-Eleven hadn't cut her hours to almost nothing. As if she had a stack of money and a rich husband waiting at home, and she just wanted to get these few extra pennies to get her nails done. As if she was no good.

She didn't notice the bus coming until it had almost passed her by. She jumped up from the bench and flagged it down. It stopped a few yards beyond the bus stop and the driver frowned as she boarded and poured her last few quarters into the box. She muttered an apology as she walked past him to take a seat.

Tasia held Sharonda close to her chest, Sharonda's head on her shoulder. She was grateful for her daughter's comforting weight and warmth. She was the only person who didn't look at Tasia as if she were a complete failure. Sharonda and Nana— although Tasia often caught Nana studying her when she didn't

40

think Tasia was looking. Nana always seemed worried. Maybe she thought Tasia was a failure, too. Maybe Sharonda was the only one who didn't think it.

She nuzzled Sharonda's soft hair and listened to the child's gentle breathing against her ear. She looked so much like Kenny, sometimes Tasia had trouble looking at her. Especially when Sharonda looked at Tasia with those big, slanted brown eyes. She had Kenny's skin coloring, too—a little lighter than caramel, and his thick, black hair. Already Tasia had to use the big-toothed comb to get through Sharonda's tight curls.

Tasia held Sharonda tighter and breathed in her scent. She used to love to do that with Kenny—just breathe him in and feel his stubble against her cheek. It took so long for her to let him get close to her. But he was determined—refusing to give up when she passed him on the street. He told her she was fine, like good wine. So corny. But he made her laugh, and she always went on her way with a smile, believing she *was* fine, just like he said.

Mamma had said she would come to Tasia's high school graduation, and then they would go out to dinner at the Inner Harbor. It was rare for Mamma to take Tasia anywhere, and Tasia doubted it would actually happen. She doubted Mamma would even show up to graduation, and Nana couldn't get off work because one of the people she worked with got injured and the others had vacations planned ahead of time. So, Mamma was it.

Mamma even paid for her cap and gown, and Tasia didn't have to be one of those kids who had to go to the guidance counselor to say she couldn't buy her graduation stuff. Mamma gave her the money nice and early too, and Tasia spent at least two weeks trying on her cap and gown in front of the mirror and practicing her walk at home.

Still, Tasia prepared herself to be disappointed, but Mamma was one of the first people she saw when she and her classmates lined up. Mamma was there, in a nice dress Tasia had never seen before, her short hair neatly combed. She seemed sober, and she jumped up and clapped when Tasia walked past. Tasia could hear her calling, "That's my baby!" when Tasia walked up on the stage to accept awards in math and science. Tasia beamed and held her head high as she walked. Neither Mamma nor Nana had graduated from high school. She was the first one. It was probably the best day of her life.

After the ceremony, Tasia came out where all the graduates and guests were milling around drinking juice and eating cake. She searched the crowd for Mamma. *Where could she have gone?* Tasia stopped briefly to hug Jayla, the only true friend she had in high school. Jayla flipped her long, bone-straight weave over her shoulder. Her brown eyes shone with excitement. Her full lips were perfectly encased in red lipstick, and she had matching nails.

"We did it! We did it, Tayz!" Jayla took it upon herself to shorten Tasia's name to one syllable in ninth grade because she said two syllables took too much work. It had been their personal joke for four years.

Tasia was distracted. "Jay, have you seen my Mamma? She was here."

"Yeah. I saw her when I was walking." Jayla looked around the crowd. "Did you look outside? Maybe she went out to smoke."

Relieved, Tasia hurried outside the building. There were several smokers standing around outside the door, despite the "NO SMOKING" signs, but Mamma wasn't one of them. Tasia walked back inside and looked around the auditorium. Sometimes Mamma fell asleep at strange times, but the auditorium was empty. Tasia felt so stupid. Mamma had gone to get high. There would be no nice dinner at the Inner Harbor. Tasia would go home to an empty house and might not see Mamma for days.

Tasia took her robe off and slung it over her arm. She didn't say goodbye to Jayla. She walked out of the school and headed home. She wanted to cry—just like she had at 5th grade graduation and 8th grade graduation when Mamma hadn't shown up at all, but she had no tears left. This was the last time anyone would do this to her. She would never depend on anyone but herself ever again. She had already filled out all the forms for community college. She would finish there and maybe go out of state to college to get her Bachelor's. No one would be able to disappoint her because she wouldn't expect anything from anybody.

43

"Hey, Fine as Wine!" she heard Kenny's voice call out. She couldn't be bothered with Kenny right now.

"What?! Shorty, you graduated? Look at you! Congratulations!"

Tasia turned around and told him, "Thank you." Kenny stopped talking when he saw her face.

"Yo, Shorty, what's up?" His eyes were wide with concern. "You alright?"

Tasia felt tears welling up and willed herself not to cry. "Yeah. I'm alright." She turned to continue walking. Kenny strode along beside her.

"So, what we doing to celebrate? Let me take you to dinner. This is big shit!" He grinned enthusiastically. It was the first time Tasia noticed how slanted his eyes were—as if he was part Chinese. Or maybe he had some kind of African in him, like Nelson Mandela. She stopped walking and turned towards him.

"For real?" she asked.

"Yeah!" Kenny patted his hip pocket. "I got dollars. Where you wanna go? Just name it and we'll go." No one had ever said that to her before. She stopped to think. Maybe she would choose somewhere really expensive—just to see if he was full of shit.

"Red Lobster!" she finally announced.

Kenny grinned. "Yeah! Let's go! My car is parked right down there."

And that had been the start of everything. The start of

allowing Kenny to tear down her carefully constructed walls, of letting someone get close, of losing her heart, of being abandoned all over again.

She stood up with Sharonda as the bus approached her stop. Sharonda continued to sleep soundly as Tasia walked home. Tasia shifted her from one shoulder to the other. Sharonda was getting heavy and Tasia wished she hadn't sold the stroller Kenny bought, but she needed the money and the pawn shop gave her enough to buy a week's groceries. The seven blocks felt like twenty today, but she finally got home and laid Sharonda on the bed. Tasia grabbed a bag of chips and sat on the couch.

It had all started so perfect. Kenny took such good care of her and he was fun to be around. They went out every night that summer. He took her out to eat at nice restaurants and to the movies. He wanted to go on walks and hold hands. He showered her with gifts, like cute clothes and shoes, and took her to get her hair and nails done. He would sit in the salon and watch with a big smile on his face. He told her every day that she was beautiful and talked about "when we're married." Tasia had never had this much attention in her life. She spent the first few months expecting him to disappear like Mamma, but he kept showing up and eventually Tasia began to depend on him.

Tasia knew Kenny did things that weren't right, even though he wouldn't talk about it. She knew that what he did was

45

probably dangerous. He always had cash, and he didn't have a job. He was exactly the type Nana always talked about— "walking trouble" she called them. Tasia knew it was dangerous to get involved with Kenny, but she was caught up with his soft pink lips, his thick black hair, and his slanted eyes. Nana warned her she was headed for trouble with him, but by then Tasia didn't care.

He started taking her home to his apartment, a first-floor one-bedroom apartment in a row house in Franklin Square. He told her it was "their" place, and she could move in and go to college and he would take care of her. This sounded like a great plan, because Mamma hadn't paid the rent for months and they would get kicked out soon. When Mamma hadn't been home for more than a week, Kenny took Tasia to pack her things and she moved into his apartment. She took out a student loan, which Nana cosigned for, and started at Baltimore City Community College that fall.

Kenny was Tasia's first, and she delighted in the long nights of lovemaking. He had a lot of energy and was very interested in her pleasure. He was patient and gentle with her and only finished up himself when he was sure she was satisfied.

Tasia was shocked at how perfect life was. She went to class during the day, came home and cooked dinner. Kenny came home in the early evening and they ate. She did homework while he watched television. Sometimes he went back out at night, but he always texted her to tell her when he would be home.

Tasia knew she could get pregnant but really didn't think

about it. The only thing she ever heard about getting pregnant was from Nana, who said, "Don't have sex and you won't get pregnant." Tasia didn't have a period for four months before she realized she was pregnant. She was too scared to tell Kenny. This is where she heard things typically fell apart for other girls. But Kenny was excited, picking her up and spinning her around, talking about, "our baby's in there" while rubbing her belly.

Kenny bought everything they needed for the baby—an expensive bedroom set with crib, dresser, and changing table, a huge stroller, diapers, and formula for a year. He got more excited as the time grew closer for the baby to be born. He went with Tasia to the clinic and asked for sonogram pictures to keep in his wallet. When Tasia went into labor, Kenny came home and took her to the hospital. He did everything the doctors and nurses told him, and he kissed Tasia's forehead with every contraction and whispered that it would all be worth it when Tasia saw "our beautiful girl."

When Kenny brought Tasia and Sharonda home, he was the proudest Daddy ever. He fussed around them and wanted to make sure everything was perfect. When Nana came to visit her new great-granddaughter, she walked in with her lips pushed out, prepared to find fault in how the baby was being cared for. But Kenny and Sharonda won her over. Kenny made a big deal of putting Sharonda in Nana's arms, and Sharonda contentedly sucked on her fist as Nana held her. Tasia knew it impressed Nana to see how gently Kenny held Sharonda and how proud he was.

Even though her lips were pushed out, Tasia could tell Nana was trying not to smile.

In the two years she had known him, Kenny never talked about *his* family. Whenever Tasia asked about them, Kenny responded, "I have a mom, but we aren't communicating right now. One day, I'll take you and Sharonda to meet her." He wouldn't say anything else, no matter how many questions Tasia asked. She really wanted to meet his mother. She dreamed about Kenny's mother, Nana, and Mamma (clean and sober) sitting in a park watching Sharonda play, and Kenny and Tasia close by holding hands. It was her favorite dream, and she was certain it would happen one day.

Since Sharonda was born in September, Tasia missed the start of the fall semester her second year, but Kenny told her to go back in the spring and he would pay someone to watch the baby. They found a young woman a few blocks away who kept a few kids, and she took good care of Sharonda. Tasia did really well in her first year and was headed for a straight 4.0 GPA. She would have to stay in school for an extra semester, but she was okay with that. Tasia had been looking at the University of Baltimore for the last two years, and was excited about the prospect of going there. School was perfect. Her little family was perfect. Life seemed to be just perfect.

When Sharonda was six months old, Tasia knew something was wrong with Kenny. He started coming home late without texting to tell her he would miss dinner. She set the table each night and texted multiple times to see where he was. He never responded. In the early hours of the morning, he would come home smelling of liquor and crawl into bed with her. He seemed deep in thought all the time, and he didn't smile like he used to. He stopped playing with Sharonda and barely said anything more than "yes" or "no" when Tasia talked to him. He was like a different person. Tasia asked him, for weeks, what was wrong, but he wouldn't tell her.

"I got some problems out there," was all he would say. "I'ma handle it."

Kenny suddenly didn't have any money, and he only gave her enough to buy the bare necessities around the house and pay the babysitter. He didn't come home to drive her to the market like he used to, so she had to shop from the corner store, where everything cost twice as much. She had less food, diapers, and formula to work with. It was beginning to feel like living with Mamma again.

One day, Tasia complained about him missing dinner. Kenny snapped at her, telling her to get off his back. He had never spoken to her like that before, and she was frightened. When he saw the look on her face, he softened and pulled her to him with an urgency that increased her anxiety.

"You know, you and Sharonda are the most important things in the world to me, right?" he said. Tasia nodded, her face against his chest. "I'm just havin' some trouble right now with some niggas from the east side. I'm tryin' fix it." Tasia felt him lean his head back and look up at the ceiling, his voice catching. "I'm gonna fix it."

The next morning, Kenny left and Tasia never saw him again. She waited, texted, and called for days, but he never responded. The thought slowly dawned on her that he might be somewhere injured. She didn't even know his mother's name, much less how to reach her, so she called the police station and the hospitals, but no one knew anything about him. She watched the news every night, but there was no word of him. She didn't have money to pay the babysitter, so she had to stop going to school right before finals.

One week later, when Tasia and Sharonda returned home from visiting Nana, Tasia recognized some of her stuff on the ground in front of the building—her older shirts and jeans and some garbage bags of pots and utensils. She stood on the sidewalk for a moment, leaning on the stroller, trying to make sense of what she was seeing. *Why was their stuff outside?* It took a moment for her brain to register that their belongings had been tossed outside by the landlord, and that people on the street had already taken most of it. Kenny hadn't paid the rent for months and they had lost their home and everything they owned. It was only then that Tasia began to consider the idea that Kenny might be dead.

Chapter Four

Lisa found a table while LaTanya went to the bar to order drinks. They were at the Friday evening happy hour a little later than usual because Lisa had stayed behind to set up her lesson plans for the following week. She didn't want to take work home for the weekend. LaTanya was an assistant principal at a school in East Baltimore and didn't get off work until 5 p.m. anyway, and Lisa wanted to catch up.

They had been hanging out every few weeks since Lisa began working in Baltimore. It was a time to laugh, vent, and support LaTanya's ongoing search for a man. Lisa had gotten in the habit of scouting men for LaTanya, since right after college, and was keenly aware they had very different tastes in men. LaTanya determined whether she wanted to get to know someone initially based solely on physical attraction. Lisa's search for a husband, on the other hand, had been closely curated by her mother, and every possible suitor was compared to a long list of eligibility criteria, which included things like educational pedigree, generational wealth, and earning potential. Her husband, Kai, had been closely vetted before her mother accepted him as a potential son-in-law. Sometimes Lisa wanted to fight back against her mother's strong opinions about her life, but she didn't have the energy. She often wondered how different her life might have been if her mother wasn't so controlling. From personally managing Lisa's preparation for her debutante ball (including etiquette, posture, and ballroom dancing lessons), to directing every step of her wedding coordinator's work (including choosing her wedding dress and flowers), Diahann Preston was an ever-present force in her daughter's life. *Would she do the same with her own daughters?*

Lisa looked around at the growing crowd. They had missed the usual happy hour crowd where teachers getting off work behaved like middle-school kids in the cafeteria— drinking, flirting, and gossiping until they could hardly stand or pay attention to whom they went home with. The Wild Hours, as Lisa and LaTanya called it, usually started at about 3:30 for the teacher crowd, and as the evening went on, the young professionals from nearby office buildings started filing into the bar, loosening their collars and ties and ditching their jackets, eager to shed the workweek and let loose.

Lisa texted Kai to remind him that she would be home late and to make sure he had ordered pizza for himself and the girls. Jessica and Mia would be anxious to eat dinner and settle down to play video games. Lisa and Kai allowed them to go to town with their video games on Friday evenings, because they were not permitted to play them on school days. The girls devoted Saturdays to volleyball and soccer and Sundays were for chores.

52

But Friday nights were for each person in the family to do whatever he or she wanted, and for Kai and Lisa, this usually included lounging on the couch in their study, with a glass of Malbec in hand, watching movies or binge-watching whatever television series they were currently focused on, happy the girls were preoccupied and not clamoring for their attention.

But not tonight. *This* Friday, Kai was on his own with the kids, and Lisa was out with LaTanya. He would be happy to watch anime all night without feeling any guilt that she wanted him to watch something else with her.

After a thumbs-up from Kai, Lisa put her phone away and scanned the bar. It was a typical Inner Harbor bar, hosting a variety of locals, and a few tourists. Most of the clients fit a particular type: young, white, focused on their cell phones as they sat with friends, steadily becoming more and more drunk. They stood three-deep at the bar, either talking to each other, or trying to get one of the bartenders' attention.

Several televisions around the bar showed the latest poll results of the upcoming election. The Republican candidate, Reginald Sumter, or *The Sump*, as his followers called him, was riling people up at a rally in Memphis. His blond pompadour remained stiffly in place as he gestured wildly in what looked like a bizarre dance. The crowd loved it, and although there was no sound, it was clear they were screaming and shouting their approval of him. Behind him stood several local sheriffs and police officers. While they did not scream and chant, the look of admiration and devotion on their faces reminded Lisa of idol worship. Her stomach churned.

Unfortunately, Lisa's mother liked Reginald Sumpter, thought he would be good for the country, and contributed significantly to his campaign. Lisa felt instinctively there was something almost obscene about her mother's devotion to this politician, but she didn't know how to put her concerns into words. Lisa avoided discussing politics with her mother. She always folded under Diahann's strong opinions. Even her father had stopped talking about politics in the house. During the 2020 election, Diahann had been incensed to discover her husband voted for Democrat Daniel Jackson, the second Black president, instead of voting for the white Republican incumbent. She had barely spoken to her husband for months after the election. Four years later, Grant Preston knew better than to once again incite Diahann's wrath.

LaTanya elbowed her way through the crowd, carrying two glasses of red wine. She set them down on the high table and pulled her petite frame up onto the stool with a sigh. She followed Lisa's gaze up to the television. Instantly, her nose wrinkled, and her full lips turned down at the corners.

"Oh, that fool!" she exclaimed. "There is no way he can win. I don't even know why the press gives him so much airtime. It's sickening."

Lisa shifted uncomfortably in her seat. "I don't know. I know some folks who really like him. It's a little frightening." She thought of Danielle. For the hundredth time she wondered why she was friends with her.

"Like who?" LaTanya demanded. "Who do you know that would actually vote for that ass?"

Lisa hesitated and looked away.

"Oh, no!" LaTanya scoffed. "Don't tell me." Her voice became high-pitched and perky. "You must be talking about Dan-i-elle." Her eyes rolled upwards.

Lisa didn't respond. She was never sure what to say when Danielle gushed on about Reginald Sumter, how he would change the country, bring back law and order and solve every problem known to man. Sumpter said he would return "America to Americans" and that he would stop the "illegals" from taking American jobs. He wanted to cut all social programs and "instill a strong work ethic" in U.S. citizens. "If people don't work, they shouldn't eat," he said, and he was determined to prosecute all people who claimed illness and disabilities were preventing them from earning a living. "Laziness" would become a crime. We would all see that when the handouts went away, and hunger took their place, people would suddenly find they were able to work after all. "Only then," he proclaimed, "would America truly be the great nation God intended her to be."

Lisa knew many of the problems he focused on involved oppressing people who looked like herself, and making white people more dominant than they already were. She knew his supporters, nicknamed The Alt, could be found in every corner of government, law enforcement, criminal justice, and business. She knew The Alt wanted the return of a completely white America, but she didn't know how to put her feelings into words when with Danielle. She felt like a traitor defending Danielle to LaTanya, who did not hide how she felt about the white woman, even when she was present.

LaTanya shook her head. "I'm going to leave you alone, but I just want to remind you that you're nothing but Danielle's pet Negro. She likes being able to say she has a Black friend. She will turn on you faster than your hair turns back on a humid day in August. I guess you'll just have to learn that for yourself."

"Well . . . there are Black people who like Sumpter, too," Lisa pursed her lips, looking down at her hands.

LaTanya studied Lisa for a moment and sighed. "Ok. I'm done. I'm not talking about your momma. You have to figure that one out for yourself." LaTanya smoothed her hand over her short natural cut. With her caramel-colored skin and petite frame, she looked like a teenager, instead of a 31-year-old. Only her curvy figure and worldly air revealed she was, in fact, an adult. Diahann did not like LaTanya at all, and felt she came from a background that was beneath Lisa's station in society. This was the only instance in Lisa's life where she defied her mother; she and LaTanya had been friends for the past ten years, since meeting in a new teachers' program.. The only fight Lisa had ever had with her mother was about having LaTanya as her maid of honor. Lisa won, but that fight almost ended up in a cancellation of the

56

wedding because Diahann threatened to withdraw her substantial financial support. The compromise had been that LaTanya could be in the wedding, but none of LaTanya's friends or family could attend, even though LaTanya's family had treated Lisa like one of their own since they met.

"Girl, what a week. I am *ready* for the weekend!" LaTanya rested her elbows on the table and sank her chin into her hands, looking around. "And the local wildlife is gathered around the watering hole, jockeying for position and power," she whispered in the conspiratorial tone of a narrator in a wildlife documentary. She chuckled as she sipped her wine.

Lisa patted her straightened bob. The mere mention of her hair turning back made her want to go to the bathroom to check. She had spent a lot of time and money in the Dominican salon getting it bone straight, and she wanted it to last for a few more days. She loved the way it moved like a curtain every time she shifted her head. She was thankful to change the topic.

"Yeah? So, what type of wildlife are we?" Lisa sipped her wine and wrinkled her nose. *Tasted like this bottle had been open for way too long.*

"I'm feeling like a hunter tonight. And I have some prey in my sights." LaTanya nodded toward a group of five men sitting at a table together nursing tall glasses of beer.

Lisa looked at them skeptically. "Which one are you eyeing?"

LaTanya stopped perusing the men abruptly and cut Lisa

the side eye, one eyebrow raised. "Are you serious?" she asked, pulling her neck back into her head, her chin almost touching her breasts. "Are you serious." This time she was not asking a question.

Lisa shrugged and looked over at the men. "I don't know. Maybe you're feelin—"

"Never!" LaTanya cut her off with a wave of her hand. "You know I don't stray from the brothers. You're crazy."

Lisa examined the men more carefully. The one Black man at the table was probably in his mid-thirties. He had dark chocolate skin and a smoothly shaven head with a full, neat beard. His shoulders were broad and square, and muscles rippled under the rolled-up sleeves of his dress shirt as he reached for his beer. When he brought the glass to his mouth, it was difficult not to notice the thick fringe of dark eyelashes that fluttered downward as he drank. Lisa wanted to see those lashes up close, if they looked so long and thick from across the room.

"Uh, hello? Are you trying to make it obvious or have you forgotten how to do this?" LaTanya interrupted Lisa's smiling gaze and she quickly looked away from the table of men. But they had already noticed. One of the white men nudged the Black man and he nodded towards them. The Black man looked up as if he had not noticed them, although they were the only other Black people in the bar. He said something to the other men, and they laughed. Lisa turned away, suddenly feeling very warm.

"Sorry," she mumbled. "How embarrassing!"

"Yeah, well, you might have ruined my chances of playing it cool and making him beg for my attention," Lisa fussed. "How long have you and Kai been married? Have you really forgotten how to flirt?"

Lisa shrugged. "I guess so."

She turned her attention back to the television. With seven months to the election, the commentators were discussing Reginald Sumpter's chances of winning. Meanwhile, Sumpter had been endorsed by the KKK, the National Rifle Association, and the National Brotherhood of Police. Lisa had never even heard of the last organization, but apparently, they were members of law enforcement agencies and military branches across the country. They wholeheartedly endorsed Sumpter and his proclamation he would return the country to law and order. The commentators interviewed a Georgia sheriff who proclaimed he had been "waiting many years" for a leader like Sumpter to come to power and "deal with those thugs and criminals who are ruining our country" and to "make it great again."

LaTanya hissed through her teeth. "When was this country ever great? When Black people were in shackles? That's what they mean, you know." She turned her eyes to Lisa. "They won't be satisfied until they own us again."

Lisa sighed and sipped her wine. She didn't know what to think. She knew there was something wrong with the way Danielle thought, but she also knew that, as a Black woman, she had worked very hard to get where she was. Why couldn't everyone else do that, too? Was it so wrong to expect each person to be responsible for their own progress? Who did *she* have to blame when she wasn't successful? The parents of her students seemed to think that society owed them something. Diahann was right; the whole racism excuse was old and overplayed. We left slavery behind a long time ago, and as Diahann liked to say, "the playing field is now even, but some people just don't want to sweat."

Still, something in the air had changed in the past year. Her white neighbors and colleagues were a little less friendly. She noticed small things, like the grocery store cashiers where she had shopped for the past eight years, now suddenly asking to see identification when she wrote a check, even though they knew her name. Or that her mail carrier, who took everyone else's packages up to the front door, now tossed hers onto her driveway without getting out of the mail truck. This past Christmas, some of those packages had been ruined by rain and snow. When she asked her neighbors if they were having the same experiences, they stared blankly and shook their heads. She also found out their block had a holiday party but had not invited her family, although they had been invited the previous years. Lisa brushed most of these events off, thinking she was being overly sensitive, but she could not shake the feeling that the white people around her now had permission to treat her with suspicion and disdain. Nonetheless, as Diahann would say, *that was their problem*. It didn't change the fact that Black people were responsible for pulling themselves up by their own bootstraps. She didn't understand why LaTanya couldn't see that.

"But you have to admit, there are a lot of people who aren't doing what they're supposed to. Some parents of the kids I teach are just living on welfare and aren't even taking care of their kids. Those kids are suffering because of their parents." Lisa shook her head, thinking about her students. "There isn't a single kid in my class who hasn't seen or heard someone get shot. It's disgraceful. Who's taking care of them?"

LaTanya's eyes shot fire. "I used to think that, too. When my mom drank herself to death, and I went to live with my aunt in the projects, I saw a lot of violence. That was rough. And when I got that scholarship to Morgan State, I wanted nothing but to leave that entire life behind, along with everyone I knew. But I learned that my mom drank to numb her pain, and my aunt did the best she could to take care of me and her own kids . . . " LaTanya's voice trailed away as she stared at the television absently.

"But what do you do when the schools only give you a minimal education because the law says they need to park you somewhere, but don't care if you actually learn something?" LaTanya continued. "What kind of job can you get with barely a fifth-grade reading level? My mother graduated high school and had minimal skills, even though she went to school every day. She couldn't get a job. After a while, she believed that living on welfare was what she was supposed to do, because there were no other choices for her. How long can someone keep hope alive?"

61

LaTanya looked at Lisa keenly, waiting for an answer. Lisa shrugged and shook her head.

"You like to think that you would be able to overcome all the things that life throws at you if you were in her situation. But you wouldn't, Lisa. You would have been just like my mother. The only thing you have that my mother didn't have is all external—your family, the opportunities given to you, a good education. You're not a better person than her. You just had better circumstances."

Lisa sighed and turned her gaze back to the television. The Georgia sheriff was now debating with a commentator on the benefits of allowing the military to patrol cities and "get tough on crime." She shook her head again.

"I would like to take you someplace to learn more about this. I know some people who can teach you a different way of thinking." LaTanya's voice was gentler this time. "I can take you, but it's a place that you can't discuss with anyone else."

"I don't know." Lisa was reluctant. "What kind of place?"

"A place where people are trying to figure out how to change circumstances for Black people in this country."

"How? How can they do that?" Diahann's voice played in her head: *stay away from those Black people who wear their race like a badge of honor. Remember, you are always judged by your company, and trouble begets trouble.*

LaTanya toyed with the stem of her wineglass for a moment. She picked the glass up and looked across the bar at the table of men before she took a sip. One of the white men stared boldly back at her. She sighed, shook her head, and looked at Lisa.

"I don't know, Lisa. Let me know when you're ready and I'll take you."

Donovan watched two women sitting across the bar. They were pretty enough, as Black women go, but he was far more interested in a different group of women clustered at one end of the bar. They were white, ranged from late twenties to early thirties, and were steadily getting drunk. One of the women, a petite blonde with her hair pulled back in a ponytail, wearing thick black mascara and pink lip gloss, caught his eye. She flashed him a shy smile from time to time and pretended not to notice him looking at her. They would play this game for a while before he finally made his move.

Steve slung his arm across Donovan's shoulders and picked up his beer for a long swig. He smacked his lips appreciatively and licked the foam from his top lip.

"So, you're not gonna go check out the sisters, huh, Don?" Steve teased, rocking Donovan's body from side to side. His face was getting red, and his voice was loud. This was the part Donovan did not like. When Steve got drunk, he lost the few filters he had. The result was a series of racist and sexist jokes, which Donovan tried to ignore. Steve was generally an okay guy, and had a lot of influence in the company as a senior associate, so it was in Donovan's best interests to hang out with him. Steve held many choice accounts at the firm, and a positive word from him during the next promotion cycle could help Donovan move from associate to senior associate. What was more, Steve understood his power and the fact he could be a critical force in building Donovan's career. This knowledge emboldened him and made him feel comfortable crossing boundaries not usually crossed in the workplace.

"Donovan has his eyes somewhere else," Rick pointed out. He nodded towards the group of white women. "Let me guess—blonde ponytail is your type."

The other guys laughed, and Steve slapped Donovan on the back. "Are you sure? Sister over there has a rack on her I wouldn't mind getting to know better. Just smile at her and get her over here and I'll take it from there." Steve raised his beer to his lips, his eyes fixed on the Black woman with the short hair and large breasts. "Look at those lips . . . " Steve licked his own lips suggestively. "Bet she knows how to use them, too."

Donovan laughed uncomfortably. "Go for it. Not my type."

"I know you're not into the sisters. But I am. Just get her over here." Steve lifted his left hand to his mouth, sucked on his ring finger before sliding the hand into his pants pocket, from which it emerged without his wedding ring. He held his hand up triumphantly to raucous laughter from the other men. "I'm ready." He nudged Donovan with his body. "Hook a brother up," he drawled.

64

Donovan laughed again. *Why did white people think Black people would pimp for them?*

"You're on your own with that, my man," he drawled back. He pointed to the pale mark on Steve's hand where his ring had been. "You might want to tan a bit before you go flashing that hand around."

While the men continued to tease Steve about the woman at the other table, Donovan turned his attention back to the blonde, who made eye contact and smiled at him again. He would wait just a few more minutes, and then go over. It would be a good night.

It was an old school on the western outskirts of the city, almost in the county. The school sat far back from the road, high on a rolling hill. A painted wooden sign at the bottom of the hill, next to the sidewalk, announced that this was the *Baltimore Training Academy*. The large brick structure covered the entire block and was surrounded by a tall wrought iron fence with a gate, the only thing visible from the road. A long driveway led through the open gate and into a parking lot, adjoining a small courtyard. Once inside the gate, Corey thought the building looked abandoned, its windows so cloudy with dirt and age, he wondered if the people inside could even see out.

Piles of leaves, that hadn't been raked up from the previous fall, stood in small hills around the courtyard in front of the large, metal front door. The wind whipped the leaves up into

65

the air and swirled them around Corey and Devonte as they approached the door. Corey was sure they were in the wrong place—they had to be—but he stood silently behind Devonte as he pulled on the handle and the heavy door swung slowly open. Inside the door was a vestibule and another heavy door. A tall, broad-shouldered man stood in front of the door. He and Devonte exchanged nods and Devonte handed the man his cell phone, which he placed in a basket of phones.

"You have to give him your phone," Devonte told Corey. "And he's going to pat you down."

Corey handed over his phone and cringed as the man ran his hands up and down Corey's outstretched arms, legs, and trunk. His thoughts flashed to the police groping his body, and he had to force himself to breathe deeply to put down the rising panic.

Once satisfied that Corey was not carrying any weapons or recording devices, the man stepped aside and nodded toward the door. Devonte thanked him and pushed the door open. As they walked inside, Corey realized the abandoned building look was merely a facade. The building was teeming with activity and full of people. A small group of men stood just inside the doorway— weapons ready—a second level of security. Those men nodded to Devonte and eyed Corey up and down, not in an unfriendly way, but definitely with an air of caution.

They passed several people in the hallway, all of whom seemed to be hurrying somewhere with purpose. As they passed classrooms, Corey saw groups of people dressed in black, learning martial arts. Some students held sticks and seemed engaged in a dance-like fight. In one of the martial arts classes, all the students were teenagers. In other classrooms, teachers taught history or politics to adults, writing dates and events on the board. There were classrooms that seemed to be about gardening, as students walked between tables of plants over which hung grow lights and irrigation hoses. In other classrooms, people seemed engaged in animated discussion. Some classrooms were filled with children involved in arts' projects. In another room, people meditated, sitting cross-legged and silent on the floor with their eyes closed. Everyone was Black; everyone was happy and full of purpose. Corey had never seen a school like this.

Devonte laughed at Corey's expression as they walked. "Yeah, man. This is what I've been trying to tell you."

"I thought we were going to a meeting. You didn't say anything about all this," Corey muttered, his head turning from side to side as he tried to peer into each classroom they passed. "What are they all doing?"

"You will find out in a minute. And you will get to ask all your questions. Just wait." Devonte seemed happy, blissful almost. Corey stopped walking and stared at him with suspicion.

"This ain't no cult, is it?"

Devonte gave his shoulder a slight push to make him keep walking. "No, man. This ain't no cult. This is about Black people doing things for themselves and not waiting for Wypipo to come save us. Just wait. You'll find it all out at the meeting."

They continued walking down the long hallway. Many of the people they passed nodded to Devonte or greeted him by name. Most were dressed in white, and all seemed very busy as they rushed along. Corey also noticed there wasn't any of the *sizing up* or *flexing* that men typically do to each other. Women didn't seem interested in flirting or looking cute. People were too busy for that, instead flashing a smile or greeting as they passed and continued on their way. There was a sweet, earthy scent in the air that Corey could not place. It smelled like perfume or incense. He didn't know what it was, but it was warm, heady, and inviting.

Devonte noticed Corey sniffing the air and smiled. "Frankincense. Incense of royalty. That's what we are." Corey frowned, confused, but Devonte hurried him along, "Come on— it's gonna start now."

Finally, they reached the auditorium, which seemed to be quickly filling up, and Devonte led the way down to the front. The main lighting came from bright stage lights, while wall sconces around the room provided a warm yellow glow. The dark red velvet stage curtains stood wide open where a huge red image of the African continent could be seen. Beneath it, the word *Welcome* was projected on the white screen at the back of the stage. People sat in groups holding whispered conversation.

Devonte ushered Corey into a row and they were seated. Bob Marley singing "Exodus" played from speakers on the walls. Corey's eyes were wide as he looked around the dim room. Most of the people wore short sleeves, probably because the auditorium was very warm. Corey slipped out of his hoodie and draped it over the back of his chair.

After a few minutes, four people walked out onto the stage; the music faded, and the room became quiet. People continued to enter the auditorium and find seats without speaking. The two men and two women were dressed in white T-shirts and white pants, which looked like medical scrubs, and sneakers. They stood silently and looked around the room, smiling.

One of the men stepped forward and outstretched his arms. He was in his late forties, with mahogany-colored skin and salt and pepper hair, mustache and beard. "Sanibona!" he pronounced, smiling widely.

"Ngikhona!" the room replied loudly. Corey looked around. *What kind of language is this?* he wondered.

As if reading his mind, the man continued, "For those of you who are here for the first time, Sanibona is Zulu for 'I see you.' Ngikhona means, 'I am here.' I see each one of you in your beauty, your strength, your magnificence, and all your inherent potential. Our very existence depends on each other. I do not exist without you, and you do not exist without me. I am because you are, and you are because I am. We need each other."

At this, the crowd erupted in clapping, cheering, and foot-stomping. Despite his suspicion and confusion, Corey smiled. The atmosphere in the room was warm, comforting, and joyful. It was infectious.

One of the women on the stage stepped forward. She was

young, late twenties, with shoulder-length braids. "Welcome to the Baltimore Cell, headquarters of the Black Resistance Movement. There are Cells like this all over the country, all planning the liberation of Black people from white supremacy. We will take care of ourselves, develop our own economies, our own food sources, our own education systems, and our own security. Most of all, we will end our dependence on white systems, governments, education, welfare, and laws.

"We are preparing for the rise of The Alt, which will begin this year, with the upcoming election of Reginald Sumter. This has been predicted by the ancestors, who have told us to prepare for incredibly difficult times for our people. Many think we have been freed from enslavement and segregation, but our ancestors tell us we are entering a time of tribulation, similar to the Red Summer of 1919, where whites rampaged through this country, indiscriminately killing Black people. If you look around, you will see the signs of rising white dominance. The Alt has freed white people from the narrative that says they should integrate with us and make equity a basic tenet of this society. The Alt's narrative is that white people should take their country back, and many are listening.

"Our ancestors have predicted that, in this year, 2024, white people's alternative interpretation of history, which they have been forced to suppress for decades, will finally be realized. This interpretation says we are inferior, unpredictable, dangerous, and that we do not belong in this country. Despite the fact we have been freed from chattel slavery, they will seek to either kick us out of the country or return us to chains. We must be prepared in every way possible to fight them."

The other woman stepped forward. "This does not necessarily mean we will engage in violent resistance, but we are prepared to do so if we need to." She had a West Indian accent and swung her long, thick locs over her shoulder. "We will be prepared to engage in armed battle as well as unarmed resistance. This is why every person who has breath must know how to fight with their body, fight with their mind, and fight with their will. We must put aside the ways that white people have used to divide us—that we have bought into—how we dress, our skin color, our hair, our possessions. We must resist the ways in which white supremacy has classified us, and instead find a new classification for ourselves. There is only one class—it is human, beautiful, and full of potential. We must stop begging them to see us, recognize us, and honor us. We must stop begging them to give us resources and develop our own. We must stop using them as a benchmark for our success, and develop our own benchmarks based on values that would make our ancestors proud. This is not about hating white people. This is about loving ourselves."

The last man stepped forward. "But the work begins inside us. We have much to do. First, we need to decolonize our minds. Most of us do not realize that white supremacy affects our values, our interactions, and our self-concept. We are constantly striving to be more like white people. We have been taught that we must straighten our hair, shave our heads, our beards, anything that makes us too Black. We have mistakenly adopted the individualistic views that belong to the European, instead of the collectivist views from Mother Africa. We believe it is every man or woman for themselves. We have become like crabs in a bucket, willing to step on each other on our way to success. Our original values have been beaten out of us. We have been taught that we must strive to have the education of the white man, the house and garden like the white man, the fancy cars like the white man. Some of us even think that when we have sex with or marry white people, we become more normalized, more successful. In the Black Resistance Movement, we reject those values and return to the values that say, Black is beautiful, brilliant, and beneficial. If you are tired of living in white systems that say you are nothing and want to become part of a community where your beauty and brilliance are recognized, you need to join us."

By the time the last man finished talking, Corey was breathless. He had never heard anything like this before, yet something inside him reacted with joy, relief, acceptance. His body pulsed. He felt strangely alive and awake. As the audience rose to its feet with thunderous applause, he joined them. He looked over at Devonte, who seemed enraptured. This time, Corey did not scoff about cult-like behavior; he got it. This felt like something he had been waiting for without actually knowing what it was. All the rage that had slowly boiled inside him since the day Uncle Tony died finally had an outlet. The cloud of smoke usually

72

swirling around him was gone, and his vision was clear. He could finally do something, and this was where it would happen.

Chapter Five

Donovan stuffed papers into his briefcase. He was seething inside, but kept a blank expression on his face. *He would never let these motherfuckers know he was pissed.*

"See you tomorrow, Don! Have a good night!" Steve called out as he and Rick walked past. "I know you will, too." Steve gave Donovan a suggestive wink, a leering grin on his face. "Say hi to Kirstie for me."

Steve dragged out Kirstie's name as he turned to face Donovan, walking backwards to the entrance. He stared at Donovan; the grin fixed on his face, but something in his eyes told Donovan he was not as amused as he appeared. He paused for a moment, as if he wanted to say something else, then turned on his heel and hurried after Rick's disappearing back.

Donovan was not fooled. He knew Steve didn't like the fact that he was dating Kirstie. Steve had been pissed when Kirstie left the bar with him the night they met. It was fine for married Steve to want to fuck every Black woman he saw, but he did not like the fact that Donovan dated white women. Donovan took secret pleasure in the fact that Steve couldn't do anything about it. It gave him a sense of power he did not feel at any other time in the firm.

He grabbed his briefcase and headed for the door. He didn't want to be late for his dinner date with Kirstie. Thankfully, the restaurant was just a couple of blocks from the tall glass building that housed the finance and accounting firm of Taylor, Braddock, and Smith. As he rode down on the elevator, he removed his jacket, loosened his tie, and rolled up his sleeves. He was ready for a glass of wine and the opportunity to put the day behind him. He was ready to fully immerse himself in the beautiful Kirstie.

They agreed to meet at Phillips Seafood on Pratt Street, but Kirstie wasn't there yet. He positioned himself at the table so he could watch her walk in. He loved to watch her—gleaming blonde hair, petite frame. She was perfect.

His phone rang. He looked down to see his mother's number. He sighed. She had been calling him all week. He looked at his watch. Kirstie probably wouldn't arrive for a few minutes. He stifled a sigh as he answered the phone.

"Hi, Mom." He tried to force a smile into his voice.

"There you are! I thought I had lost you." Melva Franklin's voice was deep, warm, and rich with a strong Jamaican accent. "You dash mi 'way like ol' shoe." She chuckled.

Donovan felt the usual irritation rise in him. *Why did she always have to start every conversation like that?* "I've just been busy, Mom. You know, it's tax season." He tried to keep his voice neutral.

"Yeah man, mi know. But that don't mean I don't miss you. When you comin' by? Come for Sunday dinner."

"I don't know, Mom. I might have to work. I'll see."

"Work on a Sunday?" Her voice was incredulous, as if he had said he planned to kill someone. He didn't hide his sigh this time.

"Yes, Mom. This is a busy time for accountants. I might have to catch up on work. I'll see." He saw Kirstie enter the restaurant and look around. The hostess leaned in to talk to her. Kirstie pointed towards him and began walking over.

"I've got to go, Mom. I will see if I'm free on Sunday."

"Okay. Feel free to bring a friend. I'm cookin' oxtails and rice and peas and cabbage." She paused. She knew she had his attention. His mother's cooking was unparalleled. "See you Sunday. Be 'dere by t'ree."

He hung up and greeted Kirstie with a hug and a kiss. He loved the way her hair felt against his neck as he hugged her— like spun silk. He helped her off with her coat and pulled the chair out for her.

Kirstie nodded towards his phone, her eyebrows raised. "Still working?" she asked.

Donovan sat across from her. "No. That was my mother." He chuckled. "She wants me to come over for dinner." He picked up the menu. He could tell he had piqued Kirstie's curiosity.

"Tonight?" she asked.

"No. Sunday. She's cooking my favorite meal." He

turned his attention to the menu, hoping she would do the same.

"Oh, really?" Kirstie leaned her elbows on the table and eyed him. "And what would that favorite meal be?"

It was no use. She would not be distracted. He put the menu down. He always ordered the same thing here anyway.

"Oxtails, rice and peas and cabbage." He felt strange talking about his mother to her. She and Kirstie were worlds apart.

Kirstie wrinkled her perky nose. "Oxtails? You mean like cow tails?" she asked. "That's . . . interesting." The corners of her pink lips turned down like a petulant child. She was so cute.

Donovan chuckled. "It's just something we eat in Jamaica. She cooks it for hours in the pressure cooker until the bones are soft. It's really good."

Kirstie sat up straight. "Your family's from Jamaica? I didn't know that. How have we been dating for almost three months and you never mentioned that?" She looked hurt.

Donovan shrugged. "It never came up, I guess." His family was the last thing he wanted to talk to Kirstie about. Most times, he didn't even want to think about his mother, her new husband, or her new children. They really weren't a part of his life.

Kirstie leaned her elbows on the table again. Her hair was loose and flowed around her shoulders like a straight, shining golden sheath. Donovan had the memory of it trailing across his bare chest. He started to get hard.

77

"Tell me about your family. Were you born there? How long has your family been here?" Her blue eyes were open wide, and she rested her chin in her hand. "All you've told me is that your undergraduate and graduate work was at Hopkins. But I don't know about your life before that."

The waiter appeared, poured their water, and took their drink orders. Kirstie waited for him to leave before turning her attention back to Donovan. She didn't say anything, but her raised eyebrows and pointed stare told him she wanted him to answer.

Donovan sighed. "Okay. I was born in Jamaica. My mother left me in Jamaica with relatives so she could come to the States and work when I was five. She sent for me almost ten years later, and I came to Baltimore in ninth grade. I lived with her and her new husband and her two new children. I got really good grades in school, and was offered a full scholarship to Hopkins. End of story. There's nothing more to tell." He took a long drink of water. "Oh yes, and I really like oxtails and rice and peas when my mother cooks it."

"Where does your family live? In Baltimore?"

"In Baltimore County. Catonsville." He picked up the menu. "Do you know what you want to order?" he asked.

Kirstie opened the menu and gave it a cursory glance before closing it. "Yep," she replied. "How old are your siblings?"

"My brother is nineteen. He's studying computer science and my sister is twenty-one. She's about to graduate from Morgan State."

The waiter appeared with glasses of wine and took their order. Kirstie turned back to Donovan.

"That's so cool! And you have a stepfather, right?"

"That's right." Donovan could not hide his look of disgust.

"You don't like him?" Kirstie raised her eyebrows again. "Did he treat you badly when you came to live with them?"

Donovan took a sip of his wine and slowly placed the glass on the table. "No. He didn't treat me badly. I just don't like him."

"Why not?" Kirstie pressed.

"He just . . ." Donovan was suddenly irritated. "I don't know. I just never liked him. My mother left me in Jamaica. She came here and created a whole new family. Things were hard for me back home. My aunt was very poor. She struggled to raise me, even with the money my mother sent; it wasn't enough. Meanwhile, my mom is here and has time and energy and enough money to make a whole new family. *Then* they send for me. I come here, and they expect me to help take care of those little brats that got everything that should have been mine."

Donovan stopped suddenly, surprised he had let loose in that way. He looked away from Kirstie. He didn't want to see what was in her eyes.

Kirstie reached across the table and took his hand. "I'm sorry," she whispered. "That must have been so hard."

Donovan took a deep breath. He forced himself to look at

79

Kirstie and smile. "It's okay. I'm over it. That was a long time ago." He fought the urge to pull his hand away. He didn't want her to feel sorry for him. He was fine.

Kirstie paused. "I got the sense when I walked up to the table, that you were already tense. Is that because you were talking to your mom?"

Donovan paused. He and Kirstie had not been dating for long and he wasn't sure how she would react to him sharing so much.

"I'm fine. It was just a tough day at work."

"How so?"

"I just . . . I just don't feel the firm is distributing clients fairly. I was upset about that today." He sipped more wine.

"They're giving you bad ones?" Kirstie picked up one of the warm buns that the waiter had placed on the table and buttered it.

"They're not bad, per se. They just aren't the choice ones. I keep getting the little start-ups that have no money. There's only so much I can do with them. It's the good clients that get you promoted."

Donovan did not add that the firm kept giving him all the Black clients and the nonprofit organizations. None of them had a large enough budget to be noteworthy. Steve commented that Donovan would be able to "relate to them" better than the other associates. Donovan wondered if that meant they thought he

80

couldn't relate to white clients? Or clients with large budgets? Or maybe they really just thought those clients couldn't relate to him.

Kirstie smiled at the waiter when he brought their appetizers. "Well, just tell them. Just tell them you want different clients—that you aren't happy with the ones you've got." She spread her napkin across her lap and reached for a shrimp roll. "I'm sure it's just an oversight."

Donovan took a deep breath. She was so naïve. But that's what he loved about her. Kirstie thought the playing field was level for everyone. Why would she think otherwise? Based on her experience, the field *was* level for everyone. At least, it was for *her.*

He smiled and picked up a shrimp roll. "I will have to try that." He bit into the shrimp roll and took his time chewing so he could steady his breathing. "So, tell me about your day. How's life in the world of pharmaceutical sales?"

Tasia couldn't believe the change in Jayla when she opened the door. The bone-straight weave her friend had worn for as long as Tasia had known her was gone, replaced by smooth, shiny Senegalese twists that flowed around Jayla's face and down her shoulders, making her look like those pictures of African princesses you see in books. Gone were the expensive, name-brand clothes Jayla loved to rock. Instead, she wore white scrubs and white sneakers. Tasia paused in the open door and gawked.

Jayla chuckled, "You look like me when I cut that weave out—minus the tears. You gonna let me in or we gonna stay out in the hallway?"

Tasia opened the door wider and stepped aside. Sharonda clung to her, skirting away from Jayla as she entered, yet never letting go of Tasia's leg.

Jayla threw herself into a chair and turned her gaze to Sharonda, "You gonna come over here and give Auntie Jay a hug? You don't remember me?" Jayla's beautiful, full lips turned down on the edges in mock sadness. She held her arms out but Sharonda clung to her mother's leg so hard she almost tripped Tasia as she walked to a chair.

"Nana at work?" Jayla asked.

"Yup." Tasia pulled Sharonda onto her lap. "She's working another double. They think there's gonna be snow so she has to stay on." Tasia shook her head. "She really needs to retire. She's too old for this." She pushed the guilt away and turned her attention to Jayla. "So, what's going on with you? What kind of job you got that you're wearing that?" Tasia nodded towards the scrubs. "And why were you so anxious to come over here tonight? I know when something's up with you. Spill it."

Jayla shrugged and examined her nails. They weren't as long as before, but they were still nicely painted in a natural color. "A lot. Learning how to defy the white man." She looked up at Tasia in order to gauge her reaction.

Tasia shook her head in confusion. "What white man?"

82

Jayla leaned forward in her chair. "Not just any white man—white supremacy. Tayz, I learned some things about how white people continue to create poverty and injustice for us. And most of us don't even know it." Her eyes sparkled with energy and excitement. Tasia had only ever seen Jayla this excited over some expensive new name-brand item she had acquired. Tasia was confused.

"I . . . I don't understand." She bounced Sharonda on her knee. "I don't even see white people unless I go to the unemployment office. So, I don't see how they do anything to me."

Jayla sat back in her chair looking contemplative. "I don't know if I can explain it yet, because I'm still learning. I met this guy a few months ago who offered to take me to a meeting. He was real cute so I said yes because I liked him. And he took me to this meeting where they told me I had everything wrong. Everything I thought was important was all about upholding white supremacy.

"I just want to take you to meet these folks who can explain it to you." Her eyes sparkled pleadingly. "They opened my eyes to things I still don't really understand, but I know my eyes have been closed for so long. And I keep looking around at my friends and family. And we all have our eyes closed—like little sheep—letting the white man keep us locked up in this shit we're living in!"

Tasia shook her head in confusion. "What shit?"

"Come with me to a meeting so you can hear about it. Let me introduce you to some people. They can tell you better than I can."

Tasia's eyes grew wide. "Ohhhh. This is like that stuff you were selling, where you took me to meet those folks and they tried to get me to sell it, too." She shook her head again. "No, thank you. I'm good. I can't sell anything."

Jayla laughed. "OK. Yeah, that was when I was selling those knives door-to-door. No. This is not multi-level marketing. I'm not trying to get you to sell anything." She leaned forward again. "I'm trying to get you to open your eyes about what is happening around you!" Jayla's hands traced the air in excitement.

Tasia frowned at Jayla in suspicion. "I don't have anywhere to leave Sharonda. I can't go to any meeting."

Jayla grinned widely. "See, these folks want you to bring Sharonda, and they have playgroups for kids, and great teachers. Bring her and come. These folks love kids. They are the future of Blackness."

Future of Blackness? White supremacy? Tasia still didn't know what Jayla was talking about, but the thought of being able to leave Sharonda someplace safe so she could get a moment to herself sounded really good. She had been with Sharonda round the clock, except when she was working. She couldn't describe how tired she felt. And even if she had to sit through some stupid sales meeting, she would have a moment to herself. She didn't

84

have to listen. She could just sit there and zone out. She sighed at the thought of it.

"When is this meeting?" she pulled her earring out of Sharonda's grip.

"There's one tonight. I could take you." Jayla offered eagerly.

"Tonight?!" Tasia had planned to lie in bed and watch TV—yet another night 7-Eleven said they didn't need her.

"Yes. Tonight. Let's stop at that Jamaican place and get some food, and then we can go. It's not that far from there." Jayla read the look on Tasia's face. "I got you. I'm buying."

Tasia shrugged. *They needed to eat, and Nana would be out 'til late.* She had no more objections.

"Okay."

"Good. Go get some clothes on. We need to leave now if we're gonna stop and eat."

Corey sat on a chair in the small office. He was nervous to meet the Black Resistance Movement elder assigned to him. This was his fifth time in The Cell Block, as the old school was called, and each time he left invigorated, with his mind racing, eager to understand more about what he had heard. At night, he and Devonte sat up talking, with Corey asking questions about Black liberation and what the Baltimore Cell was planning. Devonte answered as many questions as he could, but suggested Corey

85

meet with some of the elders of the Cell. Each time Corey went to the meetings, he peppered the organizers with questions.

At first, he thought they would be annoyed that he constantly pestered them, but their gentle smiles and patient answers in response to his questions made him realize that this was exactly what they wanted, that they were excited by his curiosity, and they encouraged his seeking. Eventually, Shelly, the young woman with braids who had spoken on the stage at his first meeting, suggested Corey might be ready to develop a relationship with an elder who could guide him and answer his questions. His elder was to be Samuel, and Corey was there to meet with him for the first time today.

Corey looked around the office. Pale afternoon sunlight filtered through the dusty windowpanes. The setup looked like his old high school guidance counselor's office, with a few chairs, a desk, and a bookcase, but that's where the resemblance ended. Instead of the drab, putty-brown walls of his high school, these concrete block walls were a bright canary yellow. On the wall was painted a huge map of the world, with Africa at its center. The continent was painted in bright stripes of red, green, and black, and the other countries on the map were all painted the same shade of light green. Arrows coming out of Africa pointed to Europe, the U.S., South and Central America, and other parts of the map. In huge red letters painted above the map were the words, "THE DIVINE DIASPORA." Corey wondered what it all meant.

The office door opened, and a tall, thin, brown-skinned

man with salt and pepper hair, walked in. Like most of the elders and organizers, he wore white scrubs and white sneakers. He smiled at Corey and extended his hand.

"Samuel. Nice to meet you, Brother Corey." He pulled up a chair across from Corey and sat slowly.

Although his face was almost completely unlined, Corey realized from the careful way in which he lowered himself to the chair he was much older than he looked. His eyes mesmerized Corey. Large and soft brown, they regarded Corey calmly, with wisdom, kindness, and . . . amusement. Corey didn't know why he thought of those words when he looked at Samuel.

Corey suddenly realized he had not responded to Samuel's greeting, and that he was still grasping Samuel's long, thin fingers as the man sat in his chair. He pulled his hand away, embarrassed.

"Hey. What's up?" He wanted to kick himself. *That's not how you're supposed to talk to an elder. What does that even mean, anyway?* He knew it wasn't just about age, but this man was much older than Momma.

"Oh, you know." Samuel settled into his chair and crossed his long legs, gently swinging the ankle of the top leg back and forth. "Trying to keep the white man's foot off my neck." He chuckled, his eyes never leaving Corey's.

Corey couldn't help but smile. "Don't I know it." He stared at Samuel. He sat down, not knowing where to start.

"So, I'm told you want to learn more about BRM—the

Black Resistance Movement," Samuel began. He said the name of the movement slowly, seeming to savor every word. He stopped for a moment, contemplating his own hands, crossed in his lap. He examined perfectly clean, clipped nails before looking up at Corey. "I've heard a lot about you." He smiled, watching and waiting for Corey's reaction.

Corey felt a sense of dread flood him and realized his armpits were wet. "About me?" His voice cracked. Oh shit, had he been that much of a pest? "Wh . . . what'd you hear?"

Samuel smiled again. "Oh, that you're smart, curious, energetic, driven. We like those characteristics here at the Cell."

Corey sighed with relief and chuckled. "Well, I don't know about all that, but I do have a lot of questions."

Samuel tipped his head to one side and regarded Corey solemnly. "I have many questions for you, too."

Corey shrugged. "But I don't know anything."

"Oh yes, you do. You know your history, and that history will shape where you go in your future, as it does for all of us."

Corey sat silently, trying to follow.

"Do you know about Marcus Garvey?" Samuel asked.

"Uhh . . . I don't think so. Who is he?"

Samuel smiled and slid down in his chair as if getting comfortable to tell a good story. His leg swung slowly from the knee now, and he leaned his head back, as though lost in thought.

"Marcus Garvey was a Black man. He is now considered one of the national heroes of Jamaica. He lived in the 1800s and

88

taught us about Black empowerment. Have you heard of it?" Samuel brought his chin down and regarded Corey.

"No. We didn't learn about that in school."

"Of course, you didn't. Why would the white man teach Black children about Black empowerment?"

"Some of my teachers were Black. They didn't teach me."

"Black teachers learn white supremacy, and that's what they teach. I'm not surprised." Samuel laced his hands behind his head and looked back up at the ceiling. "But you see, Marcus Garvey taught us that we must know our history because history is the landmark by which we are directed in our lives. The history of a movement, a nation, and a race are the guideposts of that group's destiny. And, of course, we keep hearing that any nation or group that ignores its history is destined to repeat it." Samuel looked at Corey with a piercing, but not unkind gaze.

Corey felt as though Samuel had pinned him to his chair with the look. He took a deep breath.

"So, what is your history, young Brother Corey? What has brought you to this moment?"

"I . . . I don't know where to start." Corey wasn't prepared for this conversation. It all felt too raw.

"Start from the beginning." Samuel's eyes were understanding and kind, but unrelenting.

"Ok. Well, I was born in West Baltimore . . . " Corey began. He told Samuel the whole sordid story of his life—about

Momma, Calvin, Aunt Doreen, Uncle Tony, Mrs. Minkus, Devonte, the police, and the swirling cigarette smoke, which he described as anger because he didn't know what else to call it.

The words came tumbling out so fast he could barely even understand himself. When he got to the part about Momma and how she was when she came out of jail, his voice shook, and tears fell. He let them fall, wiping them with the back of his hand, and kept talking until his nose ran, and his shirt became soaked with tears.

He talked about Calvin and his struggle with heroin. He talked about school and his dreams for graduation and a career, and how the police took that all away from him in a moment. He talked about the broken nose and the sadness—how he hadn't eaten a full meal for a month—how he kept calling out of his part-time job at the laundromat and knew he would lose it soon. He talked about how he still had nightmares and was afraid to sleep, how he kept a little light on in the room to keep the bad dreams away. He talked about his shame that someone could have done that to him, and his confusion about what to do next, how to pick up his life. He talked about how he felt like he could explode and take someone out.

While he spoke, Samuel nodded at one moment, and shook his head at another. Corey felt as though Samuel already knew his story, that it was already familiar to him, although Corey had never told it to a single soul. Ever.

When he had cried all his tears, spoken all his words, and

was completely spent, they sat in silence as Corey breathed heavily. By then, the sun was going down, and the room was shadowy. Samuel got up and turned on a lamp on the desk. Out in the hallway, Corey could hear the chatter of children walking past the door. But he and Samuel sat without speaking for a long time. In some strange way, Corey knew Samuel's silence was in honor of his story, a tribute to his history, and he appreciated the gesture.

When Samuel spoke, it was with an air of gravity. "Brother Corey, what do you know about the history of white supremacy in this country and particularly in Baltimore?"

Corey wiped his nose with the sleeve of his sweatshirt and shook his head. "Nothing." He felt ashamed.

"You see, what you and your family have experienced, was all planned. It was all created, and if you think that it was an accident, or that it all started with Mrs. Minkus, or those police officers, that's exactly what you are supposed to think. But this is a much bigger and more complex story." Samuel uncrossed his legs and placed both feet on the floor, leaning forward, elbows on his knees.

"Let me tell you about the civilizations we created in Africa, the scientific inventions we made. Let me tell you how we were doing brain surgery when white people were still learning to hunt and forage, how brilliant we were and still are as a people, and how we were stolen from our homes and brought to this country to build it and create wealth for white people."

91

Samuel told Corey the history of Black people as royalty, engineers, warriors, and scientists from Africa to the American South. He continued through enslavement to the Black Codes and Reconstruction to Jim Crow. He talked about the mass migration of Black people to the North, and how whites considered this migration an infiltration, causing mass fear and anger. How, from practices started in Baltimore, the federal government learned to shuffle Black people into certain neighborhoods, where the rents were high and the infrastructure nonexistent, where they experienced overcrowding, disease, frustration, and hopelessness. How the modern police force was simply a reincarnation of the slave-era overseer, designed and appointed to watch over, control, and subdue Black people. How the courts and the laws were created to uphold the overseers' work and keep Black people poor, dependent, ignorant, and powerless. How the social service system was another reincarnation of the plantation system, how the education system was created to reinforce the idea that Blacks were inferior. Samuel asked Corey just how much of what he had learned in school was created by Black people?

When Corey shrugged and shook his head, Samuel smiled and continued. He talked about how little had changed for Black people over the last fifty years, regardless of who sat in the white House, and that Black people, in large number, had even given up voting, because they had been taught that the electoral system was not for them. He talked about Black Wall Street and Rosewood, and how whenever and wherever Black people create success, white people come to burn it down while, at the same time, telling them they never accomplished anything. He talked about Sumpter and his supporters, The Alt coming to power, how this was simply a culmination of all that had come before, and that with the election of Reginald Sumpter, white people were reliving their dreams of returning Black people to the plantation, providing free labor, because it would get to the point where they were so broken and so poor that even the sting of the overseer's whip would feel like an improvement over what they had now.

When Samuel stopped talking, Corey was wide-eyed. He had never heard anything like this. His mind was spinning. He couldn't process it all. He felt like he could hardly catch his breath.

Samuel smiled. "So, that's a lot to think about. I'm sure you will have many questions, but that's enough for tonight." He glanced at the watch on his thin wrist. "I smell food out there, and it's almost nine o'clock. How about we go to the kitchen and see what they've got? I know Brother Carl will have something good for us."

Samuel stood and reached his hand out to Corey, who felt planted in his seat. Samuel took Corey's hand and pulled him to his feet. He stood close to him and put his hand on Corey's shoulder, looking him in the eye. "Remember what I told you that Marcus Garvey said about history?"

Corey nodded.

Samuel squeezed his shoulder affectionately. "Brother

93

Marcus also said that what you do today, that is worthwhile, will inspire others to act at some future time. He said that chance has never yet satisfied the hope of a suffering people, but that action, self-reliance, and the vision of self and the future, have been the only means by which the oppressed have seen and realized the light of their own freedom. Remember, when you become enlightened, you understand that it is no longer about your success alone, because as long as some of us continue to suffer, we will all suffer. So, I ask you, young Brother Corey, what action will *you* take to realize the freedom we as Black people will have in the future? What will be your role?"

Chapter Six

Kai brought the last of the burgers and hot dogs in from the grill, and went upstairs to shower, while Lisa arranged the chicken in a glass bowl. She laid out the burgers, dogs, chicken, rolls, buns, potato salad, and kale salad on the table. Danielle would bring dessert and drinks. It was always like that. Danielle and Ryan professed that they liked Lisa's cooking so much they felt "intimidated" to cook for her. So, they always brought items they could purchase from the store.

Lisa didn't mind. She was pretty sure, from watching and smelling what Danielle brought to work for lunch, that she didn't want to eat Danielle's cooking—even though they had been friends for four years.

"Jessica and Mia, time to get off the video games," she said over her shoulder. No answer. She walked into the family room and stood behind the couch. Both girls stared at the large television intently, controllers in hands. They weren't even blinking as they played.

"Uh, excuse me, Ladies. I am speaking to you."

Jessica dragged her eyes away from the screen briefly to glance at Lisa, and then continued playing. Mia never even looked up.

"Hi, Mom!" Mia said cheerfully, as she made her character jump to avoid a group of rolling tumbleweeds. "What's up?" Her older sister hunched down further into the couch and pushed the controller closer to the television. The tip of her tongue snaked out the side of her mouth as she played.

"I told you both it was time to stop playing," Lisa said between clenched teeth. She glanced toward the dining room table, visible in the open layout of the house's first floor. She mentally went over all the food again. It was done. She could relax. "Josh and Cora will be here soon and you both need to get some clothes on." She turned back to the kitchen. *Why was she so irritated?*

"Mom, can we just finish—?" Jessica began, finally looking up.

"No!" Lisa whipped around on her heel so fast, Jessica almost dropped the remote in surprise. "This is my third time asking, and I don't think I should have to keep repeating the same thing over and over." She breathed hard and slow, forcing herself to calm down. She lowered her voice. "Please. Do what I asked of you, so that the next time, I don't have to just walk over and turn the game off."

Jessica hissed between her teeth and threw the remote onto the couch. Mia got up and turned the television off. She sighed, shrugged her shoulders, and danced off toward the stairs humming, her plaits flopping.. But Jessica gave Lisa a nasty side-eye, hissed again, and twisted her lips as she walked away.

Kai passed Jessica at the bottom of the stairs, and she nearly bumped him with her shoulder. He stopped and watched her stomp up the stairs. He turned to Lisa with eyebrows raised. Lisa shrugged.

Kai walked towards the table, reaching for a hotdog. Lisa slapped his hand playfully. When he pulled his hand away, she wrapped her arms around his waist and buried her head in his chest. He smelled like a fresh mixture of fabric softener, soap, deodorant, and aftershave. She closed her eyes and breathed him in, her face against his soft T-shirt. He held her and smoothed her hair. He always knew what she needed, and it had been like that since they met in college.

"What's up, Little Spoon? Puberty drama?" he chuckled against her head. "It's gonna get worse, you know." She felt him look down at her, but she pressed her head harder into his chest. She felt him shake his head and knew he was smiling. "It's okay. If she gets too difficult to manage, I'm sure we can sell her to someone. By the time she's fifteen, she will make a good live-in nanny somewhere."

Lisa leaned back, feeling his stubble brush her forehead, slapped at his chest and moved away. She walked over to the mirror by the front door to make sure her hair wasn't messed up. The Brazilian blow-out was holding firm. She regarded herself in the mirror. Sometimes, it felt like Jessica was staring back at her from the mirror. Straight black hair, just past her shoulders, cocoa-brown skin, pointed chin, dimples, and almond-shaped eyes behind fashionable black glasses. Jessica had even chosen glasses like her mother's although she would likely die before admitting it. Mia looked a lot more like Kai, with her bronze skin and curly—frizzy really—red hair.

Lisa fluffed her hair over her shoulders and smoothed her black sweater. Why was she feeling so apprehensive about Danielle and Ryan coming over? She had avoided Danielle since the day of the shooting, mostly because she felt so embarrassed about the way she talked about her own students, and even more embarrassed that she allowed Danielle to talk about them the way she did.

In the month and a half since, Lisa had made a greater effort to get to know her students better, to try and understand the root of their behavior, and they had responded well. She now knew which kids were sleeping in class because they had come late and missed breakfast. She kept granola bars in her desk, which she slipped to them when no one was looking. She also understood that when a child acted up in class, there was likely an underlying issue. She would pull him/her aside and give the student a hug. In the beginning, they struggled in her arms. Sometimes, they told her what a bitch she was. But now, they simply collapsed in her arms and sobbed. The story would eventually emerge: a parent was high or drunk, someone had died, they spent the night alone or hungry, or they had seen someone beaten by the police or shot.

There were so many stories—all of them heartbreaking. She listened without judgment, and often talked to the school social worker about getting help for the kids. They trusted her now, and she understood why they hadn't trusted her before. She didn't deserve their trust. Four years. For four years she taught in that school before she truly saw her students. Her stomach turned over at the thought of how many children she had failed.

She wanted to tell Danielle about what she had learned, wanted to appeal to the part of Danielle that became a teacher in the first place, but she had already established a relationship with Danielle based on their middle-class sense of superiority over the kids they taught. She didn't know how to change that. She didn't think Danielle would understand.

Sometimes she wondered why she and Danielle had become friends. Danielle had been teaching at the school for three years before Lisa started, and in the beginning, she had been overwhelmed with the behavioral problems she encountered with her students. Danielle was the first teacher to come into Lisa's classroom to offer support. Unfortunately, she also offered her opinions of the students and their families. Lisa soon realized Danielle confirmed many of the ideas Lisa already had about the Black students in low-income West Baltimore. It had been easy for Lisa and Danielle to slide into a "them versus us" relationship with the students. Lisa also acknowledged that Danielle was the type of friend Diahann would approve of, and she secretly downplayed her relationship with LaTanya and highlighted her relationship with Danielle to her mother. When Diahann and Grant came to visit, Lisa always made an effort to invite Danielle and Ryan over for dinner and superficial conversation, but LaTanya never even knew when Lisa's parents were in town. The thought of her betrayal of LaTanya made her stomach ache.

The doorbell rang and Lisa saw Ryan's tall shadow through the frosted panes at the top of the door. She reached over and opened the door, prepared for Danielle's high-pitched hellos and hugs. She felt the irritation rise in her again. Danielle always seemed surprised to see her, even when she was coming to Lisa's house. She brushed the irritation away, forced a smile onto her face, and hugged first Danielle and then Ryan. Josh and Cora raced around her to the family room, looking for Jessica and Mia.

Lisa led her guests into the kitchen. Ryan headed over to the man-cave where Kai was already pulling some beers out of the small refrigerator. Ryan's big voice and laugh filled the entire downstairs. Kai didn't like either Danielle or Ryan. He thought they were fake, but he humored Lisa and entertained them. He even made the effort to go out for drinks or golfing with Ryan, but always came back irritated, vowing he wouldn't do it again. But he would, because Lisa asked him to, and if there was one thing Lisa knew about Kai, it was that he would do almost anything for her.

Danielle placed two shopping bags on the counter. She sighed and looked around, pursing her shiny, pink lips. "It looks good in here. Do you have new curtains?" Danielle walked into the family room for a closer look. "These are really nice! Where did you get them?"

Lisa began unpacking the bags to put the drinks and dessert on the table. "Oh, you know me—always shopping online."

Danielle continued looking around. She seemed to inspect every corner of the family room, dining room, and kitchen. She always did this, exclaiming as though she was surprised that Lisa and Kai had such good taste. She had been doing it for years, and Lisa always found her behavior mildly annoying, but not like she did today. Today it truly pissed her off.

"So, when are you going to invite us over? It's been a long time since we've been by. I want to see what *you've* changed." Lisa hadn't intended to say it, but it came out anyway.

Danielle rarely invited Lisa over. Lisa had begun to realize, with rising resentment, that while she often invited her white friends over, they rarely reciprocated. Meanwhile, it was not uncommon for Lisa to find herself sitting cross-legged on LaTanya's bed drinking a glass of wine and watching LaTanya try on clothes, and vice versa. *Why was that?*

Danielle shrugged her thin shoulders. "I don't know. We'll have to make it happen." She leaned in to smell the scented candle on the counter. "Mmmmm. So delicious." She walked over to the table where Lisa was emptying tortilla chips into a large bowl. Danielle took the cover off the tub of store-bought guacamole she brought, and Lisa's scalp prickled with irritation.

What is the matter with you? she fussed at herself silently. *This is one of your best friends. Why are you being such a bitch?*

She chuckled because that question was more characteristic coming from Danielle than from her.

Danielle looked up as Lisa chuckled. "What's so funny?" she asked, popping a guacamole laden chip into her mouth.

"Nothing." Lisa walked to the door of the man cave and gestured to Kai that the food was ready. "Just me being silly." She handed Danielle a paper plate, and Danielle began helping herself to the food.

During dinner, the kids sat at the table and the adults walked into the all-season sunroom overlooking the large back yard. Since fences were not permitted in Columbia, the Wilsons' yard backed up to the yards of houses on a street that ran parallel to theirs. With only a line of young trees to separate the neighborhood yards, they merged together and looked like a park. Although the trees were still bare, forsythia bushes in several yards lit up the landscape with bright yellow blooms. Spring would soon be here.

Lisa and Danielle sipped wine as they ate, while Kai and Ryan chugged cold bottles of beer. They sat in comfortable silence, listening for any sign coming from the dining room that an adult was needed.

"So, it seems Sumpter is looking strong for the election." Ryan put his empty plate on the wicker coffee table and stretched out his long legs. "We've been needing a leader like him for a long time." He sighed with contentment. "Lisa, that food was amazing—everything!"

Lisa caught Danielle shooting Ryan a pointed look—warning him to stop there, but Ryan was gazing out over the yard, and didn't see her warning. Lisa's scalp prickled again. So, Danielle really did understand just how offensive Lisa found what he was saying. That meant, all the wide, blue-eyed surprise whenever Lisa objected to Danielle's open admiration of Sumpter, was fake. *What the fuck?*

Kai raised his thick red eyebrows and looked over at Lisa as if to say, *They're your friends. Handle them, because you don't want me to.* His nostrils flared, and he looked down at his feet.

"Well," Lisa began tentatively, "I don't think Reginald Sumpter is what we need right now in this country." She stopped to think of what she wanted to say.

"He's exactly what we need right now," Ryan jumped in. "There are too many people out there looking for a handout." He looked over at Lisa and Kai apologetically. "No offense to you guys." He looked away quickly.

Lisa saw Kai furrow his brows and his brown freckles stood out on his nose. It took a moment for Lisa to realize this was because his skin was turning so red..

"What do you mean, offense?" Kai's voice was soft.

Ryan suddenly seemed less enthusiastic about the conversation. His voice became quieter. "Well, you know what I mean. All the folks looking for a paycheck without work. You know. Assistance."

"You mean welfare? I'm not on welfare. Lisa's not on

103

welfare." Kai's voice was quiet and insistent. "So why are you apologizing to us?"

Ryan stopped and thought for a moment. Danielle's gaze was fixed on the backyard. Ryan seemed to be weighing what he wanted to say. Then, he took a deep breath and went for it.

"Well, you know a lot of the crime is committed by Black people. And a lot of Black people are on welfare." He looked up at Kai with a smile. "I know you guys aren't like that. You've worked hard for all you have. But, you see? That's how we know everybody can do it. Some folks just want it easy, and we need to deal with that."

Lisa's heart sank. She often had similar conversations with Danielle. And she was a willing participant each time. Shame flooded her. She had lost herself in her middle-classness. She had basically weaponized this white woman.

"Do you know there are a lot more white people on welfare than Black?" Kai's voice was still quiet. "And are you aware of the 13th Amendment?"

Ryan frowned. "No. How can you say there are more white people on welfare? All these welfare queens—" His voice rose defensively.

"Look it up," Kai interrupted. "So, you don't know what the 13th Amendment is, and how it shaped the criminal justice system's relationship with Black people?"

Ryan opened his mouth to speak, but Kai interrupted him. "Look it up."

"Well, I didn't go to law school like you—" Ryan began, but Kai interrupted him again.

"Yes. Well, I can understand why you don't know about it. Because our educational system is scrubbed of everything that explains the systemic issues we see today. But that's not an excuse, Ryan. You're educated; you have access to the internet. Look it up. If you don't know, it's because you don't want to— you choose not to know."

Kai rose to his feet. Lisa knew he wanted to finish with, *now get the hell out of my house.* But instead, he gathered up the plates and walked into the kitchen.

Lisa, Danielle, and Ryan sat looking out at the yard in frozen silence. Finally, Danielle stood.

"It's getting late. We should go." She avoided Lisa's eyes as she stood. "Gotta find my purse." She headed for the family room with Ryan following her. He didn't look at Lisa either. They usually stayed much later than this, but there was no pretending the evening could be salvaged.

Lisa followed them inside, and helped Danielle find her purse and gather up the kids. None of the adults spoke to each other—all conversation was directed to the children.

Lisa and Kai followed their guests to the door. The four kids chattered and hugged each other, begging to stay longer, completely unaware of the heaviness in the air. Ryan and Danielle made a big fuss of saying goodbye to Jessica and Mia. Lisa and Kai made a big deal of saying goodbye to Josh and Cora.

Kai and Lisa sent the girls up to take baths and put their pajamas on, while they stood in the doorway, watching the Hogans back into the street and drive away. When Kai closed the door, Lisa didn't have to look at him to feel his anger. She could feel it pulsating in waves of heat.

As they worked silently together to clean up the kitchen, Lisa didn't know what to say to him. She had befriended Danielle and brought her and Ryan into their family. And she had participated in conversations about Black people that now left her feeling ashamed.

She stole a glance at Kai. His jaw was clenched under his red facial hair and he avoided looking at her. He moved methodically around the kitchen, filling the dishwasher and wiping the counters. She wondered whether he was angry at her, too. She had never told him about her conversations with Danielle, but clearly in the twelve years Lisa and Kai had known each other, she must have made her thoughts about some of these topics clear to him.

This wasn't the time to talk to him about it. Besides, she didn't know what to say. She had a lot to figure out—about herself. One thing she did know, was that her friendship with Danielle was over.

Tasia stood in the doorway watching the kids play. Sharonda struggled to break away so she could join the other kids, but Tasia held her firm. *She wanted to see what was happening here before she left her child with these people.*

They had passed several classrooms of kids on the second floor of the school. There were kids of every age, from infants to teenagers, in small groups in different classrooms. This was one of the two toddler classes, and two teachers, dressed in white scrubs, sat on the floor with about fifteen kids. There were two activity centers going. One in which the teacher read a story in a loud dramatic voice, acting it out and making the kids giggle. On the other side of the room, another teacher knelt next to a low Legos table. She had a group of children working away there, listening to the story.

From time to time, a child would knock all the Legos down and the teacher would laugh and help knock the rest down. Then, she made a game of having the group pick up all the Legos and start building again. The teachers weren't shouting at the kids or scolding them. They were completely engaged. Tasia knew Sharonda would be in the active group. No way she would sit quietly and listen to a story with so much to look at and touch.

Jayla waited patiently while Tasia watched. She didn't push, which was so unlike Jayla, and Tasia appreciated it. As she stood there struggling with Sharonda, an older woman with a short Afro walked up and introduced herself.

"Hi. I'm Pat. I'm one of the directors of the children's program. The woman extended her hand to Tasia, who jostled Sharonda onto her hip so she could shake her hand.

"Hi. I'm Tasia," she said shyly.

"And who is this beautiful young lady?" Pat asked, stroking Sharonda's arm. The toddler reached for her instantly, and Pat took her into her arms.

Tasia stood for a moment in shock. Sharonda didn't go to anybody she didn't know. If too much time went by without seeing Tasia's mother, Sharonda would turn her head away and cling to Tasia when her grandmother tried to take her.

"Were you thinking of leaving her with us, Tasia?" Pat's eyes twinkled as she smiled at Sharonda, who feigned shyness and buried her head in Pat's shoulder, her arms around Pat's neck. "We would love to have her. We just need you to fill out some paperwork so we know a little more about both of you. It will only take a moment."

Pat put Sharonda down on the floor, and she promptly headed off to the Lego table.

The teacher let out a squeal of delight. "Ohhhhh! We have a new friend. Welcome, friend!" She looked up at Pat with a question in her eyes.

"Sharonda," Pat told her.

"Welcome, Sharonda!" Sharonda threw herself into the teacher's outstretched arms and gave her a big hug. "Oh, how nice. We're so happy you're here. Do you want to play with us?" Sharonda nodded, and the kids moved over and made space for her. The teacher handed her some blocks and Sharonda began building.

Tasia watched this exchange as she filled out the information sheet. It asked basic questions about Sharonda and whether or not she had any allergies, health issues, or took medication. When she was finished, Pat took the clipboard and handed Tasia a pager.

"Hold on to this and we will page you if we need you. Just because we page doesn't mean there's a problem. It might just be a question. Okay?" Pat looked over at Sharonda. "Is she wearing a Pull-Up?"

Tasia nodded, waiting for the disapproval that often came with that question.

"Great. No problem." Pat smiled and waved Tasia away. "We have lots of those. See you later. We close at 9 pm. Have fun!"

Tasia waved goodbye to Sharonda, but Sharonda was too busy to look up. Tasia shook her head in amazement. Sometimes, even when she left Sharonda with Nana, she cried. *This was so strange.*

Jayla read her expression. "Kids instinctively know when they're somewhere that's good. And look at how many friends she has to play with now. She's fine." Jayla headed towards the door and Tasia followed reluctantly. She looked back over her shoulder at her daughter who didn't look like such a baby anymore.

Out in the hallway, Tasia continued her wide-eyed examination of the old school. The place looked like a wreck from outside, but was filled with people, was brightly lit, and smelled great. Most of the people were dressed in white scrubs with white sneakers, like Jayla.

"Okay. What's with the scrubs?" She eyed Jayla up and down.

Jayla laughed. "Okay. The scrubs." Jayla waved at a young woman walking by. "Well, the scrubs have two purposes. One is that having everyone wear something so plain, where everyone has the same outfit, removes the pressure we have to compete with each other. You see, when Black people were enslaved, we were given the white people's castoffs to wear. Sometimes, we were practically naked. We never got to feel good about how we looked. So, when we got to freedom, clothes became a status symbol for us—just like cars and houses. And you know what they say, "a Black man will be wearing thousands of dollars in clothes or driving a luxury car and not have a single dollar in the bank." This attitude holds up white supremacy. The very same people who brought us here, and took away our self-respect, now profit from our need to buy clothes, houses, cars, and other stuff to feel important. They are continuing to make money off our backs."

Tasia tried to wrap her head around what Jayla was saying.

"At the same time, the white man has encouraged us killing each other for what we have. We sell drugs for it; we steal for it; we lie for it. These are attitudes that white people have encouraged, because as long as we are focused on superficial material objects, we can't build true economic power, and aren't a threat to the white man. We are only a threat to ourselves."

Jayla guided Tasia down a wide flight of stairs. "I had to kill my love of white hair and white labels. And I had to kill the idea that my power lay in how I look rather than who I am, what I do, and what I stand for."

Tasia shook her head, as if that would calm her swirling thoughts. "Wow. Okay. Coming from Miss Name Brand herself. Just wow." She eyed Jayla up and down. "What's the second reason for the scrubs?"

Jayla laughed again, "Because the people in the neighborhood around this school have been told that we run a home health aide training program here. So, no one thinks twice about all the Black people coming and going from here all day and most of the night. They just see us in our scrubs and think we are becoming good, productive Black people. They love it."

Jayla looked over at Tasia. "You will be wearing scrubs soon, too!"

Tasia shook her head again. "I don't think so!"

Jayla stopped and took Tasia's hand, "These folks can help you, Tayz. I mean, really help you. All you've been through with your mom and Kenny. They understand, and we help each other." Jayla gripped Tasia's hand—hard. "No one goes hungry, no one gets evicted, and no one struggles to buy diapers for their kids. We are all in this together. Tell them what you're struggling with and they will help you."

Tasia didn't know what to say. She was confused.

Jayla took her hand and pulled her into the dimly-lit auditorium. The meeting began almost as soon as they sat down.

Tasia looked around. The room was filled with Black people of all types, ages, and sizes. Many were wearing white scrubs. A few, like Tasia, were dressed in street clothes, and sat looking confused and overwhelmed. Beside each confused person in street clothes was another in scrubs, looking excited, reaching over to whisper encouragingly to their guest.

This place was different. There was a feeling of warmth and acceptance. Maybe, it was the soft jazz playing in the background. Or the sweet smell that reminded her of the time Nana took her on the church bus trip to Ocean City, with all that sunlight and ocean. Or maybe it was the fact that people smiled at her as she walked by.

Tasia felt something bubble up inside her, but didn't know what it was. She felt tingly inside, like this was something she had been waiting for. *But what was it?* She felt confused, but the happiness here was contagious. She found herself smiling, not knowing why.

She thought of what Jayla said: "No one goes hungry. No one gets evicted. No one struggles to buy diapers for their kids." The weight of all she had experienced over the past two years felt as if it would crush her. *Was it really possible to be peaceful, to stop struggling?*

A man stepped out in white scrubs. "Sanibona!" he said, smiling, his arms outstretched.

"Ngikhona!" the room replied loudly.

Tasia began to cry.

Donovan pulled up outside his mother and stepfather's small, brick house. In the passenger seat, Kirstie was chattering about something related to work, but he wasn't listening. He really didn't want to be here. Several weeks had passed since he told his mother he was coming to dinner and hadn't shown up. But his mother's last call had not been an invitation—it had been a directive, as only a Jamaican mother can give. He knew better than to not show up this time. He was here, although he had missed the 3 p.m. dinner Melva served every Sunday afternoon. But he was here. He brought Kirstie along to give himself a reason to escape early. He hoped Kirstie would distract his mother from focusing so much on him, and Melva would enjoy feeding her.

He sighed. He didn't know what to expect. Well, he knew what to expect from his mother. She would be polite and pointed in her questions to Kirstie. What he didn't know was how Kirstie would respond. She didn't know very many African Americans, aside from the Black men she often dated. She most certainly didn't know much about Jamaicans. "We can be a strange breed," his mother often said.

It took him a moment to realize Kirstie had stopped

113

talking and was looking at him questioningly. "Are we going in or is this curbside service?" she asked.

He laughed. She busted his chops like no one else, and he loved it.

"We're going in. Just trying to get myself together." He turned off the ignition.

"Is it really that bad?"

"Yes . . . no . . . not really. I don't know." He ran his hands over his forehead. "I've been an ass to my mom and she really doesn't deserve it, but I just can't stand my stepfather."

He opened the car door and set one foot outside on the ground. "Just forget it. Let's go." He got out of the car.

He didn't want to explain to Kirstie that his anger at his mother began decades ago, and that it spilled over to his stepfather, half-brother, and half-sister. His mother hated those terms, always reminding him that, in their culture, there was no such thing as "step" or "half" family. There was full family and full love, she said. But, in his mind, he had been abandoned by his mother, and she replaced him with three other people. He didn't know if he would ever forgive her.

He rang the bell, instead of using the key his mother had given him. He didn't even know where it was.

Melva Franklin opened the door with a wide smile. She opened her arms and he stepped into them without hesitation. Despite all his anger, there was something about his mother that disarmed him, comforted him, turned him into a little barefoot boy, longing for her again.

When his mother released him, he stepped back and smiled at her. He couldn't help himself. Her warmth was contagious. Melva was a slight woman, short and thin, with smooth dark chocolate skin and short black hair with a patch of brilliant silver on one side. She had dark, intuitive eyes, and the amazing ability to see right into him, find his hurt, and tend to it. Sometimes he hated her for that. It made him feel too vulnerable.

Donovan stepped aside so Melva could see Kirstie. The shadow that crossed Melva's face was almost imperceptible, and Donovan only saw it because he was watching for it.

"Mom, this is Kirstie," Donovan muttered.

Melva stepped forward and opened her arms for Kirstie. "Kirstie, it's so good to meet you." Her voice was deep and rich, with the island lilt Donovan had worked so hard to erase from his own speech.

Kirstie hesitated and looked up at Donovan. He smiled at her. For some reason, he wanted her to feel the happiness he felt in his mother's arms. Kirstie stepped forward and leaned down into Melva's arms, barely allowing their shoulders to touch. Kirstie patted Melva awkwardly on the back as they hugged.

When Melva released Kirstie, she stepped aside and welcomed them into the house. Donovan indicated to Kirstie the shelf on which she should store her shoes, right inside the door.

Donovan's stepfather, Conrad, was sitting on the couch watching television. He looked up when they entered and smiled tentatively, rising to greet them.

Donovan sighed in disgust. Conrad was, as usual, wearing a white, sleeveless mesh undershirt, and cargo shorts. Melva liked to refer to the undershirt by its Jamaican name, *marina*. But Donovan preferred the derogatory American term, *wife beater*. It better fit his view of his stepfather. This is what Conrad wore, year-round, in the house. Donovan would never be caught dead in one.

"Conrad, this is Kirstie." Donovan gestured to her. Out of the corner of his eye he saw Melva shake her head. He knew calling a parent by their first name was considered disrespectful in Jamaican culture, but he did it anyway. "Kirstie, my stepfather." He felt, rather than heard, Melva's sigh. When Melva sent word to Donovan in Jamaica that she had gotten married, the betrayal he felt had made him physically ill. He developed an unexplained malady that sent him to bed for several weeks while his aunt fretted over him. She took him to multiple doctors, who could find nothing physically wrong with him. During this time, he had feverish nightmares that his mother had replaced him with this man she met in America. He had nightmares where she wouldn't send for him because she didn't love him anymore. The birth of each of her American children sent Donovan back to bed again, and in his recurring nightmares he saw a dark, swirling mass of his mother, her husband and her two children encased in

116

a bubble together with him on the outside doing everything he could to get in. He was never successful in his dreams, or in real life. No matter what his mother did, he was determined not to ache for her as he had when he was in Jamaica. His disdain for Conrad was palpable.

Conrad stretched his hand out to Kirstie. She looked relieved as she stepped in to shake it. "Nice to meet you, Conrad," she said.

Donovan felt a moment of surprise. Kirstie had been instantly affectionate with him. He assumed she would be the same with his family, but she seemed reluctant to hug either Melva or Conrad. He filed that away to ponder later.

Melva invited them to sit. "We have already eaten, but we have your plates set aside." She looked at Donovan with a wide grin. "I made something special for you. Oxtails, rice and peas, fried plantain, boiled banana and cabbage."

Donovan pumped his fist in the air. "Yes! Thank you!" He hated so much about being an immigrant, but he could not resist his mother's food. He looked over at Kirstie in excitement. "It's good, Kirstie. My mother is the best cook I know," he assured her excitedly.

Kirstie's smile was frozen on her face and her eyebrows were up around her blonde hairline. "I can't wait to eat . . . oxtails."

Donovan frowned. He wanted Kirstie to enjoy being there and meeting his family. But he hadn't exactly set good expectations, with all his negative talk, so he could hardly blame her.

Melva went into the kitchen and began bustling around, walking back and forth from the kitchen to the small dining room, placing plates out on the table. Donovan tried to identify the hymn she hummed under her breath.

He looked around the room. It was a small house, with few windows, but Melva managed to make it feel light and airy. She had a special skill with fabrics. The windows were draped with gauzy, textured, white curtains. In the spring and fall, when the windows were open, the curtains blew in the wind. When he was in high school, he used to stand in the window and watch the kids playing outside on the street. He never joined them. He had decided they were not worthy of his company.

The couch and armchairs were old pieces from the Salvation Army, but Melva had covered them with a rich, navy tapestry fabric, with contemporary gray cushions strewn around. Antique coffee and side tables in dark wood were polished to a deep shine and held modern lamps with shimmery silver shades and dark gray, tapered stems. The light gray rug, with a swirling navy pattern covering the wood floors, was probably the only thing in the room Melva had purchased new, but the room felt bright and modern. Large, white-framed collages of the family adorned the taupe walls. Donovan avoided looking at the pictures of himself in his aunt's yard, wearing short pants and flip flops, with hens running around his scrawny legs.

118

It felt like home, and although Donovan was relieved when he moved out to go to college, he hated that it pulled him into its inviting warmth whenever he returned. He wanted to curl up on the navy couch with a pillow under his head and watch television or play video games like he used to in high school. The smells of familiar food coming from the kitchen didn't help.

The seduction of his mother's house was a major reason he avoided coming back. He preferred to harbor his anger and resentment toward his family. He nursed that anger like a small spark he carried inside, making sure it never went out, and fanning it into a full flame whenever he felt himself weakening.

Donovan sighed and looked over at Kirstie. She sat stiffly in a chair, feigning interest in the soccer game on the small television Conrad watched, the sound off.

"So, where do you live, Kristy?" Conrad chuckled awkwardly.

"Kirstie." Donovan corrected him. He tried hard to keep the irritation out of his voice.

"Oh, sorry." Conrad glanced anxiously at Donovan and chuckled again. "Kirstie."

"You're fine. I live in Fells Point, in the city." Kirstie looked at Donovan and smiled. She seemed to be relaxing. Her eyes told him to do the same.

"Oh, yes. That's a very nice area." Conrad nodded. "A lot to do down there."

"Yes. It's fun." Kirstie nodded.

Donovan's half-brother, Paul walked slowly down the stairs, wearing his usual home attire of flannel pajama pants and a white T-shirt. Donovan wondered, for the hundredth time, if anyone in this house ever wore street clothes, besides his mother.

"Hi, Donovan," Paul muttered, fixing his brother with an unblinking stare. He paused at the bottom of the stairs, and Donovan knew he was unnerved by the fact that Kirstie was there, although he didn't look at her.

"Hey, Bro." Donovan bounded up from his chair and went to slap Paul on the shoulder. Although Paul kept his eyes fixed on the chair Donovan had just vacated, he smiled with pleasure.

"Hi," Paul repeated. He finally moved his eyes from the chair to look at Donovan's chest. "I didn't hear you come in."

"Just got here. Come and meet Kirstie." Donovan turned Paul to face Kirstie. He kept his hands on his brother's shoulders. "Kirstie, this is my favorite brother, Paul."

Paul grinned and fixed his eyes back on Donovan's chest, although he had to turn his head to the side to do so. "I'm your *only* brother," he muttered, smiling broadly. He glanced quickly in Kirstie's general direction, and back to Donovan's chest.

Kirstie was standing in front of her chair. "Nice to meet you, Paul." She extended her hand and began to step forward but stopped when Donovan shook his head at her.

"Nice to meet you, too," Paul muttered, his eyes still on Donovan's chest. He shifted uncomfortably and turned as if to go back upstairs, but Donovan stopped him.

"Where're you going so soon? Come hang out with us." Donovan led Paul away from the stairs. "The video games can wait for a while."

Paul headed for the kitchen. "I wasn't playing video games. I was writing the program for a robot I designed."

Donovan headed back to his seat. "That's what I'm talking about." He winked at Kirstie. "One of the smartest guys I know." He called out to Paul's retreating back, "When you're running the NSA, remember your poor old brother here."

Kirstie smiled, but her eyes showed confusion. She would have a lot of questions later.

Melva came to the kitchen door. "Dinner is ready," she announced, her arm outstretched toward the dining room.

Donovan led the way through the kitchen and into the dining room. As always, Melva's table was impeccably set, with a white lacy tablecloth, which was protected by woven navy placemats. On the center of the table were white Pyrex dishware containing dark, rich oxtails swimming in a flavorful stew; rice and peas; steamed cabbage with slices of carrots; boiled green bananas, and fried plantains.. A glass pitcher sat on one end of the table, and Donovan's mouth watered at the thought of the freshly-squeezed carrot juice sweetened with condensed milk, ginger, grated nutmeg, and cinnamon. *Why did he resist coming here so much?* He could eat like this every Sunday, or whenever he wanted.

121

Donovan ushered Kirstie into a chair and sat next to her. Paul was already sitting at one end of the table staring intently at his nails. Melva bustled around, uncovering the serving bowls and pouring carrot juice into tall glasses.

"Okay, Kirstie. Please help yourself," Melva said looking satisfied.

Melva went to pour Kirstie's juice, but pulled back when Kirstie indicated, with her fingers, that she only wanted a drop of the juice. Melva looked at Donovan as if to say, *Ah wha dis yuh bring me?* But instead, she smiled graciously and poured an inch of juice into Kirstie's glass.

Kirstie picked up the glass, swirled the juice around, and sniffed it, before gingerly tasting it. Donovan grimaced. He had forgotten to tell Kirstie how Jamaican cooks feel about people sniffing their food.

Kirstie exclaimed in delight, "This is good!" She sounded surprised.

Donovan glanced over at Melva, who was sliding into a chair across from him. Only a slight raising of her eyebrows indicated she heard Kirstie. Melva picked up a serving dish of rice and peas and handed it to Kirstie.

Over the next half hour, Kirstie sampled every dish on the table and exclaimed in excitement with each forkful. From time to time, she closed her eyes and sighed as the food entered her mouth. She lavished Melva with compliments about her cooking and asked for second helpings of everything.

"I don't usually do spicy—anything! But this food is *so* good!"

"I'm glad you like it," Melva responded, her eyes twinkling with amusement. Donovan could tell she was warming up. "You should eat Jamaican food more often." Melva looked over at Donovan. "My son is a very good cook, despite whatever he tells you." She chuckled.

Kirstie whipped her head around and looked at Donovan, her eyes wide. "You know how to cook like this?" She sipped from her full glass of carrot juice and winked at Melva. "I've only ever gotten fake Italian and really bad Mexican food from you. You've been holding out on me."

"Wait until you hear about the calories in oxtail," Paul proclaimed, staring at the table. "You won't want to eat like this all the time."

"Oh, I bet! What do you eat the rest of the time?" Kirstie reached for more cabbage.

"We eat a lot of chicken and fish," Paul responded, this time looking at his mother.

Melva nodded. "That's true. We don't eat like this all the time. It's not healthy. But we splurge on the weekends."

Donovan turned to Paul. "So, tell me about this robot you're building."

Paul shrugged. "I'm building it for school." He remained expressionless, although Donovan could tell he was excited about his robot.

123

"What can it do?"

"Lots of stuff. It can perform a sequence of tasks that I've programmed it to do."

"Like what?" Donovan was accustomed to pulling information out of his brother. Paul was brilliant, but as a characteristic of his autism, very sparing in his use of words.

"It can throw balls and pick them up. It can put things in a basket. It can pick up rings and stuff and take them places. It can even dive underwater and do everything I tell it to." Paul chewed on his nail, seemingly lost in thoughts about his robot. "I'm writing the program now."

The front door opened, and Donovan heard his sister's cheerful voice. "Hello, folks!" the door slammed hard, causing Melva to wince. "I think my big brother is here."

Karen walked into the dining room and straight over to Donovan. Before he could fully rise from his seat, she had wrapped her arms tightly around his neck.

"I haven't seen you for so long!" she squealed, rocking him from side to side. "Where have you been?"

Karen stepped back from Donovan and looked him up and down. Her locs had grown since he last saw her, and she had shaved both sides of her head, piling her hair in a high bun on top of her head. She was short and slight, like their mother, with dark, smooth skin and large, dancing eyes. Donovan always thought she looked as if she was up to mischief.

Donovan grabbed her chin and turned her head from side to side, surveying her. "You have more piercings? Oh my God! How many is enough?" he teased.

Karen laughed and pushed at his chest. "Oh, be quiet!" She reached over to shake Kirstie's hand. "Karen." She nodded at Kirstie and walked around the table to kiss Melva loudly on the top of her head.

"Well, you've already seen my septum." She pointed to the semi-circular piercing in the middle of her nose. "Since then, I've gotten a conch." She pointed to the stud inside her right ear. "And a tragus." She pointed to the tiny hoop in the flap of her left ear. "And a new helix and a couple more lobe piercings." She slid into a chair next to Melva. "That tragus hurt like a mother—" She glanced at Melva and blew her a kiss.

"Chups!" Melva hissed her teeth in response, but she was clearly pleased to see her daughter. She slapped Karen's hand as she reached for a plate. "Did you wash your hands?"

Karen sighed and got up, walking into the kitchen and over to the sink.

Donovan noticed, for the first time, that she was wearing white cotton pajamas and white socks. He frowned. Karen was about to graduate from college with a BS in mechanical engineering.

"What are you wearing?" he asked as Karen walked back into the dining room, drying her hands on a paper towel.

125

Karen glanced down at the white pajamas as she sat down at the table. "Scrubs," she replied briskly, reaching for a plate.

"Scrubs? For what?"

Karen piled food on her plate. "Just a club I'm involved in. It's kind of like a uniform."

She shoveled rice and peas onto her fork with her knife as Donovan watched. It had taken him a long time to stop holding his knife in his right hand and fork in the left while he ate. When he came to the States, he forced himself to adopt the American style of putting the knife down after cutting his meat and moving the fork to the right hand to eat. At first, very little food made it onto the fork and into his mouth. It took him an hour to eat each meal. He was always amazed that Karen and Paul, born and raised in the United States, ate as if they had been raised in Jamaica.

"What kind of club makes you wear scrubs?" Donovan persisted. "Is that at the university?"

Karen stopped with her fork halfway to her mouth. She gave Donovan a long, unblinking look, seeming to weigh her response. Her mouth opened, as if she would speak, then her gaze moved to Kirstie, and she made a decision. She shrugged as the fork went into her mouth, chewing slowly, her eyes moving back and forth between Donovan and Kirstie.

"Maybe I will tell you another time." Karen held Donovan's gaze for a moment. She was trying to read him. She glanced over at Kirstie and then back at Donovan. "I'm not sure you're ready yet."

126

Chapter Seven

Tasia stretched out her arms to accept the white scrubs being handed to her.

"Two pairs of adult medium," Donna muttered, turning around to look back at the stacks of scrubs organized by size on the floor-to-ceiling, built-in wooden shelves. She had a slight accent, but Tasia didn't know where she was from.

Donna looked at Tasia's feet. "Do you need sneakers, socks, underwear?"

Tasia gazed down at her frayed sneakers, which had seen better days. She clutched the scrubs to her chest, looking away from Donna and nodded silently.

Donna didn't seem to notice Tasia's embarrassment. "We've got that! What size?" she looked at Tasia, smiling, her eyebrows raised.

"N . . . nine."

Donna walked to the end of the shelves and ran her hands along rows of shoes, looking for the right size. She reached for a pair of bright white sneakers and grabbed a few pairs of rolled socks.

"Here you go." She deposited them into Tasia's arms on top of the scrubs. "Underwear? Bras?"

Tasia shook her head silently.

"Okay!" Donna clapped her hands together in satisfaction. "I think we're done here." She turned to lead Tasia out the door of the huge classroom-turned-storeroom but stopped suddenly. "Wait, you have a toddler, right?"

Tasia nodded.

Donna turned to a set of shelves on the other side of the room. "What do you need for her? We have diapers, formula—oh wait, she's probably too old for formula. Pull-Ups?"

Tasia looked at the row and rows of diapers, training pants, and cases of formula. Sharonda was wearing her last Pull-Up. She followed Donna over to the shelves.

Donna took the stack of clothes out of Tasia's arms. "Let's get you a box for these, while you grab a couple packs of Pull-Ups." She walked to the other side of the room and found a box for the scrubs.

"A couple packs?" Tasia muttered weakly.

Donna turned, stooping to put the clothes in the box. "Yeah. You should get a few packs, unless you want to come back here every week," she chuckled. "I don't mind, but you might get tired of coming here."

Tasia found Sharonda's size and took three large packs of training pants off the shelf. She glanced at Donna to see her reaction, but Donna walked over and held the box out so Tasia

128

could put the packs of pants in it. She placed the box in Tasia's arms.

"I will give you a ride home with all that later. Okay?"

Tasia nodded and followed Donna out of the room, carrying the box. They walked down the wide hallway to the staircase. The Cell Block was quieter during the day, while many people were at work, and the older children were at school, but still the hallways bustled with activity as members scurried about on various tasks. Tasia wondered what they were doing.

Donna led Tasia into an office and pointed to a chair. She sat behind the narrow desk and pulled out a notepad.

She smiled at Tasia. "It's okay. I just want to learn more about you. Then, we can figure out what your role will be in the Cell."

"My role?"

"Yes. What you have to offer the liberation movement."

Tasia shrugged. "I don't think I have anything to offer."

Donna smiled and picked up a pen. "Of course you do—you and—Shar . . . Sharonda, right?"

Tasia nodded, as Donna wrote on the notepad. "I don't understand."

Donna smiled again. "You will in time." She leaned back in the chair and looked up at the ceiling. "Tell me, Tasia, when you dream about your future, what do you see yourself doing?"

Tasia cocked her head to one side. No one had ever asked her that before. She had lots of dreams, but most of them involved

Kenny. She felt her eyes begin to fill with tears. She tried to turn her head away from Donna's watchful eyes.

"I don't know. Being a good mother." Despite her best efforts, a tear fell onto her cheek. It felt like she cried every day lately. "Giving my daughter a good life." She looked down at her hands, and felt her chest beginning to heave. She didn't even know this woman. She didn't want to cry in front of her.

Donna leaned forward, her elbows on the desk. "It's okay." Her voice was soft, soothing. "You're not alone anymore. We're here now, and you are one of us. We're here to help. Tell us what you need."

Donna's soothing voice just made Tasia cry harder. "I don't know." She sobbed and wiped her face with the back of her hand before noticing Donna pointing to a box of tissues on the desk.

Tasia took a tissue and wiped her eyes. She didn't know what was wrong with her these days. Maybe it was all the stuff she was learning about racism and white supremacy. She felt like they were telling her story—about Mamma and Nana and Kenny and now her and Sharonda. She had never heard of redlining, or block busting, or the prison industrial complex. She only knew that Mamma used to have a good job in a store, and then she got sick and lost her job and couldn't get another one. And she had a lot of medical bills that kept getting bigger and bigger because she couldn't pay them. That's when Mamma started drinking, sleeping all day, and staying out all night, leaving Tasia to fend for herself. Then some boyfriend introduced Mamma to heroin and Tasia's life became a new version of hell. And she never fully forgave Mamma for abandoning her.

When people in the Cell Block started telling Tasia that what she experienced in her life, and in West Baltimore, had been deliberately created to keep Black people down—the peeling lead paint on the walls in public housing that poisoned kids so they couldn't learn; the vacant houses left to rot; the lack of public transportation so people couldn't get to where the jobs were; the low-paying jobs that didn't offer health insurance (businesses hiring a bunch of part-time people instead of a few full-time people so they didn't have to pay for insurance); the way the police were always trolling around looking to shake down Black people and put them in jail for no reason, and the introduction of drugs into Black communities as a means of dependence, control, and profit for white people. Tasia had been shocked. And overwhelmed. Her head hadn't been right since.

She wiped her eyes again as Donna waited patiently. "I used to dream about being in communications," she offered hesitantly.

Donna wrote on the notepad. "That's great. So, what happened?"

Tasia hung her head. "I got pregnant." She didn't look up. She didn't want to see the judgment in Donna's eyes. "And then my boyfriend disappeared." She began shredding the tissue, absently.

131

Donna reached across the desk and gently took the tissue from Tasia's hands. Tasia began picking at her cuticles. She didn't look up at Donna.

"You know, I had my first child at sixteen," Donna said softly, as she balled up the tissue and threw it into a wastebasket under the desk. "And my baby's father left me, too. I thought I was going to lose my mind."

Tasia stopped picking at her fingers and looked up at Donna. She was probably in her early forties, and looked so well put together, with her curly, natural hair pulled back into a neat ponytail, her smooth copper skin and clear eyes. She didn't look like the kind of mess Tasia felt. At least, Tasia hadn't gotten pregnant until she was nineteen.

Donna laughed softly at Tasia's look. "Yup. I was a mess." She shook her head. "But you want to know what I've learned?"

Tasia nodded.

"I have learned that the child I had at sixteen—he's grown now—was my greatest treasure, my legacy, and that I should not be ashamed that I had him. It might not have been the best planning, but once he was here, he was a treasure."

"But it's so hard!" Tasia blurted out. Her chest began to heave again, and she grabbed another tissue.

Donna reached across the desk and took Tasia's hand. "I know it's hard, but you have help now, so it should get easier."

Tasia nodded. She didn't know this woman, and she had

132

no reason to believe anything she said, but she did.

Donna picked up her pen again. "We need to figure out how to get you to finish your studies so you can help us with communications. Did you finish high school?"

"Yes. I was at Baltimore City Community College. I was studying communications there, and I was going to go to University of Baltimore. But then . . ." Talking about Kenny was so hard.

Donna nodded and wrote on the notepad. "So, we need to get you back in school so you can finish up. Maybe you should just go straight to the University."

Tasia shook her head. "I can't. I don't even have a job. Plus, I defaulted on my student loans."

Donna smiled. "Don't worry about that. We've got you. We need you, so we will make it happen."

Tasia looked at Donna incredulously.

Donna continued, "I need you to get your transcripts, find out how much you owe, and figure out what you need to do to get into the University. Bring me the bills. I will take care of them."

"But how? Where do you all get this money? How are you doing this?"

Donna smiled and put the pen on the desk. "We have figured out, the Black people in this city and around this country, that we are stronger if we pool our money and make sure everyone is taken care of. Have you ever heard of *money susu*?"

Tasia shook her head.

"*Susu* is a form of community wealth-building that Black people brought from Africa, to the Caribbean, and around the world. It is a way of saving money as a group, and not entrusting it to Backra's bank."

Tasia frowned. "Who is Backra?"

"Backra is an old name for the white master. We know that the U.S. economic system benefits the white master, but not people like you and me. So, we don't give our money to him. Instead, we pool money every month. Those who have more give more, and those who have less give according to what they can manage. We have been able to secure millions of dollars in this way. We take care of our own people."

Tasia's eyes were wide as Donna continued.

"Right now, you need to take. But one day soon, you will also contribute. This is the only way we will be free of Backra."

"I don't have a job. I was getting food stamps—"

"And that's another thing," Donna interrupted her, "we will no longer take Backra's money. You will have a job in one of our businesses, and you will be paid a fair wage. We will also take care of Sharonda when you are in school. When you start working, you will give some of your earnings back to the susu. We each have to play our part."

Tasia nodded, but she was struggling to take it all in. "There are businesses?" she stammered.

Donna smiled again. "Yes, there are. I think, perhaps, I will put you with the communications group and you can start helping them. It won't be fancy. You might be cleaning up the production floor or making copies. But don't let pride get in your way. Work hard, learn everything you can. Every contribution matters."

Tasia stared at her silently. She couldn't wrap her head around what Donna was saying.

Donna picked up her pen again. "Okay. Let's figure out your budget so we know how much you need to earn. Tell me about your rent."

Corey bounced on the hard seat of the old school bus. Emotions surged through him that he couldn't name. He knew he was excited, but he was also scared, and there was something else, but he didn't know what it was. His foot tapped the stained floor, and his palms sweated. He wiped his hands on his jeans and shifted in his seat, half of his body out in the aisle, looking around the bus. Devonte sat in the very back row, next to a curvy young woman with smooth, onyx skin. She had short hair, almond eyes, and high cheekbones. Devonte was quite taken with her, and they talked quietly, their heads close together. Devonte looked up and nodded at Corey. Corey smiled and nodded back. *Devonte was a solid brother. He deserved a good woman.*

In the seats around him, men and women—most dressed in dark sweatshirts and jeans, others in dark fatigues—chatted with each other. Through the large window at the rear of the bus, Corey saw a second school bus behind them, and a third behind

135

that. The convoy of small buses traveled steadily north on Highway 83, winding their way through the Friday evening traffic, as the sun sank lower in the sky.

In the seat beside him, Samuel looked out the window, his thin fingers laced through each other, resting in his lap. This was the first time Corey had ever seen Samuel in any clothes other than his white scrubs. Today, he wore a black turtleneck, dark gray jeans, and a black skullcap. Over the last two months, Corey had learned that Samuel spoke only when he had something important to say. He sat silently beside Corey, gazing out the window, and occasionally smiling at Corey's excitement about the trip.

As they passed the sign welcoming them to Pennsylvania, the man with salt and pepper hair and beard, who spoke during Corey's first meeting at the Cell Block, stood up from his seat in the first row and turned to face the passengers. Corey now knew his name was Langford, and that he was a physician and administrator at Johns Hopkins Hospital.

"Okay, everyone." Langford rubbed his hands together as he spoke. "We are about thirty minutes from the Farm. I want to talk about what will happen when we get there."

Corey settled back in his seat, noticing how quiet the bus was, and how intently people listened to Langford.

"The truck that went ahead of us has already arrived at the compound, and the brothers and sisters who traveled with the truck are unloading the weapons and your luggage as we speak."

136

He stopped talking for a moment as a cheer went up from the passengers. "It will be dark when we get there, so we will have a light supper and retire to our cabins. We will be up and at breakfast at five a.m." Langford stopped and looked around the bus. "What time will we be at breakfast in the morning?"

"Five a.m.," the passengers responded in unison.

Corey felt the unnamed feeling rising in him again. He felt as if he would explode out of his seat at any moment. He tapped his foot with increasing speed.

"That's right. Anyone, who is late, gets to stay behind and wash dishes with the kitchen crew while we all go out to the field."

A murmur rose up in the bus as passengers shook their heads and proclaimed to their neighbors that they would not be late.

Langford smiled. "Okay." He clapped his hands lightly and the group settled down immediately. "So, you should all have been assigned your teams. You will share a cabin with members of your team. There is a blue cabin with a male bunk room, a female bunk room, and a few private rooms for nonbinary folks and whoever else needs it. Same thing for the green, red, purple, and yellow teams. Is there anyone who doesn't know what team they are on?" He waited for a response. Receiving none, he continued "Okay. Good. If you labeled your luggage as you were instructed, your bags will be in your bunk room. If your luggage is not there, you didn't follow instructions and you will need to come find me. A few of us will be staying in the main hall so you can find us easily.

"Each cabin will have two leaders. They will identify themselves when you move in. We are going to go ahead and collect your cell phones now. There is absolutely no photography permitted at the Farm, and you may not use your cell phones at any time. Please go ahead and turn off your GPS or any other type of location setting."

Langford stopped and waited while people took their phones out and looked for the location settings. He watched the group carefully. A young woman in a black Malcolm X T-shirt walked down the aisle with a pillowcase, collecting phones.

"If you are wearing a watch with GPS or location services of any type, please go ahead and put it in the bag. Unfortunately, you will not be accessible by the outside world until Sunday evening. If you have an emergency of any type, please come and see me and you can use the office phone. But it is critical to maintain our radio silence while we are in the compound. If we reveal our location, or what we are doing there—we will jeopardize the Cell, the compound, all our partners, and this entire movement."

Langford stopped to allow his words to sink in. The passengers nodded solemnly. "Speaking of partners, there are six buses coming from New York, carrying brothers and sisters from the New York cell, and from La Lucha. There will also be buses from New Jersey, Virginia, Delaware, and Ohio joining us. I expect there to be about five thousand people coming and going throughout the weekend. Please take time to get to know some of our partners. We will be fighting back-to-back with them. We need to know them."

Corey turned to Samuel. "La Lucha?"

Langford returned to his seat just as the bus exited the highway and turned onto a narrow country road.

"La Lucha is the Latinx counterpart of the Black Cell," Samuel replied quietly. "They are launching their own liberation movement, but we are working on several issues together. We're doing much of our arms training together. Their numbers are considerable in the western and southwestern states. They are fighting The Alt's anti-immigration movement, and are gathering in large numbers near the borders. We will fight together if we need to."

And suddenly, there it was, the unnamed emotion Corey was experiencing. It felt as if his entire body burst open like a flame and heat crept up his spine, through his neck, into his face, and threatened to burn his scalp off. The intensity of the feeling took him by surprise, and he could barely breathe.

This feeling was not new to him. It had consumed him when Mrs. Minkus pulled his hoodie off him. He pushed it away whenever he looked at the shell that was now his mother. He tried to stifle it when the cops threw him over the hood of the police car. He tried to breathe it out whenever he looked at the swelling on his nose. He had spent his life squashing the flame down to a

139

thin ribbon of smoke that swirled around him every day and threatened to ignite at any provocation. He had been able to keep it down, always present, but pushed into the background of his consciousness. Suddenly, he could no longer push it away or stifle it. The smoke burst into flame with an intensity that knocked him back on the hard bench and made him glad he was seated. He leaned his head back against the seat, squeezed his eyes shut, and took some deep breaths.

He felt Samuel's hand on his shoulder. "It's okay, little brother. Let it out." Samuel squeezed his shoulder gently. "Your time is coming."

Corey nodded; his eyes were still closed. His heart pounded so hard it felt as though his entire body was throbbing with every beat. He tried to slow down his breathing. What was happening?

His butt left the hard seat and slammed back down as the bus bumped along the gravel road. He opened his eyes and smiled his thanks at Samuel, who nodded and removed his hand from Corey's shoulder, returning his attention to the window. It was almost completely dark now, and Corey could only see the black silhouette of the treetops against the dark gray sky.

The road was rough, winding, and sloped steeply upward. The bus gears shifted loudly as the vehicle struggled up what seemed like the side of a mountain. Corey turned to see the other two buses zig-zagging up the narrow road behind them. Their fluctuating lights revealed, at moments, the winding road, tall evergreen trees, a post and rail fence on the right side of the road, and a steep rock mountain wall on the left.

The bus slowed and turned right onto another gravel road, this one even rougher and sloping downward. Corey had to brace his arm against the seat in front of himself to stay in his seat. After half a mile, they drove past several long, low, wood cabins. They eventually swung into a parking lot in front of a big, well-lit, wooden lodge with a wraparound, covered porch, behind which a huge mountain of rock stood out against the dark sky.

The passengers filed out of the bus and into the Farm's lodge. The building looked much larger inside than it had from outside, and Corey realized the lodge did not just back up to the mountain, but was built *into* the mountain. The first three hundred feet of the huge structure looked like a regular building, with large windows on both sides. Beyond the windows, there were enormous steel double-doors, at least eight inches thick, which now stood wide open. Beyond those doors, the building went on indefinitely, and Corey saw a wide set of stairs ascending to the floors above, and a set of elevator doors, in the distance.

Pushed along by a large crowd of people, as other groups entered, Corey moved to the right and found himself in a spacious dining room. Large round tables held groups of people laughing and talking. Others were walking away from a steaming buffet with trays of food. Samuel placed his hand on Corey's shoulder, and steered him to a table with a few other people.

"Bro. Manny!" Samuel called out as they approached the

table.

A brown-skinned man with straight black hair looked up and smiled broadly. "Bro. Sam!" He rose quickly from his seat to hug and dap Samuel. "How are you, my brother?" He looked at Corey as he pointed them to sit at the table.

"Manny, this is Corey. He's new with the Cell."

Manny reached over to dap Corey. "How're you doing, Bro. Corey? Good to meet you!"

Corey sat at the table and was introduced to the others. There was Yolanda, whose name Manny pronounced with a J instead of a Y, Mateo, and Luis. They were all much older than Corey, probably closer to Samuel's age. They greeted Samuel and Corey as if they were all old friends.

Corey and Samuel went up to the buffet and got themselves fruit, sandwiches, a bottle of water, and a cookie. Workers in aprons and hair nets scurried back and forth restocking the five buffets situated around the large room. More groups arrived and Corey estimated there were more than five hundred people in the space. The noise level rose to a steady rumble, but Corey noticed how much laughter, hugging, and back patting was happening around the room.

Everyone in the lodge was Black or Latinx. Corey nodded towards a table of interesting-looking people and asked Samuel if they were male or female. Samuel said they were trans people. Corey asked Samuel to explain what trans meant, and when he told Corey that gender was a continuum, that there were more genders than just male and female, Corey felt like his mind was blown. He had never heard this before. His immediate response was to wrinkle his nose in disgust, but the simple, matter-of-fact way Samuel explained it made it sound as commonplace as saying some people have black skin and some people have white skin. Corey decided to accept it as simply as Samuel explained it.

There were people of all ages, including three tables with teens in one corner of the room. The people were all shades from light-skinned, who could have passed as white, to the darkest black. He had never been anywhere like this before. Back at the table, as he ate, Corey listened to the other five catch up on life.

Manny, Yolanda, Mateo, and Luis were all from the New York cell of La Lucha. They told Samuel about the ways in which The Alt had infiltrated the New York City police force, and the increasing number of incidents of shooting, choking, and sudden disappearances of Black and Brown New Yorkers. Activists who spoke out against injustice disappeared inexplicably, or were found dead, with a ruling of suicide. Sumpter visited New York frequently for campaign rallies, and had drawn huge crowds of supporters, as well as protestors. At the rallies, police beat peaceful protestors mercilessly, leaving many people critically wounded. Participants of street protests were hunted down and arrested—*or found dead*. With each rally, the number of protestors grew smaller and smaller while the number of Sumpter supporters grew larger. The fear in communities of color was palpable and, at the same time, white people were growing bolder and more expressive in their racism. In mixed-race communities, tension existed between neighbors and when the police were called to address conflicts, it was always the person of color who was hauled off to jail or, even worse, beaten in their homes for disagreeing with the police. In all these cases, the police report cited "aggressive behavior" on the part of the person of color as the reason for their response with batons or fists. Another common occurrence was white neighbors calling the police on their Black and Brown neighbors. The police would burst into some unsuspecting family's home, their guns blazing. The death rate of New Yorkers of color rose rapidly.

The four New Yorkers shared how their numbers had grown exponentially, as people decided to take their organizing underground. They created a number of businesses to hire Latinx people, in order to take care of their own and reduce dependency on the social service system or white businesses. They talked about the reinforcements they were sending to the southwest borders to protect incoming immigrants and prepare to fight The Alt at the borders. They shared stories about their protection of the Middle Eastern/North African cells that had formed to protect Middle Eastern and Arab New Yorkers from harassment, even though it had been more than two decades since the September 11 attacks, because The Alt couldn't tell the difference between Latinx people and Arab-Americans.

Several meetings had been called between different communities of color to discuss how to handle the rising racism

144

in New York. They understood that The Alt would be put on alert if they knew Black and Brown people were working together. They planned to stage conflicts between Black and Latinx communities in order to satisfy The Alt that people of color, in New York, could not band together for a shared revolt of any type. Several East and South Asian communities agreed to "play the part" of passing disinformation to The Alt. The white racists believed Asians were more similar to them, which meant they would be more likely to believe what the Asians told them. Little did they know, the Asian communities were deeply embedded in BRM and La Lucha activities. At this, everyone at the table threw back their heads and laughed.

Corey listened intently to everything. At times, their stories were so rich and colorful, he forgot he was supposed to be eating, and sat listening, his eyes wide.

"It's almost nine o'clock!" Samuel exclaimed. "That four-thirty wake-up call will come soon and," he winked at Corey, "You know what will happen if you're late to breakfast."

Corey pushed his chair back quickly and stood. He had no intention of being left behind when his team went to arms training.

Everyone stood, picked up their plates, and went to one of two busing stations. Corey noticed the large bin marked, "Compost" and wondered what went in it. As he got closer, he saw the careful instructions. He threw his fruit peel and brown napkin into the compost bin, his water bottle into the recycling bin, and the rest of his waste in the trash. He placed his plate and utensils on a conveyor belt that took them out of his sight.

Waving goodnight to their table mates, Samuel and Corey walked back towards the front door. Across the foyer, on the other side of the building, there was a large living room, with furniture pushed back to the walls. In the center of the room, a number of people organized rows of automatic and semi-automatic weapons. Beside them were wooden crates of ammunition, where a woman was prying the tops open and unloading boxes from within.

The sight stopped Corey in his tracks, and someone bumped into him from behind. He mumbled his apologies and continued staring at the weapons. He had never seen so many guns in his entire life. Again, he felt a mixture of fear and excitement. But the spark that had been lit within him on the drive up was much stronger. It was becoming a comfort to him.

Later that night, as he lay in his bunk in the male room of the purple team's cabin, he listened to the breathing and snoring of the fifty or so men around him. He closed his eyes and searched for the flame. It was there, bright and now familiar, seated deep in the pit of his belly. He encouraged it to grow, and it burst into his chest and up his neck. This time, it didn't frighten him. For the first time since Uncle Tony was killed, Corey welcomed the flame, encouraged it, breathed it in without trying to put it out. This was why he was in The Cell. This was his time to find his place in the world. And all the Mrs. Minkuses and racist cops in the world couldn't extinguish his flame. He would let it grow, and it would scorch everyone who tried to put him down, from here on out.

Chapter Eight

Lisa knew as soon as she got home that something was wrong with Jessica. The girls were sitting in the kitchen, eating a snack, when she walked in and put her bags on the counter. There was nothing unusual about that. It was the way Jessica stared at the counter as she chewed slowly and didn't look up or move when Lisa came in that told her Jessica was in a bad space.

Mia jumped up, as usual, and ran to throw her arms around Lisa's waist. "Mommy!"

Lisa hugged Mia back and looked at Jessica, who sat unmoving, staring at the counter. "Hi, Pumpkin." She rubbed Mia's red ponytails. "Hi, Jessica. What's up?"

Jessica looked up with a start, and Lisa realized she was so lost in her thoughts she hadn't noticed when she came in.

"Hi, Mom." Jessica's voice was subdued and hoarse, as if she might cry at any moment.

Lisa released Mia, who pranced back to her stool and hopped up to finish her chips and grapes. She walked behind Jessica and placed her hand on her shoulder, swiveling her around on the stool. "What's wrong, Jes?"

148

Jessica hung her head and shrugged. One tear slid down her cheek. Now Lisa was concerned, as Jessica almost never cried. Attitude, yes. Really stank attitude, absolutely. Tears, rarely.

"Sweetheart. What's happened?"

Jessica let out a loud sob and threw her arms around Lisa's neck. She clung to her mother, her shoulders shaking, tears flowing freely.

Lisa held her daughter and rubbed her back. Jessica's hot tears soaked her collar and flowed down inside her blouse, but she didn't care. When Jessica's sobs slowed to an occasional hiccup, Lisa reached across the counter for a napkin, gently held Jessica away from her, and wiped her face.

"Now tell me what happened," she said firmly.

Jessica sighed. "It's just so unfair!" she wailed, sobs welling up again.

Lisa gave her a stern look. "Take a deep breath. What happened?"

"I don't know why Mrs. Thompson doesn't like me," she said.

"What do you mean, she doesn't like you? How do you know?"

"She always talks to me like I'm in trouble, or like I've done something wrong. I don't know why. She doesn't talk to the other kids like that."

"Okay. Give me an example." Lisa shooed Mia, who was listening intently to the conversation, off her stool and sat on it.

She turned Jessica's stool around to face her and placed a leg on each side of Jessica's stool. "Tell me."

Jessica took a deep breath. "It's been like this all year. She always talks to me like I'm a bad kid." She looked at her mother pleadingly. "I'm not a bad kid!"

"I know that Jes. Of course, you're not a bad kid. Why do you say she thinks you're a bad kid?"

"Well, like the first day of school, I forgot my pencil case. Remember?"

Lisa nodded.

"So, when she asked me why I didn't have my pencils she was really mad, like I've been leaving my pencils at home all year. But it was the first day of school! I didn't understand why she was so mad, and I wasn't the only one that forgot something. But she didn't get mad at them. She was all like," Jessica mimicked Mrs. Thompson's high-pitched voice, with a pleasant, sing-song tone, "Okay, Natalie, you have to remember to bring your folder every day. Don't forget, now." Jessica pasted Mrs. Thompson's wide smile on her face. "And Natalie forgets her folder at least once a week! All year! And Mrs. Thompson never gets mad at her." Lisa nodded, understandingly.

"But she gets mad at me every day for something. Even if someone talks to me first, and I just nod, she yells at me for talking. She never says anything to them. When I ask a question, she sighs and answers me really slow, like I don't understand English, or like I'm really stupid or something."

Lisa frowned. This was beginning to anger her.

"If I ask to go to the bathroom, she rolls her eyes, like I ask all the time, but I don't. And now when I ask to go to the bathroom, everyone in the class rolls their eyes just like she does. And the other kids have started talking to me like she does," Jessica continued.

"Even Chris?" Lisa hoped the one other Black child in the class would stand up for Jessica.

Jessica nodded. "Chris is one of the worst. I guess if he doesn't laugh at me the other kids will turn on him, too. Sometimes, he starts the laughing and the others just follow him." Lisa shook her head with dismay. "So, what happened today?"

Jessica sighed, and her eyes filled with tears again. She hung her head. "I . . . I had a really bad day," she stammered, avoiding her mother's gaze.

"Tell me exactly what happened." Lisa leaned in, one elbow on the counter, the other arm pulling Jessica's stool closer to her.

"Well, when we were lining up to come in from lunch, Ruth pushed me, she always pushes me or hits me, and I never do anything about it. When I tell Mrs. Thompson, she doesn't believe me. But I guess I was tired of it today, so I pushed her back, just a little bit. And Mrs. Thompson saw when I pushed her, so she grabbed my arm and pulled me out of the line." She looked at Lisa hesitantly.

151

Lisa took a deep breath and tried to control her expression. She nodded encouragingly at Jessica, urging her to continue.

"She made me sit in the classroom when the rest of the class went to gym."

"Did you tell her Ruth pushed you first?"

"I tried, but she didn't believe me. I don't believe she didn't see Ruth push me because it all happened in a few seconds, and she was right there!" Jessica shook her head. "But she said I was a liar."

"She actually called you a liar?" Lisa was incredulous.

Jessica nodded. "So, I sat in the classroom during gym, and Mrs. Reinhardt came in and they were talking about me."

Lisa flushed with embarrassment. She had done this in her own classroom with Danielle. "What did she tell Mrs. Reinhardt?"

"That I was out of control and that I was a little hol . . . holgo . . ." Jessica struggled to find the word.

"Hooligan?" Lisa offered.

"Yes! Hooligan. I don't even know what that is. And she was talking about some people being in her class and how she didn't want them there. She kept saying, 'they keep sending their children to our schools,' but I didn't know who she was talking about. Then she said, 'at least the Indians know how to act.' Then, Mrs. Reinhardt said our new president would take care of that and Mrs. Thompson said, 'yes.'"

Jessica continued. "She wouldn't let me color or anything. She just made me sit there. I asked if I could go to the bathroom and she said no."

"So, what happened when the class came back?"

"I asked again if I could go to the bathroom. I usually go right before gym because the locker room is right there, and I don't have to ask. But I didn't go to gym, so I missed my time to go, and I needed to go really bad."

"And she said no again" Lisa filled in.

Jessica nodded. "But she gave me this lecture in front of the class about how I needed to learn to act properly, and that violence was not how I should be in the world. And that I would end up in big trouble one day. And the whole class was laughing, especially Chis and Ruth and Natalie." Jessica shook her head. "It was like she was deliberately making the class laugh at me."

Jessica hung her head. "I kept asking to go and she kept telling me no. And I held it for as long as I could, but just before the bell rang, I couldn't hold it anymore, and I . . . I . . . ." she stopped. Lisa suddenly gained the realization of what happened. "You had an accident?" she asked, her eyes wide.

Jessica nodded, looking away from Lisa. When she spoke, her voice was high and pleading. "I didn't mean to. It was an accident. I tried really hard to hold it, Mommy. I really did. I'm sorry." The last few words were a squeal, and Jessica buried her face in her hands.

Lisa reassured her quickly. "It's okay. I'm not mad at you. I'm mad at your teacher." She pulled Jessica into her arms. "So, then what happened?"

Jessica buried her face in Lisa's neck. "They all saw it on my pants. And they were laughing at me. And Mrs. Thompson laughed too, though she tried to hide it. And I had to go on the bus like that. And they all kept laughing at me on the bus the whole time, and Chris was calling me Stinky Butt. It was terrible."

Lisa noticed, for the first time, that Jessica was freshly showered and wearing different clothes than she was wearing this morning. Her face burned with anger.

She grabbed her daughter by both shoulders and held her away from her. "Listen to me," she spoke firmly. "This was not your fault. Your teacher did this, and I'm going to go talk to her about it. Don't you worry."

Jessica's eyes grew wide. "No, Mommy! Please don't! That will only make it worse. Then she'll be even more angry at me. Please don't!"

Lisa looked at the fear in her daughter's eyes and felt her heart breaking. *How had she not known Jessica was going through this? The school year was almost over. How had she missed this?*

"Okay. Let me think about this. I promise I won't make it worse for you," she reassured Jessica. "But I can't let this go. I have to address it. Otherwise, it won't get better for you, okay?"

Jessica nodded silently.

154

"Why don't you go watch a little television or play a video game to relax."

"Video games? On a weeknight?" Mia's head popped up from the couch, and Lisa realized she had been listening to the entire conversation.

Lisa and Jessica laughed. Lisa nodded. "Yep. One hour, then on to homework."

"Yesss!" Jessica hopped off the stool and ran into the living room.

Lisa heard the television turn on and the video games begin. She put her purse and a few groceries away and began pulling items out of the fridge for dinner. She worked robotically—her mind was preoccupied with what Jessica had told her. She was incensed, but didn't know what to do about it.

She put glass trays of seasoned chicken and cut potatoes into the oven and walked up the stairs to her bedroom. She wanted to call LaTanya but didn't want the girls to hear the conversation. In her bedroom, she inserted her ear buds, dialed the number and began changing her clothes.

LaTanya answered immediately. "Hey girl. What's up?"

LaTanya never wasted time on trivialities. Sometimes that offended Lisa's sense of etiquette, but today she was grateful for it.

"Girl, I need some advice." She launched into a description of what Jessica shared with her. LaTanya listed carefully, with an occasional exclamation, but said little else.

155

When Lisa was finished telling the story, LaTanya sat silently for a moment.

"Jes is in what, third grade?" LaTanya asked.

"Yep. She's been in this school since Pre-k."

"Mmmhmm. And how many Black students and Black teachers are there at the school?"

Lisa sighed. She and Kai had talked about this issue many times.

"There is one other Black kid in Jessica's class—a little boy. But he's on survival mode. He stands with the other kids, I guess, and seems to take part in the bullying. It's either bully or be bullied, and there are only two of them in the class. There are a lot of South Asians. Mia has one other Black boy in her class. The school has very few Black kids, and I think there is one Black teacher in the whole school, and he's the gym teacher."

Lisa paused, thinking about what she had just said. "You know, we deliberately bought a house in a neighborhood that had good schools. I remember last year when they wanted to change the neighborhoods zoned for that school. They wanted to include Elm Forest and a few other low-income villages. We all came out and fought it. So, then it didn't happen."

"You fought it?" LaTanya's voice was incredulous. "I didn't know that."

Lisa suddenly felt ashamed. "I did," she almost whispered. "I thought those kids would bring our school down."

"Those kids? You mean Black kids?" LaTanya's voice

was not unkind, but Lisa knew there would be no coddling.

Lisa sighed and nodded. "Low-income was a code word for Black."

"And how do you feel now?"

Lisa sighed again. "I was wrong. I thought we were safe because we have good incomes and a nice house. But our neighbors don't see any difference. It was a false sense of safety. I realize that, now that I see what's happening to Jessica." She sat on the edge of the bed and sank her head into her hands. "Oh my God, what will I do?"

LaTanya made some sympathetic noises.

"Kai was so angry with me after that community meeting. He told me I had taken bougie to a whole new level, and that it would come back to bite me. I really wondered if our marriage would survive it. He loves me, so he let it go, but I'm not sure he has forgiven me. I was so sure I was right!"

They sat in silence for a while, and Lisa knew LaTanya was trying to figure out how to say what was on her mind. LaTanya had been checking her since their early days of teacher training. Normally, Lisa would jump in to change the subject, but this time she waited. She needed to hear what LaTanya was thinking.

"You know you can't send your kids back to that school."

"You mean until it blows over? I need to go talk to the principal. I just need to figure out—"

"Ever. They can't go back," LaTanya clarified. "Ever."

157

"Wait. What?" Lisa stood up and began pacing in her bedroom. "No. It's just this teacher. We need to get her dealt . . ."

"Lisa, wake up!" LaTanya's voice rose. "What universe are you living in? How are you being so naïve right now?"

Lisa stopped pacing. LaTanya had never yelled at her.

"Are you really so caught up in your own internalized racism that you're willing to sacrifice your own children so that you don't have to change your way of looking at the world?"

Lisa bristled, offended. "I would do anything to protect my children."

"Well, then open your eyes, and stop acting as if racism isn't a thing and that this society is not trying to move backwards two hundred years when it comes to Black people. Do you really not see what's happening here? Or are you just hoping it will go away and you can go back to your nice little bougie life where you're Black, but not really?"

Lisa blinked rapidly. Kai had said something very similar to her when they had the blowup over the school zoning. She frowned, unsure of how to respond.

LaTanya's voice softened. "Lisa, I have been waiting more than ten years for you to wake up and recognize the bubble you have encased yourself in. I had hoped it would happen before any harm was done, but you are so resistant."

Lisa sat down on the bed, hard. When she spoke, her voice was hoarse. "Are you saying it's my fault this happened to Jess?"

"No. I'm saying you closed your eyes to the circumstances

158

we are in, you colluded with white supremacy, and so you didn't see it coming. It was going to happen, but because you would not see what was happening, you could not protect her from it." LaTanya's voice was soft and insistent. "I'm not blaming you for what happened, but if you don't act, and stop further harm from coming to your children, then you *will* be fully to blame, because you now have knowledge."

Lisa's mind spun. "Should I move them to a private school? There's a Catholic school—"

"No. I'm saying you should move them to a Black-centered school where the teachers look like your children, and value them, love them, want to teach and protect them. And where the teachers don't answer to a system that pathologizes Black children and prepares them for prison."

"I don't know any schools like that," Lisa responded quickly.

"I do," LaTanya fired back just as quickly. "Are you familiar with the Freedom Schools of the sixties and seventies?"

Donovan was excited to share his news with the Managing Director. He emailed Bill and asked if he had time to talk. Bill responded immediately that Donovan should stop by his office. He gathered up his notebook and the file he had been compiling. On his way up to the penthouse, he looked over his documents. This new account was such a big break, would bring millions to the firm over the next several years, and would be a critical part of his portfolio during the 2025 promotion cycle. He had endured all Steve's racist shit in the hopes that Steve would put in a good word for him, but as Melva often said, *God bless the child that's got his own.* And he wasn't confident Steve truly had his back. It was Donovan who was bringing in this big account; it was Donovan who would demonstrate his value to the firm through the balance sheet, and it was Donovan who would show them he deserved to be Senior Associate. *Fuck Steve.* Donovan had been at the firm for five years. It was time.

Bill's assistant, sitting at her desk, was on the phone and looked up as Donovan walked into the suite. She waved him into Bill's office.

Bill looked up from his computer and leaned back in his chair as Donovan walked into the brightly lit corner office overlooking the Inner Harbor.

"Don!" he exclaimed in his deep, loud voice. "How are you, my brother?"

Donovan cringed. He hated when they called him Don. And the whole "brother" thing was something he commonly heard from the white associates. It wasn't worth the effort to say something about it. Besides, the last Black associate who complained about the way he was treated at the company, suddenly found that he couldn't do anything right with his bosses, and was soon let go. Donovan wouldn't let that happen to himself.

160

"I'm well. I'm well." He sat across the desk in the chair Bill motioned him to. "How are you?"

"I'm good." Bill tipped the springs on his swivel chair back, picked up a pen from his desk and clicked the tip of it up and down absently with his thumb. "What's on your mind?"

Donovan leaned forward and placed his folder on the desk. "I was talking to a friend of mine from college. He works at the Ashton Foundation, headquartered in D.C. Do you know them?"

Bill nodded silently, his eyebrows raised, his thumb stilled at the top of the pen.

"Right. So, they're huge, and they have eight offices around the country." Donovan opened the folder and read from a sheet of paper. "D.C., New York, Chicago, Miami, San Francisco, Seattle, Portland, and L.A." He glanced up at Bill to find him listening carefully, his chin pointed slightly to the side, eyes on Donovan.

"They're looking for an accounting firm, and my buddy suggested they talk to us. So, they want to set up a meeting. They want a proposal."

Bill nodded enthusiastically. "That's awesome! Really great!" He leaned forward in his chair. "Have you started gathering information?"

"Yes. They hold about $3 billion in investments and liquid funds, and another $16 billion in assets. They fired their last accounting firm, but I have all their tax returns and balance sheets for the past five years."

Bill's eyebrows crept higher. "How did you get that so fast?"

Donovan smiled slyly. "I had some inside help."

"Nice! When do they want this proposal?"

Donovan's collar suddenly felt tight. "Well, that's the issue," he began. "They want it in two weeks."

Bill brought his chair upright abruptly and frowned.

"But I can do it. I've already started working on it. I can make it happen in two weeks," Donovan continued hurriedly. "Don't worry. I've got it."

Bill nodded. "Rhonda and Jacob can work with you on it. I'll let them know." He turned to his computer and began typing an email. "I see some long nights ahead of you." He glanced up at Donovan and smiled. "Better tell that cute little girlfriend of yours you won't be seeing her for a while."

Donovan nodded as he wondered how Bill knew about Kirstie. *Steve.*

"Rhonda and Jacob can help me with the research, but I'll be writing the proposal."

Bill sent off the email with a flourish and nodded. "Suit yourself. Let me know when the meeting is scheduled. Steve can go with you."

Donovan's heart sank but he knew better than to argue.

162

How would he make sure this didn't become Steve's account?
"Sure. That would be good."

Lisa sat in the passenger seat and stared at the nondescript brick building. It was long and low, and resembled a re-purposed post office. Kai opened the door for her and stood waiting. Mia jumped up and down excitedly in the back seat, but Jessica sat quietly. She had said very little in the past week. She responded politely when spoken to, but didn't initiate conversations, and rarely joined in with the rest of the family during mealtime conversation.

Lisa turned to look at Jessica, who was also staring at the building, a blank expression on her face. That had been her facial expression since the incident at school. Blank. Unreadable. Broken.

Kai opened the back door of the SUV for his daughters and extended his hand to Lisa. She allowed him to help her out of the car and stood looking at the building. She didn't want to go in. While Kai and Mia could barely contain their excitement, Lisa and Jessica stood silently. She didn't know what Jessica was feeling, but Lisa was feeling dread.

They opened the heavy metal door and entered. They were in a vestibule with another heavy metal door in front of them. Lisa could see a window to their right, beyond which sat an office, with people walking around and sitting at desks. The glass was thick and cloudy. Was that bulletproof glass?

163

A woman slid the thick glass open and looked at them. She was light-skinned, with a short, red, curly afro.

"May I help you?" she smiled as she spoke, looking from Kai to Lisa, to the girls. Her gaze lingered on Jessica.

"Yes. We're here for a tour. Last name Wilson," Kai stepped forward.

The woman consulted a clipboard. "Oh yes! Jessica and Mia. Welcome. I'm going to buzz the door. Come right on in and I will meet you in the hallway."

When they stepped through the door, Lisa thought she had entered another world. The hallway was painted in large stripes of black, green, and red. A huge, black painting of the African continent was on the red wall directly in front of them. Above the continent were the words: Welcome to the West Baltimore Freedom School. Directly beneath those words were painted the words: Separate and Superior.

To their left and right, the hallway was broken by wood-framed glass doors, which Lisa assumed were classrooms, and children were seated in groups on the hallway floor, their heads together as they worked. There was a steady din of children's voices, broken occasionally by the voice of a teacher rising above. Lisa heard clapping and singing in the background.

The woman with the curly red afro met them in the hallway and extended her hand.

"I'm Sonia, the school secretary."

Kai and Lisa shook Sonia's hand before she turned to

Jessica and Mia, who were both looking around. Mia jumped up and down with nervous energy and excitement, but Jessica stood perfectly still, her brows furrowed as she watched the children in the hall.

Sonia extended her hand to Jessica. "You must be Jessica. I'm Ms. Sonia. Really nice to meet you."

Jessica dragged her eyes away from the kids in the hallway to look at Sonia. She shook the woman's hand silently.

Sonia turned to Mia and extended her hand. "And you must be Mia!"

Mia stopped bouncing and took Sonia's hand. "I am!" she pronounced proudly, with a big smile.

Sonia laughed. "Welcome! Would you like to look around?"

Mia nodded animatedly, while Jessica merely shrugged and looked uninterested. Sonia looked at Jessica thoughtfully for a moment and nodded slowly. She glanced up at Lisa and winked, as if to say, *I've got her.* Something about Sonia made Lisa relax a little.

"Let's go!" Sonia led them down the hallway to the left, pointing out the gym, cafeteria, classrooms, computer rooms, and labs. "We are one of hundreds of Freedom Schools around the country. There are eight in Maryland, two in Baltimore City, one in Baltimore County, two in Prince Georges County, two on the Eastern Shore, and one in Western Maryland. More schools will begin in September. All Freedom Schools are year-round, and

165

families may choose to take a two-week break during the summer, if they desire, but this school is available all summer."

She glanced at Jessica and Mia's horrified faces. "But summertime is sooooo much fun. We take a lot of trips and do fun things. It's really like camp," she added quickly. "Not all parents can afford to pay for separate camp, and we like to keep our scholars with the peers they know. It encourages them to build and maintain community. This school is pre-kindergarten through eighth grade. Ninth through twelfth grade takes place at the Block, and then many of our kids go to college."

"What's the Block?" Kai asked.

Sonia stopped for a moment and looked at Kai for a moment. "You were referred by LaTanya Malcolm, right?"

Lisa and Kai nodded.

"We can talk about the Block in a little while," Sonia responded before she began walking again.

They passed a large health suite, guidance counselor's office, and pre-kindergarten and kindergarten classes, with students sitting in centers, and two teachers in each classroom. The school was well-equipped, with a rock-climbing wall in the gym, stacks of laptops on tables in every classroom, big-screened smartboards on the walls, and cases of books. The classrooms and hallways were decorated with children's work and motivational posters. Some of the student artwork on the walls accompanied essays on heroes like Marcus Garvey, Malcolm X, and others Lisa didn't recognize. One whole wall featured Bob Marley with didn't with essays about his song lyrics.

"The purpose of the Freedom Schools is to grow young Black scholars in an environment tailored to their specific needs. This is an Afrocentric environment, built on collectivist values found in Africa and the diaspora. We teach our children about Black scholars, philosophers, and scientists, dating back to early civilizations in Africa. It's our goal to provide a space where scholars can learn about our ancestors and begin to see all the possibilities for their own lives."

Lisa followed Sonia, Kai, and the girls, glancing around in amazement. Every child in this school was Black or biracial, as was every teacher and staff member. There wasn't any yelling coming from any of the classrooms. Students bounced along the hallway unrestricted and seemed intent on their tasks or on reaching their destinations. Several students made eye contact with Lisa, Kai, and the girls, and said "hello" as they passed. Everyone was busy and engaged. There wasn't anyone hanging around in the hallways or any extreme horseplay going on.

Sonia led them into the library, a large, well-lit area at the back of the school, which spanned the width of the building. Windows lined three walls, and there were rows and rows of books, a computer section, a large empty area that looked like a meeting space, and a reading area for young children, separated by low bookshelves. Strewn around the room were brightly colored beanbags. Several children were comfortably reading on the bags.

"An important goal for our young scholars is to be self-directed and to think critically. In order to do that, they need to have time and space to make their own decisions and learn from their mistakes in a safe environment. For that reason, every scholar from third grade and up has a free period during which they may make choices to play outside, come to the library to read, do some work on the computer, or finish projects. We trust them to make good decisions when they are not closely monitored, and they rarely disappoint us."

Sonia pointed outside the rear windows, where Lisa saw a large playground, with swings, slides, and a basketball court. "This is where scholars can play during recess or their free period."

She pointed to a large, fenced area adjacent to the playground. "This is our community garden. Each grade has a plot, and they're growing ornamental plants, fruits, and vegetables. Families can come and pick what they need. Our scholars are very proud to eat the food they grow."

She led them past a fourth-grade classroom where a student stood at the front of the class, teaching. A teacher could be seen sitting at a desk in the back of the room.

"Our students all practice oratory skills and debate from second grade on. By fourth grade they are expected to be able to present their work and respond to questions and challenges from teachers and classmates."

Sonia led them back to the office and ushered them in. "I would like to introduce you to our Director." She pointed them to a conference room with a large table. They sat and waited silently.

Lisa glanced around the table at her family. Only Mia seemed like her regular self. Jessica looked around the room, the now-familiar empty look in her eyes. Kai stared at the table, nodding from time to time, as if he was listening to music. Lisa knew this meant he was thinking deeply. And she, Lisa, sat feeling lost and confused.

A tall woman with waist-length locs walked in carrying a notebook. She paused just inside the door and surveyed the room. She smiled as her eyes scanned each face. They rested on Jessica for a few moments before moving on.

She pulled out the chair closest to the door, at the head of the table, and seated herself.

"Hello, Wilson family. My name is Dr. Campbell. I'm the school's Director. How are you all?"

"I'm Mia!" Mia bounced in her seat. "I'm in first grade!"

Dr. Campbell clapped her hands in delight. Her tone matched Mia's. "You are?"

Mia nodded.

"I would have thought you were in fifth or sixth grade!"

Mia beamed and shook her head. "Nope! First."

Dr. Campbell nodded. "It's very good to meet you, Mia." She turned to look at Jessica, whose eyes never left the table. "And is this your big sister, Mia?" she asked softly.

Mia nodded. "Yep! That's Jessica!"

Dr. Campbell's eyes seemed to drink Jessica in. Lisa wondered what information she was gathering.

"Jessica, how are you today?" Dr. Campbell's voice remained soft, cautious, as if she were approaching a nervous animal.

Jessica's eyes rose from the table.

"Excuse me?" she asked, looking around the room. Her eyes settled on Dr. Campbell. She frowned, as if wondering when the woman had appeared.

"How are you, Jessica?" Dr. Campbell repeated.

Jessica shrugged. "Fine." Her eyes drifted to the wall above Dr. Campbell's head.

"What grade are you in, Jessica?"

"Third." Jessica's eyes didn't move.

"Fabulous. Our third-grade class is building the most amazing robot. Do you like robots?"

Jessica's eyes focused on Dr. Campbell's face and she tilted her head to one side, thinking. She finally nodded. "What kind of robot?"

Dr. Campbell smiled. "Would you like to see it?"

Jessica nodded and stood.

"Come on. Let's go." As Lisa started to rise, Dr.

Campbell gave her a look that made her drop her butt back onto her seat. Dr. Campbell smiled and nodded, satisfied. "Your parents can stay here." She stood up.

Mia stood, too. "Can I come?"

"Of course! Let's go." Dr. Campbell followed both girls out of the room.

Left behind, Lisa and Kai sat in silence for a long while.

"I have a good feeling about this place," Kai said, nodding his head. "I have a good feeling."

Lisa sighed. She didn't know what she felt.

Kai continued. "Our girls need a loving place. Jessica needs to heal. Can't you feel how different this place is?"

Lisa shrugged. "I don't know. I'm so confused." She turned to Kai. "I'm so worried about messing her up even more. I don't even recognize her."

"She's been traumatized, Lisa. She needs to heal. And she needs to heal with Black people who will love and nurture her. Nothing else will work."

Lisa grimaced. Guilt bubbled in her belly. "I just don't know about pulling them out of public school. I don't know if these folks—"

"Lisa, just stop!" Kai banged his open palm on the table, making Lisa jump. She looked at him in surprise.

"Look at what the all-white public school system has gotten us. Look at what your need to have our children rub shoulders with white people has gotten us." His voice broke as he

171

pointed at the door, jabbing his finger with every word. "Our baby—our baby is so hurt—I don't know if she'll make it back. She is damaged!"

Kai placed both palms flat on the table and braced himself against it, taking a deep breath. "I have gone along with you all this time. I have gone along with your need to live some middle-class, white-bred dream where if you squint your eyes and don't quite look at us, you might think we're white."

He took another deep breath. His voice was quieter now. "I've gone along with all you wanted to do. You wanted to be in that school system, so I agreed. You wanted the big house in the neighborhood where we're the only Black family, so I agreed. You wanted to fight to stop low-income people from coming to our school, so I agreed." Kai made air quotes with his fingers around the words, "low-income."

"You wanted to bring white people into our lives who don't respect our race. I went along with it, but didn't like how all of it changed you."

Kai turned his body around in the chair and looked at Lisa. "Has it been worth it? Was this what you wanted— subjecting our daughters to the racism they have experienced? Was it worth it?" He waited for Lisa to respond.

Lisa shook her head, looking down at her hands. She didn't want to meet Kai's eyes. Her face burned with shame. She opened her mouth but didn't know what to say. At that moment, Mia bounced back into the room, followed by Jessica and Dr.

Campbell. For the first time in over a week, Jessica was smiling. Lisa sat up straight, looking at her daughters.

Dr. Campbell indicated to the girls that they should sit and took her seat.

"Well, I think the robot was a hit. What do you think, girls?"

Mia nodded her head enthusiastically and looked at Jessica.

"It was so cool, Mom!" Jessica grinned widely and grabbed Lisa's hand. "Can we come here?"

"Yes! Can we, Mom?" Mia added, bouncing in her seat. Lisa blinked, not knowing what to say.

"What do you like about the school?" Kai asked.

"The teachers here are so nice." Jessica responded. She looked at the table and lowered her voice. "And the kids here aren't … mean." Her voice sank to a whisper. "I don't want to go back to my old school." She looked up at Lisa, her eyes wide and pleading. "Please, Mom?"

Lisa nodded her head, a lump in her throat and her eyes filled with tears. She looked at her daughter. There was nothing she wouldn't do for her right now. Nothing.

Chapter Nine

The Block was bustling as Corey entered the building. He heard the buzz of voices and feet, and it seemed as if a lot of people were running around. As he stepped into the main hallway, he paused; he had never seen so many people in the Block at the same time. Gone were the white scrubs; most of the men and women were dressed in black or dark jeans, black turtleneck shirts, and black baseball caps or black knitted skull caps. Each cap sported a patch with a raised Black fist—the logo of the Black Cell.

There was a line of people pushing big flatbed carts piled high with crates toward the loading dock at the back of the building. Corey heard loud truck engines and the clanging of the heavy metal loading dock doors banging against the brick wall outside.

Someone grabbed Corey's arm firmly and pushed him towards one of the storage rooms.

"Go get out of those scrubs. There are clothes in the storage room. We got to go." A male voice said behind him.

Corey turned to see who had pushed and spoken to him, but it could have been any one of the people running past. He walked into the storage room and saw several men and women in the room, grabbing items off shelves. He scanned the shelf of jeans, found his size and looked for a turtleneck top and cap.

He looked around, trying to figure out where to get changed. His felt disoriented as he headed for the door. The door swung open, more people ran in, and he stepped out of the way. He remembered he had forgotten to get shoes and walked back, found a pair of black boots in his size and grabbed them.

Corey changed quickly in the bathroom, then walked into the auditorium to drop his backpack and clothes in a corner. The large-screen television was on, and there were a few people standing around watching CNN, shaking their heads. The white reporter on the street in Charlottesville, Virginia, was surrounded by people wearing backpacks and carrying signs.

"It has been seven years since the 2017 Alt march in Charlottesville and we are here again, in 2024, waiting for another rally." The camera panned across the crowd. "You can see some of the signs The Alt supporters are carrying here."

The camera zoomed in on a few young white people carrying signs like, "America for Americans," "Make America white Again," and "Go Home Rapists."

Corey had never seen so many white people in one place. As he scanned the screen, he could not see a single person of color. The crowd was packed so tightly behind the reporter that it was difficult to see anything but a sea of white people. The camera panned across the crowd. There were several muscular men

175

carrying rifles and wearing ammunition vests mixed in with the sea of colorless, hate-spewing Alt supporters. Since his arms training at the Farm, Corey could now recognize each of the rifles he saw on the screen, the type of ammunition used, how many rounds were standard for that rifle, and the best positions for firing. He had never so much as held a gun before his trip to the Farm. Now, he felt quite comfortable with most types of guns, and his twice-weekly trips to the indoor firing range in Baltimore since returning from the Farm continued to build his confidence. He could almost feel the weight of each weapon as he watched the television.

"We expect the majority of Alt supporters to show up in the next two hours or so. Let's talk to some people and hear what they are doing here."

The reporter walked up to a wide-shouldered young white man dressed in a camouflage jacket, sunglasses, and a baseball cap with ALT superimposed on an American flag. He carried a sign that said, "This is Our Country."

"Hi! What's your name?" the reporter asked, shoving the microphone in his face.

"Bill." The young man handed his sign to the woman he was with and crossed his arms across his wide chest rocking back on his heels.

The reporter brought the mic back to his own mouth. "Nice to meet you, Bill. So why have you come out here today?"

Bill nodded and pursed his lips as the mic returned to him.

He seemed to think for a while. "Well, we are out here today to support The Alt, and to take back America."

"Oh. Okay. Tell us who you're taking America back from," the reporter pressed.

"From the . . ." Bill cleared his throat and affected an announcer's voice and leaned into the microphone. ". . . from the people of color who have come into our country and tried to take over." He chuckled and returned to his normal voice. "They don't belong here. We don't want them here. America belongs to Americans, and everyone else can get the—"

The reporter pulled the microphone away from Bill's face. "Thank you, Bill.

He turned back to the camera. "We will be here all day. We expect counter protesters to begin gathering soon and we would love to hear what they have to say. Stay tuned as we follow this evolving story." The camera panned around the scene.

Someone switched off the television and the members in the auditorium ran out, with Corey following them. People were running toward the loading dock, and Corey was swept away with them. Out on the dock, the cool spring air hit him, and he was grateful for the thick turtleneck. A man was collecting cell phones and GPS watches. Corey threw his phone into the pillowcase and stood behind a crowd of people waiting on the dock.

Three large trucks pulled away from the dock, and several motorcoaches pulled into their places. Corey entered a coach and took his seat by the window. As soon as the coach was full, it pulled away from the dock. For the first time since Corey had begun traveling with Cell members, there was absolute silence on the bus—each member engrossed in their own thoughts.

One of the Cell leaders, Monica, got up and stood at the front of the bus. She was a tall, thin woman, probably in her late forties, with an imposing presence. Her hair was pulled into a ponytail under her black cap and she had an empty black leather holster strapped to her right thigh. She surveyed the bus grimly.

"Baltimore Cell, the hour is here for our unveiling. It is time to let the world know of our existence," she said in a clipped British accent. "This is the moment we have been planning for years. We are about to change history."

There was a low murmuring of agreement on the bus before everyone fell silent again, listening.

"We are on our way to Charlottesville, and we will be met there by members of the New York, Dover, and Philly cells. Richmond is already there doing reconnaissance. Other cells are on alert, including La Lucha. If we need them, they will come. But we don't expect to."

Monica widened her stance, put her hands on her hips, and swayed from side to side as the coach bumped along. "I want to remind all of you what we have discussed. It is not our goal to kill anyone. This is the first time the world will learn about the Black Resistance Movement, and this is simply a show of force. We want The Alt to know that we exist, and that we will fight back. We will have weapons, and live ammunition, but we do not plan to fire a single shot today." Monica stopped and looked around the bus to ensure she had everyone's attention. "If we fire shots, we have failed in our mission. Are we clear?"

"Yeah!" the riders on the bus shouted their agreement.

"We will only use weapons if we need to defend ourselves. It is important that we all hide our identities. Keep your sleeves rolled down to hide your tats, keep your caps on, and we will be handing out black masks and dark glasses. Keep them on. If you have tats on your hands, please take a pair of gloves."

People on the bus began rolling down their sleeves as a young woman walked down the aisle handing out masks, sunglasses, and black leather gloves. Corey looked at the black, fabric mask she handed him, and then glanced around the bus. Several people had donned their masks, which covered their noses, mouths, chins, and hooked around their ears. The wide, black sunglasses covered their skin from the cap to the mask, so there was literally no skin showing, and there was very little way to differentiate one person from the next. They made a formidable group, and Corey shivered at the thought of meeting a group of a few thousand of these people carrying weapons.

"Our goal is to march toward The Alt, show our force, and retreat. They should not know who we are or where we came from. We will have to move quickly and decisively. We will march as instructed, retreat to the buses and disappear as suddenly as we came." Monica paused and looked around again. Her eyes were piercing. "Clearly, executing this with three thousand people will require a lot of discipline. Remember why you are there and pay close attention to your leaders. You will be organized by your assigned teams. Please find your leader as soon as you get off the bus. We will have signs showing where the teams are gathered." Monica took her seat at the front of the bus and put on her own mask and sunglasses.

As Corey hitched his mask behind his ears, he felt the now familiar, and not unwelcome, smoldering begin in his belly. The warmth rose up into his chest. He felt the heat radiating from himself, and he didn't want to put it out. The flame fed him. It gave him energy, fueled his anger, and gave him purpose. He closed his eyes and breathed into the flame. When he opened his eyes, he felt clear-headed, calm, and ready for what was to come. This is what he had been waiting for. This was it.

Tasia had been sending messages all morning, since before 6 a.m. when Carla picked Sharonda and her up. Her fingers flew across the computer keyboard as she typed, and Carla fed her information for the messages as it became available.

The first set of SMS messages that went out to every cell in the country, from the Baltimore headquarters of the Cell and La Lucha's headquarters, contained the same five words: *Unveiling in Charlottesville happening today.* As the hours wore on, she sent additional messages advising which cells had been dispatched to Charlottesville. It began with *5 dispatched.* The Richmond cell, or Cell #5, was on its way to the rendezvous point; it was the closest

180

cell to Charlottesville. Then, she added *3 dispatched* (Philly cell), *1 dispatched* (New York cell), *2 dispatched* (Dover cell), and *4 dispatched* (Baltimore cell).

Carla leaned over and pushed a sheet of paper in front of Tasia. It contained intelligence from the Richmond cell, who was first on the scene. Tasia typed another message: *Expecting 300-450A; 3,000+C* (expecting up to 450 Alt members, and more than 3,000 Cell members). Then another message: *3 rendezvous at NW Center Street and Paul Street at 1 heading N* (Philly cell meet at the northwest corner of Center Street and Paul Street at 1 p.m. and march north). And a final message: *1 rendezvous at NW Carlie Road and Fifth Street at 1 heading S* (New York cell meet at the northwest corner of Carlie Road and Fifth Street at 1p.m. and march south).

She sent messages detailing where to park trucks and coaches so they were scattered around the city and would attract little attention. She began plotting truck and coach locations on an electronic map. All GPS systems loaded on the equipment trucks had gone dark, so she had to enter their locations manually. Cells sent her their coordinates each hour so she could update the map. Before long, her map showed more than 60 motorcoaches and 15 trucks carrying equipment and weapons, all heading toward Charlottesville, VA.

Once she had sent messages to the dispatched cells, she began messages to the cells that were to be on alert: *6 standby* (Hartford), *7 standby* (Springfield), *8 standby* (Durham). It was

181

unlikely these cells would need to dispatch, but they needed to be in a heightened state of alert, and cells as far west as Chicago and as far south as Miami needed to be prepared to rendezvous in Charlottesville.

She paused for a moment and looked around. Carla was on the phone talking fast and loud to someone about "intelligence failures" and asking, "How did we not know about this?" She looked up, nodded at Tasia and gave her a thumbs up. That meant she could relax for a moment.

Tasia leaned back in her seat and pushed the rolling chair back from the computer. She was exhausted, but her body buzzed with excitement and fear. She leaned back towards the desk and double-checked that each coach and truck was reflected on the map. She thumbed through the papers Carla gave her, making sure she hadn't missed anything. When she was satisfied that she had done everything, she leaned back again.

She looked around the large communications room. All the windows were painted over with black paint to darken the room, and large-screened televisions lined the wall, each one tuned to a different news channel. Dedicated newsgatherers sat at their computers watching the television screens and typing information. Most of the information went to Carla, who also gathered information from the surveillance groups on the ground in Charlottesville. As she gathered information, she disseminated it to different groups for action. Tasia was responsible for communicating with the multiple cells around the country and keeping them apprised of what was happening on the ground.

Tasia took a deep breath, cognizant of the importance of her role. She had expected to spend her time cleaning the communications room and making copies, as Donna promised, but she only ended up doing that for a couple of weeks. It did not take long for Carla, the Director of Communications, to begin giving Tasia more complicated tasks.

Tasia, eternally grateful for the job, the salary, the childcare, and the support she received from the Cell, threw herself into her work, giving it everything she had. She showed up to work early every day. She listened carefully when Carla gave her instructions, and tried to go above and beyond what Carla asked. She began anticipating what Carla would ask for next. She started preparing reports she knew would be needed and gathering information she knew would eventually be wanted. When Carla asked, Tasia would send it right away, and Carla was increasingly impressed. Over the next few weeks, she became Carla's trusted right hand.

"You're very good at reading people. You understand what they need, and what will speak to them. And you have a great head for communications strategy," Carla often told her. At first, Tasia didn't believe she had anything special to offer, but as the weeks went on, she received such positive feedback from members of the Communications Team, she began to believe them. She was now able to give Nana money for rent, utilities, and food. She didn't have to ration Sharonda's training pants or anything else they needed. She didn't have much extra, but she contributed what she had to the Cell's susu, and was happy she could give as well as receive. Tasia felt strong, proud, happy, and a part of something much bigger than herself. She didn't spend her days obsessing over Kenny anymore. She knew he was dead, and that one day, she would find out the truth. But she wasn't alone anymore. The Cell had changed her life.

Carla gestured to Tasia, the phone still glued to her ear. She pointed at the row of locked cabinets against one wall. Tasia nodded and went to get the key. As soon as she unlocked the cabinets, several people rushed in, dressed entirely in black. Tasia helped them sign out cameras and recording devices. They would transmit pictures back to the Communications Team to be used to document the event and recruit more members.

A new set of coordinates popped up on the SMS system. Tasia returned to her computer and plotted them on the map. Within one hour, all the buses and trucks would arrive at their rendezvous points. She looked up at the television screens. The Alt marchers were gathering on two blocks and it looked like hundreds of people. Anti-Alt protestors gathered one street over. The aerial views showed crowds of people moving towards the two gathering points. Reporters hopped from group to group, thrusting microphones in people's faces. Tasia could hardly bear to read the closed-captioned text of the racist insults coming from The Alt marchers. They praised Reginald Sumpter and promised to take America back for white Americans. They chanted, "Hey, hey, ho, ho, niggers and spics have got to go!"

Tasia shuddered at the hate spewing from the lips of The Alt supporters. The Cells were coming and would march with equal passion to meet them. The plan was for this to be a peaceful march on the part of the Cell, but anything could happen. Tasia shook her head. She couldn't believe this was *finally* happening. The Cell had planned this day for years. But were they really ready? Tasia knew they would find out in a very short time.

Chapter Ten

Donovan cursed with annoyance when the game was interrupted by breaking news. He hadn't paid attention to the newscasts, but as he paid for the pitcher of beer and headed back to his table, he glanced up at the large-screen television to see the camera focused on a white man carrying a sign that said, *Niggers Go Back to Africa!*

Donovan pulled up short, staring at the screen. Someone bumped him from behind, making him spill a quarter of the pitcher on himself.

"Damnit!" he muttered, shaking the liquid off his arm.

"Look where you're going, moron!" the tall, blond-haired man said. He turned to walk away and muttered under his breath, "stupid nigger."

Donovan stood rooted to the spot, feeling as though the air had been knocked out of him. He watched the man's back as he disappeared into the crowd at the bar. Looking back up at the television, he saw what looked like a huge protest, with hundreds of white people carrying signs that said, *America is for white People*; *No Illegals*; *whites are Superior*; *No More Welfare Queens*, and a slew of other offensive signs. Many of the people carried semi-automatic rifles. The banner at the bottom of the screen announced that this was an Alt march in Charlottesville, VA.

He turned and walked back to his table, where his friends, Michael and Phillip, stared at a big screen on the wall near their table, eyes open wide.

Donovan set the partly empty pitcher on the table. His eyes went back to the television. He felt sick as he slid into his seat. Michael looked at him and must have noticed the expression on his face.

"You okay?" Michael asked, his eyes pulled back to the television. He ran his hands through his straight brown hair anxiously. Donovan felt, rather than saw, Michael's eyes moving back and forth between Donovan and the television. When Donovan didn't respond, Michael's eyes remained on his friend. He ran his hands through his hair again.

Donovan felt light-headed, as though he hadn't eaten all day, or like the time he had the stomach flu and couldn't keep fluids down for three days. His head spun. He looked up at the television. *What was happening?*

It took a moment for Donovan to realize both Phillip and Michael were now staring at him. He kept his eyes on the television, avoiding the eyes of his two white friends. A group of men at the bar cheered loudly as the camera panned across the protest signs. He heard the cheers, felt the energy growing around him, and sensed the air of excitement in the bar. Panic rose up in him.

Dragging his eyes away from the screen, Donovan forced himself to pour beer into the three tall mugs on the table. His hand shook and beer hit the table. He took a deep breath and brought his left hand up to steady the pitcher as he poured. His brain spun. *How could he talk about what he was feeling with his two white friends?*

When he had finished pouring, he set the pitcher on the table and picked up his mug. He stared at the foam on top of the golden liquid before taking a sip. He closed his eyes and tried to steady his mind. *What was happening right now?* His mind was attempting to grasp something that eluded him. His heart beat rapidly, and he struggled to steady his breathing. *How did things get to this point?* As he took deep breaths, it dawned on him that he had seen several signs of this hostile atmosphere escalating but had ignored them. His mind flew back to comments Steve and his other colleagues had made in passing over the previous few months. They had become more crude in their comments about Black people than they were before. Some of the things they said shocked Donovan, like Steve's increasingly insulting narrative about Black women and their bodies. One of the associates had suggested that, when Donovan was back in Jamaica, he used to swing from trees in the jungle. Two of the firm's clients had asked that Donovan be replaced as their accountant, citing some nonsense about him not being a "good fit" for their company. And Donovan had noticed he was followed around in more than one store—even more than he had been before. Cashiers were more rude than usual. At the gym, he noticed the staff scanning members in, who were usually smiling and pleasant, presented him with sour, hostile looks that he did not see them give to white gym members.

Donovan had viewed each of these events separately, assuming they were isolated incidents having nothing to do with his race. Or, at least, when the idea of racism presented itself, he pushed it away. But now, in this moment, he could no longer deny that the general atmosphere in society was becoming increasingly unfriendly to Black people.

He took another sip and it became immediately clear that the beer was a bad idea, given the current state of his stomach. He placed his mug on the table before looking at Michael and Phillip, who were both staring at him with great concern.

"Sorry. I just . . . I just. . . . " He didn't know what to say. He had been friends with Phillip and Michael since their undergraduate days at Hopkins. His friends had both gone into law enforcement, and joined the National Guard, while he became an accountant. They had remained friends over the years, getting together for drinks every month or so, or to watch a game. While they had been friends for a long time, their conversations centered around sports and women. Like with most of Donovan's friends, he had never discussed anything serious like politics or race with them and didn't know how to do it now.

"Hey, man, this is terrible. I don't know what's happening in this country right now," Michael said.

"I don't recognize this country," added Phillip somberly.

Donovan nodded silently. Between the man who bumped into him, what was happening on the television, and the excitement of the crowd in the bar, he was experiencing so many emotions he didn't know how to voice anything. The only feeling he was sure of, in that moment, was the feeling of insecurity that his physical safety was at risk.

He gazed around the bar. He was the only Black person in view. His heart sank, and he suddenly realized that this unease was an unfamiliar feeling for him. He usually felt proud to be the only Black person in a space. A space filled with white people was an indication of space he had infiltrated, one that had not been created for him. This usually made him feel proud, with a sense of achievement. Today, it made him scared.

"Hey, man," Michael said again. "Don't worry about those assholes." He gestured at the television. "That's just a few crazy people trying to get some attention on TV."

Donovan frowned. A few weeks ago he might have agreed with Michael, but right now, he wasn't so sure. *How could anyone look at what was happening in Charlottesville, combined with the change in atmosphere across America, and not think something serious was brewing?* He had ignored news reports about the growing influence of The Alt. He couldn't see what they had to do with him. But, now he did. He opened his mouth to speak but wasn't sure what to say. Instead, he nodded and looked up at the television again. It looked like more than a few crazy up to him.

The camera panned to a temporary stage set up in front of Colonial Square. Reginald Sumpter's running mate, Alice Warner, walked toward the stage, surrounded by a tight group of armed Secret Service agents. She strolled up to the mic, her silver hair shining in the late spring sun. The view of the stage from where the reporter stood, looking over the heads of the crowd, was momentarily hidden from view as the crowd raised their posters in the air and pumped their fists. Although the sound was off on the television, Donovan could tell they were cheering loudly.

Alice Warner smiled at the crowd and waved. She seemed to revel in the applause and allowed it to continue for a long time. Finally, she motioned to the crowd to be quiet and removed the mic from its stand.

Donovan was suddenly aware of the hush in the bar.

"Hey! Turn up the sound!" someone shouted and was met with cheers of agreement.

"My fellow Americans," Warner began. "Candidate Sumpter . . . I'll just go ahead and say, President Sumpter—" at which the crowd on television and the crowd in the bar erupted with cheers and applause. She grinned and motioned for them to be quiet. "President Sumpter and I are so happy to see the work you are doing here in Charlottesville. We want you to know that —we—are—with—you!" She pumped her fist in the air to punctuate the last four words.

191

The crowd erupted in cheers, as did the room. Donovan felt his skin crawl and wondered how he could get to the door without going through the crowd of people near the bar. She waited for a moment before continuing. "Many of us have been waiting for this moment for a very long time. We are about to take our country back!"

The cheers erupted again, and she waited for them to die down.

"Mark your calendar. This is the year for us to expel, from our country, people who don't belong here."

To this the crowd began to chant, "Kick them out! Kick them out!" People in the restaurant joined in.

She continued, pausing between each phrase to allow the crowd to respond.

"All the rapists trying to cross the border to attack our women and children."

"Kick them out!"

"All the criminals in cities like Chicago and Baltimore and Detroit."

"Kick them out!"

"All the people who are too lazy to work and want to sit home and collect checks."

"Kick them out!"

"We are returning our country to God-fearing Americans, who work hard for what they have, and who have been building this country for their own families. We need to return to our values

192

and reject those who threaten them. We need to provide for our children and grandchildren—the ones who belong here."

She stood for a moment, surveying the crowd. They stood silently, waiting. The bar was also silent.

"This November, do what you know is right. Go to the polls. Let your voice be heard. When you cast your vote for the Sumpter/Warner ticket, you cast your vote for the future success of America. You can be sure we will clean this country up and work for your children's futures!"

The crowd erupted as the camera zoomed in on Warner's face. She looked pleased. "We will see you at the polls in November, and in the White House in January. God bless you, and God bless the United States of America!"

At this, the crowd on television and the crowd in the bar erupted. The camera switched to an aerial view of the protest. The streets were crammed for several miles in every direction, crowds converging on the stage. Donovan estimated there were thousands of people.

Out of the corner of his eye, Donovan saw a black mass moving towards the protest from the north. As the helicopter moved over the area, Donovan noticed another mass of black coming from the east, another from the west, and another from the south.

What is that? he thought, peering at the screen.

As the camera zoomed in, Donovan saw that each of the black masses was a group of hundreds of people dressed in black.

They moved smoothly, as one unit.

"Rick, what are we seeing here?" the reporter in the newsroom asked the reporter in the helicopter.

"I'm not sure, Beth. It looks like a big crowd of people. In fact, there are several groups, it looks like."

"Could you pan in a little closer?" Beth asked.

The camera zoomed in, and the bar fell into shocked silence. There were thousands of men and women, dressed completely in black, marching toward the protest. They were heavily armed, with automatic and semi-automatic rifles. They all wore black hats, dark glasses, and black face masks that covered the lower half of their faces. They were unrecognizable, but something about the way they walked, and a few locs showing under some of the black hats, told Donovan they were Black people. They were *his* people.

Donovan turned and looked at Michael and Phillip, who were staring at the television, their mouths open. He looked back at the television. The aerial view had disappeared, and the camera was focused on the reporter in the newsroom.

Beth smiled, but her eyes seemed panicked. "Well, that's it, folks! We will check in from time to time with our crew in Charlottesville." She sounded breathless. "Let's go now to coverage of the upcoming election." The music started, and the animated words *2024 Election* swept onto the screen.

Michael and Phillip jumped at the same moment and reached into their back pockets for their phones. They both read their messages and exchanged glances. Michael looked at Donovan for a long moment. "We're being called to the barracks. They're mobilizing the National Guard."

Phillip seemed stunned. He stared down at the table, avoiding Donovan's eyes. "They are calling us out to Charlottesville." He paused and slowly raised his eyes to look at Donovan. "I've never felt so conflicted in my life. I don't know how to feel about . . . those people, and what they're doing." He glanced up at the television and then back at Donovan. "This doesn't feel right, but I don't have a choice." Phillip seemed to want Donovan to say it would be okay. Donovan just looked back at him; his tongue felt dry and swollen and he was unsure whether he could talk. *Besides, what would he say?* He looked up at Michael, who was already standing and reaching for his jacket.

"We've got to get going, man," Michael shrugged apologetically.

Phillip stood up and counted out a tip to put on the table. He looked down at Donovan, who felt rooted to his seat. "Want to walk out with us? I don't want to leave you here."

Donovan nodded. They elbowed their way, single file through the crowd, with Donovan sandwiched between Michael and Phillip. A few people stopped and pierced Donovan with angry gazes. When they saw his two large friends, they turned away. Out on the street, Michael and Phillip walked Donovan to his car. They waited while he got in, started the car, and drove off. Without thinking, he turned towards his mother's house.

195

Corey took the AR-15 and an extended magazine from the woman handing them out from the back of the truck. He slammed the magazine into the well and checked that it was secure. He pulled back the charging handle and listened for the satisfying click of the round entering the chamber. He savored the weight of the weapon in his hands, for a moment, before slinging the strap over his shoulder. He was ready.

The purple tactical team had already moved out and Corey fell in line as the group marched five across, with members on either end of the row, marching partially sideways to cover the flanks of the group. They moved silently in the middle of the street, listening for instructions from the front.

Holding his head straight and high, as he had been taught, Corey's eyes shifted from side to side behind his sunglasses. His heart pounded, and he felt breathless. He wasn't sure if he was scared, or excited, or both. Either way, he felt free, as if he had been chained up for a long time and finally released. Through his mask, he opened his mouth and took in deep breaths of the cool air. His entire body buzzed.

Be cool. Just be cool. He told himself.

On the sidewalk, people stopped and stared, their mouths open, pointing at the Cell members. Corey was suddenly aware of helicopters overhead. He had been trained to prepare for this, and understood they would follow the Cell members, filming them, running their faces through facial recognition software. But they would come up empty, because the members' faces and all identifying characteristics were completely covered. In some cases, the member's gender was not even clear. They would be very difficult to recognize without removing their face coverings.

As they marched through the cross streets, they passed an armed Cell member who held up traffic so they could pass unobstructed. After the group passed the side street, those members joined the back of the convoy, walking backwards to cover the exposed rear of the group, and two members at the front of the group would take up their posts at the next cross street. The group moved as one machine—smooth, disciplined, well-trained, and prepared for anything.

It was only a few blocks to the center of the protest, but it felt like miles. Corey saw police officers pushing protestors back from the sidewalk, and several cops knelt behind their parked cars, guns trained on the Cell marchers, but they only watched. They made no attempt to stop the group. Corey understood how intimidating it must be to see thousands of people with guns. He thought about how much he would enjoy watching the footage of this later.

Corey heard a command shouted from the front, and the group came to an abrupt halt. They stood for a while, awaiting further instructions, and Corey heard shouting coming from the front. The group was being challenged, but Corey couldn't see what was happening.

A chant started among the protesters. It was faint at first, niggers and spics have got to go!"

Eventually, the people on the sidewalk all around Corey were chanting, pointing at the Cell members, or pumping their fists in the air with each word. Corey and the other members kept their heads high and their faces expressionless. They maintained their forward-facing stance, eyes scanning the crowd, looking for weapons pointed at them, or any other threat. Although many of the white people on the sidewalk carried large guns, no-one pointed them at the Cell members. They held their guns across their chests and chanted words of hate, their eyes wide and piercing, mouths turned down at the corners in a sneer.

With another command, the group moved forward. The people on the sidewalk seemed to press in on the flanks of the group. They moved between parked cars into the street and came close enough for Corey and his row to touch them. As they yelled, Corey's heart pounded harder and harder, and it became difficult to breathe behind his mask.

A big man with long red hair and a bushy red beard, carrying a black rifle, marched alongside Corey's row, his face inches from the member on the left flank. The member ignored him and continued marching, his head straight.

"Go back to Africa!" The man yelled, spit flying from his mouth. "Go back to the jungle! Go back to swinging in the trees. Go back to fucking your ugly bitches!"

Corey took a deep breath. He felt the fire begin in his belly. It wasn't slow and gentle this time. It grew from a smoldering ember to a roaring flame in a matter of seconds. His body was on fire, and flames crept up his chest into his neck. He wanted to tear off the mask and the turtleneck and expose his skin to the cool air, but he kept marching, eyes straight ahead.

The man stepped into Corey's row. He was moving along in front of Corey and his row mates. He walked up to each person, screaming in their faces, walking backwards as the row kept moving.

He stepped up to Corey, so close Corey could smell the sweat from his body and alcohol on his breath. His eyebrows furrowed into one straight red line as he screamed.

"Ugly, fucking monkey!" He moved in step with Corey, keeping his face close enough that Corey could see the dark flecks in his blue irises. His spit sprayed Corey's mask and sunglasses. He resisted the urge to wipe his face.

"I bet you look like your ugly monkey momma. I'm gonna fuck your nasty monkey momma, and—"

Corey felt as though his head exploded, and all he could hear was a loud roar. He momentarily lost sight of the man's face and wondered for a second where he went. That is, until he realized he had knocked the man down and was now pummeling him on the ground with his fists.

The man's eyes were wide. Corey noticed the intense fear in his eyes and felt a level of satisfaction. Yes. This was for Minkus and the asshole cop who slammed his face on the patrol car. This dick would never talk about Momma again.

"You motherfucker!" someone was screaming. "I'ma kill you!"

Blood covered the man's face. Corey's fists felt numb as he continued to hit the man even after he lay still. He felt his feet lifted off the ground from behind, and he kicked his feet wildly, trying to get back to the man on the ground.

"Stand down, Brother Corey. Stand down!" a deep voice commanded.

Corey continued to kick his legs and swing his feet blindly. His limbs did not connect with anything, and he felt himself moving forward. He was completely surrounded by Cell members. They carried him as he kicked. He realized someone was holding his arms and his legs, and that he was actually unable to move them. He looked up and could see only Cell members. They cocooned him, and carried him silently, their heads held high. He could no longer see the people on the street, and he doubted they could see him. Yet, he heard their chants and insults continuing.

Corey allowed himself to be carried, sobbing quietly. The fire inside him was gone and he felt confused and exhausted. His mask was soaked with tears, sweat, and snot, and his glasses slid down his wet nose. There was a heavy weight on his chest, and he struggled to breathe. He realized he was holding his body stiff and tried to relax.

Calm down, he thought, attempting to regulate his breathing. *Get your ass together!*

200

"Are you ready to walk?" the deep voice behind him asked.

Corey nodded.

"Okay. Put him down."

They rested him gently on his feet, even as they continued to move. They did not step away from him. He walked within a tight circle of members. There were two women on either side of him, someone behind him and someone in front. He could feel a firm hand on each of his shoulders, moving him briskly along. His gun was gone, and he wondered what happened to it.

The group stopped suddenly. A command sounded from the front, and the members, with the exception of the team surrounding him, thrust their guns in the air.

"It is our duty to fight for our freedom.
It is our duty to win.
We must love each other and support each other.
We have nothing to lose but our chains."

The Assata Shakur chant was loud and guttural. Even the members holding Corey chanted loud and strong, without releasing their grip on him. Over and over, they chanted. The street was surprisingly silent, except for their chant. All the yelling and insults stopped. Corey wished he could see what was happening, but the members around him were too tall to allow him to see anything but their rifles lifted in the air.

After the fifth time chanting, another command sounded at the front, and the group moved out again. They turned down a side street. The coach was waiting on the street for them, and Corey was hustled up the steps and into a window seat. The tall man with the deep voice who had been walking behind him sat next to him, almost as if to ensure he stayed in his seat. No one made eye contact with him. Corey turned his face towards the window in shame. *He had totally fucked up. What was wrong with him?*

It took less than three minutes to get sixty people on the coach and to start moving. Corey looked at his watch. They had been on the street for less than thirty minutes. The goal was to make an appearance and leave before the City of Charlottesville could scramble police and National Guardsmen to the scene. The Cell appearance was a flash which, if the protestors blinked, they would have missed. But there was no way they could have missed, or would ever forget, more than three-thousand armed Black people marching in the streets. They had achieved their goal—the world knew of their existence.

There was silence on the bus. Monica talked to the other coaches and the Block using a satellite phone. Apparently, there were a number of decoy buses, with trusted white drivers, waiting under bridges and overpasses. The coaches split up and headed for their decoy points. Surveillance members in cars sent information to the buses about the location and activities of the helicopters.

The coach drove under an overpass and pulled up behind an identical coach, which was waiting under the overpass. As the decoy bus pulled off, no one on Corey's coach so much as shifted in their seat, and Monica's was the only voice heard.

"Baltimore 3 at rendezvous location, awaiting further instructions," Monica said into the satellite phone. She listened for a moment and then hung up.

"Let's get our weapons stowed," she said.

At that, the bus sprang into action. Two young men collected the weapons and stowed them in a hidden compartment at the bottom of the bus, accessible via a trap door behind the rear seats. They collected all hats, sunglasses, masks, and turtlenecks, which were thrown into the hidden compartment, and an array of different colored T-shirts were handed out. When everyone was changed, the members returned to their seats and sat, waiting for instructions.

Corey sat in misery on the silent bus, forcing himself to breathe normally. Of over three thousand Cell members, he was the only one to have screwed up. He didn't know how he knew that, he just did, and his heart felt like it would stop at any moment.

He stared out the window at the trail of water dripping down the square gray stones making up the walls of the underpass. He counted how many patches of moss were growing on the stones. He tried to identify the types of trash strewn on the ground.

Anything to keep him from meeting the eyes of the other Cell members.

After thirty minutes, the satellite phone squawked. Police had stopped five decoy coaches. At that, Monica gave the driver the order to get on the road, and the coach pulled off quickly.

They travelled fast on the darkening roads, staying off major highways as much as possible. When they got to Baltimore, Corey heard the collective sigh of relief inside the tense bus. They got back to the Block and drove around to the loading dock.

The bus emptied quickly, and Corey waited to get off last. As he stepped off the bus, Samuel waited for him on the dock, and Corey's heart sank. He wouldn't be able to slink away quietly, as he had planned on the ride. He would have to deal with this tonight. He nodded politely at Samuel and tried to follow the others into the building.

Samuel nodded at Corey and placed his hand on Corey's shoulder, stopping him. "The elders are waiting for you," he said.

Corey sighed. "Okay."

He followed Samuel into the building and down the main hallway. Samuel stopped at the open door to a large classroom and ushered Corey in. There was a circle of ten chairs in the middle of the otherwise empty room, and all but two of the chairs were occupied.

Samuel closed the classroom door behind them. Corey looked around at the men and women seated in the circle. They were all older, probably around Samuel's age, and they looked at him solemnly. Samuel pointed Corey to one of the empty chairs and sat to the left of him in the other.

The room was silent for a full minute as the elders looked at Corey. His throat was dry, and he could hear and feel the pounding of his heart. It sounded like a drum beating in his head. He took a few deep breaths and tried to stop his hands from shaking and his foot from tapping. The silence felt like an hour, but he knew it could not have been.

Finally, one of the women spoke. She had thick, gray locs piled high on her head, around which was wrapped a silky white cloth. Her voice was deep and rich, and she looked unblinkingly at Corey as she spoke. She looked and sounded like someone he wouldn't mess with, but she did not seem unkind.

"Brother Corey, you have been brought before the Council of Elders to account for your behavior at our unveiling today. Please tell us what happened."

Corey took a deep breath and swallowed. *He really didn't want to be here. Why didn't they just throw him out of the Cell so he could get on with his life? He didn't want to do this.* But, in his months at the Cell, he understood the importance of respect for the elders. *He had to do this. Maybe if he showed his respect, they wouldn't kick him out.*

"I . . . I fu . . . I mean, I messed up today," he began.

The woman nodded slowly, her eyes never leaving his face.

"I . . . I don't know what happened." He fought back tears. *He was always fucking crying these days.* "I was marching, and then this white guy got in my face, and I was cool, you know? I was cool at first." He looked around the circle, pleadingly.

The elders nodded, listening.

"Go on, Brother Corey." The woman with the locs said.

"But then . . . but then he said he was gonna fuck . . . I mean, he said. . . ." Corey trailed off. He couldn't even repeat the words. His voice sank to a whisper, and the elders all leaned in to hear.

"He said he was gonna fuck my monkey momma, or something like that," he whispered. "And I don't remember anything else. Until they picked me up off him." He looked at the floor. Shame flooded him.

The elders were silent for a moment.

"What did that mean to you, Brother Corey, when he said that?" the gray-locked elder asked. "Why did that trigger you?"

Corey swallowed again. He wasn't sure of the answer. When he opened his mouth to speak, he didn't know what he was going to say.

"Because I couldn't protect her before," he said slowly, realization dawning on him. "I couldn't protect her when she went to the school to deal with Mrs. Minkus. And I couldn't protect her when she went to jail." The words tumbled out faster than his tongue could wrap around them. They were jumbled and almost unintelligible, but the words kept coming, accompanying hot tears, which he didn't bother to wipe.

"And I couldn't protect Aunt Doreen, and I couldn't protect Calvin. I still can't protect Calvin. And I couldn't protect myself from the police. And I just couldn't . . . I just couldn't."

He looked up at the elders. "I failed them all," he whispered, shaking his head. "I failed." He looked back at the ground. "And I failed the Cell, and all of you." He looked over at Samuel. "And I failed you too, Brother Samuel. I'm sorry." He fell silent, but the tears continued to stream down his face.

The man to Corey's right, put his hand firmly on Corey's shoulder, and the touch was surprisingly comforting. They all sat in silence for a moment.

"Brother Corey, do you know why that white man got in your face?" One of the men asked.

He shook his head.

"Or why he called your mother a monkey?"

He shook his head again.

"Because ever since white people came in contact with Africans, their efforts have been designed to dehumanize us. They create a set of circumstances in which they treat us as animals—they enslave us, they beat us, they rape us. When they could no longer use us as free labor on their plantations, they began using us as beasts of burden in their prisons. When we excel, they burn down our businesses and neighborhoods and tell us we can never rise up. When we make brilliant inventions, they hide that fact from the history books and tell our children we have never created anything. They bring their drugs and guns into our neighborhoods. They deny us opportunities for a good life, and then when we finally believe all they have said we are, when we react to all they have done to us, it confirms what they have always thought about us—that we are less than human."

He stopped to make sure Corey was listening. He was. Intently.

"But the truth is, it's their humanity that is at stake. Because if they acknowledge we are human, it shines a light on their own inhumanity for how they have treated us. As long as we are animals, their treatment of us is justified. But if they acknowledge us as human, they have to justify to themselves, and to their God, how they could have been so wicked."

Corey nodded. It made sense.

"So, our movement is about recognizing and reclaiming our humanity, our birthright to be sovereign over our own destinies. And the more we assert our sovereignty, the more they will attempt to assert our inhumanity. Even those who claim to support us have not truly taken into account what this country will look like if Black people are free. When threatened with our freedom, even those white people will seek to maintain their power."

Corey nodded again. The other elders murmured their agreement.

"Our task, Brother Corey, is to rise above their

inhumanity, so that we do not meet them on their animalistic level. Because we are better; we are greater, but even more important, we are aware of what they are trying to do."

"The task for you, Brother Corey, is to find your own sovereignty," the man beside him said. He moved his hand from Corey's shoulder to his chest. "It is right here, inside of you. And when you find who you are, when you walk in your power and beauty, and you recognize who you are as a sovereign being, it won't matter what they call you, because you know the truth."

"Brother Corey, your focus is on the wrong thing." Samuel said, prompting Corey's head to swivel toward him. "Remember I have been telling you about Brother Marcus Garvey?"

Corey nodded.

"Brother Marcus told us to be as proud of our race as our fathers were. We have a beautiful history, and we will create a future that is as beautiful as our history before we encountered white people. He said the future we will create will astonish the world."

"That's right," the woman with the gray locs added. "As long as your focus is on what they have taken from you, you will always be trying to get it back. You will be trying to catch up, or take revenge, or win against them somehow. They will always be the center of your universe. When your focus is yourself and your community, and how to build and grow together—you won't care what they say. You will create your own story."

"You want to know how to protect your mother?" Grey Locs asked.

Corey nodded.

"Help us build a powerful Black nation. Focus your energy on that. Build a nation your mother will be happy to be a part of, where she will be protected."

Corey nodded again. It all made sense. He didn't know how to build a strong Black nation, but he wanted to try.

Grey Locs looked around the circle and nodded. The elders all stood, and Corey joined them.

"Brother Corey, what you need to focus on is learning about your history and disciplining your mind and body," Samuel said. "I will walk with you on that journey."

"So, I can stay?" he asked, amazed.

The elders all laughed.

"We don't throw anyone away, Brother Corey. We believe in accountability, and discipline with love. But we don't abandon."

As the circle disbanded, each elder walked up to Corey, put their hand on his shoulder and gave him words of encouragement.

"I believe in you, Brother Corey."

"I want to walk with you, Brother Corey."

"The ancestors have brought you here for this time."

"We need you with us, Brother Corey."

"Your passion will bring us great success."

When they had all spoken to him and left, Samuel walked out with him.

"How do you feel?" Samuel asked.

Corey shook his head. "I really thought you all would throw me out."

Samuel nodded.

"But I don't think I have ever really experienced this type of . . . " he didn't know what to call it.

Samuel chuckled. "Community? Love? Compassion? Solidarity?"

Corey nodded. "All of that."

Samuel turned, his hand on Corey's shoulder. "Remember when I said you weren't alone anymore?"

Corey nodded.

"This is what it means to not be alone."

Chapter Eleven

Lisa sat in the crowded cafeteria of the West Baltimore Freedom School on Monday evening, anxiously waiting for the meeting to begin. The benches attached to the folding lunch tables were fully occupied with parents and community members, fanning themselves in the humid room while chatting quietly. There was a tension in the air, which was uncharacteristic of the few Freedom School meetings Lisa had attended. Many parents were dressed in white scrubs and white sneakers, and Lisa wondered where they worked. The students were in the library and the gym, engaged in activities with teachers while their parents attended the meeting.

Dr. Campbell entered, wearing white scrubs and sneakers, and the room fell silent. Her face was grim, and her tall frame stooped slightly. She looked burdened and troubled.

"Sanibona!" she said.

"Ngikhona!" the parents replied.

Lisa looked around, wondering what they were saying. She seemed to be the only one confused.

"As many of you know, our country is entering a time of great tribulation, as predicted by our ancestors. Every Black and Brown person in this country will have to make a decision about their role in this struggle. Many of us have chosen to fight, figuratively and literally. Some people will decide to uphold the systemically racist systems that undergird our society. I want to be very clear; we are either doing one or the other. There is no middle ground. Each of us who decides not to engage in the struggle, by the very nature of that decision, has chosen to fight against it."

Murmuring arose in the room, and several people shook their heads and raised their fists in the air. Lisa frowned. She had no idea what Dr. Campbell just said.

"As you know, the Black Resistance Movement unveiled its existence at the Charlottesville Alt rally on Saturday. It was a beautiful, brilliant show of force designed to put The Alt on notice that we will not go back into chains easily or peacefully. I'm sure you have noticed that our unveiling has not been aired by local or national media, although they were all there and filmed it."

Lisa finally began to understand. She had heard about the Black people marching in Charlottesville but had been unable to find any footage on television or any description of the event in the newspapers or online. Danielle had texted her several times in the past two days asking if she knew anything about it. She didn't, and she hadn't responded to the texts.

"But our cameras were there," Dr. Campbell continued. "And we captured it. We know that it is time for us to stop relying on white media to tell our stories. They only tell the stories that support their narratives about us—that we are weak and dependent. When we show that we are strong and independent, we become a threat, and they will seek to put us down like rabid animals."

She stopped speaking and looked around. "This is where we are right now, my brothers and sisters. As we speak, The Alt is mobilizing their militias and sending them to majority Black and Brown cities. We know Baltimore will soon see an influx of white nationalists coming to make sure we are not supporting the Black Resistance Movement."

A parent raised his hand and Dr. Campbell nodded for him to speak.

The man stood. He was one of the parents dressed in regular street clothes, like Lisa. "Dr. Campbell, I don't understand this," he began. "How can President Jackson allow this to happen? How can he let The Alt rise up against us like this? Won't he stop it?"

Dr. Campbell shook her head, sighed, and thought for a moment.

"Brother Richard, you seem to think the rules that were made for whites in this country also apply to us. They don't. This is one of the first myths we need to get rid of as a people. Whites are held to a different standard than we are. The laws that protect them don't protect us. Don't you understand that the Bill of Rights was written while we were in chains? Do you think it was written for us? We were still property, and white people believe that is our station in this society." Dr. Campbell pierced Brother Richard with a sharp gaze. "Don't you understand that the rise of The Alt

214

is in direct response to this country electing its first and second Black presidents? President Jackson, himself, is the reason The Alt has gained such power."

She stopped and gazed around for a moment. Lisa thought she looked sad.

"We elected a Black president and many of us felt proud, recognized, and strong. But don't you see? That was purely symbolic. Nothing actually changed for us, except that white America can claim we must be post-racial, since we have had a Black man in charge. But how many Black people have been killed since he was elected? How many Brown people have been kidnapped at the border and put in prison?"

To this, the parents murmured agreement and nodded their heads.

"We have bought into the lie that one man can reverse four hundred years of abuse. He can't. The white establishment won't let him. White supremacy is too deeply rooted in this country. We need to let go of the story we keep telling ourselves. We are responsible for our own liberation, and that is what the Black Resistance Movement is about."

Lisa shook her head, wondering if she was dreaming. She didn't understand what was happening, but knew it was serious. She wished she had told Kai about the meeting, but she hadn't even known what it was about. She had assumed it was a regular parent-teacher meeting to discuss changes to class schedules, or a food drive. She had no idea issues like this would be discussed.

"So, we need to ensure the safety of our children," Dr. Campbell continued. "We called all of you parents here to explain that, beginning tomorrow, we will have armed guards stationed in all Freedom Schools. Please explain to your children that these guards are here to protect them, and that they should get to know them and follow their instructions in an emergency."

"Our students will begin drills where they learn how to protect themselves, in the event the school is attacked. As some of you know, this school, and all Freedom Schools, have multiple ways we can evacuate the building without going through the front door. Your children will come home talking about some of these routes." She paused and looked around, speaking slowly for emphasis. "It is imperative. That you do not. Share this information. With anyone at all." Her gaze seemed to focus on the people wearing street clothes. When her gaze met Lisa's, the intensity of the warning in her eyes made Lisa shiver.

"If you break confidence, you jeopardize the lives of all the children and employees in this building." She paused again. "Is there anyone in this room who does not understand what I am saying?"

The room sat silently. Lisa nodded her head. She understood.

"We have a special texting service that will allow us to notify all of you if there is an emergency or need for immediate action. If you want to be notified, please put your name, cell phone numbers, and children's names on the list by the door."

With that, Dr. Campbell hurried out of the room and the parents began to leave. Lisa waited in line to add her cell number to the text list.

As she walked out of the cafeteria, she noticed several muscular men dressed in black, filing into the building carrying guns strung over their shoulders. They entered the building and split up, walking down each hallway, peering into classrooms and offices. Lisa was glad Dr. Campbell had warned them, because this would have been an alarming sight for any parent.

Lisa walked over to the library to get Jessica and Mia, who sighed and frowned before packing up their games and leaving with her. Out on the normally bustling street, it was eerily quiet as Lisa ushered the girls into the parked SUV.

As she pulled away from the curb, she only half-listened to Jessica and Mia chattering about the game of Go Fish they had been playing in the library. She felt overwhelmed. She had so much to tell Kai. She had so many questions. The first thing she would do after briefing Kai would be to talk to LaTanya. There was something big happening, but she had been on the outside of every movement for so long, she had no connection to anything even remotely socially conscious. But not anymore. She was done with lying to herself. She had been blind for a long time. Black people were organizing, and she wanted to be a part of this movement.

*****

217

Donovan spent all weekend at his mother's house. On Monday morning, he left to go home and get work clothes. Then, he returned to her house after work Monday evening. While he was home, he packed a full bag, at least a week of clothes, and hunted for the key to his parents' house. Uncharacteristically, as he looked around to make sure he had not forgotten anything, he took no pleasure in his luxury one-bedroom apartment overlooking the Inner Harbor. All the things he had found so pleasurable—the expensive charcoal leather couch that felt like a high-quality glove; the pure white sheepskin rug in front of the fireplace; the bold watercolors hanging on the walls— were all unimportant to him at the moment. He just wanted to get out of this building and get to his mother's house, where he knew people loved him.

For once, he didn't complain about being there, and he even enjoyed lying in his old bed on the top bunk at night, talking to Paul on the bottom. Paul's matter-of-fact pragmatism and unfiltered conversation was always refreshing to him. Despite his complaints about his mother's American children, he found Paul brilliant, pure, and without guile. He knew Karen loved Donovan, second only to their mother, despite his occasionally brusque treatment of them both. As reluctant as he was to admit it, this was a safe place, and while the world seemed to be falling apart outside, this was the only place he wanted to be.

Melva didn't ask him any questions about why he was there, but several times he caught her looking at him intently, trying to read his mind. When he showed up Saturday after

218

leaving the bar with Michael and Phillip, she welcomed him, quickly concealing her surprise. She made him a plate right away, from the pots on the stove of spicy stewed peas with salted pork and fragrant white rice. When he sat at the table, she slid a bowl of kale and carrot salad next to his plate and watched him devour his food. She knew he didn't want to talk, and he appreciated the silence.

When he was finished eating, he sat in the living room, across from Conrad and watched re-runs of Columbo. They laughed at Peter Falk's antics, and joked about a remake of Columbo with all Black people.

"Just one more thing . . . " Donovan said, imitating Columbo.

"The Jamaican version is *stick a pin, tell me sumptin*," Conrad added in his thickest Jamaican accent.

"The African-American version is: *hold up, hold up, hold up!*" Donovan clutched his side. He couldn't remember the last time he laughed this hard.

Every once in a while, Melva stuck her head out of the kitchen and looked back and forth between the two men, eyebrows raised, before shaking her head and returning to cleaning up.

After his parents went to bed, Donovan sat up watching the news. There was continuing coverage of The Alt march, but absolutely no mention of the thousands of armed Black people he saw marching toward Colonial Square. He hadn't imagined it. Why wasn't this in the news?

At eleven o'clock, Karen came home with her girlfriend, Amani. They walked in laughing hysterically about something and were so busy removing their shoes and putting them away, they didn't notice Donovan sitting on the couch.

"Hey, ladies," he said in a creepy voice, making both women jump.

Karen squealed. She threw her entire body across him on the couch. He usually rolled his eyes and tolerated her affection, but this time he welcomed it. He squeezed her tightly. When he released her, she pulled back and looked at him in surprise.

"Hey, Amani." He got up and hugged her. She was slight, 5'2" with caramel skin and curly hair pulled back into a big, bushy ponytail. Donovan knew not to be fooled by her size. Amani was a powerhouse of knowledge and passion for a number of issues. *Lickle, but tallawah*, Melva called her. It meant small, but mighty in patois.

Amani and Karen had been dating since freshman year of college, and every time he saw them together, they seemed closer and closer. Going into their senior year now, they would almost certainly move in together after graduation. Sometimes, he felt jealous of their tight bond, but he assured himself they understood each other particularly well because they were both women. He didn't expect to find that type of bond with a member of the opposite sex. Yet, when he looked at Melva and Conrad, he wondered if he was mistaken.

The women grabbed plates of food Melva had left for

220

them and sat in the living room with Donovan. They would not have eaten in the living room if Melva were up.

"When the cat's asleep . . . " Donovan chuckled as they sat down, plates in their laps.

"Shhhhhh!" Karen said, looking up the stairs.

Donovan noticed that both women were wearing the same white pajamas he commented on last time he visited.

"Okay. Tell me about these pajama things you both are wearing."

Karen and Amani exchanged glances.

"Really, I'm not letting you brush me off like last time," Donovan leaned back in the couch, crossed his legs, and waited. "Really," he repeated.

"I want to tell you, Donovan, but I don't think you'll understand," Karen said.

"Try me," he responded, crossing his arms over his chest, "I may surprise you."

Karen sighed. "I'm not so sure about that," she said.

She thought for a moment. "Did you see the Black Resistance Members marching in Charlottesville today?"

Donovan put both feet on the floor and sat up. "Yes! Did you see them too? I can't find anything about it on the news. It's like it never happened!"

Karen nodded her head. "Well, the news will never carry anything that shows Black people as brilliant, strong, and able to fight back. We can only be shown as weak, helpless, criminal, and dependent."

"Wait. What?" Donovan cocked his head. "Are you guys into some type of conspiracy theory?"

Karen sighed again. "Donovan, really?" She shook her head. "You don't think there are systems that keep Black people down?"

Donovan frowned. "No. I think there are bad people who are racist, but I don't know about the whole system thing."

Amani got up, took hers and Karen's empty plates and walked into the kitchen.

"Okay. If it's just about some racist people, then why is there nothing on any of the local or cable channels about the Black people marching? Not on one single channel. Explain that." Karen said, smiling her thanks at Amani.

Donovan thought for a moment. "I've been trying to figure that out," he admitted.

"And what have you come up with?"

"Nothing," he shrugged. "I can't figure it out."

"How do you think a country, that has kept a group of people subjected for more than four hundred years, will respond to those people seeking their liberation?"

Donovan shrugged. "I think the country becomes enlightened and sees the error of its ways."

"Really? Has that been your experience? That white

people in your life recognize the wrong they have done and want to make up for it?"

Donovan shrugged again. "Well, we have a Black president."

"Yes, we do."

Amani returned and squeezed into the armchair with Karen. She turned sideways and threw her legs over Karen's legs.

"So, what has changed for Black people since we've had a Black president?" Amani asked.

Donovan frowned. He had never considered the question. "It has demonstrated all we can be."

"Exactly!" Karen exclaimed. "It shows that we are not the stupid, bumbling animals that white supremacy has said we are. So how do you think white people will respond to seeing what we can be? Celebrate us?"

Donovan was silent. He didn't know the answer.

"Well, let me put it this way. If you had treated your dog badly, abused him, beat him, starved him, kept him chained up for years, what would you expect him to do to you when he gets free?"

Donovan shook his head. "He probably would be so scared and subdued he wouldn't do anything."

"Well, that's what you would hope for," Karen replied. "And for many dogs that would be exactly the case. You could remove his chains, but he would act as if he was still chained up, because you had established chains in his mind. You didn't need

223

them on his body." She paused. "But what would you do the first time he came towards you with a snarl?"

"I would have to put him down." Donovan didn't hesitate. "It would be him or me, and I would have to prevail."

"Exactly!" Amani replied. "That's what we're seeing right now."

"The Alt is responding just like that. We have become a threat. They plan to put us down." Karen pushed Amani's legs aside in her excitement and scooted to the edge of the chair. "That's what you saw in Charlottesville. The sudden rise of The Alt, Sumpter's popularity with whites—all this is a response to having a Black president. How dare we go from naked and toiling in the field to sitting up in the White House? They had to try to put us back in our place."

Donovan shook his head, confused. "Wait. What are you talking about? We have made such strides as a race!"

Amani straightened up in the chair. "Really? What have we achieved as a race that isn't purely symbolic?"

"And I'm not talking about individuals that are considered . . ." Amani made air quotes, ". . . exceptions. I'm talking about as a race. How are we doing?"

"I don't know," Donovan admitted.

"Well, let me tell you. As a race, we continue to sit at the bottom of all races on every indicator of well-being. And we have not made any significant economic gains in the past century," Amani continued.

"That's because many of us don't want to work hard."

"No," Amani bristled. "That's because every time we build something, white people see us as a threat and burn down what we've built."

"Like what?" Donovan bristled in return.

"Like the success of Black Wall Street. Like the prosperity we built in Rosewood. Do you remember learning about those in school?" Amani asked.

"No." Donovan shook his head. "I don't know about those."

"Exactly. You don't know about them just like you wouldn't know about the thousands of Black people who marched in Charlottesville today. Those narratives are suppressed in our educational system, by our press. And because so many Black people don't know our own history, we can't even see that we are chained up. Many of us have no idea we were even ever free."

Amani continued, "A friend of mine always says, 'if you don't know your history, you're like a newborn baby, born yesterday. Anyone can tell you anything, and you will believe them.' So, we're like that dog. You can unchain us, and we won't dare try to leave the yard. Because we believe the dominant narrative, which is that everything we experience is based on personal responsibility. So, if we aren't successful, that's because we didn't work hard enough, not because the conditions in this country make sure we don't achieve success. We are so conditioned." Karen stopped and looked at her brother keenly.

"You are so conditioned," she said solemnly.

Donovan sat silent. This was a lot to take in. He realized he had never really thought about issues of race in this way. He had only thought of working to become successful, and that usually meant doing what white people were doing, being with white people, achieving what white people achieved, not being the person who they thought swung from trees in the jungle back where he had come from. To him, it had meant doing what it seemed other Black people couldn't do, like fitting in seamlessly with white people, and that made him feel proud and superior, although he had never thought of it in those terms. This was a lot to absorb.

"So, what does this have to do with the pajamas?" he asked, finally.

Amani looked like she would say something, but then glanced at Karen and stopped. They sat in silence for another few moments.

"You know, Donovan, there are Black people doing things to fight The Alt, but we need to be very careful who we share this with, because we have so much planned," Karen said.

"Like the folks who were marching today?" Donovan asked.

"Yes. We are prepared to mount up armed resistance. We really don't want violence, but we are prepared to go there if we need to. By any means necessary," Karen responded.

"We? Are you part of the group?"

"Yes. We were out there marching today. We have been to arms training. We are prepared to fight."

Donovan laughed. "Wait. What? You two have been to arms training?" He pointed back and forth between the two women. "No way!"

"Yes way," Karen replied. "Amani is an expert shot, and I'm pretty decent. The arms teacher told us that women are often superior shooters to men. Another hidden narrative."

"Okay. So, the pajamas are the uniform for the resistance?" Donovan asked. "When you're not terrorizing people on the street with guns, that is," he added, chuckling.

"They're scrubs, and yes, that's what we wear when we go to our operations center," Amani responded.

"Why?"

Karen sighed. "Why do you wear $2,000 suits?"

"Because I like the quality and the fit, and I look good in them," Donovan responded quickly. He thought for a moment and sighed. "And because that's what the most successful people in my firm wear. They signal that I'm successful, too." He lowered his voice as he added the last statement. *Shit.* He had never thought like that before. He was starting to get what Karen and Amani were saying.

"So, the scrubs remove that type of hierarchy and make everyone the same," he added.

"Not the same. Of equal worth. We will never be the same—we're all individuals. But, although we are individuals, we still work towards collective goals, *not* as individuals each with our own agenda, which is what white individualism has taught us we should do." Karen stood and pulled Amani to her feet.

"We're headed to bed. Let's keep talking about this, Big Brother. I would love to introduce you to our group."

After Karen and Amani went upstairs, Donovan sat staring at the muted television for a long time. It was hard for him to believe what the women were saying, but considering what was happening at work and in society, it was difficult to completely dismiss. He had a lot of thinking to do.

For the rest of the weekend, Donovan peppered Karen and Amani with questions. They got their computer out and made him watch the documentary, *Thirteenth*, about the systemic incarceration of Black and Brown people. They played him speeches by Malcolm X, Marcus Garvey, and Frederick Douglas. They flipped through pages of *The New Jim Crow*.

Donovan had always been a good student whose thirst for knowledge fueled his success in learning new things. He soaked up the new knowledge like desert sands soak up rain, and his questions became more and more sophisticated as his knowledge grew. Karen and Amani delighted in his developing thinking and curiosity. They spent the entire weekend teaching him, while Melva and Conrad looked on with interest.

During the weekend, Kirstie called and texted him several times, but he didn't know how to tell her what he was feeling or learning, so he just texted back that he was at his Mom's house and would call her later. He didn't call her until Monday evening, and by then, she was pissed.

Tasia stood in front of the library behind Sharonda's stroller, watching the parade of trucks roll down Pennsylvania Avenue. The Maryland governor was on television this morning announcing that she had called out the National Guard, but Tasia hadn't known what that might look like, until this moment. She now understood this was a frightening development. The governor had also set a curfew between 10 p.m. and 6 a.m., after which time people would be arrested for being on the streets. She did not make exceptions for anyone aside from healthcare workers who were required to show documentation of their jobs in case they were stopped by the police. Nana, who usually picked up a late shift at least one evening a week, had been forced to change her schedule so she could get home before curfew.

Pedestrians hurried along, trying to get everything done before they were required to go home. When the National Guard vehicles drove by, people on the street stopped and stared, and traffic slowed down. There was an ominous air—one Tasia understood very well. When Black people came into contact with law enforcement, the results were usually very bad for the Black people.

Two of the trucks broke off from the row and pulled up to the corner of Pennsylvania and North Avenue, where the occupants got out. They began fanning out in pairs, stationing two people on each corner. The Guardsmen wore fatigues and boots, dark glasses, helmets with visors, and each carried a huge M16-A1 weapon across his chest. They did not smile or greet the people they passed on the street, instead they looked straight ahead as they walked. Tasia had learned, during arms training, to recognize the guns they carried, and that they were likely scanning the crowd for threats behind their dark glasses. Arms training was required for all Cell members, although those on the tactical teams received more intensive training and were required to practice weekly. People like her, who worked in communications or finance, were only required to know how to handle weapons and how to shoot with reasonable accuracy. She visited an indoor range monthly.

As the Guardsmen approached, pedestrians crossed the street to avoid them. When two walked past Tasia and Sharonda, Tasia stepped back towards the library and turned her head away to avoid eye contact. She had seen far too many people thrown over the hood of a police car because they were unfortunate enough to make eye contact with a cop. She had no reason to believe these military folks were any different.

When she turned back around, Carla was pulling her small Honda up to the curb. She hopped out, grabbed Sharonda's car seat from the trunk, and began putting Sharonda in the car. Tasia broke down the stroller and stowed it in the trunk. When Sharonda was safely strapped in the back seat and looking at one of her picture books from the library, they headed towards the Block.

There were National Guardsmen at every major intersection in the city, pulling people over and requesting identification, seemingly at random. They drove past several young men sitting on the curb, their hands cuffed behind them, while Guardsmen surrounded them, rifling through their backpacks. Carla drove slowly to avoid attracting attention. Tasia knew Carla carried weapons, like most of the Cell leaders, and would not want to have her car searched.

There were armed white men in street clothes, standing in front of many businesses carrying rifles and displaying grim expressions.

"Who are those people—National Guard, too?" Tasia asked, pointing with her chin. She didn't dare point with her finger.

"Those are the armed militia who have come to Baltimore to protect white people and white businesses."

Tasia's head swiveled sharply. "What? What are they going to do?"

Carla chuckled grimly. "We are in the time of tribulation as Black people in this country. Remember, we talked about this? That white people would throw off all pretenses of accepting us as equals, and that this would be the Red Summer of 2024? Right?"

Tasia nodded.

"Well, this is the beginning of that. Buckle down. Things are going to get so much worse," Carla replied.

Tasia sat wide-eyed in the passenger seat, staring out the window. What was playing out on the streets of Baltimore looked like some futuristic horror movie. There were Guardsmen and women and cops on every block. She passed more people thrown over the hoods of police cars than she could count. All the people being searched were Black, but so were some of the Guardsmen and cops. Tasia was confused.

"What do you think about the Black people who are cops or in the Guard? Can they say they don't want to do this?" She asked.

Carla shook her head. "No. They have to follow the chain of command."

"Even if what they're doing is wrong?" Tasia pressed.

Carla shook her head again, her lips pursed. "Wrong is subjective. What they are doing is legal, because the governor has the right to call out the Guard. Is it ethical, or right? No, it isn't. But it *is* legal."

Tasia frowned. "And President Jackson won't stop it?"

"President Jackson is tied up fighting a number of battles himself. He's probably preoccupied with his own struggles in Congress. He is in an unwelcome and hostile place, and doesn't have a lot of support—even from his own party." Carla sighed. "I'm sure when he was elected, he had many good intentions. But good intentions can't overcome white supremacy, and I'm sure he has since learned that, President or not, he's Black first, and white people will oppose him at every step."

232

Carla turned the car into the driveway of the Block. The tall black iron fence was now topped with five rows of barbed wire, and the usually-open gate was closed, blocking the entrance to the parking lot, and behind the building, to the loading dock. The barbed wire and closed gate had been added since Charlottesville.

The gate slid open as they pulled up, and Tasia knew there were spotters on the roof of the Block, looking into the car through their high-powered scopes. When a car approached, these spotters communicated with the guards whether or not it was safe to open the gates. If they didn't recognize the people in the car, the vehicle would have to wait while the driver and passenger's faces were run through facial recognition software and were confirmed as members.

Carla pulled the car into a parking space. "Even liberal and progressive whites don't really want to give up their power. They say they do, but pay attention to what they will say about Black people asserting their right to liberty. It will be fine with those whites as long as no white blood is spilled or none of their property damaged. But let Black people protest too vehemently, and you will see those very same whites turn against us, telling us we must have peaceful expression, or they won't support our protest against our own genocide. President Jackson is busy fighting those people in his own party. He can't help us."

Tasia's heart sank. She had always believed, naively she now understood, that politicians had her best interests at heart, that they would protect regular citizens and respect their rights. But her own experiences had not shown this to be true. She wasn't sure where she had gotten this idea, this expectation. Maybe it was all the civics lessons in school about our "good policemen" who would protect us, and our "caring lawmakers" who worked to ensure Americans have the best lives possible. Apparently, those civic lessons didn't apply to Black people.

Tasia got out and lifted Sharonda from the back seat, hoisting the heavy toddler onto her hip, walking into the building through the back entrance. She nodded at the armed guards, who broke their serious expressions for a moment to flirt with Sharonda.

"There she is! Little Miss Smiley Face." One of the guards shifted his gun to one shoulder and reached out to tickle Sharonda's neck. She giggled, tucked her chin down and swatted at his hand.

As Tasia and Carla continued down the hallway, Sharonda threw her arms around Tasia's neck and waved at the guard over her mother's shoulder.

"Bye!" she called out.

"Bye, Miss Smiley!" he called back.

Things in the Block were hectic. Tasia recognized there was an action underway, but Carla would not tell her what until they were in the Communications Center.

"By the way, I've been meaning to ask you," Carla began, "What was the name of Sharonda's father? Kenny what?"

Tasia's heart galloped at the sound of Kenny's name.

"Milford. Kenneth Milford. Why?" She was breathless.

"There's a lady who has been attending our seniors' group—by the way, I meant to tell you I think you should invite your grandmother to that—anyway, there's a lady there who has been talking about her son. His name is Kenny, and I wasn't sure . . ." Carla's voice trailed off and she smiled at Sharonda before gazing away.

"I just think you might want to meet her. She will be back in the Block for the meeting next Wednesday at 5:30 p.m. Maybe ask your grandmother to come. I can pick her up."

They stopped at Toddler Room 1, dropped Sharonda off, and then climbed the stairs to the Communication Center. Tasia moved robotically, overwhelmed with emotion. *Would she really find out what happened to Kenny? And could she handle what she might hear? She shuddered. Was Kenny's death about to become real to her? Could she possibly grieve any more?* The very thought made her exhausted.

In the Communications Center, things were bustling, and when Tasia sat at her computer, she was quickly pulled into the work and stopped thinking about Kenny for a few hours. The Communications team was called into a briefing with the intelligence team—a very secretive group of men and women who were known only by code names. They were active in several fields: government, law enforcement, military, and corporations. They worked like everyone else, but kept their ear to the ground and sent back information to The Cell. Most of them did not come to the Block, as it was unknown whether they were being surveilled by the FBI. They communicated with the Block using a series of coded messages sent via text and email. Only the intelligence leaders came to the Block.

Maurice, the head of the intelligence team, was a short, thick man with huge muscles. Although he was only two inches taller than her, Tasia thought how afraid she would be if she faced him in a combat situation. The Communications team gathered around Maurice. He held a notebook, which he consulted occasionally as he spoke.

"Okay, folks. So, as you can see, the governor has called the National Guard to town, as well as a number of white militias who have come from around the state and from the Midwest. They are here to warn Black folk not to engage in any type of protest or civil disobedience. What we have seen so far is just the tip of the iceberg."

He consulted his notebook. "Our intelligence tells us that 2,000 Guards have been dispatched, and more are on standby. At this point, we do not know how many militia groups have arrived. The Alt is fairly disorganized, and doesn't have a central dispatch system. These are all folks who scrambled themselves to arrive here. But don't get comfortable. The Alt is becoming more and more organized every single day. And they are counting on Reginald Sumpter getting elected so they can have official presidential backing."

236

Tasia scribbled fast in her notebook, trying to keep up. She would type up the notes later for the Communications team.

"National Guard and white militias have arrived in every largely Black and Brown populated city: New York, D.C., Chicago, St. Louis, Miami, Boston, etc. Everywhere there are enough of us to cause concern, is being flooded with police, military, and deranged white people with big guns."

The team chuckled.

Maurice continued. "So, every Cell across the country is on alert, as is La Lucha. We are planning a counter-operation against the militias and the National Guard. We are making every effort to send a strong message without any lives being lost. Doing so will require absolute secrecy and flawless execution."

He looked at Carla and Tasia. "We are calling this Operation Duckpin One. The plan is to blow up parked and vacant militia vehicles. This is Duckpin One, National Guard vehicles will be Duckpin Two, and police vehicles will be Duckpin Three. We don't know yet if we will launch all three operations."

He waited a moment for what he'd said to sink in, and then continued. "We will use low velocity explosives. As we speak, members are out planting them. They will all detonate tonight around 9:00 p.m. Each unit will be detonated individually, because we want to ensure the vehicle is not occupied when it explodes."

Tasia's breathing stuck in her throat, and she swallowed hard. This was big. And she was involved.

"Carla, you and your team need to send out the message that the Baltimore Cell will launch Operation Duckpin One at 9:00 p.m. All Cells across the country will launch at the same time."

Carla nodded, while Tasia wrote furiously.

Maurice looked grim. "I cannot stress to all of you how much this operation is going to change the game and piss off The Alt. All members need to be on high alert. We are spreading the word that if anyone feels at all threatened, in their homes or in their communities, they are to get their family members and come to the Block. We can move folks to the safe houses, and there's lots of space on the Farm."

He looked around and weighed his words very carefully. "If this location is breached, we will all need to be prepared to bring our families and retreat to the Farm. Please spread the word that everyone needs to have bags packed and a means to get here or to the Farm."

Carla and Tasia nodded. The rest of the Communications team murmured as they digested this information. The group disbanded, and Tasia began sending messages across the country. Thoughts of Kenny surfaced from time to time, but she pushed them away. She didn't have time to nurse that beast tonight. The pain would have to wait. She had a great deal of complicated work to do in the next few hours, and it would be a long night.

Chapter Twelve

Corey and Devonte, in their dark sweatshirts and black jeans, slid along the deserted sidewalk trying to blend in with the shadows of buildings.. They looked out for police and Guardsmen, who would apprehend them for being out after curfew.

Corey held the duffle bag carefully, trying not to jostle it too much. Monica told them the explosives were very stable and would not detonate accidentally, but Corey couldn't help feeling nervous carrying a bag with enough explosives to take him off this earth ten times over. Sweat beaded on his forehead as he moved. It was bad enough they had to wear long sleeves and hats, but it happened to be a particularly warm late-May night and he felt like he was going to suffocate.

The old stone church that housed a number of militia members made an imposing presence against the darkening sky. The glow of lights shone through thick panes in the building adjoining the main church, and he assumed it was the fellowship hall, where the militia members were likely eating after a long day patrolling the streets.

They crept around to the back of the church, moving smoothly in the shadows created by the wooden fence surrounding the building. Behind the church, a couple of dozen pickup trucks and SUVs were parked. Corey counted them. Between himself and Devonte, they had enough cylinders—thirty in total. They would return to the Block with a few remaining.

They knelt behind one of the trucks, put their duffle bags on the ground, and slowly began removing the explosives. The metal cylinders had magnets attached to them. Corey and Devonte were supposed to attach the cylinders to the undercarriage of the vehicle, near the engine.

Carrying two cylinders at a time in their gloved hands, Corey and Devonte left the duffle bags in the shadows and crawled on their backs alongside each vehicle, reaching under and attaching the cylinder wherever it would stick. They went back and forth to the bags to gather more cylinders. When they had attached a cylinder to each vehicle, they retrieved the bags and crept back to a dark corner of the parking lot. Corey checked his watch. It was eight-thirty. They had half an hour before they were to begin detonating the explosives.

Corey took the tablet out of his bag, opened the cover, and switched it on. He turned his back to the building, and Devonte knelt behind him to help shield the light coming from the tablet. He removed one of his gloves and pulled up the program Monica had loaded, which showed each cylinder by number. They each had to be armed individually. Once armed, they could be detonated individually, or all at once.

"Shit!" he whispered to Devonte. "I forgot we were supposed to pay attention to which cylinder we put on which vehicle, just in case we need to abort one. We were supposed to put them on the cars in numerical order, but I didn't look at the numbers. Did you?"

Devonte shook his head, his eyes wide. "I didn't!" he whispered back. He shrugged. "I guess it won't matter, since we're going to detonate all of them, right?"

Corey shrugged. "I guess so." He pulled the bag closer and noted the numbers on the five cylinders left in the bag. He took those five off-line and armed the others. At exactly 9:00 p.m., he would press one button and detonate them all.

"Corey, Corey!" Devonte's whisper was urgent. "Turn it off, turn it off!"

Corey closed the tablet, shoved it into the bag and zipped it up, hiding the glow from view. As soon as he placed it in the bag, he heard voices. He and Devonte flattened themselves on the ground against the fence, listening intently. Corey's heart beat so loud it was almost all he could hear. *They had to be able to hear it, too.*

"Alright. I hope y'all have a good night!" a man's voice said. The door to the Fellowship Hall opened, and two men walked out.

"Pastor, I just want to thank you again for your kind hospitality," the other man said.

"It's no problem at all. In fact, it's our pleasure. I'm glad y'all are here. Something needed to be done," the pastor responded. "You have my cell number. Let us know if you boys need anything. Anything at all."

"We will, Pastor. Thanks, again."

Corey heard the hall door slam shut, and at the same time, a vehicle door opened. Corey buried his face in the ground and held his breath as the truck backed up and its headlights swung in their direction. The driver didn't see them and Corey didn't release his breath until the truck turned and headed out of the parking lot. When he looked up, he saw taillights behind a light-colored SUV.

Corey and Devonte sat up, opened the bag, and took out the tablet. They looked at the screen and then at each other. How could they know which cylinder just drove away?

"Oh my God, we've fucked up!" Corey whispered.

Devonte didn't respond. In the glow from the tablet, his eyes looked wide and wild. He shook his head, his breath ragged through parted lips.

Corey forced himself to take deep breaths. "Okay. Let's think about this. Monica said these explosives work with Bluetooth technology. That means it can't detonate an explosive that is out of range, right?"

Devonte nodded, "Yeah. I bet that's right. So, what do we do?"

Corey looked at the time on the tablet and thought for a moment. "It's 8:45. By the time we detonate, in fifteen minutes, he should be way out of range, right?"

Devonte nodded again. He looked relieved. "Right."

"Okay. Let's go 'round front so we can get out of dodge real quick after we detonate."

Devonte nodded again, and the two men grabbed their duffle bags, and while staying close to the fence, crept around to the front of the church. They moved to the other side of the street and ducked into an alley..

Crouched in the alley, Corey took out the tablet while Devonte confirmed their escape route. The alley led from the street the church was on, through the block to a large thoroughfare running parallel. They would escape through the alley to the other street.

Corey checked his watch. Five minutes. He double-checked the tablet. All cylinders were armed and ready to go.

Devonte crept back beside him and gave a thumbs up. It was time to detonate. Once he pushed the button, they had thirty seconds to flee before the explosives detonated.

Corey took a deep breath. The old, familiar flame was gone, and he almost wished he had that anger right now. Instead, it was replaced with cold hard fear. Although the night was warm, he shivered as the sweat cooled his skin. There was no going back now.

He placed his finger over the detonation button and looked at Devonte, who nodded. Devonte stuffed Corey's empty duffle bag into his own and pulled the straps over his neck and across his chest, so the duffle bag sat across his back like a backpack. He was ready to run. He nodded again at Corey.

Corey took a deep breath and pressed the button, slamming the cover as he started running. They ran through the alley to the main road and Corey slid the tablet into the waist of his jeans, under his sweatshirt. When they got to the street they walked at a normal pace, staying close to the buildings. The street was empty because of the curfew, and they ducked into a doorway whenever a car drove past. They had almost made it to the rendezvous point where the car was waiting for them when they heard the explosions begin.

The two Cell members in the car held the back doors open as they ran up. They jumped in as the car took off. With the doors closed they could barely hear the explosions. It sounded like loud pops and could have been firecrackers. Corey looked behind him and saw small fingers of fire shooting into the sky.

Corey breathed a sigh of relief as they turned the corner onto Charles Street. They were far enough away now. He leaned back in the seat and looked out the window, trying to still his thudding heart. He looked over at Devonte, who was staring straight ahead, eyes wide. He finally looked over at Corey and nodded in a way that Corey could relate to. It said, "We did it!""

As they drove down empty Charles Street, they heard sirens, probably fire trucks. The young woman driving the car, with her locs in a bun piled atop her head, zigzagged through back streets, trying to avoid all vehicles. The woman in the front passenger seat was also young, with her hair in a frizzy ponytail. She was on the phone, probably with the Block. They were telling her which streets to take.

The driver introduced herself. "I'm Karen." And pointing to the passenger. "This is Amani."

"Hey. Corey and Devonte. Nice to meet you," Corey said, staring out the back window. Emergency lights flashed in the distance behind them.

Five blocks from the church, Karen began to turn down a side street, but stopped when she saw an SUV pull into a parking space. She decided to turn down the next street so they would not be seen. As they passed the street, they heard a loud explosion and saw flames from the SUV shooting into the sky.

Corey and Devonte looked at each other—*the last cylinder*.

Donovan tried to be patient. "Kirstie, I'm sorry. I didn't mean to disappear. It's just been a really terrible time."

"But you won't tell me what you were doing all weekend, so I *can't* possibly understand," Kirstie insisted.

He sighed. "I told you. I've been at my mother's house. I was here all weekend."

"Okay. So, why couldn't you call me? I would have come over, but you didn't return any of my texts."

Donovan paused. How did he tell her he didn't call because he was learning about racism and white supremacy from his sister and her girlfriend? And that he didn't want her to come over.

He decided to try a different approach. "Did you hear about the march in Charlottesville on Saturday?"

"Yes. What about it?"

"Well—it really messed me up," he confessed. "I was at Martini Mike's in Fells Point when it came on television."

"Okay . . . " she said slowly. "And?"

"And . . . it was terrible. People were using the "n" word and stuff. It was terrifying."

"Martini Mike's was terrifying." Kirstie repeated.

Donovan wondered if he imagined the note of sarcasm in her voice. "Yes. It was."

"So that's why you couldn't call me this weekend? Because you were terrified at Martini Mike's?"

Donovan sighed again. "Kirstie, have you seen what's happening in the world?"

246

"What do you mean?" She sounded as if she really didn't know what he was talking about.

"The Alt marches, Alice Warner's speech, the tone of the country right now?"

"What does that have to do with you and me?"

Donovan was dumbfounded. "I don't know if you've noticed, Kirstie, but I'm a Black man."

There was no mistaking the sarcasm in her voice this time. "I know that, Donovan," she said slowly. "But those Alt marches aren't about you. They're about the illegals coming across the border and the folks who want to sit around not working while getting handouts. Not you."

"It *is* about me. And people like me. And my family."

"No, it's not," she insisted. "You're hardworking. You came here legally. You're not looking for a handout."

Donovan didn't know how to explain it to her. He had spent so much time rehearsing what he would say to Kirstie about what he was going through. In his mind, she had been concerned, compassionate, and understanding. It wasn't working out that way.

"I don't know, Kirstie. I have to go to work. Can we talk about this later?"

"Are you cheating on me, Donovan?" Kirstie asked.

The question was so jarring, he was silent for a moment. *How had she gotten to that?*

"Cheating?" He wanted to make sure he heard her correctly.

"Yes, Donovan," she spoke crisply. "Are you seeing someone else?"

"No!" The word burst from his lips. "Is this really what you're thinking? Whether I'm cheating on you while the world is falling apart around us?"

Kirstie was silent, and he realized he had spoken more forcefully than he ever had to her.

"I've got to go. I'm late for work. I'll talk to you later," he said more gently.

"Ok," she said tersely and hung up.

He sat on his mother's couch. He was fully dressed for work, but really didn't want to go. He didn't want to see Steve and the others. Yesterday had been awkward and uncomfortable in the office, and he finally realized many of his colleagues were avoiding him, which was just fine because he didn't want to engage in small talk with them anyway. He looked at his watch. It was after eight, and he needed to leave. Instead, he leaned back, crossed his legs and turned on the television, the sound off. His mother bustled around in the kitchen where she had gone to give him space while he called Kirstie.

The front door opened, and Karen and Amani walked in. For the first time in the last few days, they were dressed in dark street clothes. Donovan realized they had been out all night and looked exhausted.

248

"Hey, Bro," Karen muttered as she took off her shoes.

"Hi," Amani mumbled.

Melva was coming out of the kitchen, probably to see who was at the door, when Amani threw herself into Melva's arms, burying her head in the older woman's neck. Melva's arms closed around her, pulling her close. Her eyes met Karen's over Amani's head. The question was clear.

Karen shrugged and sank into an armchair. "Rough night. Really, really rough."

Melva gently held Amani away from her with one hand, wiping Amani's face with the other.

"What's happened?"

Amani's slight body shook with sobs. She whispered something, almost as if to herself.

"What was that?" Donovan asked.

"We killed him!" Amani said more loudly. "We killed that man!" she wailed, before throwing her arms around Melva's neck again.

Melva rubbed Amani's back, looking concerned and confused. "Here, let's sit down." She led Amani to a chair and helped her sit. She glanced over her shoulder at Donovan.

"Go get her some water."

Donovan headed for the kitchen, as Karen walked to Amani's chair, squeezed in beside her and encased Amani in her arms.

Donovan handed Amani the glass of water and sat on the couch beside Melva.

After Amani had taken a few sips of water, Melva leaned forward with her elbows on her knees.

"Now, tell us what happened. Who did you kill?"

Amani opened her mouth to speak but, instead, pointed at the television.

"Him!"

Melva and Donovan turned to look. A picture of a middle-aged white man wearing a clerical collar flashed on the screen, with a chyron that said, "Pastor killed in truck explosion."

"Turn up the volume," Melva gestured at Donovan.

"Reverend Michael Milkin, pastor of New Hope Emmanuel Church in Baltimore, was killed in a series of truck bombings that shook the city last night," the reporter said. "Reports of similar bombings are being discussed on Twitter from around the country—New York, Miami, Chicago, Detroit, Cleveland, St. Louis, with more confirmations coming in."

At this, Amani burst into a new spate of sobbing and Karen buried her head in her hands. Melva and Donovan exchanged glances before returning their attention to the television, where aerial views showed a series of parking lots with burned-out vehicles, a banner announcing the location of each scene.

"Reverend Milkin is the only reported fatality in these bombings thus far, although there are reports of minor injuries to

250

bystanders and some property damage. We will be updating this emerging story throughout the morning."

Melva gestured for Donovan to turn off the television. They sat in silence for a moment, listening to Amani's sobs.

Finally, Melva turned to the two women and spoke softly. "Okay. Tell me what happened. What part did you two play in this?"

Karen uncovered her face. "The plan was to blow up white militia vehicles that have come to town to protect the white businesses and to harass us. We—me and Amani—were supposed to pick up two Cell members after they planted and detonated the bombs. So, we did that. The two guys jumped in. We drove off. We heard the bombs explode. It was all good."

Amani stopped crying and wiped her face. "But we didn't know one of the bombs was planted in a car that someone got into and then drove off in," she added.

Karen nodded. "Right. I think the two guys thought it wouldn't matter because the truck the guy . . . " She pointed to the television. ". . . that pastor, drove off in was out of range of the Bluetooth when they exploded the device, so they went ahead. But—" she looked at Amani helplessly.

"Go on," Melva prodded.

"But it turns out we were driving right behind the truck with the bomb and it seemed like the program was able to connect to the bomb and detonate it," Amani said. "And he was still in the truck."

251

They sat in silence. Donovan felt a knot in his stomach. *What the hell was happening? Wasn't this just a bunch of Black people talking about racism? How did it get from that to bombings?* Donovan sat dumbfounded, staring at Karen and Amani.

When Melva spoke, her voice held a firmness and conviction Donovan had never heard from her before, not even when he was in trouble. "Wipe your face and straighten up your spine."

Karen and Amani looked at her in surprise but sat up straight.

Melva stared at Donovan and Karen. "Have you forgotten who you are? Who your ancestors are? You are both direct descendants of the Maroons. Do you remember?"

Karen nodded. "They were enslaved Africans in Jamaica who escaped from the plantations and then came down periodically to free more slaves, kill the slavers, and burn the plantations down."

Melva nodded slowly. "That's right. There were Maroon colonies in Jamaica and many other islands. They would not be enslaved. They would not be subjugated. They insisted on their liberty, and the white man was powerless to stop them."

Donovan leaned forward with interest. He had forgotten this history.

"All throughout our history, as Black people in the African diaspora, we have had to fight for our freedom. The white man will never give us our freedom without bloodshed. It was slave rebellions across the Americas that led to the abolition of slavery in many countries. And our leaders, like Sam Sharpe, Nat Turner, and Malcolm X, have shown us over and over again that, as Black people, we need to demand and take back our liberty. If we are waiting for the white man to give it to us, it will never happen. Why would they?"

Melva spoke slowly, her voice thick with emotion, her accent clipped and strong. The three younger people listened intently.

"We have always known the time would come, in this country, when those who have been oppressed would rise up. The government has done everything in its power to derail this, but we always knew the chickens would come home to roost. It has been foretold."

Donovan looked at his mother in surprise. *How did he not know this side of her?*

Melva looked at Amani and Karen, her eyes narrowing, her voice crisp. "Stop your crying. The time for tears is long gone. Right now, we must fight. This man would not have been killed if he had not supported the white militias. He came into the fight of his own volition—and lost. Get over it. He is no longer your problem. Got it?"

Karen and Amani looked at each other, their eyes wide. Donovan was glad he wasn't the only one surprised right now.

"Yes, Ma'am," they both muttered.

Melva's gaze pierced Donovan. "And I have held my tongue all these years, while you have tried to become white."

Donovan frowned, but remained silent. This was not the time to interrupt his mother.

"You will need to choose sides, my son. You can't straddle this fence. Either you are fighting with us or you are fighting against us. Decide now."

Melva looked at him. He started, as he realized she was waiting for an answer.

"I . . . I . . ." He stopped, overwhelmed with emotion. Images of his life flooded him, his anger at his family, his desire to go into spaces where he wasn't welcome, his feelings of achievement. All these things had brought him to this moment, where his mother thought he wanted to be white. His eyes burned. He hadn't known of her disappointment, or maybe he knew and just chose to ignore it. He wasn't sure if she was right about him wanting to be white. If it was true, it was a deeply shameful fact. What he did know, in this very moment, was that he wanted to be with the struggle, not against it.

He stood abruptly and looked down at his sister and Amani. "When are you going to the Block next, and where can I get some of those white pajamas?"

Lisa paid the pharmacy technician, took her prescription, and headed for the supermarket exit. She thought about stopping to grab a few groceries but changed her mind, and instead headed for the door. She had waited for almost an hour for the prescription. She wanted to give this first dose of antibiotics to Mia to get her ear infection under control. She could always come back later, or send Kai if Mia was too fussy and clingy.

As she neared the exit, she heard chanting coming from outside. Several shoppers were stopped with their carts near the glass doors, watching something happening in the parking lot. She walked past a Black woman who stood near the door. The older woman reached out and grabbed her arm, stopping her. Lisa turned to see the woman's face creased with concern.

"Don't go out there," she whispered. "Those white folks outside are stopping all the Black people. It's not safe."

Lisa peered outside. Kai said he would take the girls to the drive-through to get lunch while they waited for Mia's prescription. He should have been back a long time ago. She didn't see the SUV outside the store where he usually waited for her.

The woman was still holding Lisa's arm. She leaned in close, and Lisa guessed she was probably in her late eighties, although her face was barely wrinkled. She leaned heavily on the shopping cart in front of her.

"All them white folks out there with guns. I never thought I would see anything like this in my life. I grew up in Tulsa, and my mother told me about what they did there. You know about that?" She peered at Lisa, eyes wide.

255

Lisa nodded. "Yes, Ma'am, I heard about it." The truth was that she had heard about the Tulsa race massacre, but she really didn't know very much. She made a note to do some reading.

"Well, this is how it started." She shook Lisa's arm with every word. "Them white folks walking around with guns, looking at Black people all evil. And then finally they went crazy—going around shootin' everyone. They chased women and children down on the street and shot 'em. They killed my grandfather and uncle like that. In cold blood."

The woman shook her head. "I never thought I would see this. I thought things were changin', what with President Jackson and all." Her voice shook, and tears pooled in her eyes. "But it don't mean nothin'. I was born in 1934, and ain't nothin' changed." She shook her head again. "Nothin' at all."

Lisa felt chilled. "Do you want me to walk out with you?"

The woman glanced at Lisa with what looked like pity. "Sweetheart, I done lived long enough. Don't you worry about me. I ain't scared no more." She moved her hand from Lisa's arm to her face, gently cradling her cheek. "You got babies?"

Lisa nodded. "Yes, Ma'am."

"Go get your babies and get to someplace safe. They ain't safe." She put her hand back on Lisa's arm and squeezed, pulling her closer. "Bad times are comin'. This time we can't let them slaughter us in the street. We can't live through that again. You hear me?"

Lisa nodded. The woman nodded back at her, released her arm, and walked out the door, holding her head high. Lisa quickly lost sight of her in the sea of people crowding the doorway.

Lisa pulled out her cell phone and called Kai. He didn't answer. She hung up and called LaTanya.

"Girl! Where you been?" LaTanya asked. "I've been calling you for hours!"

"I took Mia to urgent care for an ear infection, and then I came to fill her prescription. But something's happening outside the store. Have you heard?"

"Yes! The white militias are on a rampage because of the truck bombings. They are out of control in the suburbs. Is Kai with you?"

"Yes. He's outside with the girls. But he's not answering the phone. I'm getting ready to walk outside, but I'm scared."

"You all need to go home and stay there. If it gets too crazy, come to the Freedom School. It's the safest place for you to go."

The sound of chanting and yelling outside swelled.

"Okay. I'm gonna go out now. "Where are you?" Lisa asked.

"I'm at the Block," LaTanya responded. "Text me when you get home." LaTanya hung up before Lisa could ask her what the Block was.

Lisa took a deep breath and squeezed between the people at the door. When the automatic doors slid open for her, she

257

stepped outside into what looked like a scene from a movie. White men and women with rifles and handguns marched outside the store yelling. She couldn't understand what they were saying, but she recognized the anger on their faces.

Across the parking lot, a Black man was curled up in a fetal position on the ground with a group of armed white men standing over him. They were punching and kicking him and he was soon obscured from Lisa's view by a sea of flying limbs.

To her left, there was a group of angry white women yelling at a Black woman. The Black woman was trapped in the middle of them, scared. Her groceries were scattered on the ground around her feet, and she shifted, trying to avoid turning her back to any of them.

Lisa looked around frantically for Kai and the SUV. She didn't see them anywhere. She paced back and forth behind the line of shopping carts, doing her best to stay out of sight of the crowd of armed whites. She was partially blocked from their view by a huge concrete column abutting the exterior wall of the supermarket, and she peered out from behind it, scanning the parking lot.

A pickup truck pulled up and stopped on the other side of the column. She pushed herself further into the shadows. Five white men with guns got out of the bed of the truck and joined the chanters. When the truck pulled off, Lisa pushed her head out from behind the column and saw Kai's SUV all the way across the parking lot, facing away from the supermarket, almost in the adjacent shopping center. The brake lights flashed twice at her.

Ducking back behind the column she pulled her phone out and dialed Kai. He answered immediately.

"Where have you been? I've been calling you."

"Hi, Babe. We're just out here waiting for you. Are you still in the store? That prescription is taking a very long time."

Kai's voice was light and cheerful, and Lisa experienced a moment of cognitive dissonance. It took her several seconds to understand that Kai was trying to downplay the scene for Jessica and Mia's benefit. The car stereo blasted Kidz Bop, probably to drown out what was happening outside. She suddenly understood why the car was facing away from the fiasco happening in front of the supermarket.

"Can you see me?" she whispered.

"Yes. I know, you're still in the store," Kai responded. "We just went to get some McDonalds. You can blame the girls. They convinced me."

"Hi Mommy!" Mia yelled over the music. Her mouth sounded full.

"Okay. I can see you, but I don't know how to get to you." Lisa watched as one of the white women, who surrounded the woman with the spilled groceries, shoved her to the ground. She tried to get up, but one of her tormenters pushed her down again. She remained on her hands and knees as they leaned in to yell at her.

259

Lisa tried to make herself as small as possible behind the column. "I'm so scared, Kai."

She told herself not to cry. This was not the time for tears. She had to figure out how to get out of there.

Kai was silent for a moment, and Lisa knew he was trying to get his voice under control.

"It's okay, sweetheart," he said evenly. "You just stay there and shop as much as you want. We will figure something out. Just stay right there."

At that moment, her phone beeped, indicating a text was coming through. "Hang on, Kai."

"Don't hang up!" Kai's voice was suddenly panicked. "Stay on the phone with me while you shop," he added more calmly.

"I'm not hanging up. I just need to stop talking while I check my text. Be right back," she whispered.

Pulling the phone away from her face she saw that LaTanya was texting her.

"*BRM on the way to Columbia. Send me a pin to your location,*" the text said.

Lisa had no idea what BRM meant, but she sent LaTanya a pin to her location and texted back. "I'm hiding outside the store. Can't get to Kai and the girls."

"Stay where you are." LaTanya texted back. "They are five minutes out."

Lisa texted a thumbs-up then put the phone back up to her

ear.

"There are people coming to help us in about five minutes," she said.

"Okay, sweetheart!" Kai put on a cheerful voice. "Just stay on the phone."

"Okay," Lisa looked around, shivering, although the day was warm. More militia pulled up in an array of vehicles, as the crowd grew. Their chants became more and more vicious.

"Hey, hey, ho, ho, niggers and spics, have got to go!"

The woman on the ground crawled back to her car, reached up to open the door, and pulled herself in. Lisa could hear her crying, screaming hysterically. She started her car and drove away, driving over the landscape strip separating the parking lot from the street. The bottom of her car ground against the curb, but she didn't stop. She flattened bushes and tore into oncoming traffic, narrowly avoiding vehicles entering the shopping center.

The man, who had been kicked and beaten, lay beside his car unconscious, or dead, Lisa couldn't be sure which. The armed men moved on, walking up and down the long strip of stores, peering in. Lisa guessed they were looking for more Black people. She squeezed herself deeper into the shadow of the column, keeping her back against the wall so no one could creep up behind her.

"You okay?" Kai sounded anxious.

"Yeah," she whispered.

More vehicles pulled into the shopping center, screeching

to a halt in front of the supermarket. Lisa peeked out to see five huge black SUVs with completely blacked out windows. Men began pouring out of the vehicles, dressed in long-sleeved black shirts and black jeans. They wore black hats, dark glasses, and black masks. They carried guns slung over their shoulders.

Lisa pulled her head back behind the column. Her heart sank. More militia. When would this end?

There were several loud clicks, what sounded like guns being armed, and Lisa held her breath. The chanting died down slowly. She peeked out again. About forty men, dressed in black, surrounded the protesters, holding their guns in the air. The chanters crowded closer together and stared at the men in black, their eyes wide. Lisa marveled at how quickly they had gone from hateful aggression to absolute terror.

The armed militia, who a moment before, were peeking into stores hunting Black people, came running down the sidewalk, their guns cradled in both hands across their chests. As they neared the chanters, half of the men in black turned outwards, so they were standing back-to-back in two concentric circles—one facing out, one facing in. The inside circle pointed their guns at the chanters, and the outside circle pointed their guns at the militia on the sidewalk. Across the parking lot, and on the street, there were dozens more men in black, pointing their guns towards the militia. Some of them held cameras trained on the group of chanters. Two were bent over the man lying on the ground, offering him medical attention. Lisa held her breath as everyone seemed to freeze. She heard nothing, except for her own rapid breathing, which she struggled to control. The standoff seemed to last for five minutes, but Lisa knew it was actually only a few seconds.

One of the white men slowly raised his gun towards the man in black closest to him. In one synchronized move, five men in black turned and pointed their guns directly at him. He slowly lowered his gun, and lifted his hand, palm pointing towards them, as if to say, "chill." He backed away from the circle, patting at the air with his open palm.

Without a word, but moving as one, the masked men stood aside, gesturing to the chanters to leave. They fled towards their cars. The masked group stood their ground. When the chanters had disbanded, the armed militia backed away from the masked group. They got in their trucks. The masked group turned with them; their guns remained trained on the trucks until they had driven off.

A deep voice on the other side of the column spoke softly, "Ma'am, you can come out now. I will escort you to your car." The voice was undeniably Black, and Lisa looked around to see who he was talking to. As she began to peek around the column, he stepped into view, and she jumped back, tripping and falling to the ground in her fright. With his face completely covered, he was a frightening sight. He reached out his hand to help her up, and Lisa shrank away from him, trying to squeeze into the space where the wall met the column. He kept his hand out to her, and her eyes opened wide as she saw his brown skin. She took his hand, and he pulled her to her feet.

As the masked man led her out from behind the column, Lisa stayed close behind him, clinging to his hand.

"Where's your car?" he asked.

Lisa pointed to where Kai was parked, but Kai was already on his way towards them. He pulled up next to the curb, reached over, and threw the door open. The masked man helped Lisa into the SUV, then reached across to dap Kai.

"Thank you, man," Kai's voice shook. "Thank you."

The masked man nodded at Kai, nodded at Lisa, and closed the car door. As they headed out of the shopping center, police cars screeched down the main road towards them, sirens blazing.

"I called the police so many times when you were in the store. That's why I didn't answer when you first called me," Kai said. "They wouldn't show up for the white folks with guns, but as soon as the Black folks show up to protect us, they wanna come?" He shook his head with disgust. "I'm so tired of this shit."

Lisa turned around to look behind them. The masked group was already gone, leaving no sign of their visit. They had been there for all of fifteen minutes, and apart from the man who escorted her to her car, had not uttered a single word.

Chapter Thirteen

Corey jumped out of the SUV and ran into the Block. The vehicle sped away to the newly constructed parking structure behind the old school. From the outside, it looked like a huge trailer, like the type you see behind schools. Inside, it was a hollow structure housing a number of SUVs with tinted windows.

He had a lot to do, and very little time to do it. The mistake with the bombing had shaken him, and he had developed a growing realization of the consequences of his actions. Anger made him impulsive and reckless. Fear made him cautious and alert.

Every time he watched the news coverage of the white pastor's killing, his stomach clenched and he struggled to breathe. *He* had done that. *He* had killed that man. He could never go back and change his actions. His rage had become his master. It controlled him. It caused him to be focused on his own revenge, rather than the movement. His anger was selfish—not because he had no reason to be angry but in the sense it made him focus on making himself feel better, instead of helping to meet the goals of the movement. He now understood that the movement's focus on liberation of all Black people was bigger than his individual need for revenge.

Whether it was attacking the protestor at the Alt march, or ignoring Monica's instructions for the militia bombings, he continued to jeopardize the movement. The police going door to door, pulling innocent people out of their homes, or beating folks on the street, had a new frenzy, a new sense of justification and a need for revenge that *he* had created. Of course, they would have been looking for the bombers even without his screw up. But the killing of the pastor had given The Alt a new mission now, and it had pushed the movement into a phase of activity they had not fully planned to yet reach. That was *his* fault.

He couldn't afford to lose control again. After the mistake with the pastor, he understood how much was at stake. He needed to always be clear-headed. The only place for anger was behind a clear-minded focus on the movement's objectives. At the shopping center in Columbia, just now, when he faced the white militia, his focus had not been on them, but on his own self-control. He kept hearing Monica's warnings. *This is not about killing white people; this is about showing that we have the capacity to kill white people if needed to defend ourselves. If we kill them, we have failed.*

At the door he dapped up the guards and kept moving. Taking the stairs two at a time, he entered the Communication Center which, as always, was buzzing with activity. He looked around for Carla's assistant, the real fine girl with the long twists. He saw her sitting at a computer, typing furiously, her nose almost touching the screen. He stood and watched her for a moment, feeling something that felt like hunger, but in his chest instead of his stomach. Even in the midst of all his turmoil, there was something comforting about her. Something in her eyes told him she had experienced pain. He felt sure he could tell her about Momma and Calvin and the police, and she wouldn't judge him. He needed that right now. He wanted to hug her, although he didn't even know her.

She looked up and caught him staring at her. *Busted.* Her face creased into a frown, and he quickly looked around the room, as if looking for someone else.

"You here to return the camera?" she slid her rolling chair in his direction.

"Huh?"

She nodded at the digital video camera in his hands. "You returning the camera?"

"Yes." He smiled coolly at her, hoping she didn't think he was sweating her. Which he was.

"Okay," she responded, getting up and walking towards him. He tried not to look her up and down, although she was built just the way he liked a woman—like a brickhouse. Thick and curvy. He forced himself to keep looking at her face. But that was real pretty, too, so instead he looked down at the camera in his hand.

She took the camera from him. "Did you take out the card?" she asked, turning the camera over in her hand.

He shook his head.

"Okay." She ejected the card and looked up at him. "Do you need the camera back now with a new card, or are you done with it?"

He shook his head again. *Why couldn't he speak? Dumb ass. Dumb ass. Dumb ass.*

"I guess that's what I get for asking two questions at once," she chuckled. She had the most beautiful dimples Corey had ever seen. "Let's try that again. Do you need the camera back with a new card?" Her eyes twinkled up at him, and he had a sneaking suspicion she was enjoying his discomfort.

Corey had to laugh back. He was totally busted. "No, I don't need it back," he said.

"Okay. Cool." She turned to walk back to her computer.

"But I did want to ask what you do with the videos," he added quickly.

She sank into her chair and turned back towards him. "Want to see?"

"Yeah. Sure," he said it too quickly, and immediately wanted to slap himself.

She raised her eyebrows and looked at him before gesturing to a chair. "Pull up a seat and let me show you," she said in a mock-serious voice.

Corey sank into the chair and watched her insert the card into a slot in the computer. While she was pulling up the video, he watched her out of the corner of his eye. She knew her stuff.

"I'm Corey, by the way. What's your name?"

268

"Tasia," she replied, looking at the computer.

"Nice to meet you, Tasia." He felt a little bolder.

"Nice to meet you, too." She kept her eyes on the computer, but he was sure she blushed. Nice.

She pulled up the video from the Columbia parking lot. "Okay, so I will look at the entire video. We'll decide which clips we want to use. Most likely some of the footage of these folks here with all the nice things they had to say." She hovered the pointer on the white chanters. "And these folks here." She hovered over the white militia. "Then we will show some of this." She fast-forwarded to the standoff between the Cell members and the militia. "Then we'll show them running away." She laughed, fast-forwarding to the militia getting in their vehicles."

She turned and looked at him. Not for the first time, he noticed her smooth dark skin, thick eyelashes, and high cheekbones. "You did good." She smiled shyly. "You gave me something to work with."

Corey smiled back proudly. "I'm glad. It was my first time filming."

She turned back to the computer. "So, I will string all the clips together in one video, and we'll use it to recruit members, and to show potential members that the white folks who threaten us, do so because they are afraid of us."

Corey's eyes were wide. "Ohhhhh! So how will you get the video out?"

Tasia turned to him, her eyes full of excitement. "We

269

have a number of social media platforms we use, including Twitter and Instagram. We have a lot of dummy accounts that we send these videos out on. It looks like it comes from many different people at first. I flood the Internet with it, and eventually folks start forwarding it on their own social media platforms and it goes viral. All I have to do is get it started." She giggled, clearly proud of herself. "It's the bomb."

Corey drank her in. *A beautiful, smart, conscious sister. Damn.*

"Did you have any other questions?" She looked away, clearly embarrassed at the way he was staring at her.

He jumped to his feet. "No! That was it. Thanks for the lesson."

She nodded.

Corey sat back down in the chair. "Well, actually, there's one more thing," he began.

She looked at him questioningly.

"I was wondering." His voice cracked. *Damn.* He didn't even remember how to ask a woman out; it had been that long. He cleared his throat. "I was wondering, when things calm down," He chuckled nervously. "God only knows when that will be. But I was wondering if I could take you out to dinner . . . " He gazed down at his hands, afraid to look at her. ". . . Or coffee, if that works better," he added quickly.

He looked up at Tasia. She was staring at him with an expression he didn't recognize. He had made a mistake.

"I'm sorry," he began, pushing his chair back to stand up. His body felt hot, and he just wanted to get out of there.

"No!" She put her hand on his arm, and then snatched it away, as if she didn't know how it got there. "I want to . . . It's just. . . ." She stopped and looked around frantically, her voice barely a whisper.

"It's what?" he leaned in, trying to hear better. "You've got someone?" he asked.

Tasia shook her head. "No. Not like that." She looked up at him and sighed. "I've got a daughter. She's almost two." Her voice trailed away as she faced the computer and stole a glance at him out of the corner of her eye.

Corey smiled, relieved. "Okay. That's it? That you have a daughter?"

Tasia nodded, her head still turned toward the computer.

"Well, I hope I get to meet her someday. What's her name?"

"Sharonda." Tasia turned to face him, a mixture of emotions on her face. Relief, maybe. Surprise, definitely.

Corey sat back in the chair. "Okay. Now we've got that out of the way, what's your answer?"

This time Tasia blushed full out. She lowered her head and nodded yes, peering up at him through her thick lashes.

"Something to look forward to." Corey jumped to his feet, feeling bold. "I will see you soon, beautiful Tasia." He said her name slowly. Savoring it.

Corey bounced out of the Communications Center. *Tasia.* He was going to get to know her *and* Sharonda. He needed to become a better man for them; not a man controlled by rage, but the type of man Brother Samuel always said he could be. Disciplined, conscious, loving. He had a lot to look forward to, and he couldn't wait.

Tasia watched Corey walk out of the Communications Center. She wanted to kick herself. *Why did she do that? Why did she tell him about Sharonda like that?*

She turned back to her computer, and although her eyes were on the screen, she didn't see it. All she could see was Corey's face. He was so cute, with his bald head and smooth face; she definitely wouldn't mind getting to know him better. Her face grew hot and she leaned her elbow on the desk, cradling her cheek in her hand. She hadn't talked to another man since Kenny. *Oh, Kenny!* Tasia looked around anxiously. She was supposed to meet this woman Carla told her about.

Immediately, she felt ashamed. She might be about to find out what happened to Kenny, and here she was flirting with some other man. She looked at the clock on the computer. It was almost seven already. The elders' group would be ending just about now. She stood up and walked quickly out of the Communications Center, and down the stairs. She jogged along the main hallway, looking for the classroom where Carla said the elders were meeting.

272

The meeting was over when she got to the classroom, but several people stood around talking.

"Dimples, there you are!" Nana said, walking over to Tasia. "I think Carla's going to take us home."

"Okay. How was the meeting?" Tasia asked, her eyes scanning the room.

Nana hesitated. "It was good. Trying to understand everything they were saying." She shook her head, clicking her tongue. "These are terrible times. I never thought I would see anything like this again in my life. I thought the fifties and sixties were bad, but this—"

"Yes, Nana. It's—" She stopped suddenly, looking at the older woman on the other side of the room. She stood facing Tasia, talking to a tall, regal-looking woman with long gray locs piled high on her head. The woman Tasia was looking at had to be Kenny's mother.

Tasia stepped towards her. She was short, with light skin, thick black hair pulled back in a bun, and those eyes. Tasia would never forget Kenny's almond-shaped eyes.

She walked up to the woman and stood close, to get a better look at her. The woman with the gray locs nodded at Tasia, said goodbye to the other woman, and walked away. The light-skinned woman turned to look at Tasia questioningly. She even had the same way that Kenny had of raising one eyebrow slightly higher than the other. She smiled hesitantly at Tasia.

"I know what you're thinking. I was thinking it all during the group," Nana said from behind Tasia. "If Sharonda don't look just like her."

The woman glanced from Nana to Tasia, confused. "Sharonda?" she asked.

Tasia stepped closer and extended her hand. "I'm Tasia," she said. How do you ask a woman if her dead son is your child's father?

"Nice to meet you, Tasia. I'm Cathy." She shook Tasia's hand and turned to Nana, her hand outstretched. "And you're Minerva, right?"

Nana shook Cathy's hand. "Yes. That's right. I've got a great-granddaughter that looks just like you."

Cathy's eyes widened. "Great-granddaughter?" She looked at Tasia. "Your daughter?"

Tasia smiled. She couldn't take her eyes off the woman's face. "My daughter's name is Sharonda." Tasia's voice sank to a whisper. "Her father's name is Kenny—Kenneth Milford."

The smile faded from Cathy's face and she stepped back from Tasia, as if she had been pushed. She mouthed, "What?"

Tasia stepped forward and grabbed Cathy's hand. "Is Kenny your son, Miss Cathy?" she asked, her heart beating fast and hard.

Cathy nodded; her eyes filled with tears. "Kenny was my baby boy. And we lost him. They killed him and threw his body away in an alley. The police didn't even look for his killer."

274

Tasia closed her eyes. *What had she expected?* That Cathy would say Kenny had been hanging out at her house for the past year, or had gone on a long trip? She always knew he was dead, but this was so final. Tears escaped from behind her closed lids. This grief, all over again. She didn't know if she could take it.

She felt arms encircle her. She opened her eyes and Cathy was holding her tight, rocking her from side to side while sobbing. "I'm so sorry, baby girl. I wish I had known. I wish I had known. He didn't tell me. We lost touch because . . . "

They stood like that for a long time, with Cathy rocking Tasia and Nana rubbing her back. All the pain she had held within for the past year poured out. Finally, someone who understood her grief. Not that Nana didn't understand, because she loved Tasia and hurt for her, but this was different. This woman loved Kenny, too. And she probably felt the loss more deeply than Tasia, in the tragic way a mother mourns the loss of a child..

Cathy stroked the back of Tasia's head. "We lost touch because of the things he was doing. I just couldn't condone the drugs . . . selling the drugs. I told him he had to go, and I never saw him again." Her voice caught, and she paused to regain her composure. "I don't know if I will ever forgive myself."

When she was spent, Tasia stepped away from Cathy and wiped her face. She grabbed both of Cathy's hands.

"He didn't tell me what happened between you. But you taught him well. He was such a great father. Couldn't have been

275

better. I knew you had to be a good mother. Where else would he have learned to love like that?"

Cathy pressed her lips together to stifle a sob. "He was a good boy. He just got caught up. He didn't feel he had choices."

Tasia released Cathy's hands and hugged her again. She was tired, and ready to put this grief behind her and move on. It was painful to go through this all over again, but she could finally close this chapter of her life, and felt excited that Sharonda had another grandmother who could be there for her. She released the older woman and smiled.

"Would you like to meet your granddaughter?"

Donovan sat next to Paul in the back seat, while Karen drove. She and Amani were uncharacteristically quiet. Paul gazed out the window, a backpack cradled on his lap.

"So, what are you going to be doing at the Block?" Donovan asked Paul.

Paul continued looking out the window. "Working on a robot."

"What robot?" Donovan pressed.

"A robot to identify explosives."

Donovan shifted in his seat, interested. "Really?! Did you design it?"

"No. The engineering group in San Francisco designed it and sent the design to all the Cells. We just build it based on their design. We test it and program it, too."

Donovan sat back in his seat, impressed. These folks *were* serious!

"We always knew when we unveiled ourselves, that The Alt would plan to attack us, so we began working on a bunch of robots to help us identify explosives in vehicles and buildings," Amani said, partially turned around in the front seat. "Since we bombed the militia's trucks, we know it's just a matter of time before they figure out some of our identities and come after us."

"We will be ready," Paul added, his gaze still focused on the street.

"But how many robots can you possibly make?" Donovan asked.

"A lot." Paul finally turned to look at his brother. "They're very small, about the size of a salad plate. They move on wheels and fit under cars, sending a video feed to your phone, so you can see what's under the car or around corners before you get there. We're making hundreds."

"Oh." Donovan felt ancient and out of touch. Who knew his brother could build robots the size of salad plates?

"Uh-oh," Karen said, as they turned off the highway onto Martin Luther King, Jr. Blvd.

"What's happening?" Donovan shifted his body to look out the front windshield. Flashing blue and red lights surrounded them, and he realized they had driven straight into a police checkpoint. The road ahead was blocked with police cars and there was nowhere to turn around. They were in a line of cars, stopped, waiting for their turn to proceed through the checkpoint. Police officers walked up and down the line of cars, peering into vehicles, gesturing for drivers to roll down their windows and giving instructions. National Guardsmen stood by on the sidewalk, their rifles cocked and ready for action.

Amani looked at Karen anxiously and tilted her head toward the back of the car. Karen responded by nodding, and Amani's body seemed to deflate, sinking into the seat.

"What's wrong? What's going on?" Donovan asked, watching one of the white cops walk toward them.

"Nothing. Nothing," Karen replied hastily. "They're just going to harass us."

She rolled the driver side window down as the cop walked up. On the passenger side, a Black cop stood watching, his hand on his holster.

"Good afternoon, officer," she said pleasantly.

The cop bent down and peered into the car. His gaze lingered on Donovan and Paul. "License and registration, please," he said crisply.

"Of course!" Karen reached into the glove compartment and handed him the documents.

"What's going on up there?" she asked, pointing with her chin toward the flashing lights.

The cop took her documents and stepped away with them, without answering. Karen turned and smiled impishly at

Donovan, shrugging her shoulders. "Gotta play the role."

Donovan watched the cop get back in his car with the documents. The other cop walked around to the back of their vehicle, hand on his holster.

On the side streets running alongside the main road, cops walked from house to house, banging on the doors with a force that left no question about who was knocking. At one door, when a young Black man opened, the white cop outside yanked him off the stoop by the front of his T-shirt, knocking him to the ground, and bent his arms behind his back. Donovan saw the terror on the young man's face, saw him mouthing the word, "stop." Police surrounded him, struggling to handcuff him. Donovan saw the panic in the young man's eyes, and his mouth opened in a scream.

Stop struggling. Donovan tried to channel his thoughts to the young man. *I know you're panicked. Take a deep breath. Calm down. Calm down, man. They want to shoot you. Don't give them a reason.*

When the group of cops had him handcuffed, they pulled him to his feet and walked to a police car. Blood poured from a wound on his forehead, and one side of his face was pink, missing skin, which most likely scraped off on the sidewalk. He looked dazed and frightened.

A few doors down, a cop banged on another door, and a white man opened, holding a can of soda. He smiled as the officer spoke to him. They chatted for a moment, waved at each other, and the cop walked on to the next door. The white man stood for a moment watching the action outside his house. He waved to some of the cops and Guardsmen walking by, spoke to them, and gave a thumbs up. He stood, leaning on the door frame for a while, sipping his soda and watching, a smile on his face.

Donovan turned around to look at the cop standing behind the car. He stood perfectly still, in a wide-legged stance, watching them through the rear windshield. Their eyes met, and a chill went through Donovan. He quickly faced forward, as the first cop returned to the car.

He handed Karen her documents and gestured for her to move forward.

"Thank you, officer," she said as she took her documents. She slowly inched through the blockade, passing several officers who stared into the car as they drove past.

"I counted five Cell members," Paul said.

"You did?" Karen asked, surprised. "Which ones?"

"I know the names and badge numbers of all the members of the Baltimore City Police," Paul said. "Like Officer Stewart, #61472. He was the one standing behind the car."

"That was a Cell member?" Donovan asked.

"Yep," Paul replied.

"Thank God for that," Karen said. "We might have needed him."

"Why?" Donovan asked.

Amani shook her head, chuckling mirthlessly. "Because we have a trunk full of weapons. We were praying he wouldn't search the car."

"What?" Donovan jumped anxiously in his seat. "There are weapons in this car? Why didn't you tell me?"

"Because you would have behaved nervously, and they would have known," Karen replied. "That's why we didn't tell you. You can't react to something you don't know about."

Donovan rubbed his hands over his face. *What the hell had he gotten involved in?*

They passed blockade after blockade, and repeated scenes of people face down in the street, sitting on the curb, lined up against walls, or bent over police cars, their arms behind them. Karen was more cautious this time and skirted around the checkpoints.

Donovan's phone buzzed in his pocket. It was Steve. He sighed and answered.

"Hello?" He affected a hoarse voice.

"Hi, Don." Steve's voice was loud enough to make Paul turn around and look. "Sorry to bother you when you're off sick. How are you feeling?"

"I'm okay. Doing a little better," Donovan coughed slightly.

Amani turned around to look at him with a devilish grin. She shook her head.

"Good. Good. Good to hear!" Steve boomed. Donovan doubted he would have said anything different if Donovan had said he was dying.

"What's up?" Donovan asked.

Steve cleared his throat. "Yeah. So, I wanted to let you know that Bill reached out to the Ashton Foundation and scheduled a meeting for this Friday."

Donovan was silent for a moment as his brain tried to catch up to what Steve was saying.

"What? I thought I was making that appointment. The plan was to schedule it for next week."

"Yes. Well, Bill changed his mind and went ahead and scheduled it."

"For this Friday?" Donovan asked, his mind sliding through his calendar. "What time?"

Steve cleared this throat again. "Yes. Three o'clock. But here's the thing, Bill wants me and Rick to go."

"Okay. Do we all need to go? That seems a little like overkill—three people."

Steve was silent. "Right," he said, finally.

The car drove up the driveway of an old, abandoned school surrounded by a tall metal fence. The gate slid open and they drove into a parking lot. Some of the windows in the large building were scratched and caked with years of dirt; leaves and trash lay piled in corners around the courtyard. Donovan looked around. Except for the tall fence and the mechanical gate, the place looked old and creepy. *Was this really the Block?* "

"So, you and Rick are going to present to the Foundation, even though I'm the one who brought in that business," Donovan said.

"But you'll get a commission if they sign," Steve said quickly. "You know, a finder's fee."

"But you and Rick will make the ongoing commission," Donovan continued, as if Steve had not spoken. "And I will walk away with my little fee, my tip, which is a fraction of what you'll make."

"Okay, but it's better than nothing," Steve sounded annoyed. "I mean, you're just an associate. You didn't really think this would be your account, did you?"

Donovan got the distinct impression Steve was irritated that Donovan wasn't grateful for the finder's fee.

Karen, Paul, and Amani were already out of the car. Donovan got out slowly.

"Actually, I did. I worked with an inside source for months, getting our name in front of their C-suite, and gathering information. This is my account."

"Well, it's not. If they sign, it's my account. As a member of my team, you can definitely support." Steve's tone added . . . *and don't forget who you are.*

Donovan sighed. "Got it."

"Good. Hope you feel better. See you tomorrow," Steve said.

Donovan hung up without saying goodbye, put his phone in his back pocket, and stood looking up at the school. His body surged with anger. There was absolutely no reason for the firm to prevent him from managing this account. He had been a hard worker for five years; he had been a good team player, *accepting all their shit accounts*, acknowledging that he needed to work his way up, *and he had played the game*. Steve was right; an associate would not usually get to manage an account like this, but when associates brought big business into the firm, it almost always resulted in a promotion to senior associate, and the opportunity to manage the big account, with support from a more seasoned senior. But they were actually taking the account from him and giving it to someone else. That was almost unheard of at the firm. This was the reason there were no Black senior associates.

His head pounded, and his breath came hard and ragged. He felt dizzy with rage. This is what he got for all the years of hard work. His fingers felt numb, and he realized his hands were clutched into fists, his nails digging into his palm. He released his hand and felt the blood rush back into his fingers. He shook his hands out and exhaled. There was a reason he was here at this moment. He was fooling himself if he thought his good education and middle-class job shielded him from racism. It was time for his blinders to come off.

He realized Karen, Paul, and Amani were standing at the entrance to the school waiting for him. Their silent gazes told him they understood what was happening. His apprehension about joining the Cell was gone. He was ready.

Donovan shook his head and walked up to the large, metal door. "So, this is it, huh?

Karen and Amani nodded.

"I'm ready," Donovan said. "Let's go."

Chapter Fourteen

Kai pulled up in front of the long, low lodge and parked beside LaTanya's car. They all sat in the SUV for a moment, looking at the wooden structure. Even Mia and Jessica were quiet. Lisa glanced back to see them staring up at the imposing mountain rising into the sky behind the lodge. Mia's mouth was open, her eyes wide. Jessica looked uncharacteristically impressed.

The compound sat in a valley, on a clearing, surrounded by long, wooden cabins. Around them, low hills rolled as far as the eye could see, and much of the land was covered by thick forest. They were in the middle of nowhere, and besides this compound, which LaTanya referred to as the Farm, there was not another building for miles. In fact, the compound was completely hidden to anyone coming down the mountain, and Lisa imagined very few neighbors in the surrounding farms even knew the compound was there.

The lodge was built into the side of the rock mountain, and Lisa couldn't tell where the building ended and the mountain began. She suspected the lodge was much larger than it looked from the outside and wondered how far back into the rock it extended. She knew it had to be huge, because LaTanya told her it could house thousands.

LaTanya was already out of the car and waiting for them in front of the building. Lisa unbuckled her seatbelt and sat looking out the window. She still couldn't believe she was there, and couldn't believe they were forced to leave their beautiful house for their own safety. She couldn't believe her neighbors had become so hostile. She couldn't believe she had to call in sick at the end of the school year, when her students were about to begin exams.

Missing work hadn't mattered much; many of her students had stopped coming to school. Lisa suspected many families experienced disruptions because of the rabid arrest and harassment of Black people by the police and Guardsmen. Other families had likely withdrawn their students to send them to Freedom Schools. She couldn't believe her own kids had to enter and leave their Freedom School through underground tunnels. She just couldn't believe it had all come to this.

Kai and the girls were out of the car by now. Lisa opened the door and climbed out.

"Should we take our luggage out here?" Kai asked LaTanya.

She shook her head. "No. Let's get you all checked in. You will probably stay in one of the family cabins. It's a good thing you're one of the first to come. Many of those who come later will be sharing bunks in the large cabins, which house like fifty or sixty folks."

Kai nodded and reached for Lisa's hand. "Let's go." He smiled encouragingly at Lisa and squeezed her hand, pulling her close to him.

They entered through the double doors and were met by armed men stationed around the lobby area. One of the men held open a bag into which they all placed their cellphones. Kai also had to give up his prized GPS watch, which Lisa knew was difficult for him to do.

To their right was a cafeteria, with a capacity of probably hundreds, but currently occupied by only five people. The cafeteria housed multiple serving centers scattered around the room, but only the one closest to the kitchen was currently open.

"This is where you will come for your meals," LaTanya said.

To the left of the entrance was a large living room, with couches and side tables, a fieldstone fireplace, dartboard, and a foosball table. In one corner stood a bookcase filled with games, puzzles, and books. A black Labrador retriever lay on the rug in front of the fireplace and lifted its head as Jessica and Mia drifted over to the doorway.

"Oh, look! A puppy!" Mia exclaimed.

LaTanya smiled. "She's a pretty old dog, but she's important to us. That's Lia. Her name is short for Kujichagulia, the second principle in Kwanzaa. It means self-determination."

"What's self-determination?" Jessica asked.

"It is our right, as Black people, to make decisions about our own lives and our own destinies. It is our right to overcome oppression and to live in peace and security. Not only to survive, but to flourish and to thrive."

"Oh. That makes sense," Jessica said. She seemed lost in thought.

"Are you hungry?" LaTanya asked. All four shook their heads.

"Mom, can we hang out in here?" Jessica asked. Mia hopped up and down, hoping they could.

Lisa looked at LaTanya, who nodded. LaTanya poked her chin towards the armed men at the door.

"They're perfectly safe. We will be back soon."

Jessica and Mia ran off to play with Lia, and the adults continued through the lobby. They walked through a set of steel doors, which must have been a foot thick. As they walked, Lisa turned to look behind them. She imagined, with those doors closed, the lodge would be difficult to penetrate from outside. She began feeling more secure.

Inside the doors, there were no windows, so no sunlight. Light fixtures, encased in metal grills for protection, lined the ceiling, providing a warm, yellow glow.

LaTanya led them up a flight of stone stairs, built into the rock. The center of the stairways revealed a slight, smooth indent where many feet had trodden.

How long has this place been here? Lisa wondered.

On the second floor, they stepped into a hallway, stretching way into the distance, with doors spaced every few yards. Lisa tried to see the end of the hallway, but it disappeared around a corner maybe a quarter-mile away.

"How big is this place?" Lisa breathed.

LaTanya began walking down the hallway. "It's very, very big. I haven't even seen all of it."

"How long has it been here?" Kai asked as they walked.

"Probably around seventy years." LaTanya replied. "The Black Resistance Movement began back in the thirties; this land was purchased from white farmers, who thought they were selling it to a church. The cabins and the outside of the lodge were built first, and then under cover of the building, folks dug this rock out by hand. It took them many years. Some people even died during the construction."

LaTanya led them to the right, down another corridor. "Of course, most people don't know it exists. But we always knew a time of tribulation was coming—not only because the ancestors predicted it, but also because this has been our pattern in history."

"What pattern?" Kai asked.

"Okay. So, every time Black people make some progress politically, socially, or economically, the result is a violent backlash. Everyone becomes focused on the backlash and forgets about how bad things were before. So, the focus turns to getting things back to normal. But normal was never good for Black people to begin with. We just get fooled into forgetting. It's like when we were on the plantation, after you've been in the field for a while, being in the house starts looking real good. But it's all relative, right? Working in Massa's house isn't the same as being free, but compared to the field, we might accept it, even welcome it."

"Okayyyyy," Kai said.

"Okay, so check this out. We experienced a lot of racism, Black people being killed in the streets by cops, underfunded schools, extreme economic inequity, right?"

"Right," Lisa replied.

"Then we get a Black president. Everyone rejoices—we are finally free. But we aren't, because the white people block him at every turn. And he only tries so hard anyway, because he knows he's a Black man and needs to fit in with the white folks. Being "radical" would cost him votes and maybe even his life."

LaTanya turned into an open doorway, and Lisa was shocked at the size of the living room they entered. It had a high ceiling, and although the walls were hewn out of the stone and there were no windows, a number of lamps and wall sconces around the room made it just bright enough to feel cozy and warm. On one side stood a row of doors, and a woman sat behind a reception desk in front of them. She looked up from her computer and smiled.

"You must be the Wilsons," she said. "Please have a seat. We will be with you in a moment." She gestured toward the couches.

They sat on a brown suede sectional. LaTanya pointed to the pitcher of water and glasses on the coffee table in front of them, and they helped themselves.

"But white people are not happy with the suggestion that Black people might be free. Having Jackson in the White House is purely symbolic. Nothing has really changed for us. But ask any white person, even those most liberal ones, and if they are truly honest, they will say that the idea of having Blacks as full equals in this society makes their stomachs turn."

"But why?" Lisa asked. "Why is that frightening to them?"

LaTanya looked at Lisa as if she had two heads. "Have you ever watched *Birth of a Nation*?"

Lisa shook her head. Kai nodded.

LaTanya continued. "You should watch it, Lisa. Because built into the psyche of America is the idea that the Black man is primal, dangerous, and intellectually inferior. People will never tell you that directly. How many liberal white people have you met who were surprised that you were smart or articulate?"

Lisa sighed. "Too many."

"Exactly! Why are they surprised? You have the same education as them, the same experience. Why are they surprised that you are their equal or superior?"

Lisa shrugged and shook her head. "I don't know."

LaTanya sighed. "And if you pointed this issue out to them, they would be confused, because this is so deeply subconscious. So, let's get back to the pattern I was talking about before. We make progress, like finally get a Black president or develop a Black Wall Street. This is threatening to white people, and they rise up to protect their power. They elect a president like Sumpter, and you'd better believe he will be elected. Now, they are able to act out all the hidden fears and fantasies about Black people that have existed, and yet stayed hidden, all these years. Or they burn down Black Wall Street and exert their dominance through violence. Europeans have been taught to exert their dominance over "lesser humans," LaTanya made air quotes.

"Just look at all the lands and people they colonized. They have never given up any of their colonies without a fight. We, Black people, are one of the final European colonies. Did you think they would just lay down for us? Why would they?"

LaTanya sipped some water. "And at the end of the backlash, liberal white people and many Blacks are so anxious for things to go back to the way they were before we made progress, that we can't even see we are moving backward. In fact, we are often so grateful when they take their swastikas and confederate flags down and stop killing us openly in the street; we are so happy to go back to accepting the quiet cop killings and our kids getting an inferior education, or our homes being devalued, and our wealth stolen. That starts to look like progress to us. That's the pattern, and then it starts all over again. Go learn your history. It's all there. None of this is new, we just refuse to see it."

Lisa sighed and flopped back on the couch. She was exhausted. What LaTanya was saying was like nothing she had heard before, and she felt drained. She wanted to respond to LaTanya, but didn't know where to begin.

"How have you had such a clueless friend all this time?" she whispered, her eyes closed.

"Because I knew the moment would come when you were ready to hear it," LaTanya responded.

Just then, one of the doors opened behind the reception desk and a woman walked out and came toward them, with hand outstretched.

LaTanya stood hastily. Kai pulled Lisa to her feet. She stood unsteadily, and Kai wrapped his arm around her offering support.

"Mr. and Mrs. Wilson," the woman said, shaking their hands. "My name is Esther. I'm the Housing Coordinator here at the Farm. We are going to get you settled into your new home here." She looked around. "Where are Jessica and Mia?"

Lisa was surprised. These folks really did their homework. "They're downstairs playing with the dog."

Esther smiled. "Ahhh, yes. Lia is very popular around here. She's a great companion. We actually have a lot of dogs, who serve many different purposes. Some are for companionship,

294

others for comfort, but we have a whole stable of dogs who are used primarily for warning."

She handed Lisa a clipboard. "We need some basic information from you, mostly emergency and medical information. Then we will get you settled."

She turned to LaTanya. "I will leave the key to cabin six here at the desk. Do you know where it is? Over by the family cabins?"

LaTanya nodded.

Esther smiled at Kai and Lisa again. "I hope you will be comfortable. There is a lot of information in your cabin about mealtimes and our community agreements for staying here." She turned to Lisa. "I hear you're a teacher."

"Yes."

"That's great, because everyone has a job to do here, and many families will soon arrive with their children. We need to set up a Freedom School on the Farm. I will need your help."

Lisa smiled. It would be good to have something to focus on besides the craziness happening in the world.

Esther turned to Kai. "And what type of law do you practice?

"I'm a corporate attorney."

"We are buying up a number of properties for safehouses. Can you work with our contracts team?"

"Absolutely. Would love to."

When they had finished filling out paperwork, LaTanya led them back down to the lodge. In the living room, Jessica and Mia had tired of playing with Lia, or Lia had tired of playing with them, and the girls were now sprawled on opposite couches reading books from the bookshelf. Lia was nowhere to be seen. They hopped up when the adults entered.

"Mommy, can we take these books with us?" Mia asked, running over. She threw her arms around Lisa's waist as if she hadn't seen her for days. Lisa struggled to stay on her feet.

She laughed and looked at LaTanya. "You have to ask Aunt LaTanya. I don't know the rules here."

Mia looked over at LaTanya, who pretended to think for a moment. "I think that can be done, if you promise to bring it back when you're done."

Mia put her hands on her hips and looked up at LaTanya. "Of course I will, Auntie. Some other kid might want to read it!"

LaTanya laughed. "That's my girl."

They headed out of the lodge and Lisa squinted in the bright sunlight, shading her eyes.

"Yeah. That's one of the problems about being in the rock. There's absolutely no sunlight. We try to stay out of there as much as possible. People usually stay in the cabins when they come to the Farm. There are hundreds of sleeping quarters in the rock, and we are preparing for the day when we need to retreat there and hide our families while we fight," LaTanya said.

Fight? Lisa shuddered. Is this what the world had come to? "D . . . do you think we will all have to fight?" she asked.

LaTanya turned to look at Lisa. "We are all one body in the Movement. We may have different roles. Some of us will have to use weapons. Others will teach. Some will prepare equipment. Others will manage our communications. We are all working toward our liberation and overthrowing the violence of white domination. We are all fighting in different ways. So, yes, you will need to fight. And it will be your job to figure out what your chosen weapons will be.

Tasia pushed Sharonda's stroller south on Howard Street, navigating her way through the throngs of school children heading to the bus stops or walking home. Every few blocks she spied a parked National Guard vehicle or police car. Unlike before the state of emergency, the school kids didn't dance around and play on the sidewalk. Instead, they hurried on their way, occasionally throwing furtive glances towards the law enforcement vehicles.

She walked slowly, because she was way too early, but Tasia had been restless all day, knowing what she must do. As they walked, Sharonda babbled, occasionally craning her neck to look up at her mother.

She pointed towards the street. "Car!" she announced proudly.

Tasia turned to look at the car, relieved to have something else to think about.

"Yes, that's a car. What color is it?" she asked.

"Mommy, that's a blue car!" Sharonda said it as if Tasia should have known the answer herself.

"Yes! It's a blue car!" Tasia crowed. "You're such a smart girl!"

"Hi!" Sharonda yelled, waving to a woman walking by. The woman smiled and waved back.

"Sharonda, soon you're going to be two. Show me two."

Sharonda held up two fingers, struggling to keep the other fingers down. Finally, she used her other hand to tame the disobedient fingers.

"Two!" she shouted.

"Two years old!" Tasia shouted back, sending Sharonda into giggles.

Tasia's phone buzzed, and she pulled it out of her back pocket. The text was from Donna. *Pick up in front of the ER in 30 minutes.*

Tasia sighed as she put the phone back in her pocket. Her heart beat loud and fast, and she was so distracted, she almost tripped over the uneven pavement. She grabbed the back of the stroller even harder to steady herself.

Why did she agree to do this? And the crazy thing was no one had even asked her. Her nosy butt heard Donna and Carla talking about finding someone to do a cash pickup and she offered! She volunteered to walk down Howard Street with her child to pick up hundreds of thousands of dollars from an "Invisible" Cell member.

Carla was the one who told Tasia about Invisible members. Invisible members never came to the Block or to meetings, and few Cell members knew they existed. They were never seen in the company of anyone who could be tied to the Cell. Only the top leadership knew who they were, and no one leader knew them all. This way, it would be difficult to give them up if members were arrested.

Invisible members were embedded in police departments, in finance, in the judicial system, in education, and in social services. They were Black, but usually pretended to disagree with the movement, displaying disgust for its members. They were greatly trusted by the white establishment, and were affectionately called "Toms" or "Thomasinas" by the members who knew of their existence, because they played the part of full inculturation into white supremacy so well, few people ever suspected them, including their own families. In fact, they were carefully chosen and groomed, usually light-skinned, because sometimes white people would forget they were Black, especially if they were bi-racial.

Toms and Thomasinas played a critical role in the movement. Because they were rarely suspected of having ties to any Black liberation movement, they fed the Cell information from the police department, created shell businesses to hide Cell funds and to funnel money around the world. Tasia was on her way to meet one of them and pick up a large sum of money. "They will find you," is all she was told.

She paused on the corner, near the Rite Aid, and checked the time on her phone. She needed to kill fifteen minutes before she continued walking. She went into the Rite Aid and walked around the aisles, lost in her thoughts. It wasn't until she realized Sharonda was very quiet that she stepped around the stroller to see what the toddler was doing. Sharonda was leaning back, clutching an open bag of cheese puffs and munching happily, crumbs all over her face. She grinned when she saw Tasia, her tiny teeth orange from the puffs. She held out the bag for Tasia to have some.

Tasia gasped and snatched the bag away.

"Where did you get this?" she demanded.

Sharonda stared at her. She bowed her head, looking up at Tasia, eyes filling with tears, chin trembling.

Tasia took a deep breath. She always promised herself she wouldn't be one of those mothers yelling at her kids in public. Besides, she suspected Sharonda had grabbed the cheese puffs off the shelf and held it up for Tasia to see. But her mother was far too preoccupied to notice. She could hardly blame Sharonda for thinking she had permission to open the bag.

"Okay, I'm sorry." She gave the bag back to Sharonda, stood in line at the counter, ignoring the dirty looks from the cashier, and paid for the puffs. But Sharonda's feelings were hurt and she wouldn't eat any more. She threw the bag on the ground in the store and turned her face into the side of the stroller, her lips poked out.

Tasia sighed, picked up the bag, and crumpled it up in her hand, searching for a trash can.

"I'm sorry," she muttered again as she walked out of the store.

Back on the street, she realized she was a few minutes behind schedule, so she picked up her pace and headed for the University of Maryland Midtown Hospital. As she approached the hospital, she stopped to check her phone. It was just about time for the drop. She turned toward the emergency room entrance, scanning the passenger drop-off/pick-up zone in front of the automatic doors. People milled around, leaning against the building, smoking—directly under the *No Smoking Within 50 Feet of Entrance* sign. No one looked like they might be waiting for her.

She walked down the block, trying to look casual. She backed the stroller up against the building, a little to the left of the entrance. Sharonda was asleep, her face buried in the side of the stroller, forehead still creased up in a frown. Tasia stood in front of the stroller, attempting to fit in with the others who were just hanging around. She pulled out her phone and pretended to look at it, although she couldn't concentrate on the words on the screen. A text flashed across her screen from Donna. *I'm driving up now.*

Tasia looked up, panicked. The Invisible hadn't come yet. Was she in the wrong place? She turned around to check on Sharonda, and almost tripped over a small suitcase standing right behind her. Where had that come from? She looked around. No one seemed interested in her. No one looked like an Invisible, whatever that might be. She stood for a moment, staring at the suitcase. Someone had gotten that close to her without her knowing. The thought made her shudder. They could have easily taken Sharonda.

When Donna pulled up in her SUV, Tasia was standing on the pavement, clutching the handle of the stroller in one hand and the handle of the rolling suitcase in the other. There was no way she was letting go of either.

Donna took Sharonda's car seat out of the hatchback trunk and set it up in the back seat. Tasia lifted the suitcase to put inside the car. It was much heavier than expected, and she had to hoist it onto the edge of the trunk first, and then push it into the SUV. She gently lifted the sleeping Sharonda out of her stroller and strapped her into the car seat, then stowed the stroller in the car.

As they pulled away, Tasia leaned her head back against the seat. Her heart was pounding and she felt like she had just run a long distance, like when she used to run for the bus. She was so relieved this was almost over. She closed her eyes and sighed, feeling overwhelmed.

"You okay?" Donna's voice interrupted her as she struggled to regain her composure.

Tasia exhaled. "That was so scary!"

"I bet it was. What was most scary about it?"

Tasia thought for a moment. "I don't know what scared me most. That I was meeting some person and I didn't even know what they looked like, or that the Invisible person knew who *I* was and I didn't know who *they* were, or the idea that I was gonna be carrying so much money. What if I got robbed?"

Donna chuckled. "You were under surveillance the whole time. If someone tried to rob you, they wouldn't get very far."

Tasia's eyes opened wide as she turned to look at Donna. "Under surveillance?" By the Invisible?"

"Yes, the Invisible and the intelligence team from the Cell. You were never alone."

"What?" Tasia breathed deeply. "Whewwww! Why didn't they tell me?"

"What would that have done?"

"Made me less scared."

"Yep, and made you look around trying to figure out who was watching you, right?"

Tasia shrugged.

Donna chuckled. "Tell me you wouldn't have been trying to figure it out. You would have looked all nervous and suspicious. It would have attracted attention."

"I guess," Tasia said.

"You couldn't possibly think you actually could be on the street with $1.5 million in cash without protection."

Tasia's head turned so fast she hurt her neck. "How much? What did you say?" She rubbed her neck.

Donna smiled. "$1.5 million."

Tasia jabbed a thumb towards the trunk. "That's how much money is in that suitcase?"

"Yep. In one hundred dollar bills." Donna glanced at Tasia. "Heavy, isn't it."

Tasia leaned back in the seat, her mouth open. *What the hell was she thinking?* She didn't even ask how much money she was picking up.

"What's the money for?" she asked. "And why did they need *me* to pick it up. Why's it in cash, anyway? Isn't there some better way to send money?"

"Yes. There are lots of ways to send money, but the FBI is trying hard to find out how we're being financed, and we have a bunch of money stashed overseas. We can't use wire transfers because some of us are being watched. So, our Invisibles transfer money from overseas using their companies, take cash out for business purposes, and store it in a number of places for when we need it. We've had to move to a cash system to avoid detection."

Tasia's eyes opened wide.

"As far as what the money is for, most of it will be used for cash bail for the folks who have been arrested. Our legal teams are working to get people released. The criminal justice system gets to hold poor people because they can't afford the cash bail. So, we're taking care of that and waiting to see what other barriers they put up to keep folks from getting out. Most of these people won't ever be charged or convicted. They just get held in prison, sometimes for years, without going to trial, simply because they can't afford the cash bail. And we've seen how punitive the criminal justice system is for Black people."

Tasia was silent. She knew so many people who disappeared to jail for years and never came back. *Was this why? Because they didn't have money?*

"Even if they're innocent?" she asked.

"Even if they're innocent," Donna replied.

"Do all white people hate us?" Tasia whispered, almost to herself.

"What was that?" Donna asked.

Tasia struggled to hold back tears. "Do all white people hate us?"

Donna sighed. "No. Actually, we have white folks working with the Cell."

"What? We do?" Tasia turned in her seat again. "I've never seen any white people in the Block."

"And you never will," Donna replied. "But there are some white folks supporting the movement. For example, the white people who drove the decoy busses during the unveiling."

"That's right!" Tasia remembered. "What else do they do?"

"Well, we have thousands of white allies who work with us. But I'm not talking about those many liberal white folks who talk a good talk about Black Lives Matter, but only as long as they don't have to change anything they're doing, and as long as they don't have to give up the power and privilege that comes with white skin."

Donna pulled up to the gate leading to the lot behind the Block and waited for it to slide open. When it did, she passed through.

"I'm talking about white people who have decided to ride or die with the movement. They're willing to put their bodies on the line for everyone in this country to be free. It's that important to them."

She pulled up to the loading dock, put the car in Park, and looked at Tasia.

"There are white people like that, thousands in fact, but most of the others just talk. Some of them want to do more but aren't informed about the reality of our situation in this country, so many of our white allies are out there organizing those folks. They need to know this movement is about more than just marching in the street protesting. That's symbolic, which is nice, but just a small piece of what we need to do. Real change happens with government policies and laws and economics. That's what we're working for. And if our white allies really want to help, that's where they will work, too."

306

Tasia got out of the car and opened the trunk, removing the heavy suitcase.

"I'm going to go park. Leave Sleeping Beauty and her stroller and I'll take her to the toddler room. You have to drop that off up in finance," Donna said.

Tasia walked up the ramp of the loading dock. She nodded to the guards and headed down the main hallway. The Block was full. There were people in every classroom, and the main hallway was crowded. She elbowed her way through the masses of people toward the stairwell.

Finance was at the very top of the building, on the third floor. As she started to drag the suitcase up the first step, she heard someone behind her. She turned around.

"Hey, Tasia!" Corey beamed.

Tasia suddenly felt shy. She smiled at him and continued up the stairs without speaking.

"Where are you going? May I take that for you?"

Before she could respond, he took the handle from her, lowered it, and lifted the suitcase, bouncing up the stairs.

"I'm going to the third floor." She hopped up the steps behind him. He moved so fast that she was breathless trying to keep up.

"I got you." Corey paused on the second-floor landing and turned to smile at her. He looked so cute.

"How are you?" he asked before starting up the second flight.

"I'm good." She panted behind him. "And . . . how are you?"

He stopped on the third-floor landing, put the suitcase down, and looked at her. "Better now."

"I'm sorry," she began. "I know it's heavy—"

Corey laughed. "I'm not talking about the suitcase. I'm talking about seeing you again."

Tasia blushed. "Oh, okay."

Corey raised the handle of the suitcase and gave it to her. "We still need to set up our date." He had the smoothest skin. She almost reached up to see how soft it was.

"And, I still need to meet Sharonda."

Tasia stepped back in surprise. *He remembered.*

"Oh. Okay," she said again. *Why was she acting so dumb?* "We can make that happen."

His face broke into a wide grin, as he stepped back, rubbing his hands together. "Say less." He turned to run back down the stairs. "Your move."

Tasia watched him bound back down the steps, taking them two at a time with his long legs. She suddenly realized she was standing on the landing with a dumb smile on her face. She turned to walk down the hallway towards finance.

Armed guards were stationed outside the finance office, and once Tasia turned onto the main hallway, she passed several guards who looked her up and down, focused on the suitcase, and nodded her on. Every door in that hallway was metal, unlike the wooden doors elsewhere in the building, except for the doors leading to the basement, where the weapons were stored.

She stopped at the door to the main finance office, waiting for the guard to let her in. Once inside the finance office, a woman sitting at a desk looked up from her computer.

"May I help you?" she asked.

"Yes. I'm here to drop off this . . . this package," Tasia gestured to the suitcase.

"Okay. One moment, please." The woman picked up the phone on her desk and dialed a number. "Donovan, the package is here." She listened for a moment, then hung up.

"He will be right out." The woman smiled at Tasia and returned her attention to the computer.

After a few moments, the door to an inner office opened, and a young, dark-skinned man with metal glasses walked out. He walked up to Tasia, eyes focused on the suitcase.

"Great. Thanks so much for bringing this." He took the handle from her. "I take it you didn't have any problems?"

Tasia shook her head. The way he spoke was very educated. He sounded like a teacher or a politician. Tasia didn't know many people who sounded like him. She stared at him, wondering who he was.

He started to walk away with the suitcase, but stopped, turned, and looked at her.

"Was there something else?" he asked.

Tasia shook her head again.

He gave her a little smile and walked back towards the office. When the door closed behind him, Tasia turned and walked to the Communications Center. She was relieved to be finished with the important task she had been given today, but was already wondering what would be next. She had been trusted with $1.5 million in cash today, more money than she could ever imagine, and she had done a good job. She was part of something big. Very big. Kenny always told her she would be "big-time" one day. If only he could see her now.

Donovan took the suitcase of cash from the young woman with the twists and big eyes. She looked a little lost, and he almost asked her if she was okay. But it wasn't his business. The last few weeks had been tumultuous, to say the least, and he had his own problems.

He lifted the suitcase and placed it on the desk. His next task was to count and log the money. He unzipped the case and threw the cover open. The musty smell of cash, a little like dirty laundry, filled the room. He gasped at the sight of the tightly packed hundred-dollar bills. He knew how much cash was in the suitcase, had written the order for it, but was still unprepared for the sight. He stood, staring.

"Amazing, isn't it?" Chinua looked up from the computer in the corner of the room. "You can never get used to the sight." His green eyes twinkled as he gazed at the cash. He stroked his goatee and continued "No matter how many suitcases like this I see—"

Donovan nodded, stepping back from the desk so his eyes could fully take in the cash. Finally, he reached for the suitcase.

"Wait," Chinua said quickly, handing Donovan a box of latex gloves. "No fingerprints on the cash, remember?"

Donovan took the box, carefully selected a pair of gloves, and pulled them on. He couldn't take his eyes off the cash. He would probably never see anything like this again.

He turned to Chinua. "Okay, walk me through the process now."

Chinua stood up from the computer and walked over to the desk. He pulled on a pair of gloves.

"Okay," he said. "The first thing is to count it, so we need to get it all in the money counter. We will create stacks of $100,000 each—should be fifteen stacks."

Chinua grabbed a stack of bills from the suitcase and walked over to a money-counting machine on the desk next to the computer. He inserted the cash, pressed the button, and watched as the cash flipped through the counter, the machine whirring softly. Chinua walked back to the desk, opened a drawer, took out some wide rubber bands, and grabbed more cash.

Donovan took a handful of cash and followed Chinua over to the money counter. They worked quickly and silently, counting piles of bills, securing them with rubber bands, and then setting them in stacks on the desk.

311

Donovan was thankful Chinua didn't engage in mindless chatter. He just didn't have the energy for that. He was exhausted. Getting up, getting dressed, and leaving the house each day felt like it took monumental effort. Besides, he had spent the last several days packing up his apartment and moving out. He didn't know when he made the decision to move back to his mother's house. It wasn't something he ever remembered thinking about. He just started packing a few days ago and knew he didn't want to live in that high-rise ever again. With a waiting list for apartments in his building, it had been easy to find someone to sublet.

When they finished counting and stacking the money, Chinua pulled a large fabric duffle bag from the desk drawer and loaded the money inside, zipping it up. He wrote the number printed on the bag on a notepad, placed the bag on the desk, and walked over to the safe built into the wall on the far side of the room. Chinua was not a small man; he was well over six-feet tall, and the metal door of the safe towered over him. He typed in his six-digit code, and then stood back for Donovan to type in his code. When both codes were in, the electronic mechanism in the door clicked and the keypad glowed green. Chinua grasped the metal bar attached to the door, braced his feet in a wide stance, and pulled the heavy door open.

The safe was lined with shelves from floor to ceiling, and each shelf contained several numbered money bags. Donovan handed Chinua the bag they had just filled, and Chinua placed it on a shelf among the other bags in chronological order. He swung the heavy door closed and the lock clicked loudly.

Chinua walked over to the computer, pulled off his gloves, and sat down. "Go ahead, grab that notebook and pull up a chair."

When Donovan sat down, Chinua opened a spreadsheet marked "Safe Access Log." In separate columns he entered the date, the amount of money placed in the safe, and the money bag number.

He slid his chair aside so Donovan could approach. "Enter your code."

Donovan leaned over and entered his safe code in the highlighted field while Chinua looked away. The numbers he entered immediately disappeared into a string of asterisks. Chinua slid his chair back to the computer and entered his own number, while Donovan averted his eyes.

"Natalia runs an access printout from the safe every night," Chinua said. "She compares it against this log to ensure there hasn't been any unauthorized access."

He pulled up another spreadsheet, this one listing client numbers and dollar amounts. He placed the cursor over the list of client numbers.

"This is the list of Black people we know of who will need to have cash bail posted for them today or tomorrow. Each one has a unique identifying number. Only Natalia has the actual names and numbers associated with them."

He pointed the cursor to the dollar amounts. "These are the amounts of cash bail they will need. There are a number of law firms working closely with us, and we need to get this money to them so they can post bail for their clients. The goal is that no one stays in jail longer than it takes to get this cash bail posted. This is one of the ways we can disarm the criminal justice system that counts on poor Black people not being able to make bail."

"Okay," Donovan struggled to concentrate. His brain felt full and foggy, and he just wanted to lie down somewhere and sleep. *What's wrong with me?* He shook his head, attempting to clear the cloud.

"So, what we do, is determine how much money needs to go to each law firm. We have a number of businesses that will deposit the money into their banks as business proceeds, and then funnel the money to their attorneys as payments."

Chinua pulled up a general ledger. "We need to enter the money as cash, and then record the disbursements to the different businesses. Each business has a range of daily business proceeds, and we need to stay within that range so that we don't trigger a review by their bank. Okay?"

"Okay," Donovan muttered. He blinked rapidly, trying to keep his eyes open.

Chinua looked at Donovan closely for a moment, frowning. "You okay?"

"Yeah, I'm cool." Donovan said, and turned his attention to the computer. But Chinua kept looking at him, his eyebrows raised.

"Uh-huh."

Donovan shook his head again. "I don't know." He sighed. "It's been a tough week."

"Uh-huh."

Donovan looked at Chinua and chuckled. Chinua's bald head gleamed in the overhead fluorescent light, lighting his almond-colored skin in a way that reminded Donovan of a globe-shaped lamp his mother bought for his bedroom when he was in high school. Chinua was actually a pretty cool guy.

"For real? You're not gonna let this go, huh?"

Chinua smiled and waited, his gaze constant.

Donovan sighed. "Okay. I'm just a little overwhelmed, I think."

"O . . . kayyyy." Chinua dragged the word out.

"I really don't know what's happening around me. I don't even know why I'm here."

Chinua's smile disappeared. His eyes became watchful. "Why *are* you here?"

Donovan held up his hand. "It's okay. You don't have to worry about me. I'm here for the right reasons."

Chinua nodded, but his eyes remained cautious. "Which are?"

315

"Which are . . . " Donovan thought for a moment and sighed. "I'm in a state of real cognitive dissonance right now. I thought I knew about the world. I thought I knew my place in it. I was feeling pretty good. I'm successful, I've done well." Donovan closed his eyes. Steve's face floated in front of him. "I really thought it was all up to me." He opened his eyes and looked at Chinua briefly, before closing them again.

Chinua nodded again.

"But I think what I'm realizing is that all the education, good jobs, money—"

"White women—" Chinua added.

Donovan's eyes flew open as he looked at Chinua. He bristled. *Who has been telling my business? Karen?*

"What?"

"You thought your affinity with white people, particularly white women, would insulate you from the issues experienced by the rest of your race." Chinua spoke softly and slowly, his eyes unblinking on Donovan's face. "You thought you were different."

Donovan sat silently. He didn't like this view of himself at all.

"Maybe you were just a little ashamed of your people, huh?" Chinua's gaze never left Donovan's face. "Maybe you even felt a little superior?"

Donovan frowned. "I . . . I don't know." He shook his head. "Maybe."

"And how do you feel now?" Chinua's gaze was no longer cautious. There was something else there that Donovan couldn't name. Maybe sadness.

"Confused. Ashamed." Donovan swallowed hard. "Lost."

Chinua nodded. "I've been there; I get it." He pushed his chair back from the computer, rolling it around to face Donovan squarely.

"My mother is white, and my father is Black. I really thought the world would see me as a little of both. I felt like, when I was with my mother's family, I was white. When I was with my father's family, I was Black. *I* was very clear. No problem, right?"

Donovan nodded his agreement.

"And when the media showed Black people as violent, stupid, and inferior, I could feel insulated, because I'm half white, so I wasn't really like them. Make sense, right?

Donovan nodded again.

"But my tough lesson was that the world didn't see me as white. Ever. I'm not light enough to pass, so I learned about the one-drop rule."

"What's that?"

"If you have one drop of Black blood, this society sees you as Black. That's from the plantation days where the masters used to rape the women they enslaved, and then enslave their very own children because they had Black blood."

"Oh." Donovan had never heard of that. "That's messed up."

317

"Right. So, what I had to learn was that it didn't matter how much white blood I had, this society would always see me as Black." Chinua paused. "Now, I have light skin, so in many ways white people see me as less threatening than if I had dark skin, and I have certainly capitalized on that over my life."

Donovan thought about how much he had dreamed of getting married and having a light-skinned baby with straight hair. It had never occurred to him that he might have a dark-skinned child with nappy hair. He slid down in his chair a little.

"But I have come to realize, that although I am equally Black and white, I had a lot of work to do around fully accepting the part of me that is Black. I had to work to get rid of my self-hatred."

"Self-hatred?" Donovan frowned. *How did Chinua get to that?*

"Yes. Self-hatred. We often learn it in elementary school," Chinua nodded. He seemed lost in thought for a moment. "Like, I hated the Black kids who acted "too Black." But I realize if I hate any aspect of Blackness, that means I hate that part of myself."

He turned to Donovan. "What part of yourself do you hate?"

Donovan didn't know how to respond. His head now throbbed, and he felt a strong pressure behind his eyes that made them want to close. He just wanted to go somewhere and sleep, but he had agreed to meet Kirstie for dinner, so sleep was not in his immediate future.

He shook his head. "I don't know, Chinua. I feel like my head is going to pop off. Let's get this finished. I need to go."

Chinua regarded him and turned back to the computer. He started to type and then turned back to Donovan. "Just one more thing. Tell me again who vouched for you?"

"Vouched for me?"

"Yes. Who brought you into the Cell? We only accept people on the recommendation of a trusted Cell member. Who was yours?"

"Oh. My sister, Karen, and her girlfriend, Amani."

"Okay. Talk to them if you have questions. You should be sure you want to be here."

Donovan turned back to the computer. Over the next hour they worked quickly to document the disbursements. Donovan read the numbers to Chinua from the client spreadsheet, and Chinua recorded the journal entries.

When they were finished, they saved the documents and turned off the computer. They tidied up the office, switched off the light, and left. Chinua headed to the auditorium to listen to a speaker coming that night, but Donovan headed for the exit.

As he walked down the main hallway, he noticed the sweet incense again, and wrinkled his nose. Some of the people in the Block smelled like different oils—they must put it on their skin and in their hair. He shook his head. They would never be

319

able to get a good job smelling like that. Everything about you had to be neutral in the workplace: no scents, no ethnic hair, no ethnic clothes—every freshman college student knew that.

He marveled, once again, at what the Cell had created. They were organized, well-equipped, and knowledgeable. He had to admit, if anyone had told him a group of Black people could do all this, he wouldn't have believed them. Chinua's words about inferiority and self-hatred played in his ears, but he shook the thoughts off. That *couldn't* be him. Jamaica was a Black country. *How could he possibly think like that?* Chinua must have been talking about his own experience as a Black American, not Donovan's.

And all that stuff about wanting to be with white women—that wasn't him, either. He had a Black mother and a Black sister. *How could he possibly think Black women were inferior?* That was nonsense, too. He just loved who he loved. It wasn't *his* fault they tended to be mostly white. It's not like he went *looking* for white women. It just happened that, in his world, he met more white women than Black.

The more he thought about it, the greater his conviction that Chinua was wrong about him. As he walked and settled into this thought, the cloud began to lift from his head, and the sleepiness faded. He felt his energy return. He picked up his step. Kirstie would be waiting for him, and he had a lot to make up for.

320

Chapter Fifteen

Corey sent the robot around the corner to roll under a row of cars. He brightened the display on his cell phone so he could see the video images the robot sent him. Although the sun had not yet come up, it was already hot, and he longed to take off his baseball cap and the bandana covering his face and neck. But Monica had been very clear: The Alt, using the local police forces, had placed street cameras around most US cities, and they ran all Black faces through facial recognition software, trying to identify Cell members. The less of the face they could see, the more difficult it would be to triangulate those images with MVA records.

He knelt in the narrow alley, his back to the street. He steered the small, round robot using directional arrows on his phone, and watched the video display. He set the robot's thin stream of yellow light to come on each time he sent it under a car, and turn off when it moved into full view until it disappeared under the next car.

Learning to use the robot had taken a long time, and his last few days had been all about practicing turning it from side to side, controlling the speed, and working the camera lights. He mastered running it up and down the hallways of the Block, dipping in and out of classrooms. Yesterday, he felt confident and proud of his accomplishment; today, the confidence and pride were gone, and he was very aware of the consequences of a reckless mistake. He thought again about taking off his hat to let his head breathe. The wool beanie felt damp and heavy with sweat, and his scalp itched. He dug his fingers into the wool and rubbed it back and forth across his head, sighing with relief.

He moved the robot slowly, looking for anything out of the ordinary, particularly explosives. From time to time, a text message would pop up on his screen, obscuring his view of the robot's display. *Hold it there. Pedestrian.* It was from Josh, a tall, thin white man standing lookout on the corner. This meant someone was walking by, and that Corey should keep the robot under the car until the person passed. *Moving to next block. Hold position until signal.* That meant the robot had examined all the parked cars on this side of the block and was ready to cross the street to the next block. Josh would scoop up the small, black disc and move it to the next block when it was safe. Then, Corey would resume his inspection of the parked cars.

Corey turned to look at the other end of the alley. Devonte crouched there, his back against the brick building, controlling a robot on the other block. He looked like he was playing a video game on his phone: his thumbs moved rapidly across the screen and his tongue snaked out of his mouth in concentration. Devonte was working with a young white woman named Annette, who

322

stood lookout on the street. Corey didn't know much about Annette, except that when they all met with Monica on the street that morning to be briefed and split up in teams, the words "white people" and "white supremacy" rolled off Annette's tongue as if she were talking about sports or going to the store. Corey had never heard a white person talk like that, and spent the entire meeting distracted, as he tried to figure out if Annette really was white. She *looked* white. She just didn't *sound* white.

None of the whites Corey had met since joining the Cell were anything like Minkus, or the other white people he knew from high school or community college. For one thing, they didn't act like they were in charge all the time. In his college classes, they were always the first ones to speak, and they often challenged and disrespected the teacher, especially if the teacher was not white. Last year, Corey's math professor, an Indian woman, one of his favorite teachers, was so badly abused by the white students, Corey often saw her eyes filled with tears at the end of class. Since Corey's high school math was so limited, Dr. Shah spent hours with him in her office, going back over remedial math to get him caught up. She was gentle, patient, funny, and kind, and she taught Corey so much, he aced all his math exams. Yet, the white students refused to see that side of her. They rolled their eyes at her accent and told her she wasn't teaching them properly. At the end of the year, the students gave her such poor evaluations, she eventually quit. Corey thought of her all the time. He didn't know teachers could be that caring.

323

But the white people involved with the Cell were not like the others he had met. They spoke to Monica and the other Cell members with such respect, and they listened when Monica told them what to do. They didn't come to the Block, and they didn't even know where it was. Whenever Corey interacted with the white people, it was always on the street or some other neutral place.

"They may support the movement, but they're still white," Monica said. "Some white people put on and take off their anti-racist activism as it suits them. Since it's not *their* liberation on the line, they can choose to take part when it's the in-thing, and when it's unpopular, they can sell us out."

"Can't Black people do the same thing?" Corey asked.

"Yes, they can," Monica replied. "And you're right, there's no guarantee our own people won't sell us out. In fact, we can be sure it *will* happen. But they're our people and they deserve liberation, even if they don't know it. We can only hope to liberate their minds before they turn us in." She thought for a moment. "And make sure we compartmentalize our operations so no one person knows everything." She chuckled. "But you're right. Not all skin folk are kin folk."

The sun came up, warming Corey's back and shoulders under his black sweatshirt. He wiped his forehead with his sleeve. People would be out soon. They were running out of time.

"We finished that street," Devonte said behind him. "How much more you got to do?"

"This is the last block."

"Bet." Devonte squatted and leaned his back against the red brick building. "What time will the march start?"

"About ten or so." Corey maneuvered the robot under the last car. He sighed. Despite all of Monica's instructions about what to do, he was really glad he hadn't found any explosives. But at the same time, he was surprised they hadn't found anything. The march had been planned by various Black activist groups who had come together. Some were members of the Cell, and others were still being recruited. There would likely be thousands of Black people marching and protesting what they had begun calling Baltimore's "state of oppression."

"Done." He texted Josh to pick up the robot. Josh and Annette and the other white folks would meet up with a Cell member at a parking lot downtown to hand over the robots.

"You and Annette didn't find anything, right?"

Devonte shook his head. "Man, I ain't prayed for a long time, but my ass was praying *today*!"

Corey laughed. "Me too." He stood up and stretched his arms above his head, yawning. "I have had enough of shit blowing up."

He unzipped Devonte's black backpack, which was sitting on the ground against the building. He pulled his sweatshirt off as Devonte did the same. They changed into brightly colored T-shirts and stowed their black sweatshirts, caps, and dark glasses in the backpack, which Devonte swung over his shoulder.

They stepped out of the alley and walked down Martin Luther King, Jr., Boulevard, chatting casually, their eyes scanning the street. There were few pedestrians out, which was surprising for 8 a.m. on a Saturday morning. The two men walked towards the chicken place on the corner. There, they could hang out and watch the street and the vehicles they had examined.

As they walked, they looked for trashcans and other hiding places where explosives might be. They were responsible for those two blocks of the march route. There were other Cell members placed along the entire route doing the same thing: examining vehicles, looking for trashcans, and other possible hiding places for explosives.

The chicken place was surprisingly empty, so they ordered breakfast sandwiches and pulled themselves onto stools at a high table by the window. They ate slowly, their eyes fastened on the street.

Corey wrinkled his nose at the salty food. Ever since joining the Cell, his eating habits had changed a lot. They held nutrition classes at the Block, and taught him about how Black people had developed eating habits during slavery by having to make do with the foods white people did not want to eat. Many of the enslaved were given salt pork as a staple, along with other grains. Hunger was a constant companion for slaves on many plantations, and many Black people did not have access to adequate amounts of fresh fruits and vegetables. Corey could see how his diet still consisted of very little fruits and vegetables, and plenty of salt. At the Block, they pointed out how few healthy food sources were not available in most Black neighborhoods. This was due to supermarkets not wanting to invest in those neighborhoods, and when they did, the food was poor quality (castoffs from supermarkets in other communities), or it was so expensive most people couldn't afford it.

Since he started going to the Block, Brother Carl, a tall, muscular man who ran the kitchen, introduced Corey to foods he had never tasted. He learned to like brown rice, sugar snap peas, cauliflower rice, and any stew Brother Carl made, especially peanut stew, red peas stew, and fricassee chicken. He and Devonte now got rides to supermarkets in white neighborhoods, where they enjoyed trying new vegetables. Corey discovered a love of kiwi and starfruit and had become an expert at making stir-fry with asparagus, broccoli, cauliflower, cabbage, and chicken. He enjoyed experimenting with fresh garlic, lemon juice, thyme, oregano, and a variety of peppers. He was surprised to find that most of the food he used to eat regularly now tasted greasy and salty.

Corey remembered Brother Carl saying, "They stole us from our countries where we ate healthily from the land. They put us in chains and gave us their leftovers, confined us in communities with no access to healthy foods, and now blame us for our heart disease, hypertension, and diabetes." Brother Carl crossed his thick arms over his chest. "We may not be able to get rid of the stress of being Black in America, which is killing us, but

327

we can certainly work together to grow healthy food and relearn our ancestors' ways of eating. We must live longer and better."

Corey thought about Momma and Calvin. They needed to hear this, but he hadn't been able to get either of them to come to any Cell meetings. He really wanted to bring Momma to the elders' group, but he hadn't been able to get her out of the house. He was determined to keep trying, but he didn't know if he trusted Calvin enough to vouch for him. Calvin would sell anyone out to get money for heroin. Samuel had discouraged Corey from bringing Calvin to the Block, but suggested he try to get him into one of the Cell's residential treatment centers. When Calvin was sober and could think clearly, the program would begin introducing him to the BRM ideology.

Corey put his sandwich down and noticed Devonte wasn't eating either. "Can't go back, huh?" he asked.

Devonte shook his head. "I used to love this shit. I could eat three of these." He turned his lips down at the corners. "Now, all I taste is salt and fat."

"Man, for real. I want my own garden now. Did you go by that community garden Brother Carl is growing on the East side, over near Hopkins?"

Devonte shook his head. "No. Did you?"

"Yeah. I went over there one time. We had to deliver some stuff to Brother Carl. He has it hooked!"

"Yeah?" Devonte raised his eyebrows, looking interested, although his eyes did not leave the street.

328

"Yeah. He's got beehives and he let me taste some honey. I never knew honey could taste like that."

"Honey?" Devonte wrinkled his nose.

"Naw, for real, man. You gotta taste it. This shit was fire!"

"Huh!" Devonte wasn't convinced. "What else he got there?"

"Okay, yeah, so he was growing all kinds of stuff. Tomatoes, real sweet. He had corn and collards and kale and all kinds of lettuce. Did you know lettuce could be spicy?"

"You mean like pepper?"

"Yeah. He got some like that. "Like, I never liked salad. That shit don't taste like nothing. But Brother Carl says that icewater lettuce don't have no taste and it don't have no nutrition."

Devonte grinned. "Iceberg lettuce?"

"Yeah. Iceberg." Corey nodded. "Now I know you can make salad with spinach and kale and romaine lettuce."

"Yo, so how come you ain't cookin' none of that shit at home?" Devonte glared at Corey before turning his attention back to the street.

Corey rolled his eyes. "What you mean? I cook. You're just always over at Naijah's house." Corey made his voice sweet and rolled his eyes when he said Naijah's name. "How come *you* ain't cooking at home?"

Devonte chuckled. "Because I go to the Cell and eat good food from Brother Carl. And Naijah can burn. I ain't gotta cook."

Corey eyed Devonte up and down. "Yeah, I bet she can."

Devonte chuckled.

"I've been losing weight, but you're gaining."

Devonte rubbed his stomach, grinning. "Happiness."

Corey nodded. "Yeah. A good woman can do that." He thought for a moment. "I'm trying to get there, too."

"What, you want a big belly?"

"Naw. I want a good woman." Corey smiled broadly. "And I know exactly who she is, too."

Devonte's head swung sharply from the window. "Who?"

Corey smiled and took his time answering. Devonte would have to wait for this one. "Her name is Tasia."

Devonte frowned. "Tasia who?"

Corey shrugged. "I don't know her last name. She works in the Communications Center."

"What she look like?

"She's thick and brown and beautiful. Mmm." Corey could almost see Tasia standing in front of him. "She wears those braids or twists or something. And she has a cute little girl, Sharonda."

Devonte raised his eyebrows. "You gon' be a daddy?" His head bobbed. "That's alright."

Corey and Tasia hadn't even been out on a date yet, but he knew she was right for him. As Brother Samuel always said, "When you find your queen, the ancestors whisper in your ear, and you just know." Corey just knew, and that's why he wasn't in a rush. He felt like Tasia had some things to figure out, and he wanted to give her time to do what she needed to do. When the time was right, they would both be ready.

Kirstie was so angry with him she could barely make eye contact, but Donovan was happy she agreed to come out to lunch at the Inner Harbor. Phillip and Michael hadn't arrived yet, so they were seated under an umbrella at a large table on the restaurant deck. They ordered drinks and stared out over the harbor.

Donovan sneaked looks at Kirstie over his beer. Her hair was pulled back in a ponytail, and she wore very little makeup, as was customary for her on a Saturday. Her arms were folded across her chest and she toyed with the string on her hoodie. She kept her eyes on the water and seemed to take great interest in the people getting on and off the water taxi. She had already given him a piece of her mind about his frequent and unexplained disappearances, when he went to the Block. He decided to leave her to contemplate in peace.

Michael and his wife, Kathie, arrived first. They hugged both Donovan and Kirstie and sat down. Kirstie seemed to perk up a little as she admired Kathie's haircut.

"It's so good to see you," Kirstie smiled for the first time since yesterday. "You look really great."

Donovan was relieved. Maybe, by the time lunch ended, she would have forgotten she had spent the last day cutting her eyes at him.

Kathie swung her short bob from side to side and preened. Her glossy black hair looked almost blue in the sun.

"Yes, well, I just got a new job, and I have my eye on my boss' position, so, you know what they say: you need to look the part you aspire to." She chuckled. "A little cut, a little color and, voila!"

Michael watched his wife with a wide grin. "I think it's hot."

Kathie swatted at him, her blue eyes twinkling. "Behave yourself!"

Phillip and his wife, Veronica, arrived and the round of hugs began again. The women sat on either side of Kirstie on one side of the round table, and the men sat across from them on either side of Donovan.

As soon as they ordered drinks, Veronica fixed her eyes on Donovan. "So, how're you doing, Donovan?" Her round, gray eyes regarded him without blinking.

Donovan's throat became dry, and he swallowed hard. "Wh . . . what? I'm fine. Why?"

Veronica stared at him for a moment, her eyes narrowed. "Because the world is falling apart," she said solemnly, "and I'm at a loss for words, so I wondered if you had any thoughts I could contemplate." She tucked her long, brown hair behind one ear and picked up a roll.

Michael sighed loudly. "Here she goes again." He winked

at Phillip. "I'm so glad I'm not in your bedroom when you're having your debates."

Phillip laughed. "Maybe you should be. You might learn a thing or two." He nodded towards his wife. "I may complain, but it's a good thing to listen to your wife. She's taught me a lot!"

Michael laughed and sipped his beer. "Nah. You two can solve the world's problems together. I'll hold your drinks and wait for the solutions."

Veronica shook her head and rolled her eyes. She waved dismissively at Michael. "Stop." She turned her attention back to Donovan. "But seriously, Donovan. I'm really worried. There's some crazy shit happening in this country right now. As a white person, I don't know what to do, but I feel like I should be doing *something*."

"What do you feel you should be doing?" Michael asked. "You want to get a gun and go march out there with those thugs?"

"Whoa!" Veronica exclaimed. She paused, a roll midway to her mouth. "Who are you calling thugs? Not the folks marching for their freedom?" She turned to look at Kirstie and Kathie for support, but they just stared at her in confusion.

"Who said they weren't free?" Michael asked. "There's nothing stopping them from being anything they want to be."

Phillip shook his head, looking at Michael. "I'm telling you, man. You don't want to go down this road with her."

Veronica put her hand up in her husband's direction, palm facing him. "Babe, I've got this." She turned to Michael. "So, the white man is deciding whether Black people are free. Interesting." She leaned back in her chair and folded her arms across her chest. "Tell me, white man, what equips you to determine who is free and who is not?"

Michael rolled his eyes. "I've got eyes. I work with Black people. I see Black people progressing. What's the complaint?"

Veronica shook her head. She turned to look at Donovan. "I've got Black friends," she said in an affected voice, her lips turned down at the corners. "Typical white person."

Donovan wanted to sink under the table. He didn't know what was worse—that Veronica wanted to have this conversation about race, that Michael didn't think there was a conversation to be had, or that they were talking about him as if he wasn't there. He slowly picked up and sipped his beer, both to buy time and to relieve his dry throat.

"Well, Donovan and I have been having this conversation for the past few weeks," Kirstie said, "and I don't like what's going on around us, but I also don't think it has anything to do with Donovan. He's not like those folks marching and carrying on."

Veronica's head whipped around in Kirstie's direction. "How so?"

Kirstie shrugged. "What's Donovan got to complain about?" She looked at Donovan. "He's got a good life. He's not even from this country. He can't talk about slavery and Jim Crow and all those things the resistance folks are complaining about."

Donovan swallowed again. "Well—"

"But wait!" Veronica jumped in, eyes flashing at Kirstie. "What difference does it make where he comes from? He's Black in America. Do you even know what that's like?"

"Do *you*?" Michael asked.

Veronica's head whipped around again. "I don't. But I have listened, and I have heard, and it's not good. That's why I'm asking Donovan how he's doing. Because, from what my Black friends tell me, it's pretty bad right now."

"So," Donovan began again. It seemed like he needed to speak up, but didn't know what he would say. He cleared his throat.

"Wait," Kirstie interrupted. "Veronica, why do you care so much? It's not even your business. What does it have to do with you?"

"Veronica is one of those sensitive snowflakes who gets upset and wants to go out on the street and march," Michael said. "Go ahead. No one's stopping you. But, if I'm on guard duty when I see you out there, you won't get treated any differently."

"Okay, okay, folks," Phillip held up his hands. "Let's call a truce here and order some food." He nodded to the young, male waiter pacing watchfully near the table. "I don't think we're making any progress."

While the waiter took their orders, Donovan breathed deeply, trying to calm himself. He finished his beer quickly and ordered another. Even the beers didn't steady him.

When the waiter left, they sat in silence for a few moments. Donovan gulped down the third beer the waiter brought him and ordered another.

"Well, I don't know what's going on, but I don't like what it's doing to Donovan. He's been so distant and preoccupied since this all started," Kirstie sipped her wine. "I just want my old Donovan back." She glanced at him over her wineglass and looked away quickly, her eyes filled with tears.

Donovan sighed. "I'm sorry." He rubbed his forehead and covered his eyes with his hands for a moment. "I'm just confused about what to do and where to fit in."

Veronica's voice softened. "What's confusing for you?"

Donovan hesitated. *How do I discuss this with white people?* "I don't know. I just have been seeing things differently lately. Or maybe the world is just falling apart after all, but I'm just now realizing how much racism affects me. I guess I didn't see it before. At work—"

"At work, he just needs to stand up for himself more!" Kirstie interrupted, her eyes flashing. "He needs to tell them he doesn't want any more of their shit assignments."

Donovan sighed. "Well, yes. That is true, but it's so much more complicated than that."

"Okay . . ." Kirstie shook her head. "I think you're being too sensitive, and you just need to get tough with them."

"That doesn't work. The last Black associate who spoke up, got fired." Donovan wrapped his palm around the cool glass,

336

wishing he could rest it on his hot forehead. "And it's happened more than once."

"I don't think this is all about race. I don't see color, and I don't see the big deal. You're just a person to me, not a *Black* person. This is 2024." She shook her head. "I can't believe we're still talking about this stuff!"

"You can't believe we're still talking about this stuff because we should have fixed it by now, or you can't believe we're still talking about this stuff because you think it's already over?" Veronica asked.

Kirstie shrugged, her two hands out, palms up. Her face contorted as if she had heard something ridiculous. "It's over. It's done. We've moved on." She shook her head again and picked up her wineglass. "But it can't be done, because you all keep talking about it. How can we move past it if we won't let it go?"

"You've moved on," Veronica said. "Because you were never there."

Kirstie stared at Veronica, her lips pressed tightly together. "I don't know how you can say that, considering most of the men I have dated have been Black."

"And you think that means you understand what it is to be Black in America?" Veronica asked, her lips twisted. "Or does it just mean you're satisfying a fetish?"

"Okay!" Phillip jumped in. "I think we should stop this here."

Kirstie and Veronica glared at each other. Kirstie finally turned her head away from Veronica, wiping tears.

Michael shook his head, smiling, but somehow, he didn't seem amused. He glanced over at Kathie, whose wide eyes looked as if she had seen something frightening. Michael shook his head again, wiping his hand slowly over his nose and mouth.

Donovan gave in and leaned his cool, moist beer glass against his forehead, closing his eyes. Four beers had not quenched his thirst, and now he also felt slightly tipsy. He had barely touched his food. He wanted to throw up.

"Does anyone want dessert?" Phillip rubbed his hands together and smiled broadly. The rest of the table sat silently, looking in different directions. "Okay! *I* will have dessert. I'm going to order a few and we can share." He nodded to the young waiter.

While Phillip ordered dessert, Michael slid his arm along the back of Donovan's chair and leaned over to whisper in Donovan's ear, "We are looking for someone who can help us divert the disaster that's going to happen with the resistance people," he said.

Donovan frowned and removed the glass from his face, resting it on the table. "What do you mean?" he whispered back.

Michael watched Phillip talking to the waiter for a moment. He leaned in towards Donovan's ear again. "They are going to get massacred."

Donovan turned to look at Michael, who had to pull back, so they didn't kiss. "Who's going to be massacred?"

"The resistance folks." Michael glanced at the others again. Kirstie and Kathie were whispering to each other, their heads close together. Phillip and Veronica stared out at the water.

Michael turned back to Donovan. "The powers that be want to launch an all-out attack and take the resisters out. They want to drop a bomb wherever they congregate. But cooler heads are looking for another option, one that doesn't involve killing thousands of people."

Donovan thought of the thousands of BRM members who marched in Charlottesville, and all the people he had seen at the Block, and the people in all the cells around the country. Hundreds of thousands.

"Okay. That would be bad." *Could this lunch get any worse?* He felt chilled now and wiped the beer glass condensation off his forehead.

Michael nodded. "It *will* be very bad." He looked at Donovan keenly. "We need to stop it from getting to that."

"How?"

Michael slid his arm further along the back of Donovan's chair and leaned in closer. "We need to take out the leaders and save the civilians." He watched the waiter put the desserts on the table.

Donovan noticed the mixture of garlic and beer on Michael's breath and turned his head away, pretending to look out over the water. "Wow."

"I know." Michael inched in a little closer. Donovan resisted the urge to pull away. "But it's better than the alternative, which is killing all those people."

Donovan nodded, his mind racing. *Karen and Amani.*

"But we need a way in," Michael continued. "We need to get to them. We need information. That's the only way we can be specific about who we target."

"What are you whispering about over there?" Phillip asked. "Come on, guys!"

Michael held up his hand at Phillip and turned to Donovan again. "It won't be hard for you to get in. They're recruiting heavily right now." He whispered.

Donovan avoided looking at Michael.

"You just need to find someone to let you in. And then, you just need to tell us who the leaders are."

Michael's breath warmed Donovan's ear, and the garlic-beer scent wafted across his nose. Donovan's stomach turned over.

"We will take it from there." Michael leaned away from Donovan and turned back to the table. "So, what are we having for dessert?"

Chapter Sixteen

The pedestrian traffic on the street had picked up, and the police were putting up barricades along the sidewalk. They must have blocked the street to cars, because apart from the cars they had just scanned for explosives on the side street, there were no other vehicles on the road. Corey and Devonte watched the police carefully. It would be easy for one of them to slide something under the parked cars along the route.

Even from inside the chicken place, Corey felt the tension on the street. The police kept their hands on their guns, only letting go of them when moving barricades. National Guardsmen stood by watching, their rifles held across their chests. Pedestrians skirted around the police and Guardsmen as if they had something contagious, staring at the ground as they walked by, bodies stiff and alert. One mother, walking with her young child, snatched the little boy away as he tried to wander up to a Guardsman. The Guardsman stood straight and made no attempt to look at the little boy. As she pulled him away, the mother chided her child, and he pouted, gazing back at the man with the gun as his mother pulled him along. Corey tried to imagine what she said to him.

The police put up barricades. Crowds formed in groups on the blacktop. Many carried signs saying things like: *Black Lives Matter*; *Stop Police Brutality*; *Slavery Behind Us; Liberation Before Us*. The protestors were of all colors, and Corey was surprised at how many white people carried signs.

"Yo, man, you see all these white people?" Corey asked. "Where they come from?"

"Yeah, a lot of folks are coming out against The Alt and Sumpter," Devonte said. "Some of them are real upset."

"That girl, Annette . . ."

Devonte laughed. "She's a trip, right?"

"I never heard a white girl talk like that. When I was in college those girls only wanted one thing from me. And it wasn't to talk about racism!"

Devonte laughed again. "For real, right?"

"When did white people start caring about *us*?" Corey rolled up the barely eaten sandwich in his napkin. "All the white people I ever met acted like there was something wrong with me, just for being on this earth. I don't know if I can trust them."

"Well, you heard what Monica said: trust only the ones we have already verified. But don't trust them with *everything*. They can be real fickle when it comes to standing up for us. You just never know."

"That's right."

"But some of these folks we're working with have been okay. Annette is crazy, but I think she's for real. And Josh. I don't know all the others, but these ones have been real cool."

Corey nodded. There was still so much information to take in. Sometimes, he felt so overwhelmed, he just wanted to lie down and take a nap.

Devonte checked his phone. "Time to roll."

Corey gathered up their trash and threw it away while Devonte grabbed the backpack. Out on the street, the sun beat down intensely and the air was thick. The concrete sidewalk absorbed and radiated the sun's heat back into the air. Sweat beaded on his head and trickled down his face and neck. It had been a cool start to the summer, but it felt like the middle of July right now.

They wandered along the street, mingling with the growing crowds, but never losing sight of the blocks they cleared. The sidewalks on those blocks were nearly empty. Most of the pedestrians were out on Martin Luther King Boulevard, standing around with signs, waiting for the march to start. Regular pedestrians went about their business, winding their way through the groups of protestors, the police, and the Guardsmen. They moved quickly, nervously, their eyes darting around at the people standing about. Corey understood how they felt. *Who knew what was about to pop off?* He couldn't blame them for feeling unsure. *He* felt unsure.

On one of the corners, a flatbed truck was parked, blaring Bob Marley's "Redemption Song" from huge speakers. The crowds grew rapidly, until the sidewalk could no longer contain them, and they spilled into the street, pushing aside the barriers. By now, the protestors far outnumbered the police and Guardsmen, and Corey searched the faces in the crowd, looking for Cell members. Monica and the intelligence team had decided to send a few thousand members to inconspicuously mingle with the crowd, looking for signs of people who were there to start trouble, as well as to watch the police and Guardsmen for any sign they planned to attack the protesters. Corey and Devonte were a part of that team.

Other Cell members were preparing to take part in a massive peaceful action. Corey didn't know what it was, just that they would be dressed in white. There were several thousand Cell members, either carrying concealed weapons through the crowds, or hiding on rooftops with sharpshooter rifles. They also hid in buildings, and in vehicles, examining the crowds through their scopes, prepared to protect the unarmed protestors.

Corey realized the other reason he hadn't been able to eat the chicken sandwich: his stomach tumbled over and over like the time Momma took him and Calvin to Six Flags and he went on the rollercoaster. That had been his first *and last* time on any type of ride. Unlike Calvin, he didn't enjoy the adrenaline rush or the flips and turns of his stomach. It left him feeling unsettled, like he wanted to lie perfectly still until his stomach stopped churning.

344

He felt like that now; his stomach rolled and dipped, and he wanted to stop walking and stand still until it stopped. But he forced himself to keep walking, a slight smile on his face, hoping his stomach would settle down.

The crowd organized itself into rows, ten people across, and all turned toward downtown. Corey watched with amazement as, with no leadership or guidance that he could see, thousands of people began walking in the same direction, carrying their signs, singing along to the music; the truck was now blasting Marvin Gaye's "What's Going On?" When they got to the chorus, like a choir, some people sang the main lyrics and others answered with the refrain.

Corey and Devonte moved back against the row of buildings to get out of the way of the moving crowd, both in the street and on the sidewalk. The police and Guardsmen also stepped back to avoid being run over. The crowd made no attempt to move around anything in its way, but pushed forward, the force of thousands moving everyone, whether they wanted to move or not. Corey flattened himself against the building, but the crowd needed more room. He found himself being pushed along and looked around frantically for Devonte.

Two hands grabbed him by the armpits and lifted him three steps onto the stoop of a house. Confused, he looked up to see the face of a cell member, Maurice, grinning at him. Maurice set him on his feet and disappeared into the crowd. Corey looked around and saw Devonte on the stoop of the building to his right. Devonte looked as confused as Corey.

They watched the crowd walk by for an hour. The marchers sang, danced, and chanted to the music as they moved, and Corey wondered if everyone in Baltimore had come out. Many of the police and Guardsmen had also retreated onto the stoops of houses. There were far fewer of them than had been on the street before the crowd began moving. Corey suspected the others had been pushed along with the crowd. The few left behind looked scared and confused.

Powerless. The word passed through Corey's mind as he watched the police and Guardsmen. Although their hands stayed on their guns, Corey was sure they knew, as did every person who passed them, that the few bullets in those guns would not save them if this march turned bad. Sure, they may be able to shoot a few people, but it would only take a few seconds for them to be overpowered.

Corey smiled at the thought. *What happens when people who thrive on their power lose it?* He could hear Brother Samuel say, "That's what racism is all about; white people trying to hold onto their power." Corey wondered what it felt like for the powerful to suddenly feel powerless.

As he looked around, he saw Devonte raise his arm and point towards the back of the crowd. Corey squinted to see what Devonte was pointing to. The marchers stretched almost as far as Corey could see; the little dots of color streamed off the highway

346

and over the hill onto MLK Boulevard, moving towards Corey and Devonte. But, in the far distance, the little dots of color became a sea of white. Corey realized there were thousands of people marching towards them dressed completely in white.

Corey glanced over at Devonte, who watched the crowd, his mouth open. His eyes met Corey's and he nodded his head, eyes wide. He pointed towards his chest. *That's us!* He mouthed the words.

Corey nodded and turned to look back at the crowd in white. They were far away, and it would take them half an hour or more to get to where Corey and Devonte stood. Meanwhile, the crowd in front of them continued to stream past, as the police and Guardsmen looked on, arms crossed over their chests. Across the street, on the third-floor balcony of a brick house, a television crew stood filming the events on the street. The reporter, a young Black woman wearing jeans and sneakers, with hair pulled back in a ponytail, spoke into a microphone, facing the camera, her back to the street.

For the next half hour, Corey and Devonte stood on the stoops watching the white Cell members drawing close. They moved in groups of two hundred or so, separated by one lone figure walking between each group. As they drew closer, Corey noticed that they were not singing, chanting, or dancing like the crowd that marched ahead of them. Instead, they seemed to glide, walking in step, slowly and deliberately. They were mostly women, children, and elders.

347

At the front of the crowd marched the tall elder who questioned Corey after he flipped out at the unveiling. He didn't know her name, and always thought of her as Grey Locs, because of the grey locs piled on her head. She walked straight, her head held high, carrying something in her hand. Instead of the white scrubs, she and the others wore loose flowing white pants and long white tunic shirts. A slight breeze picked up the hems of their pants and shirts and they billowed out behind the marchers, so they looked like they were gliding along.

Corey, grateful for the breeze in the stifling heat, took a rag out of his back pocket, wiped his forehead, and watched the group coming closer. There was a block between the Cell members and the crowd who walked ahead of them. The chanting and singing of the earlier marchers faded into the distance, replaced by an eerie silence, as the marchers in white grew closer. The truck with the speakers was gone now. Even those people, standing on the sidewalks watching the march, stood silent. Corey's ears buzzed with the transition from pandemonium to quiet.

As they grew closer, it became clear that Grey Locs carried a small metal dish from which floated a thin stream of incense smoke. They were too far away for Corey to actually smell the incense, but his senses filled in the scent for him. He imagined its sweetness, felt the slight sting of smoke in his eyes. He smiled at the thought. It felt so familiar, comforting. His anxiety began to fade, and he felt himself reach towards the Cell marchers, as if to hug them although his arms never left his sides. These were *his* people.

As Grey Locs passed by, Corey was sure she turned her head slightly and held his gaze for a second. A slight smile appeared on her lips before she looked away. Corey bowed his head in respect. He didn't know why he did; he had never done that before, but something about her was so honorable, so regal. She inspired his reverence.

The Cell members walking between the groups were elders, and it appeared that each elder led a group of several hundred. At the very back of the crowd, it was clear that hundreds of the marchers were children, and they bounced along, hopping, skipping, and running alongside adults who walked in step with the elders. While the rest of the marchers moved in disciplined form, the rows of kids created a stark contrast with the adults. Corey smiled, wondering if Tasia and Sharonda were among them. He searched through the crowd, but they were too far away for him to see the faces at the back of the group.

Group after group of Cell marchers passed, each elder carrying incense, some also carrying carved wooden walking sticks. It took a full hour for the groups to pass. The elder leading the final group of adults and children was a stooped, bald man Corey had not seen before. He walked past Corey and stopped, holding up his stick. The group behind him stopped also. He stood for a moment, his stick in the air, before turning to face the marchers. He lowered his stick and tapped the ground with it.

Immediately, the entire group sank to the ground, sitting cross-legged. A few of the younger children danced around before joining the adults on the ground. The adults closed their eyes and sat calmly. The younger kids looked around at the watching crowd.

There was silence for several minutes. It seemed no one, either on the street or on the sidewalk, moved. Corey turned to look at Devonte, eyes wide. Devonte shrugged.

"This is the Baltimore City Police Department," a voice barked over a bullhorn. "You are instructed to disperse. If you refuse to do so, you will be arrested."

No one sitting on the ground moved, although some of the older children looked at the adults with alarm. A few of the adults nodded at the young people reassuringly and closed their eyes again.

"You are ordered to disperse," the bullhorn repeated. "Now!"

Still, no one in the street moved. Out of the corner of his eye, Corey saw several police cars coming off the highway, down the empty street, blue and red lights flashing. His heart sped up. *Some shit is about to go down.*

As their reinforcements arrived, the few police and Guardsmen on the sidewalk and on stoops regained their confidence, and several of them strode out onto the street and surrounded the sitting Cell members. The members did not open their eyes and did not move, although some of the children slid closer to their adults.

One police officer walked up to the sitting elder, pointing his bullhorn at the older man's head.

"This is your final warning!" He barked the words into the bullhorn, just a couple of inches from the man's ear. Corey flinched at the thought of how deafening that must have been, but the older man sat, his eyes closed, and did not move.

The scene on the street froze. The group sat still. They were surrounded by police. The newly arriving group of law enforcement carried rifles, shields, and riot helmets. Their numbers grew by the minute. As police cars pulled up on the side streets, officers jumped out and ran to take up position around the group.

A woman's voice rang out clear and loud singing:

I don't feel no ways tired!
I've come too far from where I started from;
Nobody told me the road would be easy
But I don't believe you brought me this far to leave me.

She sang with the kind of feeling Corey remembered from attending church with his grandmother when he was little. His eyes closed involuntarily, and he smelled the old wooden pews, ancient carpet, and burning candles of the small, storefront church on Pennsylvania Avenue. His chest felt full and heavy, and he wanted to cry. He knew the pain she sang about. He understood.

With one voice, the rest of the crowd joined her, singing in three-part harmony, their voices clear and strong. The higher voices of the children, carried over the deeper, resonant voices of the adults, and the sound was full, rich, and painful. Corey opened his eyes and choked back a sob. He looked over at Devonte, who wiped his eyes with the back of his hand. Corey nodded. *He wasn't crazy. This shit was deep.*

The cop standing behind the elder handed his bullhorn to another officer and reached down, dragging the older man to his feet. Instead of standing, the man's legs went limp and the cop found himself dragging the man on the ground. Another cop stepped in to help, and they each grabbed the man under an arm and began to pull him. He did not move or resist, and the cops seemed unsure of what to do when they had dragged him over to the sidewalk. By now, he lay on his back, his shoes left where he had been sitting, his heels bleeding from being scraped on the asphalt. He continued singing, his eyes closed, his head back.

The cops were confused and left him there. They went back to the crowd, trying to drag another man to his feet. This man also went limp and continued singing, his eyes closed. The two cops exchanged glances and abruptly dropped the man. One of them pulled his nightstick out of his belt and raised it, bringing it down on the older man's head. Blood gushed from a jagged cut on his scalp, pouring down his white shirt and soaking the ground.

The man lay perfectly still, and Corey wondered if they had killed him.

Other police pulled out their nightsticks and moved closer to the group, raising their sticks above their heads. Corey held his breath. His heart beat so hard he felt the rhythm in his ears, and his head felt light.

A loud bang rang out and a police officer fell forward into the seated crowd, his nightstick flew out of his hand and over the heads of the crowd as he dropped. He fell onto a young woman, who moved over and continued singing. He lay on his face in the street, unmoving.

The rest of the cops dropped to the ground, their guns in their hands, looking around to see where the shot came from. Corey didn't see anyone with a gun, but suspected it came from one of the Cell snipers hiding in the buildings.

"Hands up!" a voice called out.

"Don't shoot!" the crowd replied. The people sitting lifted their hands in the air.

"Hands up!" the voice repeated.

"Don't shoot!" the crowd chanted.

A woman screamed. Corey looked towards the back of the group and saw a police officer trying to drag a small child out of a woman's arms. She held the child around the waist and the cop pulled both of the child's hands. The toddler was wailing, and it seemed the cop would pull his arms out of their sockets. When the woman would not let go, the cop released the child's hands, balled his gloved fist, and slammed it into the woman's face. She slumped to the ground. Another woman, sitting next to her, grabbed the child just as his head was about to hit the ground. The woman the cop punched remained slumped on the ground, her legs still crossed in front of her body, her forehead on the pavement, her arms stretched oddly on either side of her, as if she had been flying.

Another shot rang out. The cop flew backwards. He lay on the ground, his head rolling from side to side. He seemed stunned but uninjured. Another cop stepped toward the woman who had grabbed and cradled the crying child. He raised his nightstick over her head. Another shot rang out. It must have missed him, because he ducked, then jumped back up and ran behind a nearby police vehicle.

Suddenly, the air was filled with the sound of multiple shots, coming in rapid succession, as the police ducked and ran for cover. The shots came from all around them. People standing on the sidewalks ran behind buildings and into alleys, seeking cover. The shots were aimed at the police. The wall of riot police, standing behind the marchers, scattered. Officers dropped to the ground, ducking behind their riot shields.

Corey crouched low on the stoop, his eyes wide, looking around. The elder who had been beaten by the cop lay still in a pool of blood, and Corey knew he was dead. But his attacker, who had fallen into the crowd when he was shot, had fled. The young woman he had fallen onto, and the others in the group, sat with their hands in the air chanting, "Hands up, don't shoot." They paid no attention to the chaos all around them.

Corey was confused. Between the loud bangs from the guns, and the people running for cover, he couldn't figure out what was happening. Directly across from him, a Guardsman raised his rifle, pointing it at the seated crowd. He suddenly fell backwards and lay still, staring up at the sky, blinking rapidly behind his helmet shield. He lay there for a moment before rolling onto his side and pushing himself up into a sitting position. He examined his body, feeling around his bulletproof vest. He seemed satisfied there were no bullet holes and he looked dazed.

Rubber bullets! The thought hit Corey as he watched the Guardsman sitting on the ground. They weren't using live ammunition. He sighed with relief. That made sense; Monica had been very clear they would use non-lethal methods unless they had no choice. The Cell snipers were simply there to protect the marchers, and to draw the attention of the police and Guardsmen away from the women, children, and elders.

The whir of helicopter blades caught Corey's attention and he looked up to see two aircraft circling the street. They were scouring the roofs of buildings, searching for the snipers. But the Cell members were too smart for them. They were inside buildings, and in the trunks of cars, completely hidden from view. They were causing mass chaos and panic for the police and Guardsman.

355

A loud bang sounded. A bright flash exploded in the group of crouched riot police. They broke from their line, running towards their cars, ducking behind their vehicles, guns poised over the hoods. The flash bangs exploded every few seconds, for what seemed like forever to Corey.

Devonte appeared at the bottom of Corey's stoop. He waved and pointed towards the alley. It probably *was* a good idea to move, now that the sidewalks were clear. He leaped down the steps in one movement and followed Devonte towards the alley. They needed to get to Monica to find out what needed to be done next. With more police and Guardsmen arriving by the minute, it seemed like the Cell members were trapped.

Lisa cradled the little boy in her arms, covering his head with her hands. He sobbed against her neck, his hot tears streaming down inside her loose white shirt. Jessica and Mia sat close to her, looking around, eyes wide. She was surprised they didn't cry and didn't seem afraid. Even when the cop raised his baton to hit her over the head, they braced themselves as did she, but they didn't cry. Even as the shots rang out, and the cops fell around them, Jessica and Mia didn't cry. They knew the Cell snipers were not using real bullets, and they knew the police weren't seriously injured. All the preparation, the drills, the mock protests, the rehearsals with flash bangs at the Farm, had seemed so over-the-top to her at the time, but she now understood how important it had been. All but the very youngest children sat stoically, their hands in the air chanting, "Hands up, don't shoot!" She was proud of them, despite her own fear.

She rocked the little boy slowly, humming in his ear, trying to drown out the noise and chaos around them. She reached out to touch his mother, still slumped over in front of her.

"Beverley," she called out to the unconscious woman, pulling at her shirt. "Beverley, are you okay?" But Beverley didn't respond, and Lisa noticed with concern, that her body jerked slightly, in rapid, sudden movements, her back stiffening and relaxing, then stiffening again, arms twitching as they lay spread on either side of her.

Lisa rocked the little boy and looked around. She needed to find a member of the Cell's medical team, but they probably wouldn't be able to get to Beverley. Standing or moving might be seen as signs of aggression by the cops.

"Kai, where are you?" she whispered. Kai was with the legal team, who had been diverted to preparing bail for protestors, so that they would be bailed out first thing Monday morning. He was conflicted about Lisa and the girls taking part in the protest, but Lisa reassured him they needed to do it. After everything they had experienced, they just needed to feel they were doing *something*.

Clutching the little boy to her chest, she scooted closer to Beverley, careful not to look as if she was trying to get up. She rubbed her hand along Beverley's back as she twitched. She was slumped in a strange position and, surely, it couldn't be good for her head to be down like that. Lisa pulled at Beverley's shoulder, trying to sit her up, but with the toddler in one arm, she only had one hand free and wasn't strong enough.

She looked around. Most of the Cell members sitting around her were women and children. The women remained focused on encouraging the children to chant so they wouldn't be scared. The women smiled broadly, their eyebrows raised, their heads nodding in time with the chant. The children watched them and followed along, their expressions matching those of the women.

One person was watching Lisa struggle—Esther, the Housing Coordinator at the Farm. Lisa's eyes met Esther's, who nodded at her.

"I'm coming," she mouthed to Lisa. She looked around at the chaos, waiting for two cops to run past. When it was clear, she slid onto her belly and crawled on her elbows towards Lisa. A few of the women scooted children over so she didn't have to crawl around them and could continue in a straight line.

It took forever for her to crawl half a block to Lisa; meanwhile, the toddler stopped wailing and began pulling at his mother's shirt, gasping loudly as he tried to stifle shuddering sobs. His little shoulders shook with every breath.

"Mommy. Mommy!" he called. "Mommy, wake up!"

But Beverley didn't move, and her son called louder to her. Lisa captured his hand and kissed it.

"Mommy's okay. We're going to wake her up." She didn't know what else to say. She didn't even know this child's name. "She's okay," she repeated.

By the time Esther got to them, the street had quieted down. The Cell marchers had stopped chanting and had lowered their arms. They sat silently, looking around.

There were no more rubber bullets flying, and Lisa knew the Cell snipers had retreated to take cover. Fewer police and Guardsmen were running around; instead, the air was filled with the sound of helicopter propellers. Lisa looked up and saw both police and television helicopters circling overhead.

A microphone appeared in front of Lisa's face. She looked up, startled. A young white woman wearing a baseball cap stood smiling broadly at Lisa. *How can she be here?*

"Hi! I'm Annabelle from MSNBC," she said cheerfully. She paused and looked over at Beverley. "What happened to your friend here?"

Lisa looked up at the reporter, blinking.

"Help me lift her up!" Esther said, pulling Beverley by the shoulders. "You!" She pointed at Annabelle. "Put that microphone down and help me. This woman is badly injured."

Annabelle straightened her back and frowned. "Ma'am, I'm just a reporter. I'm here to find out—"

"Well, while you're finding out, help me lay this woman on her back." Esther stopped and looked up at Annabelle. "Unless you're just here to watch her die. Is that what good reporting has come to?"

Annabelle hesitated and looked around. Flashing lights and sirens filled the air, but the police and Guardsmen were going building to building, banging on doors, and from time to time, kicking them in. They were searching for the Cell snipers and paid little attention to the Cell members sitting in the middle of the road.

Annabelle handed the microphone to the cameraman standing behind her. He stuck the microphone in his back pocket and leaned his camera in closer to the women on the ground.

"Help me lift her. We need to get her out of this position and laying prone," Esther said.

With Esther's and Annabelle's two hands and Lisa's one hand, they pulled Beverley up so that her forehead was no longer on the ground. As they sat her up, she slumped against Esther's body, her head hanging backward, mouth open.

Annabelle gasped, one hand flying to cover her mouth, her eyes wide as she stared at Beverley's face.

"What happened to her?" she asked.

Lisa pressed her lips together, her stomach churned and her skin crawled. She shook her head as she looked at Beverley's battered face. A large knot, almost the size of Lisa's fist had formed on her forehead from where her head hit the pavement. The left side of her face was so bruised and swollen, her left eye had disappeared into the space between her swollen cheek and swollen forehead. She was almost unrecognizable. Across her cheek were four bloody, crescent-shaped cuts, each about an inch long.

"Mommy!" The toddler wailed. Lisa turned his face away from his mother and rocked him harder.

"A cop punched her because she wouldn't let him take her baby," Lisa said between stiff lips.

"What? That's from a punch?" Annabelle gestured to the cameraman to film Beverley's face. She continued holding Beverley up with one hand while pulling a notebook from her back pocket with the other.

"Yep. That's what brass knuckles do," Esther said, raising Beverley's eyelids, one at a time. Her left pupil was completely dilated. "We've got to get her to a hospital. This is bad."

Esther looked up at Annabelle. "So, are you here as a spectator or are you here as a human?"

"Wh . . . what?" Annabelle slid her notebook back into her pocket.

Esther spoke slowly, as if to a young child. "Are you here to get a story? Or are you here because you care about human rights?"

"I . . . I care about human rights."

Lisa almost felt sorry for Annabelle. Esther was not one to mess with.

"Good. Then show it. Call an ambulance and go to the end blocked off by the police, and direct it over here. We don't

361

have much time." Esther pointed back up MLK Boulevard towards the highway.

Annabelle looked up at her cameraman. He shrugged, turning his lips down at the corners.

"Okay. I'll do one better." Annabelle helped Esther lay Beverley down on her back and then stood, pulling her phone out of her jeans pocket. She stepped away, talking into the phone. Lisa watched as Annabelle looked for the street signs and told someone on the phone exactly where they were. She stuck her phone back in her pocket.

"We need to clear some space on this block for the helicopter to land."

"We can do that," Esther replied. She turned and whispered to one of the women nearby, who turned and whispered to another. The word spread, person by person, and the Cell members began to move. A few brave people stood and looked around, waiting to see if the police would come, but they ran past, ignoring the Cell members. The members with small children began to dissipate, splitting into groups and moving onto the side streets where cars waited for them.

Annabelle grabbed her microphone and stood in front of the camera. "I am here on Martin Luther King, Jr., Boulevard, the site of a peaceful protest by the Black Resistance Movement. This woman was injured during the march, and we are waiting for an air ambulance to airlift her to Shock Trauma."

Annabelle leaned down and put the mic in front of Lisa's face. "Hi there. Can you tell us what happened?"

Lisa took a deep breath. "A police officer, wearing brass knuckles, hit this woman in the face because she would not release her baby to him." She shuddered. "She was completely defenseless, and he hit her." Lisa gestured to the camera to move in closer to Beverley. "You can see the damage he did to her. The police have not offered any first aid. They just left her here to die." She shook her head. "It's as if we are animals."

Annabelle swallowed hard. She turned to the camera, forcing a grim smile onto her face. "We will continue coverage of this story in a moment."

She turned back to Lisa and Esther. "Hey, listen, this is so disturbing, I want to run a story on the Black Resistance Movement." She paused and looked from one to the other. "I really am a supporter." She handed them each a card. "I know this is a much bigger movement than the two of you, but I would really appreciate it if you would give my card to your leadership and tell them I want to talk."

Lisa and Esther took the cards, nodding. Annabelle waved goodbye and went to shove her microphone in the faces of some bystanders. Beverley had stopped seizing and lay still. Her breath came in short, uneven spurts, and Esther kept her hand on Beverley's chest, monitoring her breathing.

By now, the helicopter was circling, preparing to land about a block away. The remaining Cell members formed a line on each side of the street, creating a clear path from the helicopter to Beverley. Lisa could see their loose white clothes whipped up by the helicopter blades, billowing like white sheets on her grandmother's clothesline in Alabama. Every summer she watched those sheets flap on the line and waited until Gigi instructed her to take them in. She happily obliged, clutching the warm, sun-scented cotton against her face as she tugged at the clothespins. For a moment, she longed for those simpler times. She had no responsibilities, no worries. Just those warm sheets to bury her face into. Then, looking forward to Gigi pulling back the still-warm sheets for Lisa to climb into bed before listening to the story that Gigi told from memory, not from a book. She felt her grandmother here now, her presence calm and reassuring.

Lisa found herself smiling as the paramedics ran the thruway of Cell members, pushing the stretcher. There was something so solemn, and yet beautiful about this moment. As if all the Cell members and ancestors were standing as witnesses, honoring Beverley . . . and her death.

Lisa started as the word echoed in her brain and she looked down at Beverley. Esther had placed her head on Beverley's chest, and was sobbing quietly.

"Is . . . is she . . .?" Lisa couldn't say the word.

Esther nodded, laying Beverley on the ground and moving back so that the paramedics could work on her. They began chest compressions.

Lisa turned away with the little boy who, by now, was fast asleep, his head on her shoulder. He took long, shuddering breaths, thumb in mouth. This child whose name she didn't even know had lost his mother, and Lisa hadn't been able to do anything to stop it.

Chapter Seventeen

Tasia stood in the television studio watching the production assistant pin the microphone on Carla's lapel. Carla sat very straight in the high-backed stool across from the interviewer's chair, and Tasia knew she was nervous. Carla looked very smart in her navy-blue pants suit and silky turquoise shell, her hair slicked back in a low bun. She wore the slightest bit of makeup for the cameras, but her smooth ebony skin and large, dark eyes didn't need much adornment. Tasia had never seen Carla in anything but scrubs and a bare face, her hair wrapped up with a kente cloth.

A young woman stepped up to pat at Carla's face with a makeup sponge, and Carla smiled her thanks when she was done. Carla looked over at Tasia, standing behind the line of cameras, and smiled anxiously. Tasia winked, smiled, and gave her a thumbs up. She had no doubt Carla would do great. What Tasia was far more concerned about were the complicated maneuvers they would have to go through to ensure their safety upon leaving the studios.

The leaders of the Cell had held countless meetings over the past few days to discuss the network's request for an interview. It had been a difficult time, following the murder of six

Cell members by police at the march two weeks ago. An additional eighty or so Cell members were badly beaten and hospitalized. Five members remained in critical condition. Another two hundred marchers and Cell members were arrested, and the Cell had posted cash bail for all, including the marchers not affiliated with the Cell. Some members protested about cash bail being used for white people, but Langford pointed out that a true ally is someone willing to sacrifice body, reputation, and freedom for the cause of the resistance. If white people were willing to be jailed for Black liberation, we would be there to support them. The true test would be what happened after their release.

Since the march, the ranks of the Cell members and its allies had swelled by thousands. The allies had become so large, they were meeting and organizing in churches and meeting halls around the country to support the BRM. The video coverage Tasia and Carla released of police beating unarmed, peaceful marchers had gone viral, and every day, more people came forward in support.

They considered letting one of the Invisibles represent the Cell at the studio, but they felt an Invisible would not have the depth of information Carla would have as the Cell's Director of Communications. So, the decision was made to send Carla and Tasia to New York, accompanied by a large contingent of intelligence and armed Cell members, although Tasia and Carla never saw any of them, except for the large, muscular driver of the SUV that brought them from Baltimore, and an equally large bodyguard who rode shotgun.

They knew they were being closely monitored, were never out of sight of the Cell, and Tasia was in touch with Maurice, the head of the Cell's intelligence unit by cell phone. She was told there were Cell members in the studio, but she didn't know who they were. She believed completely that she was surrounded and supported, especially after her experience with the cash pickup.

Tasia checked her phone for messages. She was to maintain absolute cell phone silence unless there was an emergency, because it was possible the FBI was monitoring all cell phone activity around the studio, trying to get more information about the Cell.

The interviewer, Olivia Rosen, walked out onto the set, a tall white woman with shoulder-length brown hair, wearing a black fitted dress and matching jacket. She reached over to shake Carla's hand, and pulled herself up onto the stool. Tasia couldn't see the interviewer's face, but the smile on Carla's face was forced and frozen in place. Tasia knew Carla well enough to know that she was reacting to the interviewer's energy. *This is not good.*

A producer stepped up to Olivia and Carla, spoke briefly to them, and stepped back, counting down from five, using only his fingers for the last two numbers. When he pointed at Olivia, she smiled and turned to the camera.

"Good evening. Welcome to Straight Talk. I am your

host, Olivia Rosen, and I'm live tonight with a special guest. Dr. Carla Sinclair is professor of communications at Morgan State University, and she is here tonight to tell us about the Black Resistance Movement. For those of you who do not know, the BRM is a radical Black group protesting conditions for Black people across the country."

She turned to Carla and smiled. "Welcome, Dr. Sinclair. It's good to have you join us." Her voice dripped with icicles, despite the smile on her lips.

Carla smiled back. "Thanks, Olivia. It's good to be here."

Olivia consulted her notes. "Dr. Sinclair, what is the Black Resistance Movement?"

Carla smiled and turned toward the camera. "The Black Resistance Movement is a very large group of people of all races, numbering in the hundreds of thousands, who are fighting for Black liberation. It is our goal to ensure our people have the freedom to move freely in the streets, without fear of police brutality, to secure economic and social freedom from oppression, and to become fully self-determined."

Tasia watched the monitor closest to her. Carla appeared strong, clear, and in control. Her voice was firm, but not aggressive, clipped, but not cold. Tasia nodded, satisfied. Their rehearsals were paying off.

Olivia's smile in the monitor was tight-lipped and didn't reach her eyes. She nodded when Carla finished speaking and consulted her notes.

"When you say self-determination, what do you mean? Aren't you already self-determined?"

Carla chuckled, but not unkindly. "Goodness, no! We are far from self-determined as a people. Black people sit at the bottom of every social, physical, and economic indicator of well-being in this country. We would hardly choose that for ourselves if we were self-determined, would we?"

Carla paused and looked at Olivia, as if waiting for an answer. Olivia smiled tightly and raised her eyebrows, her shoulders slightly raised in a half-shrug. Carla chuckled again.

"Of course, we wouldn't. No, this is exactly what we want to change. We want full access to social and economic freedom."

"And what would that look like?"

"Well, for one thing, police and white militia caught beating us on video, or in full view of spectators, would not be able to continue their lives without consequences. Our lives would have value in the eyes of this society. We would have access to the same opportunities in our communities that you find in wealthy white communities. We would have access to high quality food, healthcare, education, jobs, transportation, hous—"

"But, Carla, Black people already have all those things," Olivia interrupted.

Carla raised her eyebrows and tilted her head to one side. "Do we? Do we really? How do you figure that?"

"Well, it's been over a hundred years since slavery ended. Surely enough time has passed for the Black people who want to do better to do so?"

"Really? white people fought the end of slavery, because they had free Black labor to build this country. What have we gotten for it? When will we be paid for our labor?"

"Is that what this is about? Reparations?" Olivia scoffed. "So, you all just want money?"

Carla regarded Olivia for a moment. When she spoke, her voice was quiet.

"Olivia, walk through a scenario with me. It might help," Carla said.

"Okay."

"Let's say you are a mother,"

"I *am* a mother."

"Good. So, this shouldn't be difficult for you to understand. Besides, I've read some of your writing on gender equality, so this should resonate with you." Carla crossed one knee over the other and smoothed the seam of her pants. "So, you're a mother and your daughter is raped by a neighbor, let's say. And you know who it is. What do you do?"

Olivia scoffed. "I would call the police."

"Right. Of course, you would." Carla nodded. "But what if they refuse to come?"

"Refuse?" Olivia blinked rapidly.

"Yes. What if they tell you it's not their problem?" Carla crossed and uncrossed her hands in her lap. "But you and your daughter have to see that neighbor walking around every day, and you're worried about what *just seeing him* will do to your daughter. And you also worry about him attacking her again. What do you do?"

Olivia stared at Carla. "I don't know what I would do. I would be very angry." She sounded thoughtful and honest. "What would *you* do?"

Carla shrugged. "Same as you. I would be *very* angry. But what can I do if the authorities refuse to help me?" She tilted her head again. "Would you consider taking matters into your own hands?"

Olivia nodded. "Probably."

"And what would you hope to achieve?"

Olivia's eyes shot fire. "I would want him to pay for what he did to my daughter."

Carla nodded slowly. "So, all you would want is money?"

"Money?!" Olivia burst out. "I'm not talking about money. Sure, a civil settlement would be great, but it would take more than—" She stopped abruptly and took a moment to compose herself. She chuckled slightly, but the icicles had returned.

"Dr. Sinclair, you are very talented," Olivia wagged her finger at Carla.

Carla raised her eyebrows and waited.

"I think *I'm* supposed to be the one asking the questions."

Carla shrugged. "An interview is a conversation. That's what we're having."

Olivia nodded and took a deep breath. "I want to turn to some of the footage from BRM marches." She turned toward the large monitor to her left. "I think this is some footage from Charlottesville a few months ago."

The video came up of the armed Cell members marching in Charlottesville. The camera zoomed in on them so that it seemed there were no other protestors, only Cell members. There was no sign of the white militias or the marchers carrying racist signs.

Olivia turned to Carla. "I'm sure you can see how this sight is particularly frightening—people marching in the street, carrying guns, their faces completely covered."

Carla raised her eyebrows. "I think it's so interesting that your camera angles did not include all the armed white militias and protestors carrying signs saying, "Niggers and spics go home." Where is that footage?"

"I'm not sure I know what you mean," Olivia said icily.

"Really? Because I know you have the footage. My office sent you several videos but, not to worry, because they have gone viral." Carla looked at Olivia pityingly. "I'm sorry you haven't seen them. Most of America has."

Olivia pressed her lips together. "Does BRM want to start a race war?"

Carla smiled broadly. "No. Not at all. But we are prepared to respond to one if the need arises."

"Does that include shooting police officers?"

"Some police officers were shot with rubber bullets as they assaulted unarmed civilians. I'm sure you can appreciate the fact that, if we really wanted to kill them, we would have used live ammunition." She paused. "But we didn't. Because are not here to kill. We *do* plan to get our freedom by any means necessary."

Olivia turned back to the monitor. "Let's look at some of that footage from a few weeks ago." She looked at Carla pointedly. "And let's see if it looks like the BRM is trying to avoid harming police officers."

The monitor came on, showing footage of the police officer trying to pull the toddler from Beverley's arms. Beverley's and the child's screams are loud and painful. Tasia shuddered, watching.

Olivia glanced over at the producer in confusion. He shrugged at her, eyes wide, and rushed towards the control room.

The video continued. When the police officer punched Beverley, the production assistants gasped. Beverley slumped over and the woman next to her grabbed the child. The police officer went down when he was shot but got up quickly and ran off. Beverley did not move. The video cut to a picture of Beverley's face when she was turned over by a group of women, including a white reporter. The video froze on her battered face. No matter how many times Tasia saw this footage, it always hurt her deeply. That could have been her and Sharonda.

A flurry of activity began in the studio, as production assistants ran back and forth trying to figure out who had cued up the wrong video. Tasia smiled and shook her head. *Damn, the Cell was good!*

The video went down and Olivia turned back to face Carla, lost for words.

Carla smiled wryly. "Tell me, Olivia, *who* was harmed in that video?"

"Well, that woman was—"

"That woman was protesting peacefully, sitting in the street, unarmed, with a young child in her arms." Carla leaned forward in her seat. "That police officer punched her wearing brass knuckles. To my knowledge, that is not an approved law enforcement weapon. Was that officer arrested? His face is on camera. Was he disciplined? No, he wasn't."

Olivia bristled. "But that woman put herself in that position."

Carla shook her head. "That sounds like someone saying, *if your daughter wasn't walking on the street, she wouldn't have been raped.*" Carla paused. "Except that *we* were discussing a hypothetical scenario, and that woman—her name is Beverley Henderson—is *very* real, and she is *very* dead."

Olivia struggled to compose herself. "Well, that's all we have time for today. I want to thank Dr. Carla Sinclair for joining us tonight. We will be sure to have you back to update us on the Black Resistance Movement." She reached over and shook Carla's hand before turning to face the camera. "I'm Olivia Rosen with Straight Talk. See you next time. Goodnight."

375

Carla jumped off her stool and stepped forward to talk to Olivia, but the interviewer hopped off her stool and strode out of the room without looking back. The production assistant removed Carla's microphone and thanked her for coming.

Carla and Tasia walked toward the exit of the studio, accompanied by a tall, male production assistant with cornrows and tattoos on his neck. He looked like someone Tasia had gone to high school with. At the exit, he opened the door and stepped outside ahead of them, motioning for them to wait inside. He returned a few seconds later, accompanied by their bodyguard. The SUV awaited them at the curb, the back door open.

"Here you go, ladies." He opened the door for them. "Get home safely."

Tasia looked up at him and frowned. *Did she know him?* He smiled down at her and nodded. "Take care." He remained at the door until they had gotten into the SUV and driven off.

Carla leaned her head back on the seat and sighed. She kicked off her heels and unbuttoned her suit jacket.

"You did great. Glad it's over?"

Carla nodded but seemed deep in thought.

"You okay?"

She sighed. "Yeah, I'm okay." She rolled her head on the headrest to face Tasia. "It seemed so clear that I should be the one to do the interview."

"Uh-huh. So, are you thinking it was a bad decision?"

"No. It was the right decision." Carla rolled her head to face forward. "But I think it's just hitting me what this means for my life going forward."

Tasia frowned. "What do you mean?"

Carla chuckled, but there was no joy in the sound. "I'm now the face of the BRM." She lifted both hands to rub them over her face but remembered the makeup and lowered them. "I will have to go into hiding. My life will never be the same again."

Tasia leaned back in her seat, stunned. *Why are you surprised? Are you dumb?* She quickly quieted the rebuking voice in her head. It wasn't helpful. She looked out the window, barely noticing the bright lights, traffic, and expensive-looking stores that had so captivated her on the drive in.

"I didn't think of that," she said solemnly. "I can't believe I didn't think of that."

"Yeah. I know." Carla closed her eyes. "I thought of it, but if I thought about it too long, I would have chickened out. So now . . . here we are."

They sat in silence for a moment.

"Have you got a plan?" Tasia whispered.

Carla smiled and grabbed Tasia's hand, squeezing it.

"The Cell will take care of me. I will go to the Farm tonight and work out of the communication center there. I'll be safe."

Tasia nodded, relieved.

"But . . . my family . . ." Carla's voice broke. "I won't be able to see them for a long time. Or talk to them. They won't know where I am."

"They won't tell," Tasia reassured her.

"Well, they won't tell deliberately. But they can be *made* to tell." Carla turned her head to look out the window, still squeezing Tasia's hand. "And I can't do that to them. They will have to go through enough as it is. They will be questioned and harassed. Everyone I know will be harassed."

"We're coming up to our transition point," said Luke, the bodyguard, from the front seat. "Be ready to move. Quickly."

Carla shoved her feet back into her shoes, and Tasia noticed her cheeks were wet. She sighed and grabbed her purse, trying to figure out how to comfort Carla. *What do you say to someone who is losing their family?* She swallowed hard and rubbed her chest where it ached. It always ached. Ever since Kenny.

The SUV pulled under an overpass, behind a red SUV. Two women stood outside the vehicle, waiting. Luke jumped out and opened the door for Carla and Tasia. They got out, walking quickly toward the red SUV with its deeply tinted windows, the back door being held open by a tall man with broad shoulders.

Tasia stopped for a moment, staring at the two women. They wore identical clothing to Tasia and Carla and were about the same build. But they wore shawls with hoods and dark glasses covering their faces, so Tasia couldn't tell who they were in the

378

dim light. They nodded at Tasia and Carla as they walked towards the black SUV and got in. Luke slammed the door behind them, jumped back into the SUV and it sped away.

"Let's go. Quickly," said the man holding open the door of the SUV.

Tasia and Carla got into the car, and the man got into the front seat, beside an equally muscular driver, and they drove off.

Tasia sat quietly, thinking of what Carla had said. *They could all be killed for what they were doing.*

"Will those two women be safe? Won't they be followed?" Tasia asked Carla.

"Yes. I'm sure they will. They're going to drive around Manhattan, looking at the sights for a long time. They are booked into a hotel in our names in Brooklyn. So, they will take the long route there, and by the time anyone realizes they aren't us, we will be long gone," Carla replied.

Tasia nodded. "Man, you all are so organized."

"Yeah, well, you only see the finished product. If you saw the way the sausage got made you might not say that."

As they turned onto the New Jersey Turnpike, the walkie talkie in the front seat squawked, and the bodyguard grabbed it.

"Sojourner One," he said into the radio.

The radio loudly spat static.

The bodyguard turned a dial on the radio. "Sojourner One to HQ, come in."

The static slowly became recognizable as a man's voice.

"Sojourner One, you've got an unmarked tail. Remain steady. Prepare to engage. Stand by for instructions."

Tasia and Carla looked at each other, eyes wide. They watched the bodyguard closely, trying to see his face.

The bodyguard and driver exchanged glances.

"Sojourner One, standing by," he replied.

They drove in silence for a full minute. Tasia turned her head to look out the rear window. "Can you see the tail?" She asked.

"Turn around!" The bodyguard barked harshly.

Tasia faced front quickly. "Sorry," she muttered.

They drove in silence for a few more minutes before the radio squawked again, "Sojourner One, take a detour. Route sent to your cell."

The bodyguard scrambled to pull out his cellphone. He scrolled through the map graphic on the screen. "Take the exit up ahead," he said.

The SUV exited the highway and moved through the toll booth. The bodyguard directed the driver onto a quiet country road, lined with trees. They drove through an industrial area, with dark, towering warehouses surrounded by high metal fences topped with barbed wire, set back from the road.

"Sojourner One, proceed through for Operation Sam Sharpe," the man on the radio said.

"Copy that," the bodyguard replied.

The SUV continued down the dark, twisting road. As they

turned the hairpin corners, a lone vehicle behind them cast its headlights against the dark trees, creating an eerie yellow glow on their trunks, branches looming above, dark and imposing. Tasia shivered.

"Sojourner One, you are a quarter-mile out," the radio said.

"Copy that."

The road continued to twist and turn. As they approached a turn, a tiny light beam swept across the road ahead and disappeared. The SUV continued around the turn, then climbed a hill. The headlights behind them suddenly flashed erratically, bouncing off the trees to the right and then the left before disappearing.

"Tire strips deployed. Operation Sam Sharpe complete," the radio said. "Proceed to rendezvous point."

The SUV continued climbing the hill and turned left into a wide clearing. A white minivan sat waiting, its lights off.

"Let's go, ladies," the bodyguard said as the SUV came to a halt beside the minivan. He jumped out and opened the back door for them.

As Tasia got out of the SUV and headed to the minivan, she noticed the black lettering on the side of the vehicle: *Freedom Baptist Church*. Inside the minivan sat four people, including two white women. In the front seat were another wide-shouldered driver and bodyguard. The people on the two seats squeezed over so Carla and Tasia could each sit on the end of a row. For the first time, Tasia noticed the large gun the bodyguard held across his chest as he stepped back from the vehicle and slid the door shut. Once closed, the minivan sped out of the clearing and onto the road. It twisted and turned its way back toward the highway.

Tasia looked around at the people in the vehicle. They held guns on their laps. Tasia examined the two white women. They were both in their mid-thirties, well-built, hair hidden under baseball caps. One of the women caught Tasia looking at her and smiled reassuringly.

Tasia half-smiled back and turned to look at Carla. Her boss stared out the window, a faraway look in her eyes. She reached up to wipe tears from her cheeks. Tasia turned around to face forward. It dawned on her what Carla was probably thinking. *Those vehicles tailing them had been unmarked, and there had been no scrambling of local police to intercept them. It was unlikely this would have been an arrest. They most likely would have simply been killed on that country road. Someone inside the Cell must have revealed the plan to switch to the red SUV. And that meant someone inside the Cell had helped plan an assassination attempt on Carla which, by association, also meant an assassination attempt on Tasia.*

Donovan watched Olivia Rosen interview Carla from the corner of his mother's couch, which was deeply imprinted from Conrad's body. He chewed nervously on his thumbnail as Olivia asked her questions with icy arrogance, and Carla responded with warm

382

confidence. He grimaced as Carla led Olivia down the path of the sexual assault scenario. He knew, from meetings at the Cell, that members were coached in Black liberation apologetics, spent hours practicing and receiving feedback, and that Carla had already determined the destination of the conversation before the interview even started. He knew Olivia had no hope of winning a debate with Carla and felt sorry for her that she didn't realize it.

When the video played of the police officer punching the woman with the baby, Donovan grimaced and pulled his knees up to his chest, wrapping his arms around them. He chewed on his thumbnail until he broke the skin. The salty, metallic taste of blood flooded his tongue.

At the end of the interview, he turned off the television and sat staring at the dark screen. He tried to imagine what was happening with Carla now. He knew she would get in the black SUV and then switch to the red SUV. He had created the paperwork and transferred the money for the purchase of both vehicles under the name of a dummy corporation as part of its fleet of vehicles. He also monitored the charges on the Smart Tag, which allowed the vehicles to pass through tolls without stopping to pay. This allowed him to confirm that the two vehicles had left Baltimore headed for New York.

All he had given Michael were the make, model, and license plates of the two SUVs in return for a promise to focus *only* on the Cell leaders, and not on regular members like Karen, Amani, and Paul. Just the cars, nothing else. No names or photographs of Cell members, no location of the Block, the Farm, safehouses, or anywhere else. Just the cars.

He closed his eyes, envisioning Carla sitting on her stool in the studio, her hands crossed calmly in her lap, responding to Olivia's questions, a slight smile on her lips. Was she being killed at this moment? Would he be responsible for her death? Who else was with her?

He switched to the thumb on the other hand. Michael wouldn't respond when Donovan asked him what they planned to do to Carla. He simply shrugged and shook his head, but assured Donovan he had nothing to worry about.

Donovan had only given them information about the vehicles. Nothing else. He could not be responsible for what they did with that information. He just wanted to make sure he didn't have to face Melva as she mourned the death of her children and Amani. *Who could blame him?* It had taken him a long time to figure it out: family always came first.

Corey sank closer to the ground, watching the dark green Hummer spin around and around on the country road, its lights creating grotesque arcs of light on the trees as it spun. He lowered his head when the vehicle turned towards him, hoping the occupants were too busy worrying about their own survival to notice him hiding in the trees. They might have seen him when he threw the tire strips down, but there had not been enough time for the Hummer to avoid driving over them.

He looked to his right, at Monica, attracted by the flashlight she moved up and down towards him. *Fall back.* He followed Monica, as she retreated into the woods. He saw slight movements to his left and right, as the rest of the twenty-member security detail moved with him. Behind him, there was a loud crash, and he imagined the Hummer had finally landed on its side.

He crouched behind a ridge of rocks, pulled small, high-powered binoculars from his jacket pocket, and looked out. Another vehicle arrived, car doors slammed, and he heard men's voices, but couldn't understand what they were saying. Two other Hummers parked behind the first vehicle, which lay on its side across the road, completely blocking it, tires still spinning.

There were eight men swarming around the overturned vehicle, climbing onto the top, opening the doors and pulling passengers out. They appeared stunned but unharmed, and the four men stood leaning against the vehicle shaking their heads and breathing heavily.

Corey counted twelve men altogether, dressed completely in black, wearing bulletproof vests, helmets, and carrying M16s with extended magazines. *Military.* They hadn't come to talk.

As more vehicles arrived, Monica gave the order to move out. The security team moved silently and quickly through the woods. Corey broke into a jog to keep up with the team. He had learned that, while they left no man or woman behind, they did not expect anyone to slow them down either. Corey had seen Monica run for three hours straight without slowing down or

385

stopping. His new diet and regular exercise were required for him to remain a part of this team.

The hot, thick air stuck in his throat as he ran, panting. He wanted to stop and grab a bottle of water from the small backpack he carried, but that would slow him down too much. He swallowed hard and tried to focus on not falling as he moved over the dark, uneven ground. Monica's flashlight was several yards in front of him, moving steadily. He quickened his pace. They would be picked up on another road about five miles away and would remain under cover of the forest to ensure they were not spotted from the air.

As Corey ran, he breathed deep sighs of relief that they diverted the Hummer from encountering the red SUV. He had found purpose as a member of the Cell. But right now, his purpose was even more specific: Tasia had been in that red SUV, and he had every intention of making sure nothing happened to her.

Lisa drove more than three hours to call her mother. Just outside Youngstown, Ohio, she found a truck stop with a phone booth. Kai was not happy she insisted on going alone, and she had no way of letting him know she was okay. She no longer had a cell phone, because there was no doubt her old phone was being tracked ever since she was filmed at the march. She appreciated the silence and the opportunity to think on the long ride.

She pulled into a parking space on the far side of the parking lot, away from the cameras on the building, and adjusted her light brown wig in the rearview mirror. It was a curly afro, framing her face and illuminating her dark eyes. But it was something she would have never worn before. Her delight had been the smooth curtain of straight hair she loved to feel swing back and forth as she moved. But she had neither the time, nor the energy, to do the work required to get straight hair. Since watching Beverley die in front of her, she hadn't had much energy for anything.

She got out of the blue hatchback she had signed out from the Farm's fleet, and locked the door. She slid on large dark glasses and walked into the rest stop. She followed the signs for public phones and dug in her wallet for quarters. It had been a very long time since she used a public pay phone, and she eyed the earpiece warily. No telling what germs were on *that*.

Diahann answered on the first ring. "Hello?"

"Hi, Mom." Lisa pictured her mother sitting in the grand family room of the sprawling colonial in New Rochelle. *Elite suburbia.*

"Lisa? Lisa, is that you? Oh, my God!" It was rare for Diahann Preston to sound anything but calm and slightly superior. But she sounded uncharacteristically out of control right now.

"It's me, Mom. I'm fine, but I can't talk long."

"Wh . . . what's going on? I saw you on television. What are you doing?"

"Mom, I'm involved in this movement for Black liberation. I just wanted to let you know that I'm fine. I don't know when I'll be in touch again, but I don't want you to worry."

"But Lisa, why are you doing this? You know this isn't the way to get things done. Besides, why are you all airing our dirty laundry all over the place?"

"What dirty laundry?"

"All this talk about race. We don't talk about those things publicly. Why are you doing this?" Diahann sighed loudly. "Do you know, the police were here?"

"I'm sure they were," Lisa replied dryly.

"The police!" Diahann sounded on the verge of tears. "All these police cars in front of our house and up and down the street. They questioned us for hours! They searched the whole house and went to your dad's office. And the neighbors—"

"I'm sorry, Mom. I didn't mean to involve you."

"I think they're watching us," Diahann whispered.

Lisa glanced at her watch. Esther told her she could only talk for one minute to make it difficult for the call to be traced. She would have to hang up in twenty seconds. "They probably are."

"Well, what about Jessica and Mia? I saw them on the news. They were right next to you when that woman was killed. How could you let that happen to them? Don't you care about them?"

Lisa swallowed hard. Her mother always knew how to tap right into the source of her pain and guilt. "Of course I care about them. They're fine, Mom. They're just fine."

She looked at her watch again. "I've got to go, Mom. I just wanted to let you know we're fine. Don't worry about us. I don't know when I will be able to call again."

"Wait, wait. Don't hang up." Diahann's voice caught in a sob. "*Please.*"

"Mom, I've got to go. I'm staying close by here, so I will try to call again when I can."

"Lisa—"

"Bye, Mom. I love you. Say hi to Dad for me."

She hurried out of the rest stop and jumped into the car, pulling out of the parking lot and heading back onto the highway. She got into the left lane and pressed the gas pedal to the floor, trying to put as much distance as possible between herself and the rest stop. She pulled off the brown afro wig and sunglasses and stowed them under the driver seat. She smoothed her ponytail and reached for large, blue-rimmed glasses with clear lenses.

Blue and red lights flashed up ahead, and a convoy of Ohio State Police vehicles barreled towards her on the opposite side of the highway, their sirens blaring. She moved into the right lane and slowed down, blending with the slower traffic to avoid attracting attention. She watched them in the rearview mirror as they turned into the rest stop. It would be a long time before she spoke to her parents next. She wondered if she would ever see them again.

Chapter Eighteen

On the top floor of the Block, the Security Control Center buzzed with activity. Corey passed room after room of Cell members in teams, plotting points on oversized maps or grouped around a series of television monitors watching traffic camera footage. In one room, a forensic team examined piles of papers. Corey guessed they were reviewing accounting transactions, looking for mistakes that may have led to detection.

Corey nodded to the security guards stationed along the hallway. The activity up here was very different from the activity in the rest of the building. On the lower floors, activities proceeded as normal, whereas up here, the entire floor was in a state of high alert.

The fact that there was a mole in the Cell was a closely guarded secret. Maurice and Monica met with every member of the security detail, both those who accompanied Carla and Tasia to New York, and those who had only a peripheral knowledge of the plans for the trip. Corey only knew about the members on his security team, but he knew enough about Cell operations to be sure he had only been briefed on a small part of the plan. No one ever knew everything.

In the main Control Room, Monica stood in front of a wall of large television screens. President Jackson was speaking on a stage, denouncing The Alt's attempts to intimidate early voters. A sea of red, white, and blue *Jackson for President* signs waved in front of him.

"We have less than two months before the election," he said, as videos of armed white militia standing outside early voting sites played on the screen behind him. "We need to decide who we are as a country."

"We've already decided who we are as a country," Monica muttered to the screen as Corey walked up to her. "You're the only one that missed the memo."

"What's going on?" Corey asked.

Monica startled and looked at him. "Oh, Corey. Hi." She turned back to the screen, gesturing at it. "The Alt are sending militia to stand outside all early voting sites where there are a lot of voters of color."

"Ah, shit," he said. "Sorry," he added quickly, looking at Monica.

Monica shrugged and turned back to the screen. Corey had never seen her look so worried, and it caused his stomach to churn.

President Jackson was saying: "These racial tensions harm all of us. Reginald Sumpter and his racist rhetoric will only further harm this country. We can do better. We *must* do better! In my second term, I will bring this country together in a way Reginald Sumpter cannot. Unless we all thrive, no one in this country thrives."

The President pumped his fist in the air. *Sideways so it doesn't appear militant.* Corey shook his head slowly.

"Vote for me on November 5, and let's bring peace, unity, and prosperity to our country. May God bless you, and may God bless the United States of America!"

Monica turned away from the screen. "There's a lot going on," she said, walking towards her desk. "We are having a meeting with La Lucha to decide how to respond." She picked up a notebook and sat on the edge of the desk. "The police won't bother the white militia, but if we show up, they will arrest us. We don't want a showdown in front of the polls because that will deter voters," she sighed. "So, I don't know."

Corey watched her carefully. "You okay, Monica?"

Monica forced a smile onto her face. "I'm tired, Corey. It just keeps coming." Her voice was more clipped, more British than usual. Corey recognized it as stress. Monica folded her arms across her chest. "I knew this wouldn't be easy, but I guess I didn't think it would be *this* hard." She chuckled grimly. "Stupid, right?"

"No. Hopeful."

She smiled wryly. "Right. So much for that."

Donovan hadn't seen Carla around the Block for a few weeks. He tried to find out where she was by coming up with a reason to visit the Communications Center. He was greeted by the young woman with dimples and long braids.

392

"Hi. I . . . I wanted to borrow a thumb drive," he said when she walked up to him as he stood inside the doorway.

She tilted her head to the side, a puzzled expression on her face. "A thumb drive?" she asked.

"Uh, yes. I wanted to print something, but the printer isn't working, so I thought I would put it on a thumb drive and take it downstairs to one of the computer labs to print." He avoided her eyes, looking around for Carla. She was not in the Communications Center.

The young woman shook her head. "We don't allow thumb drives in the Block." She chuckled. "I'm sure you can understand why."

Donovan slapped his head and laughed. "Of course! How stupid of me!"

The young woman didn't laugh with him. "I can call one of our IT guys to come look at the printer," she said thoughtfully, stepping towards her computer. "The printer in the Finance office, right?"

"No, yes, well, I mean . . . no."

She stopped and stared at him, her eyebrows raised. "Yes or no?"

Donovan laughed again, too loudly this time, and she raised her eyebrows even more. "Yes, it's the Finance office, but I'm fine. I'll find another way." He stepped backwards, trying to retreat out the door. "I'm good."

"Okay, but wait." She stopped him. "I can tell IT to talk to Natalia to get that fixed. It's no problem. Really." She dimpled at him, pointing to her computer. "That's what I do . . . communicate." She giggled.

Donovan nodded. He stepped back toward the door again. *Let's try this one more time.* He looked around the Communications Center. "Where is our television star, Carla? She did such a great job on television a few weeks ago." He smiled widely at Tasia.

Tasia's smile faltered for a moment, but she recovered quickly, and seemed to force a smile onto her face. "Yup! She's a star alright. She's been so busy since she was on TV, I've barely seen her!" She grinned widely, but the twinkle in her eyes was gone. Something was wrong.

He took another step back. "Well, when you see her, please tell her she's got a fan."

"I most certainly will," she said, sitting in her chair and turning towards her computer.

Back in the Finance office, Donovan sat staring at the computer screen. He opened the general ledger document to the names of the dummy businesses through which the Cell passed funds. Michael wasn't satisfied with the information Donovan had given him. He wouldn't say what happened to Carla, only that they needed more information.

"Help us follow the money," Michael said.

The money trail sat wide open on the computer screen in front of him. All he had to do was print it out, fold it up really small and slide it into his underwear. Security randomly searched people leaving the Block, they didn't do much more than pat down pockets and purse checks. Still, he didn't want to take any chances.

He scrolled through the list of real and dummy businesses through which the Cell funds pass. Everything was here: business names, EIN numbers, and bank information. This could be very damaging, not only to the Baltimore Cell, but to all the other cells in the country, and even to La Lucha. BRM and La Lucha regularly transferred money back and forth. La Lucha's businesses regularly purchased supplies for BRM from their contacts in Mexico and Puerto Rico. Those purchases were entered in the Cell's books as accounts payable to La Lucha businesses. If he shared the ledger, La Lucha would also be exposed.

But Michael's tone had gone from persuasive to threatening. He began by calling and texting Donovan, applying slight pressure. When Donovan waffled, Michael became more insistent. Finally, Donovan stopped returning Michael's calls and texts, and his text messages began to say things like, "You are already implicated, so you might as well help us." Or, "It's too late to remove yourself from this situation." And even, "Call me back, or I'll have you arrested."

Each text message sent Donovan further and further down

a narrow tunnel of confusion, guilt, and fear. He felt trapped, used, and frightened. He had barely slept in weeks, had lost a lot of weight, and spent most of his time sitting on the couch staring vacantly at the television. He was on medical leave, with paperwork that Langford, the Cell's main physician, prepared for him, so he wasn't required to leave the house much. He caught Melva looking at him with concern when she thought he was unaware. She didn't say much. He knew she hadn't missed any of it.

He vacillated between being angry with Michael for pressuring and intimidating him and being grateful that Michael had warned him attacks were planned on the Cell leaders. Of course, Michael didn't know that Donovan's own family members were involved, but he had clearly picked up on something in Donovan's reaction to threats against the Cell, and was exploiting that weakness. At moments, he hated Michael for that. At the same time, in a very bizarre way, Donovan felt a little honored that Michael thought he could be useful. Besides being top of his class in school, Donovan had never really stood out for anything. In fact, he had spent his entire adult life trying to blend in with the people around him, particularly the white people. He had wanted them to see him as one of them and, the fact that Michael was leaning on him so hard meant he had something they thought was important, and he liked that feeling. He considered going to Karen or Langford and telling them what was happening. But he asked himself which group was more likely to win this conflict, and he was sure it was the white people. He wanted to be on the winning side.

He selected the last month's transactions and formatted them for printing. He hovered the cursor over the print button, the other hand wiping beads of sweat from his forehead. He thought of Melva's couch, and the corner he and Conrad now playfully fought over. He just wanted to lie down and curl up. It would be even better if he could put his head in Melva's lap. It had been so long since he had done that. For years, he had pushed her away, and now he wanted nothing more than to let her comfort him.

Instead, he had spent the last several weeks drinking himself into a place of comfort. Since he wasn't going to work, he started drinking early. Two or three beers with lunch had become regular for him, followed by another four or more beers between lunch and dinner, and several glasses of rum or vodka at night. He had never been a big drinker, a few beers when he was out with the guys, but never anything stronger. Now he drank his hard liquor straight, savoring the burn as it slid down his throat, waiting for the numbness and sleep it would eventually bring.

Donovan sat for an hour staring at the computer, his finger playing with the mouse. Finally, he pressed the print button. The stack of papers was thicker than he anticipated. He folded them up, stretched the waistband of his white scrubs, and shoved them into the front of his underwear. They felt cold and stiff against his sensitive skin, and the crisp folds dug into him. He turned off the computer, switched off the light, and walked into the outer office, locking the door behind him. He smiled at the two women on his way to the door.

"Bye Donovan! Have a good night!" one of the women called out to him.

Donovan mumbled something to her and hurried for the door. He told himself to walk slowly and calmly along the hall and down the main staircase. On the first floor he waved to Cell members as they passed him. As he approached the security guards at the door, he slowed his walking, *and* his breathing. His heart beat so fast, he felt as if his blood moved through his body in violent waves, surging and stopping with each beat. He could hear it . . . could feel it. He smelled his own sweat, not like the sweat he smelled after working out, but sharp and pungent, like stale onions. He had never smelled himself like that.

He forced a smile as he walked past the set of armed security inside the door. They smiled back and waved to him. *Almost there.* He stepped into the outer vestibule, where the second line of security stood. They smiled and nodded at him as he pushed the heavy metal door to exit the building.

"Uh, Brother, wait a minute," a deep voice behind him said.

Donovan's heart sank, and he thought he would throw up. Instead, he pasted the smile back on his face and turned slowly, expecting to see guns drawn. Instead, one of the guards held out the box of phones members had to turn in when entering the Block.

"Isn't one of these yours?" the guard asked.

Donovan felt his knees buckle and leaned on the door behind him to stop himself from falling.

The guard reached out to grab his arm, but Donovan put his hand up to stop him.

"Yo, Brother, you okay?"

Donovan forced himself to laugh. "Yes, I'm fine," he said. "I think I'm coming down with something." He rifled through the box to find his phone, holding it up for the guard to see. "So glad I didn't leave this behind."

Outside, Donovan wanted to lean on the door to catch his breath, but even more than that, he wanted to put as much distance as possible between himself and the Block. He hurried to his car, opened it hurriedly, and slid in. Leaning his head against the seat, he gulped big breaths, willing his stomach to calm down.

He was a traitor to his own people. But, for Karen, Amani, and Paul, it was worth it, and they would thank him. Melva would thank him.

Tasia watched the stuffy finance guy walk out of the Communications Center. There was something about him she didn't like, but she couldn't put her finger on it. He wasn't like the rest of the people she met at the Block. He seemed guarded, judgmental, like he was looking down on everyone around him.

She pulled up her SMS program and sent a quick message to Natalia, head of the Finance Department. She wished she had asked the guy his name. *Hey, Natalia. Your finance guy came down, can't remember his name, but he said the printer in the safe room is broken. Do you want me to call IT, or will you handle it?*

She needed to head home, but Carla had sent her a list of things to do. She consulted the list, satisfied that she had made a significant dent in it. She would finish the rest tomorrow. With Carla at the Farm, Tasia found herself acting as the Communications Director in the Block, with very close supervision from Carla. Carla told Tasia she was "handling it like a pro," and Tasia felt honored and proud to be trusted with so much responsibility.

As she closed her notebook, a memory of herself standing outside her apartment looking at all her belongings on the street flashed in front of her. It had only been a year and a half since Kenny disappeared and she and Sharonda were thrown out of their apartment. It seemed like another lifetime. She leaned back in her chair and swiveled from side to side, looking around the Communications Center, at all the people working on the projects she and Carla planned together. She was twenty-two years old, and she was running things! She had already enrolled in school for the fall to finish her degree. She paid her own way. She could now encourage Nana to slow down and work less. Sharonda was already learning to read, and she was not yet two! Her little girl wouldn't go to school unable to read or count like Tasia did. Even with that slow start, and all the struggles Tasia had experienced, look at what she had been able to do.

She thought of all the white teachers in school who dismissed her as unworthy of their time and attention. She wished they could see her now. The Cell had been the best thing to happen to her, and she couldn't stop thanking Jayla. She had discovered who she was, that she was beautiful and brilliant and had a lot to offer the world. She was a part of something big—not just as someone other people were helping, but as someone who had something significant to contribute. Nana couldn't stop talking about the difference she saw in Tasia. Even when Mamma came around, she mentioned that Tasia had changed. She had invited Mamma to come to a Cell meeting, but Mamma hadn't been interested. She would keep working on her. She knew the Cell could help Mamma.

She shut down her computer and tidied her desk. She had a lot to do at home before the weekend to prepare for Sharonda's birthday party. Nana was baking the cake, but Tasia had to buy the paper products and decorations. She wanted the theme to be fairies, and had found a whole set of paper plates, napkins, cups, and tablecloths with little dancing Black fairies in pink tutus at the dollar store. Sharonda would love them.

She was excited that Ms. Cathy had agreed to come to her granddaughter's party, especially since she and Nana had become such good friends. Mamma might come; Mamma might not come. Who knows? But Tasia was no longer on the same roller coaster of emotion around Mamma. She had important things to do. All she could do was hope that one day, Mamma would get herself together—before it was too late.

The other reason Tasia was excited for Sharonda's party was that Corey was coming. Corey. *Tall, dark, fine as hell Corey.* They had done nothing more than exchange glances and small talk, but the way he looked at her . . . Tasia shivered with excitement. Those looks promised to drive away the heartache from Kenny. Besides, it had been a year and a half. It was time to move on with her life.

She checked in with a few of the folks in the Communications Center. There was a big social media campaign scheduled to go out that night. Tasia had cued up a video compilation of police beating Black and Brown people, attacks on protestors, including Beverley's death, ending with scenes of armed white militia standing in front of the polls. The caption at the end said, "Why don't they want us to vote? Because our future depends on it."

As she hurried down the stairs to the toddler room, her thoughts returned to the finance guy. Something about him was really off. She thought about telling someone, but *what would she say? That he was stuck up? That she didn't like the air he gave off?* Maybe she would talk to Donna about it, but only *after* she got through Sharonda's party.

*****

Kai and Lisa stood in line at the early voting site. The line wrapped around the block, and Lisa couldn't actually see the elementary school that was the polling station. What she *could* see were the teams of armed white men and women, standing around the school. For the most part, they just stood still, staring ahead, and didn't engage with the voters. Just the sight of them frightened her.

She examined the crowd carefully, adjusting her straight black wig. Her neighborhood in Howard County was already quite white, but she noticed that she and Kai were the only Black people in line. She wondered if the white militia had frightened the Black people away.

She and Kai exchanged glances. He wrapped his arm around her as they inched towards the school.

Suddenly, something wet hit Lisa on the side of her face, bouncing off the arms of her dark glasses. She jumped and looked around. No one appeared to be paying attention to her or Kai. She gazed down at her feet and gasped. A banana peel lay on the ground beside her.

"What the fuck?" Kai exclaimed, looking around. No one looked at them.

"Damn monkey!" someone yelled out from the rear section of the line. "Go back to the jungle and stop messing up our country!"

Another peel hit Kai on the back of the head, and he jumped, turning around with his fist balled. The man and woman standing behind them stared back, a slight smile playing on their lips, a challenge in their eyes.

"Is there a problem here?" a deep voice said beside Lisa. She turned to face a short, stocky, blond-haired police officer standing beside them, hand on his gun. His cold blue eyes were fixed on Kai, even though he was standing closer to Lisa. Lisa resisted the urge to adjust her wig again.

Kai frowned and squared his shoulders. He opened his mouth to speak, but Lisa stepped fully in front of him so that she was standing between Kai and the cop.

"Nope!" she smiled broadly. "No problem here, Officer." She heard Kai exhale deeply behind her. "We're all set."

The cop's eyes met Kai's over Lisa's head, and they stared at each other for a few moments. Lisa felt Kai's anger radiating like hot waves. She prayed silently that he could regain control. There was no other way this could end well.

As Kai and the police officer stared each other down, another banana peel bounced off Kai's head and landed on Lisa's shoulder. She jumped and brushed it to the ground. The officer's eyes never left Kai's face, as if he were daring Kai to react in some way. Lisa stepped back until she was leaning all her weight against Kai, so that if he moved, she would fall, which was what she wanted. She felt around with her foot and rested her heel on his toe, pressing slightly, willing him to calm down. *Don't react, Kai. Just don't react.*

Another banana peel hit Lisa squarely in her forehead and

slid down her nose. She did not move. Another came, and another and another, until it felt like they were being pelted with rain. Kai's chest heaved against her back, as Lisa leaned harder against him, until he had to move one foot back to brace himself. The peels came from all directions, and Lisa's face was covered with sour, slimy, rotten banana liquid. She could barely see through the lenses of her glasses.

The cop stepped back to avoid being hit with the peels. "I'm gonna ask you again," he said quietly, his eyes never leaving Kai's face, even as the banana peels continued to batter them. "Is there a problem here?"

Lisa's breath caught in a silent sob. Her heart pounded, and she felt dizzy. She was holding her breath, so she didn't cry. The cop glanced behind him and broke into a wide grin. For the first time Lisa noticed the three other cops standing at a distance behind him, laughing, their hands covering their guns.

Lisa closed her eyes, forcing herself to breathe slowly. "No, Officer. As I said, there is no problem." She prayed he didn't recognize her. There were bigger things at stake here than their pride.

Behind her, Kai's chest heaved and expanded, as if he was holding his breath. His body trembled, and she leaned into him even harder. He reached out to grab her waist, steadying himself. The crowd had finally exhausted their supply of banana peels.

"You're holding up the line, monkeys!" someone yelled. Lisa opened her eyes and turned to look at the line in front of her.

There was almost half a block between her and the person next in line. She looked at the cop, who hooked his thumb into his holster. He gestured toward the line.

"You're holding up the line," he repeated, finally looking at Lisa. "Swing on down," he said with a chuckle.

She nodded and reached behind her, feeling for and grabbing Kai's hand. She stepped forward in the line, pulling Kai behind her. When they caught up to the woman in front of them, she turned around and looked Lisa up and down, her nose wrinkled as if Lisa smelled bad, *which she probably did.* The bananas smelled days-old. The liquid and pulp that covered Lisa's face and sunglasses was in her hair and stained her clothes. She lifted her chin and met the woman's gaze defiantly, but said nothing.

Behind her, Kai trembled, and she could feel anger and shame radiating from him. A few months ago, she thought the playing field was level for everyone. She had thought her privilege could protect them. She knew better now. In the presence of these white cops, she understood that Kai was in danger, just because he was a Black man and they saw him as a threat. And if she had to stand on his foot so he didn't do anything to incite the wrath of the cops, so that he could walk away whole, that's what she would do. Hell, she was ready to scrap if she needed to.

As they stepped forward, she thought how much she had learned and changed over the past few months. Lisa had been all about Lisa and sometimes about her family. Now she understood that there was so much more, and that she was part of something much bigger than herself. It both invigorated and scared her. These people around her could do nothing but throw banana peels at them. The slime would wash off, but what they were doing with the Cell—that would change the world.

The cops stood close by the entire time they were in the line, moving along with them, their hands on their guns, daring Lisa and Kai to make a move. Lisa did not look at Kai, but just kept holding onto his hand as he stood behind her. They did not talk. There was nothing to say. They were here to vote, and they needed to endure whatever they had to so they could cast their ballot. Voting had always been important to both of them, but this year they finally understood just how important it was.

Chapter Nineteen

Donovan avoided Michael's calls and texts until Michael showed up at his mother's door. When Melva told Donovan there was a white man at the door to see him, his heart sank. He stepped outside the house, where Michael stood leaning against his car.

"Why haven't you answered my calls?" Michael demanded as soon as Donovan appeared.

Donovan walked up to him and leaned against the car next to Michael, bracing his feet against the curb. "No reason," he said. "I was just busy."

"Busy?" Michael scoffed. "That busy might land you in jail."

"Stop threatening me," Donovan glared at Michael.

"Stop testing me!" Michael glared back. "You won't like what happens."

Donovan looked away, wishing he brought his beer outside with him. He folded his arms across his chest, shaking his head. He didn't know Michael could be this aggressive, and he didn't like this side of him, although he understood that Michael felt pressured to get the information. Maybe he was pushing Donovan the same way his bosses pushed him. He felt a little sorry for Michael.

"Did you get the information about the money?" Michael asked.

Donovan sighed. "I couldn't get everything you wanted."

"What does that mean?"

"I could only print one page of the general ledger. I will have to get them one at a time, so I don't raise suspicion." Donovan reached into his back pocket and removed a single sheet of folded paper. He unfolded and smoothed it with his hands before handing over to Michael.

Michael looked at the paper, frowning. "What am I looking at?"

"That's a list of companies the Cell is doing business with."

"CA Imports? What's that?"

"Central American Imports." Donovan looked up at the sky. "That company imports textiles and crafts from Mexico, Belize, and Guatemala."

"And the Cell launders money through this company?"

"Yes."

"And what about Esperanza Community Partners?"

"That's a nonprofit social enterprise training people on job skills."

Michael studied the list. "These are strange names. Why do they all sound Spanish?"

Donovan shrugged. "I don't know. I just move money. I don't name companies."

Michael looked at Donovan carefully for a moment, his eyes narrowed. "Hmm . . . okay."

Donovan met his gaze evenly, although he just wanted to run inside the house and slam the door behind him.

"Okay. Cool. My bosses are waiting on this information. They want to act right away." Michael folded the paper and put it in his back pocket. He reached over and slapped Donovan on his back. "Good work. Keep getting more. I will be back for the rest in a few days."

"I don't know when next I'm going to . . ." Donovan wanted to scream. *When will this ever end?*

"Find a reason to. My bosses are riding my back. If I can't get what I need from you, then you'll have to deal with them directly." Michael stopped and looked closely at Donovan. "Believe me, you would prefer to deal with me, because if it were up to them, you'd be in a jail cell."

Michael stood up straight and walked around to the driver side. With one hand on the car door, he looked at Donovan again. "Don't screw this up," he said before getting into the car.

Donovan walked back towards the front door as Michael drove off. He had just sold out La Lucha, and while he originally thought it was better than selling out the Cell, his sour, churning stomach obviously did not agree. *It's all worth it. I didn't have a choice.* He walked into the house and removed his shoes. When this all went down, and the Cell leaders were killed or imprisoned, he would have to explain to Karen, Amani, and Paul how he had saved their lives. It would be difficult for them to understand, but they would eventually thank him. Melva would thank him. All he wanted now was to drink, a lot. It would be a long night.

"Oh my God!" LaTanya gasped as she turned onto Lisa and Kai's street.

"What? What is it?" Lisa asked from her crouch under the blanket on the floor of the back seat of LaTanya's car. "What do you see?"

LaTanya sighed. "Nothing. These people—"

"Wait. What people? What are they doing?" The prickly wool blanket was thick and hot, and her legs and back ached for being bent in that position for more than thirty minutes. Lisa resisted the temptation to throw off the blanket and stick her sweating face out the window.

"Nothing," LaTanya said. "It's nothing. Stay down until we get into the garage."

Lisa recognized the sound of the garage door opening as they drove in. When the door closed and the car became dark, Lisa poked her head out. LaTanya was getting out of the car.

"We good?" Lisa asked as LaTanya opened the back door.

LaTanya nodded, but she seemed pale and nervous.

"What's wrong? What did you see?" Lisa asked as she unfolded herself. She got out of the car stiffly. "Did you see any of the neighbors? Did they look at you funny?" She slammed the

411

car door behind her, pulling out her house keys. She was here mainly for Jessica's asthma medication, but if they could grab some clothes while they were there, that would be great, too. They had dropped Kai off at the Block to deliver some contracts, and he made her promise she would get the meds and leave.

LaTanya shook her head. "No, I didn't see any neighbors." She followed Lisa into the house. "Let's just get what you need and get out of here. I don't want to be here after dark."

In the kitchen it was clear the occupants had left the house suddenly. There were breakfast dishes in the sink, with cereal and spoiled milk congealed on them. A moldy loaf of bread sat open on the table. The entire kitchen smelled of spoiled food. Lisa shuddered as she remembered that day at the supermarket, how she and Kai came home, set a timer for fifteen minutes, packed as much as they and the girls could grab, and jumped back into the car. That was more than five months ago, and they had not been back.

As they walked through the house, Lisa frowned at the mess in every room. Couch pillows were scattered on the floor, furniture sat out of place and askew. Drawers and closets stood open—their contents spilled out on the ground. In the study, every drawer in Kai's desk sat overturned on the floor.

"Damn girl," LaTanya breathed, looking around, "Y'all did a number on this place."

Lisa stood frozen in the kitchen, a new fact slowly dawning on her. "We didn't do this," she whispered. "We didn't leave the house like this. Someone has been here."

Both women looked around cautiously. Lisa walked into the living room and frowned, looking at the window. Something was strange. She couldn't look outside because the glass was painted red.

"What the fuck—" she said, walking towards the window. "What *is* that?"

LaTanya sighed. "Nothing you can do anything about. It's not even worth talking about."

Lisa turned to look at LaTanya, frowning. "What do you mean?"

LaTanya shook her head. "Get what you need and get out of here. I've got the heebie jeebies." She shuddered and rubbed her hands up and down her arms. "For all we know, this place is bugged, and they could be watching us right now." She turned to look at Lisa, her eyes wide. "They could be on their way here as we speak."

Lisa's heart felt like it dropped to the bottom of her stomach. "Wh . . . what? You really think so?" She looked around anxiously.

"I think we should get out of here, right now." LaTanya walked up to the window and peered through a small space between the red gook on the window. "Shit!" she exclaimed.

Lisa came up behind her. A dark sedan had pulled up across the street. The windows were tinted too dark for Lisa to see inside, but the vehicle looked official. As she watched, a police car pulled up behind the sedan.

"We gotta go." LaTanya headed towards the basement stairs.

"Wait! Where are you going?" Lisa followed LaTanya down the stairs.

"We're going out the back!"

"Wh . . . wait! What about the car?"

LaTanya turned briefly to look at Lisa. "We can't take the car. We need to get out of here. Now!" She pulled the sliding door to the backyard open and ran out. Lisa followed her, sliding the door closed behind her.

They ran across Lisa's big backyard, past the line of trees separating their yard from those on the adjacent street, alongside one of the houses, and out onto the street. Lisa followed LaTanya, surprised at how quickly the tiny woman could move.

As she ran, she thought about the fact she had lived in this neighborhood for a decade, had thought of these neighbors as friends, had even engineered her words and behavior to be seen as one of them. Yet in this moment, in a crisis, there wasn't a door she could knock on or a neighbor she could run to. They hadn't been her friends—they had merely tolerated her. And she had been completely oblivious. She realized now that Kai had not been oblivious, but she had rejected every attempt he made to show her the truth. She wondered if she would have been as patient if the tables were reversed. Now that she had removed the blinders, she saw so much: the way she was shaping her daughters in much the same way Diahann had shaped her; how instrumental she had been in keeping Black people out of her school and neighborhood—the very same Black people she could have run to right now, how she chose friends like Danielle in the hopes her association with them would reduce her Blackness.

But after her experiences at the supermarket, and in line to vote, she was sure that no amount of money or status would change who she was. She had a different destiny now—not to become more like the white people she knew, but to be more like the Black people she knew, like LaTanya and Esther. She had a lot of repair work to do, and her first task was to apologize to Kai and thank him for loving her in spite of her flaws.

LaTanya turned right and walked quickly along the block, heading onto the street perpendicular to Lisa's. At the end of the block, she paused and cautiously looked around the corner towards Lisa's house at the bottom of the cul-de-sac. Lisa peered over LaTanya's shoulder and gasped, her hand flying to her mouth. Lisa's house was surrounded by police cars. The front door and garage were open, and police moved in and out. But what Lisa did not expect, were the thick, red letters spray-painted on the front of the brick house and across the windows. *Niggers.*

Tasia stood at the Farm's lodge entrance and welcomed the elders as they drove up for the annual Cell leaders' meeting. The elders would spend the week sharing, planning, and consulting the ancestors for guidance. Coaches, school buses, and SUVs from eastern and midwestern states arrived, each containing several elders who were helped out of the vehicles or helped down bus steps and ushered into the lodge.

"Please come inside and make yourselves comfortable," Tasia said over and over, gesturing towards the large double doors. "Refreshments are waiting inside for you."

Hundreds of elders arrived, some upright and spry, others slow and bent, some fully gray, others not gray at all. Each elder smiled and nodded at her as they walked by, saying, "How are you today, baby girl?" or "Blessings, child."

When Mother Ramla emerged from her SUV, most of the elders walking into the lodge stopped to greet her. At almost ninety years old, she stood upright, her shoulders back, her head held high. She looked much taller than she was because of her long gray locs, which she wrapped around themselves and piled high on her head, a white ropy fabric wound through them. She wore a long, white robe with gold embroidery around the neck, sleeves, and hem. Her brown skin was barely lined, and her eyes were bright and watchful.

Tasia had only seen her from a distance and had avoided her because she seemed so intimidating. Mother Ramla fixed Tasia with her piercing brown eyes as she approached.

"Mother Ramla," she bowed slightly. "Thank you for coming."

The elder stopped in front of Tasia, regarding her

416

carefully. Tasia held her breath, afraid of what would come next. Mother Ramla gently grasped Tasia's face with both hands.

"You have many gifts, my young daughter." The elder looked sad. "But you have experienced much sorrow."

Tasia's eyes filled with tears. *How does she know?*

Mother Ramla smiled. "You carry your sorrow like a cloak, hiding your beauty. But it is time to take it off, to let it go." She stroked Tasia's left cheek with her thumb. "There is great joy ahead of you. Accept it."

The tears spilled out of Tasia's eyes onto her cheeks as Mother Ramla bent down to kiss her forehead. She did not release Tasia's face.

"You will do much to free your people during the Tribulation," Mother Ramla nodded deliberately. "You will need to be purified. You will need to be prepared."

With that, Mother Ramla looked at Tasia for a moment longer, her expression unreadable. She released Tasia's face and walked into the lodge.

The other elders had waited while Mother Ramla talked to Tasia; no one stepped around her to enter the lodge. When she had moved on, the other elders filed past, each one looking directly at and touching Tasia, as if to bless her. By the time the last bus had unloaded its passengers, Tasia was exhausted.

The last several weeks had been beyond hectic. Between planning Sharonda's birthday party and managing the Communications Center without Carla, she had not stopped moving. But the highlight had been the birthday party. Everything had been perfect! The decorations, the cake, Corey. She blushed. Corey had shown up with the biggest pink teddy bear she had ever seen and the sight of him standing at the door with it had melted her heart. But the best moment was watching the look on Sharonda's face when she took the bear from him. Corey had made a friend for life, and Sharonda followed him around the entire party.

Mamma had come too, sober and clean, and although she was standoffish at first, she eventually warmed up and started talking to Ms. Cathy. Mamma didn't drink the entire time she was there, although there was plenty of liquor. Instead, she and Ms. Cathy sat in a corner, their heads together, whispering intently. Tasia didn't know for sure, but she thought Ms. Cathy was walking Mamma through a standard Cell recruiting script. Mama listened carefully, nodding her head and asking questions.

At the end of the evening, as Tasia walked Corey to the door, he took both her hands, interlocking his fingers through hers, and asked her for a day and time to go out to dinner. Tasia asked him to wait until after the election, and they set a date for the second week of November. Corey said he knew a good restaurant he wanted to take her to. He leaned in to kiss her on the forehead at the door, and his lips lingered on her skin. She closed her eyes and breathed in his crisp aftershave, savoring the moment. When she stepped back, he held her gaze for an extended moment before releasing her hands and walking out the door.

She didn't know what Mother Ramla meant about her freeing her people during the Tribulation, and the thought made her heart race and throat tighten. But she liked the sound of joy in her future. If the looks she and Corey exchanged at Sharonda's party were any sign, there was *great* joy ahead, and she was ready for it. But it was not lost on her that the Tribulation would be tough. Carla had already warned her of difficult times ahead— pain and loss. Tasia wasn't excited about that, but she knew the only way to liberation was through the fire, and she was ready.

The Security Center at the Farm buzzed with activity. Corey ran back and forth between Monica and Carla with messages. In addition to the elders coming in for the annual meeting, La Lucha leaders—Manny, Mateo, and Luis—had arrived the night before to plan joint operations between La Lucha and the Cell later that week. At these meetings, plans for the next year would be laid out: house hundreds of thousands of Cell members; purchase more weapons from overseas; build underground bunkers on the Farm compound in case the rock was breached, and create more operational security to reduce the impact of insider betrayal.

Corey was tired from running up and down the stone stairs, and when he got back to the Security Center, he planned to sit on the leather couch in the corner where people took naps during long shifts.

As he stepped into the Security Center, he noticed the looks of concern on the faces of Monica, Manny, Mateo, and Luis.

419

They clustered around a computer screen. He walked up to them.

"What's wrong?" he asked, pulling up a chair.

Monica looked up, shaking her head. "The police raided several of La Lucha's cover businesses."

"Several, as in more than one?" Corey frowned. *Does La Lucha have a mole, too?*

"Several, as in twelve," Manny responded. "That's too many to be an accident."

"They arrested more than fifty people," Mateo added. "They've confiscated over a million dollars."

"Look," Monica pointed to the list of business names on the computer screen. "Do you notice anything about them?"

The three men looked at the screen for a long time, shaking their heads.

Monica stared at them. "Don't you see a pattern?"

"No. What pattern?" Luis looked puzzled.

Monica pointed to the computer screen. "Twelve names, all between the letters of A and F." She turned to look at them. "Don't you think that's strange?"

"Ohhh," Manny said. "That *is* strange."

Mateo stroked his goatee thoughtfully. "Where might someone have seen the names of these twelve businesses?"

Luis shook his head. "I don't know. A list somewhere maybe? In alphabetical order?"

"Okay. Okay." Monica stood up and began pacing, her hands drawing pictures in the air. The men watched her walk back and forth. "Let's think about this. Where do we keep lists of businesses?"

Corey thought of conversations he had with Tasia. "Communications? We send messages to all the businesses as well as to the cells."

Monica stopped pacing. "A distribution list, right?"

Corey nodded.

"We have distribution lists, too," Luis said. "Our Communications Director, Jessica, is coming tomorrow. We can ask her then."

Monica nodded. "I need to go talk to Carla. Maybe when Jessica gets here we can all meet again."

The men nodded.

"Meanwhile, let's get to our distribution lists and see which businesses might be in danger next. We need to warn them."

Luis jumped to his feet. "Okay. I will contact them to shut down, go dark. They need to get their folks out." He turned to Manny and Mateo. "Let's get the list from Jessica and divide it between us so we can move faster."

When the three men left, Monica turned to Corey. "Two breaches in a couple of months. Can't be a coincidence. I *know* we have a mole." She sank into her chair and swiveled back and forth. "Do you think they have a mole, too?"

"Could be," Corey said, "We have access to their business names, but they didn't know about our plans when Carla went to

New York. So, do we each have a mole, or is it just ours?"

Tuesday, Election Day, was sunny and cool. Even before the polls closed in all precincts, it was clear that Reginald Sumpter had won by a landslide. The voter suppression tactics of The Alt had worked, and hundreds of thousands of Black and Brown voters avoided the polls, afraid for their lives. Alt supporters began celebrating in the early evening, and news reports on the Farm's television monitors showed groups of armed white people driving through Black neighborhoods, smashing store windows, spray-painting racist slogans on buildings and brutally beating any Black people they encountered. Although Sumpter's victory had been predicted, groups of Cell members stood silently around the televisions in the lodge, watching the mayhem in cities across the country. The air in the lodge was uncharacteristically somber. Even though the annual meeting was usually a serious but joyful reunion of Cell members who rarely saw each other during the year, there was little joy this year. The air was thick with grief about what the media was reporting.

Corey spent the morning working with Mateo and Luis, planning the joint drills that would take place that weekend. The La Lucha teams would begin arriving on Friday afternoon from cities up and down the east coast. Manny was busy talking to La Lucha Miami, working with the communications team to warn businesses about the mole.

The elders held a series of meetings around the lodge. Gray Locs sat in the lodge living room, Lia beside her, her huge head resting on Gray Locs's knee. Even the dog seemed taken with the regal elder, and Gray Locs, in turn, slowly stroked Lia's head while she talked to the other elders. Lia's eyes were closed, and her tail swished slowly from side to side.

From time to time, Corey bumped into Tasia, who was running around, following Carla's directions, making sure the elders were comfortable, and that they had everything they needed for their meeting. Each time they passed each other they found a way to touch—hand to hand here, shoulder to shoulder there. Tasia blushed whenever Corey was nearby, and he grinned each time she reacted to him.

After dinner, the elders and all the Cell and La Lucha members filed out of the lodge and headed for a clearing deep in the woods. Several of the elders needed help walking, and a few rode in golf carts that zipped around the farm.

"Brother Corey." Corey turned around. Gray Locs walked close behind him, stepping carefully into the dim light, but still holding her head high.

"Yes, Ma'am." Corey slowed down to fall in step with her.

"Mother Ramla," Tasia corrected him, falling in step on his other side.

"Yes, Mother Ramla," Corey said, smiling his thanks at Tasia.

423

Mother Ramla smiled briefly. "You have a calling, Brother Corey." She looked around Corey to Tasia. "I have already told Sister Tasia about hers."

Tasia's head swung around at the sound of her name.

Mother Ramla laughed. "What? Didn't think I knew your name?"

Tasia shook her head.

The elder laughed again. "I know a lot of things." She looked from Corey to Tasia and back to Corey, a broad smile on her face. "A *lot* of things."

"Like what, Mother?" Corey asked.

"Well, some things are not to be revealed before their time," the elder said, lifting the hem of her white robe to avoid a small puddle of mud. "But I know that you both have important work to do in the time to come. That means you must remember the pain of your past, but you cannot be ruled by it."

Corey and Tasia nodded silently.

"The pain of our past is designed to prepare us for the joy of our future." Mother Ramla looked at Corey. "But sometimes our past holds us captive, so we can't even imagine what the future could be."

They arrived in a large clearing where a bonfire, several feet high and wide, lit up the sky. Hundreds of people stood around the fire, the frailer elders in folding chairs.

"That's what both of your mothers did," Mother Ramla continued. "They became victims of their pain, their past." She

424

shrugged. "Who can blame them? They experienced terrible things."

She stopped walking and turned to face Corey and Tasia. "But you can't afford to do that—neither of you. Because many will look to you in the future, and thousands will follow you." She pointed first to her head, and then to her heart. "You will need wisdom and courage and love. You already have everything you need, but you must be willing to use it and share it. *Then*, your destiny will be fulfilled."

With that, Mother Ramla walked away towards a group of elders, smiling and waving at people as she passed.

Corey and Tasia stood looking at each other for a moment.

"I guess she knows some things about us," Tasia said.

"I *guess*!" Corey took Tasia's hand and they walked up to the circle, where the members stood silently. The only sound was the loud crackle of the fire.

Mother Ramla stepped forward. "Sanibona!" she said, her voice loud and booming, arms open wide.

"Ngikhona!" the members replied loudly.

"My brothers, sisters, and others, today Reginald Sumpter won the presidency as our ancestors predicted. Our Tribulation will begin tomorrow. We will see pain, death, and sorrow like we have never seen before in this country. Even the Red Summer of 1919 will pale in comparison."

The members nodded and murmured agreement.

425

"We will not be able to escape the pain. It will feel like we have been thrown into the fire. We will see our flesh peel. We will scream in agony. It will feel like there is no end." She turned to gaze around the circle. "But our ancestors have predicted all that has happened so far. And they have told us the Tribulation is only for a season. We will emerge.

"Not everyone will survive the Tribulation. We will mourn our dead, and we will celebrate when they go to be with the ancestors, but that does not mean it will not hurt to lose them."

Tasia shivered and Corey pulled her close, wrapping his arm around her. They hadn't even been on a date yet—that would be next week. But it was already clear that they belonged to each other; they didn't even need to discuss it. At Sharonda's party he had gotten a glimpse into her life and confirmed that he wanted to be a part of it. She was his future, and he planned to do everything in his power to be the best man he could be for her. And Calvin and Momma needed him. He would continue his efforts to get Calvin into a treatment center and Momma to the Block. He couldn't afford to give up on them.

"One of the things Bakra enjoys doing is hiding our history from us. But the only way we will survive the Tribulation is by remembering the history of our people. Remember how our people have overcome in the past. Remember the strength of our ancestors. Remember, the history of a movement determines its future."

426

"The history of a movement determines its future," the crowd replied.

Mother Ramla stepped back and the crowd stood silently, staring at the fire. Corey pulled Tasia into his chest and rested his chin on top of her head. This moment felt overwhelming and solemn. He wondered if he would survive the Tribulation. *Would Tasia?*

Their way of life would never be the same again. Persecution was their future. Corey raised his eyes to the sky. The stars were so bright, they seemed close enough to reach up and touch. Maybe he would survive; maybe he would not. But in *this* moment, facing what was to come, he felt more certain, more clear-headed, more ready than he had ever felt in his life.

Discussion Questions

1. Which of the characters did you most identify with and why?

2. What are the significant differences in the experiences of Corey, Lisa, Tasia, and Donovan? How did those differences impact their life journeys?

3. Did you re-read any passages? Which ones and why?

4. Was there anything in the book that was new or surprising to you? If so, what was it?

5. What would be the impact of a real-life Black Cell? How would it affect your life and the lives of those who are important to you?

6. If you could hear this story from the point of view of one of the minor characters in the book, who would it be and why?

7. Are you still thinking about any lingering questions from the book? If so, what were they?

8. If you were making a movie of this book, who would you cast in the roles of Corey, Lisa, Tasia, and Donovan?

9. How do the events in this book relate to real-life current events?

10. If this book was the first in a series, what do you think should happen in the next book?

11. Who, in your life, do you want to share this book with, and why?

12. Is there anything you might do differently in your own life after reading Corey, Lisa, Tasia, and Donovan's stories?

About the Author

As a social work professor, Wendy Shaia has published a number of non-fiction articles examining issues of oppression experienced by Black people in urban settings and has a significant following for that work. She regularly speaks and trains on anti-racist practices and Black liberation. Her first short story, "Waiting for *Something"* was recently accepted for publication by *The Dillydoun Review* and was nominated for a Pushcart Prize. Her second short story, "Smoke," will be published in October by *Midnight and Indigo*, a literary magazine featuring Black female writers.

Please learn more about Wendy at her website wendyshaia.com.